THE BILLIONAIRE'S HOPE

ERIN SWANN

This book is a work of fiction. The characters and events portrayed in this book are fictitious. Any similarity to any event or real persons, living or dead, is coincidental and not intended by the author.

Cover image licensed from Shutterstock.com

Cover design by Swann Publications

Edited by: Tamara Mataya, Donna Hokanson

ISBN-13: 9781099004674

The following story is intended for mature readers. It contains mature themes, strong language, and sexual situations. All characters are 18+ years of age, and all sexual acts are consensual.

If you enjoy this book please leave a review.

Find out more about the author and upcoming books online at:

WWW.ERINSWANN.COM

To sign up for Erin's newsletter WWW.ERINSWANN.COM/SUBSCRIBE

❀ Created with Vellum

ALSO BY ERIN SWANN

The Billionaire's Trust - Available on Amazon, also in AUDIOBOOK

(Bill and Lauren's story) He needed to save the company. He needed her. He couldn't have both. The wedding proposal in front of hundreds was like a fairy tale come true—Until she uncovered his darkest secret.

The Youngest Billionaire - Available on Amazon

(Steven and Emma's story) The youngest of the Covington clan, he avoided the family business to become a rarity, an honest lawyer. He didn't suspect that pursuing her could destroy his career. She didn't know what trusting him could cost her.

The Secret Billionaire – Available on Amazon, also in AUDIOBOOK

(Patrick and Elizabeth's story) Women naturally circled the flame of wealth and power, and his is brighter than most. Does she love him? Does she not? There's no way to know. When he stopped to help her, Liz mistook him for a carpenter. Maybe this time he'd know. Everything was perfect. Until the day she left.

Picked by the Billionaire – Available on Amazon

(Liam and Amy's story) A night she wouldn't forget. An offer she couldn't refuse. He alone could save her, and she held the key to his survival. If only they could pass the test together.

Saved by the Billionaire – Available on Amazon

(Ryan and Natalie's story) The FBI and the cartel were both after her for the same thing: information she didn't have. First, the FBI took everything, and then the cartel came for her. She trusted Ryan with her safety, but could she trust him with her heart?

Caught by the Billionaire – Available on Amazon

(Vincent and Ashley's story) Her undercover assignment was simple enough: nail the crooked billionaire. The surprise came when she opened the folder, and the target was her one-time high school sweetheart. What will happen when an unknown foe makes a move to checkmate?

The Driven Billionaire – Available on Amazon

(Zachary and Brittney's story) Rule number one: hands off your best friend's sister. With nowhere to turn when she returns from upstate, she accepts his offer of a room. Mutual attraction quickly blurs the rules. When she comes under attack, pulling her closer is the only way to keep her safe. But, the truth of why she left town in the first place will threaten to destroy them both.

Nailing the Billionaire – Available on Amazon

(Dennis and Jennifer's story) She knew he destroyed her family. Now she is close to finding the records that will bring him down. When a corporate shakeup forces her to work with him, anger and desire collide. Vengeance was supposed to be simple, swift, and sweet. It was none of those things.

Undercover Billionaire – Available on Amazon

(Adam and Kelly's story) Their wealthy families have been at war forever. When Kelly receives a chilling note, the FBI assigns Adam to protect her. Family histories and desire soon collide, causing old truths to be questioned. Keeping ahead of the threat won't be their only challenge.

Trapped with the Billionaire – Available on Amazon

(Josh and Nicole's story) When Nicole returns from vacation to find her company has been sold, and she has been assigned to work for the new CEO. Competing visions of how to run things and mutual passion collide in a volatile mix. When an old family secret is unearthed, it threatens everything.

CHAPTER 1

Katie

My phone vibrated again in my purse. I sat in the second row of the packed Breakers meeting room at the Mandalay Bay hotel. I was also starting to sweat in my jacket. The air conditioning was set for a T-shirt-and-shorts crowd, not the business suit I had on.

My phone vibrated yet again. Someone was persistent. The repeated buzzing earned me an evil-eye glance from the man to my left.

I gave in and opened my purse. My oldest brother, Bill, topped the recent calls list. Actually, there were four missed calls, a voice mail, and a text from him.

BILL: Call me ASAP 911

My blood froze.

Mr. Cool was not easily excited. It had to be a major issue for him to call it an emergency.

This session of the conference was about the new guidance the Financial Accounting Standards Board had issued for capitalizing software.

I was in the absolute middle of a packed row. It wouldn't be easy to get out. I would have chosen the almost-empty first row, except then I would have had to keep my legs crossed in this skirt, and that would have made typing notes on my laptop impossible.

The guys had it so easy, trading suits for jeans. They weren't judged the same way we girls were.

I was deadly serious about beating them all out, and that meant makeup, a proper business suit, and heels—even at a conference in Sin City. I was determined to be kick-ass in this profession, and I intended to make the appropriate impression when I met the presenter after the session. Connections were key in this business. It was something the dolts in the rear didn't seem to get.

I packed my computer into my laptop bag and waited for the man on the stage to turn toward the screen. I didn't want him to notice me walking out.

The presentation was pretty dry stuff. It was putting most everybody to sleep, even worse than the morning session had. But that was the essence of accounting. Knowing all the rules was crucial. *Exciting* was never a word you used in the same sentence with *accounting*. This was like school. Limit my distractions, and I could nail it. I had a high tolerance for boring.

The speaker turned to emphasize something on the screen. I shouldered my Gucci purse and made my way down the row, squeezing past the other attendees as quickly as I could.

This week had been a welcome respite from the office and my boss, Russ Downey. Chewing glass was better than being around Russ. The man yelled at me incessantly, and lately he'd piled increasingly more work on me every day. And that was before you considered his BO.

Russ had stayed in Los Angeles, although he should have been here too. Half the staff called him *Rusty* behind his back, because he wasn't always up on the latest FASB pronouncements. It was sad that several of us new hires knew more than he did, but I'd learned long ago that life wasn't fair.

Anyway, whatever the reason, Russ Downey had it in for me in a big way. I was used to hard work, but the amount he assigned me was way beyond that. I hadn't done anything wrong that I could remember, nothing to make him single me out as the one second-year accountant he was trying to run out of the company, but that seemed to be his goal.

Stubbornness, though, was not something I had in short supply. I was going to leave on my own terms and in my own time. As soon as the firm signed off on my experience hours this fall, I would have everything I needed for my CPA, and I would pull the ripcord. One extra day of Russ was a day too much. The man was such a pig.

The hallway outside the meeting room was teeming with T-shirted nerds attending a computer hacking conference. Black Hat they called it. I moved away from the BO cloud given off by a gaggle of them who hadn't showered as recently as they should have.

Typical computer geeks.

I dialed Bill back.

He picked up on the first ring. "*Katie, where are you?*" he demanded.

"Las Vegas. I'm at a conference this week."

He let out an audible breath. "*Good, I was worried.*"

"Worried? Why? What happened?"

"*I have some bad news. You might want to sit down.*"

"No can do," I said, pressing the phone to my ear. The computer geeks were a noisy bunch.

"*It's Monica.*" He hesitated.

I dreaded what might come next. Monica Paisley was a psycho bitch. She had threatened my brother Steven and his wife, Emma, and even torched Emma's car a few weeks ago. Monica was trouble with a capital T.

"*It's your house,*" he said. "*It's on fire.*"

My heart stopped, and my stomach lurched. My lunch threatened to come up.

I ran toward the women's room to my left.

I elbowed open the stall door, and the phone hit the marble floor as I went to my knees in front of the porcelain bowl. I almost made it in time. I puked in the toilet, but some splashed on the seat. I couldn't control the upheavals. Remnants of the fish tacos I'd chosen for lunch filled the bowl. After the third and fourth heaves, there was nothing left to expel, but I couldn't stop the convulsions. The urge overcame me again, and I dry-heaved twice more. It felt like I'd torn a stomach muscle.

Once the sickening urges stopped, I spit several times, trying to rid my mouth of the wretched taste of vomit and bile. I picked up my phone and stumbled to a sink. I splashed water into my mouth, spitting again. Some vomit had splashed on my jacket. I wet some paper towels and wiped it off. Some had gotten on my phone too.

Gross.

Bill's call had dropped. I pulled my phone out of the case and wiped it off. I rinsed the cover in the sink, wrapping it in a paper towel to dry and setting it in my bag.

My house. How could she do that?

I had to get home.

Screw everything. This was the last day of the conference anyway. I started for my room, gathered up my courage, and called my brother back.

The elevator door closed. "How bad?" I asked when he came on the line.

"I'm so sorry, Katie. The fire department is still working it, but there won't be anything left."

His words chilled me. Things like this weren't supposed to happen. "I thought she was in jail."

"She made bail weeks ago. Katie, you need to go stay with Patrick when you get back." My younger brother Patrick had a condo in the same building as Bill, but it wasn't anywhere near my work.

"No, that's too far," I complained. My big brother was still bossing me around—the one constant in the universe.

"Just do it, and don't argue for a change." His tone indicated he wasn't going to let this go. *"You'll be safe with him, and the Hanson firm has protection for you at his place. They can keep you safe until we find Paisley."*

"But why me? I didn't do anything to her."

None of this made any sense. I had never even met her. My sister-in-law's nickname for her had been Cruella. The first time I heard it, it sounded harsh. Today it seemed entirely too kind.

"Crazy does what crazy wants," Bill said with a sigh. *"She's out of control, and there's no telling what she might do next. The Hanson people are even pulling Patrick's new girlfriend, Liz, in for protection."*

I shuddered. The lady was a lunatic. This was terrifying. Dealing with my asshole boss was one type of stress, but this was a whole other level. At least with Russ it was only words and never anything physical.

I stepped out of the elevator and moved down the hall toward my room.

Bill filled me in for a few minutes on the Hanson Security crew's efforts to find Monica and get her back into custody. At the end of the call, he made me promise to go to Patrick's condo when I got back.

I chucked my bag and purse on the bed. My next stop was the bathroom. I brushed my teeth and gargled the entire bottle of complimentary mouthwash to rid myself of that awful barf aftertaste. I stripped off my stained suit and grabbed another from the closet. I was glad I always packed extra outfits for a trip like this. It only took me a few minutes to stuff my clothes back into my bag for the trip home.

Except I didn't have a home.

Anymore.

I moved my laptop to the desk and powered it back up. The airline website yielded bad news. No seats back to LAX today. I tried Expedia. The same answer: nothing before tomorrow afternoon. My only choice was to rent a car and make the five-hour drive home, unless I wanted to wait. It was almost four... If I left soon, I could make it tonight.

I trundled my bag behind me and shut the door to the empty room. Downstairs, the lady behind the desk gave me even worse news. Because of all the convention-goers, there weren't any rentals available downtown or at the airport, but if I wanted to take a taxi or the shuttle to the airport, I could wait and see if one became available. It seemed like my only choice.

I turned for the door. I brought up the Uber app on my phone. I was typing when I bumped into him, literally. If he hadn't grabbed my arms, I would have ended up flat on my ass.

Nick

Hank's morning presentation of my cell phone hack at the Black Hat conference had gone quite well. *Black Hat* was a complete misnomer. This conference was for white hat hackers like me to let targets know how they could be attacked, and put pressure on them to fix their vulnerabilities before the real bad guys got to them.

Hank had presented on stage while I sat in the back and watched. It paid to stay under the radar in my chosen profession. As a member of the Hanson Investigations and Security team, he made a credible presenter. Hank understood the nuances of my technique and answered all the technical questions perfectly. This was the sixth hack I'd gotten out in the open at one of these conferences without anyone realizing I was behind them.

Anonymity, thou art sweet.

I had used the hack for over a year now, and it was time to publish it so the wireless companies could patch it. The feds had a similar thing going the last few years, but it involved driving a truck around with a fake cell tower system in the back. Such a kludge, and only good for a small area. Mine could be launched from my laptop and worked anywhere in the world. Much more elegant. Those feds had no idea how clueless they were.

I had discovered a new alternative vulnerability for my own use, so I wouldn't be giving up any capability when they patched this one.

I had been up to my room and back after the presentation ended, and I now waited in the large lobby to meet up with Hank for a few hours at the tables.

My phone vibrated with a text message.

BRANDI: date Monday night?

ME: bring Candy - six okay?

BRANDI: C U

THE TWINS WERE EXPENSIVE, BUT IT WAS ALWAYS A PLEASURE TO see Brandi and her sister Candy. They had great assets and talent to match.

Hank was late.

If he didn't show up soon, I was going to hit the blackjack tables without him. I was looking left, trying to locate Hank, when I heard the clack of her heels coming my way, just before I turned my head to see her.

Too late.

Little Miss Distracted was looking down at her phone and walked straight into me. She would have ended up on her pretty little ass if I hadn't caught her. Her phone bounced hard on the marble floor. She wasn't very bright. Only an idiot didn't protect their phone with a case these days.

"Careful there, sweetheart," I said. I caught a glimpse of nice cleavage and a black lace bra down her shirt as she leaned over to retrieve the phone. She had a nice figure, probably even nicer if she didn't hide it in a business suit.

"You broke my phone. You…" She looked up and recognition flashed across her face. The anger in her eyes receded. "Nick?"

I hadn't recognized her grown up and dressed like this. But I knew that voice and those eyes anywhere.

"Precious?"

It was Katherine fucking Covington. I hadn't seen her since high school. She had been a nine then, and now she pegged the meter. Her pale blue eyes beguiled me the same way they always had.

A blush rose in her cheeks. "It's been so long," she stammered, a smile growing on her face.

She tucked stray hair behind her ear and shifted her weight. Her hair was up instead of down, and her smile was even brighter than I remembered. The way she filled out her shirt sent a shock to my cock.

She looked down and tapped the cracked screen of her phone. It didn't respond.

"A long time is right, Precious."

I would have preferred her in shorts and a crop top, but she was still stunning.

Tears welled in her eyes. "My phone," she mumbled.

"You should look where you're going next time."

"You ran into me," she blurted defiantly.

Unfortunately, Katie's personality hadn't changed one bit. She'd had an attitude back then, and she hadn't mellowed.

"Well, pardon me for standing still where you wanted to walk, Princess. Now give me that." I wrenched the phone out of her hand.

She huffed. "Give it back, and don't call me that."

She didn't care to be called Precious, but she'd absolutely hated the Princess moniker. Today she deserved it. Yelling at me for standing in her way? Give me a break.

"Just a minute. I'm a whiz with these things." That was no joke.

She grabbed for it, but I kept it out of reach. She stomped her foot like the spoiled brat she was.

"Hold on." I ran through the reset sequence, and the phone began to reboot. I glimpsed Hank to my right.

He had heard our exchange. He waved and left me to handle the ungrateful princess on my own.

Katie smiled as the little apple appeared, and she moved closer, oh so close.

I could feel her body heat as she leaned in. When the reboot finished, the display was only partially drawn and the touch-screen still wouldn't respond.

"You're going to need a new screen," I told her. "And, you should get a cover for this."

"I have one," she said with a glint in her eye.

"They work better when you put the phone in them."

"It got dirty."

Typical Princess response. My cover is too dirty to use. Oh my, what will I do now?

I handed her the phone.

"Thanks for trying," she said sweetly, surprising me.

She put it in her purse as a tear escaped down her cheek. She looked lost, hurt, vulnerable, unlike the feisty woman of ten seconds ago.

I lifted her chin and wiped away the tear with a finger. "What's the problem, Precious?"

She bit her bottom lip, seeming unsure how to respond. "I have to get back to LA, and all the flights are booked. I was going to hang out at the airport and see if I could snag a spare rental car."

"Why don't you just rent a limo?"

The Covingtons had money to burn and had never been ashamed of throwing it around. As soon as the words left my mouth, I regretted being as snarky to her as she had been to me.

She huffed, and anger clouded her eyes. "You wouldn't understand. I really have to get back." She grabbed her roller bag and turned to leave.

She didn't deserve to have me ruin her day. I made a snap judgment, the kind that sometimes got me in trouble.

I jumped around in front of her. "Katie, I'm sorry. That was mean. How 'bout I give you a ride back home?"

She hesitated, but the tug of a smile at the edges of her mouth telegraphed her answer. "You sure?"

"Sure. I was leaving tomorrow anyway. This way I avoid the traffic."

"I'll pay you for the gas," she offered.

"Princess, not everything is about money. Your pretty smile is payment enough."

She smiled at the compliment, despite my calling her Princess. She was as tempting now as she had been back in high school, like the apple in the garden of Eden. One bite, and I would regret it for eternity.

I was giving the princess a ride to help her out, and that was all.

It's just a ride, nothing more.

"If you have a pair of pants in there, pull 'em out," I told her. "It'll get colder as we near LA."

Her brow creased with confusion, but she did as I asked and pulled out a pair of striped yoga pants.

I rolled her bag over to the counter and asked to add it to my bag, which was being delivered to my house tomorrow. I had planned on living out of my backpack tonight. Luggage delivery made these trips so much easier.

She started to object, but my finger to her lips stopped her. The girl had to work on her obsession with rejecting help.

"Just don't call me Princess again," was all she ended up saying.

I nodded. "'K."

The clerk finished adding Katie's bag to my account. My mom's picture dropped out of my wallet as I put my credit card back in.

Katie picked the photo up and handed it to me.

I returned the picture to my wallet, relieved that it hadn't been stepped on. It couldn't be replaced. "You wait here while I get my stuff from upstairs."

She nodded. "Thanks."

I composed a text to Hank on my way to the elevator.

ME: Heading back 2nite catch up later

I waved to Katie as the elevator door closed.

She waved back.

I was going to enjoy having that body wrapped around me tonight.

CHAPTER 2

Nick

Her jaw dropped as soon as she recognized what I was carrying. Her eyes widened to the size of saucers, which only highlighted the light blue hue that had always captivated me. When I said I'd give her a ride back to LA, I meant it literally. A ride on the back of my bike, with that tempting body wrapped around me the whole way. Six hours in her warm embrace.

I scanned her from head to toe and back again as she put her laptop down and stood. Temptingly beautiful was the description that came to mind. My cock twitched as I could already feel those nice warm tits pressed up against my back for the long ride home. I walked over with my best smile and prepared for the onslaught.

"Are you kidding?" she asked. It was less of a temper tantrum than I had expected.

"The last time we saw each other you were begging for a ride on my hawg."

That day, Katherine fucking Covington had completely

surprised me. She begged for a ride, and I had been in the process of learning how much she would trade for it. She had always been off-limits. She was a Covington, and I knew enough to keep to my side of the tracks. I'd pursued easier, more willing prey: girls I could relate to, girls I could understand, girls who wanted to be bad.

That was the day her stepbrother caught me with my hand halfway up her shirt, and yes, she was begging me for a ride. Liam didn't like me touching his sister, which was no surprise. But his anger resulted in a yell, followed by an easy to dodge fist aimed at me. He never stood a chance.

A quick jab had sent him reeling with a bloody nose, and ended my date with his sister.

Her family got me kicked out of school the next day.

I hadn't seen the princess Katherine Covington since.

She put her hands on her hips, but smiled nonetheless. "I remember, but that was a quick trip to Dairy Queen, not an all night ride to LA."

I set down the two helmets and touched her gently on the shoulder. "Precious, I can understand if you're too scared."

As expected, the challenge was too much for her to resist. "I am not scared." She straightened herself. "I'm just not dressed for it." She pointed to her skirt and jacket combo.

"No worries." I pointed to the restrooms. "Put on your leggings. I have leathers to keep you warm."

With a huff she marched off with her silly yoga pants. They might not keep her warm, but they sure would look good on her once she lost the skirt.

She returned with a sour expression on her face. "I look like a fool." The yoga pants were zebra striped, not a good match to her light blue suit. She hadn't ditched the skirt as I had hoped she would.

An elderly lady passing by couldn't keep her sneer to herself.

I led Katie outside. "Personally I think you look adorable."

It had to be hard for princess little-miss-perfect to endure all the double-takes she got.

Motorcycle parking was at the front of the garage. For this trip I had driven the Honda. It was a big CB900 with a fairing, a good touring bike for long distances, unlike the Harley.

I handed her my leathers, pants and a jacket.

She hiked her skirt up.

Her nice legs and luscious ass enticed me as I helped her zip the clothes up. The leather pants were too long for her, but they would keep her warm.

Jeans would have to do for me. I gave her the heavyweight leather jacket and slid on the lighter one. Her heels were shitty for riding but that couldn't be helped.

She let her hair down and shook it out before pulling it back into a ponytail with an elastic band. The long blond hair was a beautiful complement to her face, it was a shame to put it up when she looked so stunning with it down.

"What's this for?" she asked when I handed her the backpack.

"Are all you rich girls so clueless? You put your shit in it and you wear it."

With a grimace but no back talk for a change, she loaded her laptop bag and her thousand dollar purse in the backpack.

I helped her with the helmet and pointed out her foot pegs before mounting up and patting the seat behind me.

She swung her leg over and we were almost ready.

I punched the starter, and we were set. "Hold on, Precious."

Like a novice she put her hands on my hips. "Shit," came through the intercom as I pulled away.

"If you want to stay on the bike, you're going to have to do better than that, Precious."

She grabbed a little tighter, but not enough. When we launched into traffic. She almost came loose before she got the idea and hugged me tightly.

"Bluetooth intercom," I told her. "So don't mumble anything to yourself you don't want me to hear."

She was warm and soft against my back and legs. This was going to be a nice trip with her snuggled against me all night. She was so close we knocked helmets on the first few gear shifts until she got the hang of it. She grabbed me tighter, and my cock surged.

Having her soft warmth against me with only a few layers of fabric and leather between us was going to kill me. I might need to visit the hospital after this ride. Like the advertisements said, seek medical attention for any erection lasting longer than four hours.

~

Katie

THE INSTANT ACCELERATION JERKED ME BACKWARDS AND ENDED my reluctance to grab onto him. I looped my arms around his massive chest and held tight, clamping my legs to the outside of his. His warmth was comforting.

After realizing that I wasn't going to fall off, the ride became nice, even fun. The rushing air and the noise of the engine were exhilarating as we made our way through traffic. My nipples peaked as each gear shift pressed my breasts harder against him.

Back in high school, Nick had been the ultimate bad boy. He'd smoked, he had tattoos, and he rode a motorcycle. Not just any motorcycle, but a ferociously loud Harley. He'd derided the bikes the other boys rode as *rice burners*. Nick had cut classes regularly, and he'd given all the teachers lip, but somehow he'd always managed to ace the tests, even though he'd *claimed* to never study.

He'd scored points on the football field as a wide receiver, and his reputation had him scoring off the field with at least half the cheerleaders.

But I hadn't cared. I'd needed to prove that I could handle myself, and he was what I wanted to handle. That day I had undone another two buttons on my shirt and begged him for a ride on the back of his Harley. It had been an act of rebellion for me. I'd thought I would get it until Liam intervened.

Then Nick was gone.

Now I was clinging to him, hurtling down the interstate. Virtually the only words between us so far had been "hold on, Precious".

"Road boulder," he said as we passed another slow car.

"I thought you had a Harley," I said into my helmet.

"I do, but you wouldn't want to ride it on a long trip like this. The damn thing would rattle the fillings right out of your teeth," he said.

I laughed.

"I ride it around town, because the chicks dig being on back," he laughed. "Because it's like riding a huge vibrator."

I joined his laugh. I could understand why. The vibrator I was sitting on wasn't bad. But, it was the warmth of his body that was getting to me. Back then I had wanted a ride on his bike. Today my imagination was running away with me, and I visualized riding more than his bike.

"The picture you dropped at the front desk. That your girlfriend? She the hot date waiting for you back in LA?"

He didn't answer for the longest time and I feared I might have overstepped a boundary.

"No, that's my Mom. She died when I was young. I never knew her." He paused. "It's the only picture I have of her."

I felt terrible that I had joked about it. "I'm sorry, Nick, I didn't know." I had never known anything about his family back in school. It was touching that he would carry her picture in his wallet.

My mother had also died when I was young, but not so young that I didn't have memories of her. It still hurt when I thought about her.

"It's okay, Precious. I'm over it," he said unconvincingly. Guys could be like that, hiding the hurt they harbored inside behind the tough macho exterior they put up.

Several miles passed before he spoke again. "How's that dickhead brother of yours? Liam?"

"I don't see him much, he moved out to Boston."

"Whatever happened between him and Roberta? I never could figure out what she saw in him."

"They got married." I didn't know how else to say the rest of it. "She died." Liam had married her after he found out about her illness. The doctors had done what they could, but it had been too late.

"I'm sorry to hear that," he said as he accelerated into the left lane. "She was a nice girl."

I squeezed him. "She was." Despite the gruff biker reputation the sincerity of his voice conveyed a tenderness hidden inside.

We left the heat of Las Vegas behind, and I was grateful for the leather pants and jacket.

The occasional bug splattered on the short windshield of his fairing as we droned on across the high desert.

"So, Precious, what brought you to Vegas?"

"Getting my CPA, and this was an accounting conference."

"CPA, huh?"

"Yeah, you got something against that?" Guys were always questioning my ability to accomplish things.

"No. I just never figured you for the corporate type."

I hadn't either, but it had become my path. Accounting had been my major when I got my MBA, and the progression to CPA had seemed natural at the time. Lately I regretted my choice.

"You going to work for Daddy then?"

"No. He died over a year ago," I told him as we slowed for a pair of side-by-side trucks.

"I'm sorry. I didn't know. It must've been hard," he said with obvious compassion.

I sniffled in my helmet, unable to wipe my nose. It had been hard. Dad had been a bit of a chauvinist, but he'd just been trying to protect me in his own way. I missed him more than I could explain.

"So you have to wear suits all day and hang around with stuffy corporate types? I could never handle that. I probably couldn't go a whole day tolerating those fools." The words coming in the helmet mirrored thoughts I often had.

"Yeah, some days it's hard," I admitted.

He raised a hand to waive to a biker going the opposite direction on the freeway. "Why do it then?"

"I'm putting my hours in at Arthur and Company, so I can get signed off for my CPA. I only have to make it through the fall, then I can quit and get a nice job somewhere else with my certificate. Until then I would have to tolerate my asshole boss."

"He isn't coming on to you, is he?" His voice was laced with sudden protectiveness.

"No, nothing like that. Lately he seems to want to run me out of the company."

"If he gets to be too much, let me know, and I'll give the toad an attitude adjustment he won't forget." He chuckled.

The image of Nick punching Russ brought a smile to my face. "No thanks, not just yet."

"The offer stands, Precious. If he gets to be too much."

We passed a pickup in serious need of a muffler job.

I needed to change the subject before I was tempted to take him up on it. "What were you doing in Las Vegas?"

"Conference, just like you. The *Black Hat Conference*. A guy was giving a hacking presentation for me." We passed a minivan on the right that was going too slow for Nick's taste.

"So you're a computer hacker?" The Harley rider I was wrapped around didn't mesh with my image of a computer nerd.

"Not like you think, Precious. I'm one of the good guys."

"But you called it the Black Hat conference."

"That's the organizers messing with everybody. It's actually the white hat guys like me giving presentations about vulnerabilities that we find."

"Why?"

"The publicity makes the companies fix the problems. We used to try to work with them confidentially, but it didn't work. They never took the bugs seriously enough. Now, when we go public at the conference, the heat is on them to plug the holes quickly or they might get sued."

It made sense when he put it that way. I had seen plenty of instances of companies deciding to put things off until they were forced to do them.

"We need some gas. How 'bout a bite to eat when we stop?" he asked.

"Sounds great, but only if you let me treat." I had hoped he would want dinner, because I was famished, having upchucked everything earlier.

"I can handle that."

I stopped myself before saying something stupid about wanting to be handled.

NICK

I PULLED OFF THE INTERSTATE AT AN EXIT TO NOWHERE. WE needed gas and food. As a novice rider I was sure Katie needed a break. This exit featured a McDonald's, a Taco Bell, and a Subway.

Her first few steps on solid ground were wobbly. It didn't help that she was wearing heels and my leathers were too long for her.

“Since you're paying, why don’t you pick the establishment,” I told her.

She took a wobbly step backwards. “McDonald's okay with you?”

“Perfect. I'll take two quarter pounders and a chocolate shake with large fries. Why don’t you get us a table while I gas up?”

I couldn't take my eyes off the sway of her sweet ass as she walked away.

She held the legs of the leathers up to keep from tripping over them. As she reached the door she looked back and smiled.

I waved and went about gassing up our ride.

By the time I finished, she was at a window table with a full tray of food, but hadn’t touched it yet.

“No need to wait for me, Precious. Dig in.”

“A lady always has good manners. And that means waiting for everybody to be seated before starting to eat.” As soon as I sat, she unwrapped her burger and attacked it. She was one hungry girl. She glanced up and caught me eyeing her. “Why are you smirking?”

“Smiling, not smirking, and I enjoy a woman that isn’t self-conscious about eating.”

She unzipped the leather jacket and continued eating. “I didn’t really get much lunch,” she mumbled between bites.

I took in her beauty as I peeled off my jacket and started on my fries and shake.

With her hair down she appeared younger and less stern than she had when she first bumped into me, happier, a definite improvement. Her earlier crying had resulted in a mascara run under one eye.

I wetted the corner of a napkin with the condensation on my shake cup, leaned forward and wiped under her eye.

She didn't pull away. "Thanks."

"A request."

Her brow creased with confusion as she pondered her response. "Okay. What?"

"Let your hair loose, I want to see it down."

She pulled back, bit her lip, and complied with a loud huff. Her lovely hair cascaded over her shoulders as she shook it out.

"Precious, you look gorgeous. That's the way you should wear your hair all the time."

She instantly turned red. "Stop that." She hid her face behind her hands for a moment.

I opened my burger and took a bite, not glancing up for a bit, to give her a chance to regain her composure.

She reached over and touched my hand. Her touch, skin to skin contact, sent a jolt through me. "Thank you, Nick, that's the nicest thing anyone has said to me in a long time." Her smile was genuine, and her eyes, soft.

I smiled back. "The truth, and nothing but the truth."

I didn't tell her I imagined gripping that hair as I pounded into her. If she had been one of my usual dates, it would have been a clear signal to find a room, and quick. But she was not a date and not my usual type in any way. This was Katherine fucking Covington, princess of the Covington family, and way above my pay grade. I had learned a long time ago how they felt about her being anywhere near a guy like me, and I was sure that hadn't changed. Bill and Liam were very protective of their little sister, to say nothing of her younger brothers who couldn't have threatened me in high school, but were all grown up now and probably equally as protective.

Nevertheless, she was quite a sight, and I could look all I wanted. For tonight she was mine, just me and her, no brothers in sight. I could let my imagination run wild, so long as I kept my hands to myself.

"Tell me, why do you have to get back home in such a hurry?"

She tucked stray hair behind her ear with those red fingernails.

I momentarily wondered how those claws would feel digging into my back as she screamed out her orgasm or how those soft fingers would feel wrapped around my cock. I smiled at the imaginary scene of her underneath me. I didn't say anything, waiting for her to continue.

"There's this crazy lady who blames my brother Steven and his wife for ruining her life." She played with her fries for a moment. "She even torched Emma's car a few weeks ago. That's my sister-in-law." She sniffled. "Anyway." She bit her lip. Whatever she held back more than bothered her; it terrified her.

"That's okay. You don't need to tell me any more. I don't need to know. I'm just happy to help." I didn't want her to drag herself back through the trauma. Whatever it was, was dark enough to break her.

She took a deep breath. "She burned down my house today," she blurted out. Tears flowed as she lost it.

I went around and joined her on her side of the table, putting my arm around her shoulder and pulling her in tight. "That's terrible. I'm so sorry." What kind of sicko bitch burns down someone's house?

She gave into her grief and wrapped her arms around me, burying her head in my chest and crying. "I've never even met the bitch. Why did she have to do this to me?"

I didn't have an answer for her. I held her and stroked her hair. All I could do to comfort her was to hold her as long as she needed. "You need a place to stay?"

She sobbed. "No, I'm going to stay with my brother Patrick for a few days." She wiped her nose.

"Keep the offer in mind. I have a place for you if you need it." I shouldn't have, but I kissed the top of her head.

"Thanks, Nick." She pulled away and straightened up. "I'll be okay, thanks for the offer." She wiped her nose with a napkin and we went back to eating.

This vulnerable side of Katie was something I hadn't seen before. She'd always been the self-confident feisty one, more a tomboy than a girl back in school.

I stayed seated next to her, my thigh up against the warmth of hers. I could smell the fruitiness of her hair up close.

For a moment, as she sucked on the straw of her drink, I allowed myself to wonder what those luscious lips would feel like sucking my dick.

She smiled at me "What are you looking at?" she asked, completely unaware of my impure thoughts. If she knew she'd probably be screaming to get away from me or getting prepared to kick me in the balls.

I gave her half the truth. "Just thinking what a beautiful lady you've grown up to be."

The blush quickly returned to her cheeks, and she slapped my thigh. "Cut it out, now I have to say something nice about you."

"Is that a rule?"

"For a lady it is. In polite company at least," she retorted.

"And you think I'm polite enough?"

She giggled. "I was going to say that I think you've grown up to be quite the gentleman."

"You've got me all wrong, Princess. Not even close." She wouldn't have said that if she knew what was actually on my mind. And, a gentleman was not something I ever aspired to be.

CHAPTER 3

Katie

Nick had been so nice, so comforting at the stop, showing me the tender side that hid beneath the surface. There was much more to him than the hard, badass he projected to the world. Nick was a study in contradictions. One moment being nice and kind, and the next infuriatingly rude and insensitive. That was probably the battle he waged to maintain the hard outer shell to keep people from seeing the soft inner core of Nick Knowlton lest they take advantage of him.

He was bad all right. Back in school, the few morons who had challenged Nick had regretted it, even the Russians.

Yuri Sorokin thought that Nick had wronged his sister, and he might have been right. Yuri and his two brothers jumped Nick after school in the parking lot. The Russian kids ended up with a broken jaw and several broken fingers between them. The Principal wanted to suspend Nick for the fight, but a bunch of us witnessed the whole thing and backed up Nick's story. That was the last time I remembered anyone challenge Nick Knowlton—

until my step-brother Liam made the mistake and got his nose broken.

Now Nick was a computer guy. A computer nerd who was a hacker of the first order if he was good enough to present at that conference in Las Vegas, and the same time a rough-and-tumble biker. Whoever heard of a computer nerd riding a Harley? I wouldn't have believed it before today.

We were back in the LA basin after the long ride down from the high desert. It was a lot chillier here. The leathers helped, but I still clung to him tightly to stay warm. And not just to stay warm, but also because it felt perfect to be snuggled up so tight to such a capable man. The strength he projected was getting to me, or maybe it was just his gasoline powered vibrator between my legs.

I had hardly dated after I graduated from USC, and not while getting my MBA either.

I had been driven to finish near the top of my class in school, and now to get my CPA. The hours they worked the first and second year accountants at Arthur and Company didn't allow much time for a social life. And, my hours were worse than most thanks to my A-hole boss Russ.

As the lights of the city passed by I found my thoughts wandering to what it would've been like if Nick and I had gotten together back in high school. It had taken me forever to work up the courage to approach him that afternoon. If only Liam hadn't intervened.

The other girls saw the hot bad boy, I saw more than that. I'd been sitting next to him in algebra the day he slammed his fist down so hard he broke his desk and got kicked out of class. The other girls found his strength hot, but what had intrigued me, was I had seen what caused it. He broke the desk because the test he had gotten back wasn't an "A".

I gave myself a mental slap. It wouldn't have worked any more then than it would now, and deep down, I knew it. I couldn't stop the sensations that rolled through me being this close to him. My arms around his muscular chest. My thighs gripping his. My breasts pillowed against his back. His breathing and occasional words in my ears.

"Do you want to go by your house tonight?" he asked. "Or do we go straight to your brother's place?"

I had been so lost thinking about him on this trip that I hadn't considered the question. The lack of a moon tonight made the darkness impenetrable. "Patrick's, I think. I'll go see it in the morning. From what Bill said, there won't be anything to see, anyway."

"I'll pick you up at eight then and take you over," Nick said.

I didn't argue, I appreciated his offer. I dreaded making the trip by myself. We exited the freeway, and I directed him to Patrick's condo on Wilshire.

Nick pulled up and parked by the front door.

It was over too quickly; I didn't want it to stop.

~

Nick

It was huge, at least twenty stories tall.

I put down the kickstand. "What is this place?"

"My brothers both have condos here. My sister-in-law Lauren calls it the Battlestar Covington."

So much like a Covington to flaunt his money and have a view looking down on the rest of us mere mortals. "Looks more like the Death Star to me."

"It's better in the daylight."

The big black glass tower had a lobby of marble and chrome that reeked of money. They even had a doorman. Nobody in LA had a doorman—that was a New York thing. Out here you pumped your own gas, and you opened your own doors.

The cheery old man greeted us. "Good evening, Miss Katherine."

"Ollie, this is my good friend Nick Knowlton. He's okay to come and go as he pleases."

The man's name tag said Oliver. "I'll note his name down for the others. Pleasure to meet you, Mr. Knowlton."

We shook.

Katie punched the up button for the elevator and smiled up at me. "Thanks for the ride, I've got it from here. You don't need to come up."

I ignored her plea and ushered her into the elevator car, my hand on the small of her back. "A gentleman sees the lady all the way to her door."

I put my arm around her. "I'm just trying to help a lady in distress."

"The lady appreciates it."

When we got in the elevator, she naturally pushed the button for the twenty-second floor. Big surprise, her brother had a penthouse on the top floor of a building twenty stories taller than anything else around. She smiled up at me and snaked her arm around me, pulling in tight, the little tease.

I relished the last few minutes of her warmth as she molded her body to mine and stiffened my rod.

Upstairs, she pushed the doorbell.

When the door opened, her younger brother Patrick greeted us. His eyes turned cold, his brow creased, and his smile disappeared as soon as he noticed my arm around his sister. His disapproval was clear as his eyes challenged me.

"Patrick, you remember Nick?" Katie said in a cheery tone.

I let go of Katie and balanced my stance. I could dodge either direction if he came at me. I wouldn't throw the first punch, but I would be sure to throw the last.

Katie started to move through the door. "Patrick, aren't you going to thank Nick for bringing me back?"

Her brother moved aside to let her by and his countenance softened. "Sure… Thanks, Nick."

I chuckled. "My pleasure, Patrick, Katie kept me nice and warm."

Fury rose in his face.

I backed toward the elevator. "Precious, eight tomorrow downstairs, don't forget. I'll get the backpack and leathers from you tomorrow."

She blew me a kiss before the door closed. "Eight sharp."

It didn't matter what had brought that on. She was a typical little rich girl, all tease and no action. For some stupid reason I had promised to take her tomorrow morning to see her burned down house, and I always kept my promises. After that she would be out of my hair. My good deed was complete. She was safe and sound back with her family and I could go back to my life, with my kind of people. Normal people who worked for a living.

Sit on that and rotate, Patrick fucking Covington.

Katie

The air-kiss got to Patrick. He slammed the door, ready to blow a gasket. "What was that all about?" he demanded.

"He's just messing with you, and like an idiot, you took the bait," I chided him.

My sister-in-law Emma was on the couch with droopy eyelids. The glass of wine in her hand obviously not her first.

Winston Evers pulled something from the fridge. I knew Winston from our Sundays at the Habitat for Humanity projects.

He rarely missed a weekend. Winston was a strapping ex-FBI agent who worked both the investigative and security sides of the Hanson firm. He had always been nice to me, and my brothers trusted him implicitly.

I headed for the bathroom.

Patrick took a place on the couch with Emma. "You aren't going to be seeing him tomorrow," he announced.

I turned to face my brother. "The hell I'm not."

"That's right, you're not," Patrick repeated after a sip of his wine.

"I'm not a kid anymore, and you can't tell me what to do."

"Maybe I didn't make myself clear. You are not going to see him."

I continued to the bathroom without another word. I needed to pee badly. That convinced him he had won the argument, and he went back to his wine and talking quietly with Emma.

Leaving the bathroom I marched straight to the heavy front door. "Bye," I said as I closed it behind me.

"Katie come back here," Patrick yelled through the closed door. "It's not safe."

I boarded the open elevator and punched the button for the lobby.

I heard footsteps in the hallway coming toward the elevator. I hit the close-door button frantically, and the stainless panels met in the middle before he reached me.

I put the backpack on and hiked up the extra long leathers. When the elevator doors parted, I raced across the lobby. I had made it in time.

Nick was at the bike putting on his helmet.

"Got room for one more?" I yelled scurrying across the lobby, trying to keep from tripping on the over-length leathers. I waved at Oliver as I ran by.

"Goodnight Miss Covington," the white-haired old man said as I passed.

Nick looked surprised. He unhooked the second helmet from the back of the bike and handed it to me. “What's the problem, Princess?”

I ignored the Princess comment, took the helmet, and slid it on. “We need to go.” I climbed on the bike behind him.

Winston Evers came charging out of the second elevator and through the lobby. I wasn’t letting him carry me back upstairs if that’s what Patrick had sent him to do.

I clung tightly to Nick. “Now!” I yelled. “Go, go, go!”

Nick punched the starter, and we roared off into the chilly darkness before Winston reached us. Nick turned left on Wilshire toward the freeway.

He didn’t slow until we were a few blocks away.

“What was that all about?” he asked.

I couldn’t tell Nick that he was the cause of the argument because he was only the latest issue. It was my over-controlling brothers who were the problem. They didn’t want to let me grow up, and it had only gotten worse since dad died. Steven listened to me the best, but he had left LA, and now I had to deal with Bill and Patrick on my own. “Patrick was being an ass is all.”

“I used to like him, it’s Bill and Liam that I couldn’t get along with.” Not getting along with them was certainly an understatement, especially after he’d broken Liam’s nose.

“My brothers are always trying to tell me what to do, and I've had enough of it,” I said into the microphone.

We rode on in silence. Not surprisingly there were still plenty of cars on the road.

The car next to us had parents in the front and a blonde high school age girl in the back. She stared over at us.

I waved to her.

She smiled back. She was me those years ago. Stuck in the car, wishing to be free to ride on the back of a fast bike, hugging a hot guy, leaving the world behind, free to go where I wanted and do what I wanted, enjoying the thrill of the moment.

I had wanted that freedom when I was her age. Then I grew up to drive a sensible car with a gazillion airbags, and a motor you couldn't even hear. All without ever having had the wind in my ears, with the power of a hundred horses vibrating between my legs and screaming out the exhaust pipe as we roared off into the sunset.

Today Nick and I had ridden into the sunset on the way back. It even was better than I had imagined back then. The noise of the bike mixed with the wind erased my worries as I clung to his back and my arms felt his rhythmic breathing with the desert whipping by. The windswept sand and scrub brush giving way to the endless stretch of suburbia as we'd merged onto the foothill freeway in Rancho Cucamonga had relaxed me.

"Where am I taking you?" he asked, breaking me out of my reverie. His question reminded me that I wasn't a high school girl on an evening ride, I was Katherine Covington. I was a grown up with a job and responsibilities, not free to ride off into the sunset even if I wanted to.

Katherine would have chosen a hotel, the Beverly Wilshire or the Beverly Hilton. That was a sensible choice befitting her sensible business suit, her sensible make-up, and her sensible job.

Katherine had gotten perfect grades, worn perfect clothes with perfect makeup, had had a perfect job, and a perfect fucking future. Except Katherine's life was now a shambles. Her house burned down today, and her perfect job had turned into hell on earth with the devil himself as her boss. Sensible Katherine was not having a good day, or a good month.

Katherine would have put up with Patrick and stayed at the condo. Katherine would've listened to her brother. She would've bitched about it, but she would've given in, understanding that it was the safe, sensible thing to do.

I was tired of being Katherine.

It was time to be Katie again.

Katie was wearing motorcycle leathers and had draped herself around the baddest boy in school all afternoon and evening, except he was no longer a boy. Nick had grown up into a mountain of a man. Everything about him was dangerous and intoxicating. With Katherine's life in ruins, Katie wanted dangerous and intoxicating, not safe and sensible. Katie deserved it with all the shit she had gone through.

Katherine would've used her head and made careful plans. Katie felt like being impulsive, even reckless.

Fuck plans, what did I feel like? I knew what I wanted, and I deserved it. It had been a long time, way too long.

I disengaged Katherine's mouth filter. "I was thinking your place." I gave him a squeeze as I moved my arms a few inches lower toward his crotch.

CHAPTER 4

Nick

My cock swelled with her answer even though I knew she was not saying it the way I wanted her to mean it.

Katie grabbed me again as the light went green, only lower this time, dangerously low. She was making it hard to concentrate, which wasn't all that was hard.

Normally if a girl came to my place for the evening, there were two options: on her back or on her knees. The problem was this was still princess Katherine Covington, and I had offered her a safe place to stay the night.

I always kept my word, but this being a gentleman shit was going to kill me. I should have suggested a hotel, she could afford it. She could afford to buy a fucking hotel. And that would put her safely out of reach, not temptingly close.

I moved over to the left turn lane. "Okay, it's not far," I said into the intercom.

The little girl in the car next to us smiled and waved as we slowed and they went on through the intersection.

I could do this. Nice guys gave nice girls a safe place to spend the night all the time didn't they?

Only one problem. I never put myself in the nice guy category, not even close.

Twenty minutes later we pulled into my driveway.

I shut down the engine and put the bike over on the kickstand after she got off.

She took off her helmet. "Nice place."

"It's good enough for me." I was sure this wasn't anywhere near what a Covington would call nice, but it was mine free and clear and with two separate gigabit Internet pipes into the house it worked for me. The neighborhood was respectable and clean, with honest working-class neighbors.

I unlocked the door and quieted the beeping of the alarm panel by putting in my code. "It may not be much, but I call it home." I set the helmets down and went to the garage to put the bike away.

When I returned she came out of the bathroom and started unzipping the leathers. She kicked off her heels and then pulled the yoga pants down from under her skirt.

I chuckled. If her fucking brother Liam could see her now, taking clothes off in my place, the little bastard would shit a brick.

She finished pulling off the leggings. "What's so funny?"

"Oh, nothing." I wasn't about to admit I was thinking back to that day I had punched out her brother.

"These are Lululemon."

"I don't care if they're lala-orange, you look fantastic." And it wasn't just her legs that I was commenting on.

She smiled coyly and finished getting back to her wrinkled business suit. "I could use something to drink. Do you have any Chardonnay?" This girl was something else, expecting that everybody had a fucking wine cellar.

"Fresh out. Your choices are Bud and Jack, so what's your pleasure, Precious?"

She settled onto the couch after taking off her jacket. "Whiskey sounds good right about now."

I put some ice cubes in glasses and brought them over with the bottle. She probably wasn't ready for neat Jack. I kicked off my boots and took a seat next to her and poured us each a finger.

She combed out her hair with her fingers.

"You should keep it down, Precious. The look becomes you. It makes your eyes even more irresistible."

A blush rose in her cheeks along with the smile that I craved. She knocked her drink back before I even got started. This girl needed to slow down. She snuggled up next to me with her hand on my thigh. "How 'bout another?"

I poured her another, but kept it small. "You need to sip it, not gulp it." I put my arm around her shoulder and pulled her hot body up to mine, remembering the sensations of her behind me on the trip.

Her hand traveled back to my thigh and traced little circles. No doubt she noticed the bulge she caused in my pants.

I had almost unlimited willpower, but she was testing my almost limit. I jumped up. "Let me show you where you can sleep."

Disappointment clouded her face, but she followed me to the guest bedroom, which was a smaller second master with its own bathroom.

"I can offer you a T-shirt to sleep in, and there's a clean toothbrush and everything you need in the bathroom right here." I pushed open the door to show her.

"I sleep in the nude," she giggled.

That comment jolted my cock again.

She was right behind me when I turned.

She closed the last few inches between us and went up on her toes, snaked her hands behind my neck, and pulled herself up into a kiss.

Her breasts were even better on my chest than my back as I grabbed her ass and hauled her up a few inches to meet me. Her mouth opened to mine. She tasted naughty, with an aftertaste of whiskey. Her tongue slid over mine as our tongues began the French dance, feinting one way and going the other, seeking each other out, tongue jousting.

I had figured her for a novice kisser, but I had been wrong. She clawed at my hair and attacked me furiously. She was one hell of a kisser and her body was to die for. She was temptation incarnate.

She was in serious danger of getting herself fucked right here on the carpet.

I was in serious danger of repeating my high school mistake. The Covingtons were not a family to mess with lightly. I could handle myself against any one of them, but the combined family had the resources to bury anybody who got in their way. I wasn't afraid, merely realistic. If they thought I had wronged their little sister, I would be fighting them off for years, and they were rich enough to have the cops in their back pockets and make my life miserable.

I should have duct-taped her, thrown her over my shoulder, and dumped her in the lobby of that monster Covington glass palace.

Instead, I kissed her back hard. I had to scare some sense into her. I had my hand up the back of her shirt and with a single flick, undid the clasps of her bra, followed by a quick trip under her skirt to pull her panties to the side and insert a finger.

My aggressiveness should have sent the prim and proper little princess running for the hills, but instead she ripped at my shirt. "More," she moaned.

Now I was fucking toast.

~

Katie

KATHERINE WOULD HAVE ACCEPTED THE OFFER OF THE SPARE bedroom and called an end to her shitty day.

But Katie was in charge, and she knew what she wanted. Cosmo said men liked their women aggressive and asking for it. I meant to test that.

When he turned, I jumped him and pulled myself up into a kiss. I speared my hand through his hair, Mr. Dangerous, meet Miss Impulsive.

He met me and our tongues dueled as he kissed me with equal fervor. He smelled of spice and manliness. We traded breath and desire like wild animals. His intensity melted my panties as I rubbed up against the bulge of his arousal. I had never done anything remotely like this. I never even gotten beyond second base with a guy on the first date before, and here I was attacking bad boy Nick. Katherine would have stopped, but Katie was going to mark something crazy off her to-do list tonight.

Guys had kissed me before, but never like this. This was my first real kiss. A kiss with a man, not a boy. I had never had a kiss that brought out the animal in him and me. Never a kiss that was unbridled sensuality. I had no idea that a kiss could convey such passion, all my previous boyfriends had been gentle and subdued. Nick's mouth branded me as his, with intensity and pure panty melting lust. He was an incredible kisser—he could probably make a living at it.

In an instant he unhooked my bra with the practiced single-handed motion of a master at unclothing women. His hand moved to my thigh and lifted my skirt.

The feel of my breasts pressed up against his muscled chest was heavenly as the heat in my core built to an intolerable level.

He pulled my panties aside.

I gasped as a finger traced my drenched slit and entered my slick heat.

It was decision time. Sensible Katherine would have run, but reckless Katie was in charge. I moaned out the word, "More." I broke the kiss and tore at his shirt to get it off him. I needed to have his skin against mine, to mingle sweat as well as breath.

He pulled my shirt off, buttons flying in different directions. He lifted his shirt over his head and threw it to the wall.

I dropped my bra and pulled at his belt, but he stopped me.

"No," he told me sternly. "Now lose the skirt," he commanded. He stood there, panting, soaking up every inch of my naked chest with his gaze. The heat of his stare made my entire body tingle. He cradled the weight of my breasts in his hands and traced tingly hot strokes around my nipples with his thumbs.

I unzipped the skirt and pushed it over my hips. It puddled at my feet. I was frozen in his glare as he pulled his hands away from my breasts and stood back to watch me.

"Now the panties." His voice was firm, insistent, building foreboding, naughty heat within me. My pussy sizzled with anticipation. This was unlike anything I had experienced before. The raw power of his voice and the animal look in his eyes demanded obedience.

I slid them down and kicked them aside. If spontaneous combustion was a thing, I was a candidate for it.

"Turn around," he commanded in a low voice.

I turned slowly and stopped, facing the bed, wondering what would come next.

"All the way."

When he had told me to turn I had expected him to want to

take me from behind or something, but he was devouring me with his eyes as I turned, like a roast on the spit.

"Precious," he said with wide eyes and an even wider smile.

I trembled as I waited for his next words. My thighs were slick with anticipation, my nipples peaked with excitement, my nerves tingling with impatience for his touch.

"You look absolutely beautiful." He pulled me to him forcefully, tightly.

My breasts pressed to him, feeling his skin against mine for the first time, but I hoped not the last, as he resumed the kiss and devoured me again, sucking the breath from me.

I clawed at his neck and laced my fingers through his hair.

His hands roamed my body, leaving trails of hot sparks everywhere they went. He thumbed my nipples and fondled my bare breasts. He traced my ass cheek and tickled my belly button, denying me his fingers at my drenched pussy.

I rubbed myself up against the giant bulge in his jeans, trying to coax him to give me his cock. I tugged at his belt again.

He pulled my hand away and swatted my ass. "Wait." The message was clear. I wasn't the one in charge. I might have started this, but he was going to finish it.

He lifted me up like I was a feather, which couldn't be further from the truth, and carried me into the other bedroom. It was clearly the master. He set me down on the edge of the bigger than king bed with a wide carved headboard. He pushed me to lie back on the bed with my legs dangling over the edge. My thighs trembled as he forced them apart.

A wicked smile came to his face as he took in the sight of my spread pussy.

I was completely open to him. The lights were on and I wasn't prepared for this. I had no idea what to expect with this man. Modesty made me try to close my legs, but he held them apart.

I gasped and tried again to close my legs as his face approached my crotch, but he was too strong.

In college I was probably the only girl in the dorm that hadn't given head or received it. Katherine Covington had been a prude that way, and all the guys had been deferential to me. It must have been because of my name, they didn't try to force the issue. Sure, I had given Joe a full hand job in the shower once, but that was about as adventurous as I had gotten. Everything else had been plain vanilla nookie.

Nick put his mouth to my pussy and licked the length of my folds, parting my soaked lips with his tongue, teasing my entrance. His stubble scraped my thighs as he moved in. His tongue circled my clit several times before he sucked on my little bud.

His hands went to my breasts and fondled and teased me as his tongue worked his magic ministrations on my defenseless clit.

The sensations crashed over me, taking me by surprise, lighting me on fire in a way I hadn't expected. I hadn't had any idea what I'd been missing.

His tongue teased me, alternately circling my entrance and moving up to my clit, circling, stabbing, stroking and sucking in a delicious torture of my swollen nub.

The waves of pleasure rolled over me in ever increasing strength as I widened my thighs and pulled at his hair. I needed him closer, harder, and just more. I had never been this high off the ground as my blood boiled and the fireworks exploded behind my eyelids.

I panted and yelped with every stroke of his tongue and pinch of his fingers as he lit all my nerve endings on fire. Every cell in my body was tensing as he drove me closer to the cliff and finally over into a sea of ecstasy.

The convulsions came as my back arched and my legs

clamped around his head, threatening to suffocate him against my throbbing pussy.

He took a thumb and pressed hard against my clit, intensifying my final throes of release.

I tried to catch my breath as I came down off my high.

I had fingered myself to climax before, but he had shown me the kind of orgasm I didn't know existed.

He stood and unbuckled his belt.

I got off the bed and pulled at his zipper. I hooked my fingers in the waist band and pulled down his boxer briefs along with his jeans.

His cock sprang loose and rose against his stomach. Everything about Nick was big, and his cock was no exception. His was big enough to need its own zip code. Long and thick and beautiful.

I grasped it and pulled.

He groaned the wonderful sound of pleasure. He pushed me back onto the bed and I shimmied up. He pulled a condom package from the drawer of the nightstand, ripping it open with his teeth. He handed it to me.

The guys had always sheathed themselves, so I fumbled to pull the latex out of the package and find the right side to roll down.

He took a finger and wiped the bead of pre-cum off his tip. He put the finger to my lips.

I sucked his finger. I didn't know what I had expected the taste to be. It was salty, exciting, forbidden. I licked my lips and rolled the condom slowly down his length.

He moaned lightly as his eyes showed the pleasure it gave him to have my hands on his cock.

I lay back on the bed as I finished, my legs open to him.

He positioned his monster cock at my entrance and entered me slowly, just a little, stretching my walls.

It had been a long time, and he was by far my biggest. I bit my lip as he pushed in a little and then back out, pulling lubrication out with him before going in farther.

He'd seen me wince. "Does this hurt too much?" he asked.

"No. Keep going, I want you. Don't stop."

He was considerate as he entered me in slow increments.

I needed to repay him and take him where he had taken me. I wrapped my legs around him and pulled him to me, forcing my hips into him and him into me, deeper and deeper. The pressure was building inside me as he filled me to the limit.

I pulled him all the way in with a final, small flash of pain and rocked my hips into him as additional layers of pleasure settled over me.

"You are so fucking good, so fucking tight, baby," he kept groaning.

Katherine's mouth filter was completely offline tonight. "Then fuck me."

And he did. The animal returned to his eyes. He stopped holding back. He thrust into me as lips and teeth nibbled on my earlobe and my nipples. He sucked and fondled my breasts as he fucked me senseless. Thrusting into me and showing me how intense sex was meant to be. Sex with Nick was pleasure on a completely different level.

He drove me yelping toward another orgasm as I clawed at his back. I rocked my hips into him, matching his rhythm and losing myself to his hands and lips as he lavished attention on my breasts, my neck, and my collarbone.

I strained to control the sensations, trying to wring every last moment of gratification from him, trying in vain to match his endurance. I needed him to come for me, to repay him.

My nerves were on fire as the tension grew and he pushed me past my limit once again into the spasms of my climax. One even more intense than the first. My walls clenched around his cock and my legs clamped him to me. I ground into him, begging my body to take him deeper and push him past his limit.

With a final thrust he tensed up and groaned out his release as our orgasms collided. His breathing jagged, he slowly settled down on his elbows, kissing me breathlessly as he throbbed inside me with an intensity I had never experienced.

He rolled us over with me on top, still impaled on him. His fingers gently rubbed my back as I settled my head on his muscled chest, relaxed, completely spent, and utterly satisfied.

He rolled me off after a while and went to the bathroom. I watched him walk away, his tight ass white below the tan line, my claw marks red streaks on his back.

He turned off the lights on his return from disposing of the condom, and we climbed under the sheets.

I had denied myself seemingly forever, convinced I needed to concentrate on school and work, to achieve my goal first, before I could relax and reward myself, but not anymore.

Sex with Nick was like eating barbecue potato chips. It would be impossible to stop at just a single taste.

My shitty day couldn't have ended any better. I yielded to sleep, cuddled against his warmth, listening to his heartbeat as he stroked my back, banishing all my worries.

Nick

I'd nearly come in my pants when I'd gotten her undressed and had her turn around for me. The softness of her full tits against my back had teased me the whole way back from Las Vegas, but seeing them was something else entirely.

She had been reluctant at first for me to go down on her. That much was clear. She'd tasted sweet, so wet and trembling under my tongue. She had been a tinderbox of passion just waiting for me to light the fire. When I'd taken her to my bed, she was tremendous. So wet, so tight, so willing, so responsive to the lightest lick, the softest touch.

She showed me a taste of the rebellious girl that had begged for a ride those years ago. Tonight she was the girl who wouldn't be constrained by what a Covington was and wasn't supposed to do.

Now, as she snuggled against me and her breathing became the slow and regular rhythm of sleep, I gazed up at the darkened ceiling and wondered what I'd gotten myself into with this girl.

This was Katherine fucking Covington, and the last time I had dared to think that I could lay a hand on her, reality had taught me a cruel lesson about power. The Covingtons had it and I didn't. Last time they had gotten me kicked out of school.

Today the equation was different. I was a better-than-average hacker, a lot better. And unlike the wimpy nerds, I could use those skills to make a buck, lots of bucks, a fucking ton of bucks. I was no bum. I owned this house free and clear and had seven figures stashed away. Nobody seeing me on the street would have guessed it by looking at me, but that was by plan.

Messing with Katherine Covington was like playing with matches inches from my pile of money. There were a million ways it could go wrong, and none of them ended up with me in good shape. The Covington's wealth was stratospheric, with dozens of lawyers and probably a gang of goons if need be to put me back in my place.

I hadn't gotten where I was today by letting my cock control my life. I was always able to compartmentalize women. They were fun and good to have around on a short-term basis, but relationships were out as far as I was concerned. A woman chasing a relationship became demanding. More a distraction and hindrance than anything else. Unpredictable, emotional, and, worst of all, devious.

Girls looking for fun, for a good time without any strings, were my kind. They were plentiful if you knew where to look for them, and I could offer them a good time while they did the same for me.

Katherine Covington wasn't that kind of girl. One night would have to be enough. She was trouble wrapped in temptation.

What had I been thinking? My cock jerked up with the memory of her tightness, and I knew perfectly well what I had been thinking.

Regrets could wait until tomorrow.

I succumbed to sleep with the warmth of her soft tits up against me.

CHAPTER 5

Katie

I woke to the aroma of coffee and bacon. The sound of the bacon sizzling in the pan drifted in through the open door.

He had woken me in the middle the night for another amazing session with me on my back learning the pleasures a practiced finger and a big cock could bring.

I had returned the favor this morning before sunrise, climbing on top of him and running my saturated folds over his length as I got him hard, begging him to take me again.

Sex with Nick was a completely new experience, and something I needed more of, lots more. It didn't matter that it wasn't right, or sensible, or wouldn't lead anywhere. It was what it was, pleasure for its own sake. And Katie deserved it.

I climbed out of bed and rifled through the drawers of his dresser, finding a simple white T-shirt. I put it on and shuffled out to the kitchen in my bare feet.

Nick turned from the stove. “Morning, Precious. How do you like your eggs?”

"Scrambled, just like my brain." I giggled.

His brow arched with a quizzical look.

I padded over to him and hugged him from behind. I smiled to myself, the press of my breasts against his back reminding me of yesterday's trip. Hours pressed up against him, warm and tight, every bump in the road bouncing me against him.

He pointed me to the silverware and plates. I set the table, got orange juice from the fridge, and we were ready to go. He scooped the eggs and bacon onto the plates as we sat down across from one another.

"I'm sorry about last night," he started.

"I'm not," I shot back, and I was serious. I was done with Katherine's restrictions. Katie today was a lot happier than Katherine had been in years.

Shock registered on his face. He had expected me to regret what we had done, to want to take it back, to demand an apology.

I slumped in my seat with the realization that he regretted it. Or that it hadn't been as good for him as it had been for me. I stared down at my plate. The fear that he was already done with me ran rampant.

We hadn't said anything, and I should have understood that it was a one-night stand, that he had a different girl in his bed every night, with his skills it had to be like that. I'd had my turn and tomorrow it was some other girl's lucky night to have her world turned upside down.

He was smiling as I glanced back up. "Precious," he started. "I just didn't mean to force you into anything you weren't ready for, and, if I did, I apologize."

His words warded off that chill as I realized that it might not be over yet. "I'm up for a rematch tonight if you are," I said.

"No," he said sternly.

With that one word, he deflated my world again. It was over, and today I would have to go back to Katherine's world. I had to face the fact that I probably wasn't good enough in bed to keep his interest. I should have read more Cosmo articles. I let out a long breath.

"I will not discuss sex with you across the breakfast table." He finished another bite. "If you want to talk sex, girl, you have to do it right. You have to be in my lap so you can feel my cock under your ass."

He was messing with my emotions like they were a light switch, off, then on, then off, then on again.

I rushed over and sat in his lap, laughing at his hilarious little speech.

This guy was completely unfiltered and unpredictable compared to any of the guys I had ever known. Joe, my last boyfriend in college, would never in a million years have come up with a line like that. Joseph E. Hunsinger the third was from a proper Boston family, proper diction, proper manners, proper posture, and properly dull, I had decided when I broke up with him.

I twined my arm behind Nick's neck as he fed me a forkful of scrambled eggs.

His arm brushed my breast as he reached for the orange juice. He had been right about feeling his cock. It pulsed under me as his other arm circled me and cupped my breast. "Now, you were saying?"

"I said, I'm up for a rematch tonight, or earlier maybe." I wondered momentarily what sex on the breakfast table would be like. I had never done it on a table. Hell, I had never done it anywhere exciting.

"No can do earlier, Precious."

I put on my pouty face. I wiggled my ass over his erection, but got nowhere trying to change his mind.

"We have a lot to do. You need a rental car and some clothes. Do you need to go to work today?"

The reminder that I still worked for that pig Russ Downey

soured my mood for a moment. "No, I was supposed to travel back today, and be in the office Monday, but I'll call in and see if I can get a few days off next week."

"I promised to take you to see your house this morning at eight, and I always keep my commitments. We don't have time for a proper session."

The reminder we were due to visit the ash heap of my house brought me back to my current shitty situation. Everything I owned fit in one suitcase.

He did the dishes while I started a shower.

He joined me and we enjoyed soaping each other up, but he wouldn't relent and poke me in the shower. He said we didn't have enough time.

Joe would have had time. It rarely took him more than two minutes, which was never enough time for me. I didn't need two hands to count the few orgasms Joe had given me—it only took two fingers.

I teased Nick as best I knew how, sliding my soapy fingers up and down the length of his steely rod. I got moans of pleasure, good ones, but he didn't capitulate. I was going to have to wait until tonight. He wouldn't let me finish him either, he was in full taskmaster mode and he forced me out of the shower to get dressed. So bossy. The story of my life.

My shirt buttons had ripped off last night, so he gave me one of his. He was right that I needed clothes badly. My suitcase was due today, but that wouldn't take me very far.

Leaving the bedroom, I noticed another door in the hallway, different from the others. It was an oddly out-of-place solid metal door.

I borrowed Nick's phone to call Patrick. My brother had been annoying and bossy last night, but it came from a loving place, and it was only fair to let him know I was alright.

When he got on the line, I didn't want to fight, so I asked about his girl Liz.

The news on the Liz front was bad. My brother had gotten the fucked up notion that he would hide his identity behind a fake name while he got to know her. I had told him that was no way to start a relationship, but like an idiot he had persisted, and now he was totally fucked.

It had blown up in his face, and I reminded him how I had told him more than once that he had his head up his ass. I yelled at him for being so stupid, then I yelled at him some more. I kept lecturing him, hoping he would actually hear me, instead of brushing me off the way he had before. Also, he deserved it for being such an ass to me last night.

Then Patrick changed the subject, and I found out the worse news. My sister-in-law Emma had been at his place last night, and drunk, to get over her day. That Monica bitch had not only burned down my house but also attacked Emma.

I cringed as he explained what had happened. Poor Emma, I couldn't imagine having gone through what she had. It explained why Patrick had been so over-the-top pushy about me staying with him last night. He had been worried and trying to keep me safe.

Nick came out of the other room and I cut the call short.

I didn't want Nick to freak out about the Monica situation. I decided to tell him later, when I was ready, and definitely not when Patrick was on the phone.

I NOTICED THEM AFTER I BUCKLED MYSELF IN THE PASSENGER seat of Nick's truck. A Laker's shirt and a pair of shorts hanging from the eaves of Nick's garage, both stained.

I pointed. "What's with the laundry?"

"Kind of a pirate flag. Blood stains. I took those off a kid that spit on my bike."

I shuddered. "You didn't."

He hesitated. "Of course not. It's only paint, but the story keeps the kids away, and nobody lets their dog go on my lawn either."

I shook my head. His sense of humor was beyond me today.

We arrived at the address where my house used to be. Nick had driven me in his Chevy Tahoe with the M*y Other Car is a Harley* license plate holder. A single firetruck was parked in front of the house. The firemen were rolling up their hoses and stowing their gear.

Across the street was a car with my insurance company's name plastered on the side.

I held my mouth and tried not to puke again as I opened the door and the smoky odor hit me. The fire was out, but it still smelled, even out here at the street.

The news had been terrible, but seeing it in person was worse. I thought I was prepared for it, but I wasn't. The roof had fallen in, parts of two walls still stood, otherwise there were only some charred studs here and there.

A short balding man with a camera and a clipboard wandered the ashes, making notes and taking pictures, the guy from the insurance company no doubt.

The range, the washer, the dryer, what was left of my car in the garage, and the fireplace with its chimney were the only things that hadn't been reduced to a pile of gray and black ash. Not a thing remained. I had one suitcase to my name and nothing else.

Nick came around the truck, and circled his arm protectively around me, supporting me.

I needed it. I could barely stand as I surveyed the destruction.

The closer I came the more repulsed I became.

I didn't bother to wipe away the tears that flowed down my cheeks. "That fucking bitch." Everything I owned, all my pictures, my books, my furniture, my clothes, everything was now either ash or smoke. Monica Paisley, that psycho, had robbed me of everything, and ruined my life. For what? She didn't know me, I didn't know her, I'd never done anything to her. It wasn't fair.

Nick tightened his grip on me and leaned close. "Tell me her name, so I can find her and we can repay her for this," he said quietly into my ear. His tone was determined, ominous, and dangerous. His method of repayment probably involved gunpowder and lead.

I was tempted to take him up on it and seek revenge in Nick's way. She deserved it, but I didn't want to become a criminal myself, or get Nick involved in any of this craziness. It was my family's burden and not his. "Later," I said.

He hugged me and I cried into his chest for the longest time, lost for what to do next.

I had to start over. Completely. I had a few changes of clothes in the suitcase that was on the way from Las Vegas, my work laptop, my purse and only one color of nail polish, not even a blanket to curl up in and cry. I sobbed, my tears soaking his shirt.

"You're safe." He stroked my back. "That's all that matters. All the rest is just stuff. It can be replaced."

He was right of course. If she had meant me harm, she had missed, and I had my family to lean on, and Nick too.

I wiped away my tears and pulled up my big girl pants, figuratively. I was wearing a skirt, it was all I had. Katherine knew how to deal with things like this. Make a list, a plan, and start checking items off the list from the top. Keep at it, chin high, and don't let them see you cry. That's what Daddy had taught me.

He was gone now, after that horrible accident, and I missed him so.

Two of my four brothers had left the city. Now it was just Bill, Patrick, and me in LA.

I took a deep breath and instantly regretted it as I coughed from the smoky smell. "We need to go."

Nick helped me to the truck and opened the windows when we got clear of the smell to air the truck out.

He handed me envelopes. "This was in the mailbox."

It was junk mail, and one envelope. My mortgage bill. "Great, I have twenty-eight more years of payments on my non-existent house." I threw the mail on the floor of the truck for now.

First thing on my list was to call the devil himself. I would need some time off work to deal with this. There was no way I could fit what I needed to do in the late night hours after he let us out of the office.

I borrowed Nick's phone to place the call while he drove.

Russ picked up after a few rings.

"Mr. Downey, this is Katherine Covington."

"Yes, Katherine." His tone was the same monotone he always used with me, dripping with disdain.

"I'm sorry, sir, but I had a setback yesterday." *Setback* was a pretty mild way to put losing your house and everything you owned, but I didn't have the words.

He waited for me to continue.

"My house burned down yesterday," I told him, keeping my emotions in check as best I could. It would be a mistake to show him any weakness.

"Yes, and?" he asked with all the compassion of a crocodile. Unbelievable. I had just told him I'd lost my house and all he had to say was *"and?"*

"I'll need to have some time off next week to deal with it."

He didn't answer for the longest time. *"That will be fine, Katherine. Take the entire week. Will that be enough?"*

I would have fallen over if I hadn't already been sitting in the truck. It was way more than I expected from him.

"Yes. Thank you," I said, unsure how he had suddenly become almost human in less than a minute. I had expected a day or two, and a reminder that I could do some of my work at home in the evenings.

He reverted back to standard Downey A-hole mode and hung up without even a goodbye.

I still had my work computer; it was the only thing other than clothes that I had taken with me to Las Vegas. I planned to do some more work on the LDSI audit in the evenings. I wasn't going to let him blame me for it being late when I got back into work. The firm had committed to a schedule that was locked in stone at this point.

"So what's the word?" Nick asked.

"He said I could take the entire week off."

"Good, the first thing on the agenda is to take you shopping for clothes."

"First, I need a rental car," I said. That was not actually the top of my list. Fixing my phone was the first thing, if I was being practical, but I had no intention right now of making it easier for Patrick or Bill to yell at me. So, the phone moved to the bottom, and the car moved into first place.

Patrick knew he could call Nick to reach me if he needed, but having to go through Nick would keep him from calling.

"No, you don't. You need clothes."

"If I get the car, then I can get around and have a way to carry the clothes back," I told him. I thought my Katherine logic was impeccable.

"No, Precious, I'm your chauffeur until this sicko arson lady is caught. It's too dangerous for you to be out alone." He was being bossy again, exactly like my brother.

"I don't need a babysitter," I protested.

He stopped the truck by the curb and fixed me with a stern glare. His countenance was the most intimidating I had faced since being called to the Principle's office in middle school.

"Either I protect you," he said sternly. "Or I take you back to your jerk brother and he puts you in Winston's care. Or maybe he just locks you in the condo for a month. Now, which will it be?"

"You know Winston Evers?" I didn't even want to consider the locked in the condo option.

"Sure, Precious. I can't speak for your brother, but Winston is almost as capable as me in the protection department. Now, make up your mind?"

I crossed my arms, staring at the windshield to avoid looking at him. "Okay, already. I'll go with you." I made it sound as though it was a tough decision, but it was really easy. Nick had a way of making me feel safe. I was going to enjoy having him as my bodyguard today if I had to have one.

I was surrounded by bossy men, but at least I could pick the sexy one.

"First stop. The mall. I hope you have a good limit on your card, Precious, 'cuz you're going to need it."

That was not a problem. My black AMEX card had no limit.

CHAPTER 6

Nick

Seeing the house convinced me that she needed serious protection. The arson was no amateur attempt, and the lady behind this was unlikely to stop her attacks. Katie was in more danger than she understood with this crazy on the loose.

I had seen arson fires before. The idiots often just poured something on the outside of a house, lit a match and ran.

That often didn't result in much damage here in southern California where most of the houses had stucco exteriors. It took a long time for the fire to burn through a window or a door and reach the interior. That gave the fire department time to respond and get the situation under control.

I didn't trust anyone to keep Katie safer than I could. It might take the cops a while to catch up with this crazy, and I would be her *babysitter* as she'd put it for the time being.

We headed to the mall to get her some clothes, but only after another one of her temper tantrums. She seemed to think being rich gave her the right to be stupid.

The sooner I made it clear that she couldn't hang around, the better for me. I'd keep her safe for a day or two from this crazy arson lady, but after that I was staying as far away from those Covingtons as I could get, Katie included.

Although Liam was the Covington who hated me most, her brother Patrick had made it clear last night he shared that opinion.

I didn't ever run from a fight, but only an idiot poked the lion and then entered the cage, and I was no idiot.

If they knew what I had done last night with their sister, they'd probably burn down my house, along with my business, and piss on the ashes.

~

Katie

I ENJOYED CLOTHES SHOPPING AS MUCH AS THE NEXT GIRL, AND could have made this a three-day excursion if I wanted to, but I went fast to spare him the agony.

The nearby mall he had chosen didn't have a Nordstrom or a Saks Fifth Avenue, so casual was what I stocked up on. Work clothes could wait for another day.

Like most guys he thought clothes were only utilitarian rags that covered us up. He would've been happy if I'd bought ten pairs of socks, ten jeans, and twenty T-shirts of two different colors and called it a day. He shadowed me through the racks and aisles, not hovering exactly, but never far away.

I caught his eyes on me multiple times, not leering, but admiring. The glint in his eye conveyed a hint of lust on more than one occasion.

I made a point of bending over for him every so often.

The way he watched me made me feel sexy and coveted. I

considered dragging him into one of the dressing rooms, but only for a moment. I wasn't that brave.

The glint grew in his eyes when we passed the Victoria's Secret store, but I didn't go in. Instead, we shopped for underwear at the department store. Of course he managed to throw a few sexy bras and thongs into the basket when I wasn't watching.

I liked how his mind worked.

Nick had brought along a spare phone for me. We stopped by the phone store and got my number ported over to it. We left mine to be repaired.

I didn't want to have a phone right now, because I didn't want to listen to Patrick or Bill trying to tell me what to do, but Nick insisted it was for my safety. I was learning that there were times I couldn't argue with him, and this was one.

I still didn't have a full set of makeup, but that could wait for another day. Leaving the mall, I checked my phone and found a text message from my boss and a missed call from Patrick that I hadn't heard while shopping.

My boss wanted my new home address and phone number. It'd only been a few hours since I'd told him my house had burned down, and already he was back into full Downey A-hole mode.

I called Patrick back. I couldn't duck him for long.

"*I'm not going to be needing the Myrtle Street house,*" Patrick told me. "*I left a key under the potted plant on the porch for you. Why don't you use that for the time being, I've got it all square with Phil.*" Phil was Patrick's best friend, and the owner of the house he had been using while he'd stupidly pretended not to be himself.

"Tell Phil thanks, I'll be out of it as soon as I find a place closer to work."

"*No hurry, take all the time you need. He's cool. He's making more off of me than he would if he rented it out to somebody else, and it's ready for you tonight.*" So there it was, he was trying to get me away from Nick as fast as possible.

"I'll have to think about that."

"*Katie it's the right thing—*"

"Drop it, Patrick, and stop trying to tell me what to do." I hung up on him.

He called back, and I sent it to voicemail. He didn't call again. He might be right, but I was tired of being told what to do.

I texted my jerk boss and gave him the Myrtle Street address.

What an ass.

Nick called ahead to order a pizza, and we picked it up on the way back to his house.

Our suitcases had been delivered from Las Vegas and were sitting on the porch. He unlocked the house and disarmed the alarm with two shopping bags in his arms while I carried the pizza. "Precious, you get dinner ready, and I'll bring in the stuff."

"What's to get ready?"

"Beer and plates. Haven't you ever had pizza before?"

I sneered back at him. Sometimes he could be so snotty. I had eaten plenty of pizza. I ditched the heels which had been killing me all afternoon. I pulled two Buds out of the fridge and got plates and napkins for the table.

It took him several trips, but he got the suitcases and all the shopping bags in. He put them in the second bedroom, not the master.

I was still in his shirt and the business skirt I had shopped in all day, the same one as yesterday. It would be good to have some clean clothes for tomorrow. He didn't suspect, but I had changed into one of the thongs he had picked out while I was trying on jeans at the mall.

We sat, and he opened the delicious smelling pepperoni pizza. He popped open his beer. "To surviving the mall," he said, raising his can to me.

I tapped my unopened can against his. "To doing it again tomorrow."

He coughed up his beer laughing. "No way, Princess. You're grounded."

"Just kidding, I think this is enough to start." I popped the top on my Bud and took a sip. I hadn't had beer since college. It was cold and fizzy going down, refreshing.

He served us each a few slices, and we attacked the cheesy delight.

"What's behind the door?" I asked about the other bedroom door that I had seen down the hall. It was metal instead of the standard wood panel of the rest of the doors.

"My cave." He responded between bites.

I waited for more. "And?"

"I'll show you later."

I didn't like the sound of "*cave*". Did he have a sex dungeon or something? I hoped it was only a man-cave for watching football, but he did have a big screen out here with surround sound speakers.

"It's where I work," he continued after finishing chewing.

I let out a relieved breath. I had no good understanding what he did for a living, but I shelved my curiosity for now.

We finished off the pizza with me answering his questions about my job.

After dinner I went through the bags, finding some comfortable clothes to wear tomorrow. I still didn't have a car or a place to live. There was so much to do.

Patrick called again, and I took it on the couch. He was finally going to do the right thing, he was going to go talk to his girl and admit his stupidity and try to get her back. I only ranted at him for a little while about how much of an idiot he had been. He deserved it.

After that, I wished him well. I really did.

"*Katie I wasn't really calling so you could lecture me.*"

"Well, you should have, 'cuz you need it. You've had your head up your ass the whole time with this girl, and you're just getting stupider by the day. Didn't I tell you—"

"*Katie stop,*" he interrupted me. "*It's Monica.*"

That froze me. I waited for the bombshell to drop.

"*The cops caught her. She's in jail for now.*"

"So, it's over?"

"*For now.*"

I let out a breath. "That's a relief."

"*Where are you now?*" he asked. Naturally he couldn't leave it alone. He really didn't want me to be with Nick.

"I'm fine. Thank you."

"*You really should go and stay at the Myrtle Street house,*" he said in his condescending tone.

"And you should butt out of my life," I said right before I hung up.

Nick had been listening. "So that's it, then," he said. "You're safe now."

"Yeah, she's locked up." I had a different problem now. I got up to get another beer.

His face showed the realization that we didn't have anything keeping us together here in his house. He didn't need to be my bodyguard anymore.

"We should talk about last night," he said.

There it was, out in the open. The elephant in the room that we had ignored all day. He probably had a different girl almost every night. God knows he had the looks for it. He probably didn't want me hanging out at his house cramping his style.

The pizza congealed into a lump in my stomach. I feared he was getting ready to tell me to leave, maybe tonight as Patrick had suggested.

I didn't know how to tell him what I wanted to say. I'd had sex before, but was always part of a longer-term thing. I had heard that a one-night stand was easy. Just ghost him when it was done, don't call and don't return calls. It sounded so easy. But what if I liked the one-night stand so much? And I had.

How do I tell him I want to keep doing it?

And I did. I didn't have a number in mind for how many nights I wanted, but it was way more than one.

I needed him to understand what I wanted, what I needed, and what I couldn't give today. I wanted a friend with benefits, but we weren't even friends yet. I guess what I wanted was the benefits and maybe later a friend. Even if he did call me Princess.

He thought I was stuck up, some kind of snooty high-society type. He hated my family, and it was mutual; they'd had it in for him since that day in high school. With my brothers' long memories this could never go anywhere, but I didn't care. Katie didn't care. Katie had denied herself for too long and last night had been too good.

I wanted him. Maybe at some point he would wear off, but not yet.

He inhaled. "Precious, this is not going to work. You're not my type," he said coldly.

He wasn't even attracted enough to me to wait until the morning. That was too cruel. How was that fair?

I was pissed. "And what type is that? Not your usual one-night fuck-buddy slut from the biker bar, or not the kind you find attractive enough to fuck two nights in a row?" I should have toned it down a notch or two or more, but I was pissed.

Am I that bad in bed?

CHAPTER 7

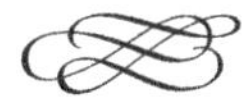

Katie

His eyes turned fierce, menacing. I had ticked him off, but he deserved it. Then he laughed in my face.

He laughed.

I was a joke to him.

"Princess, I'm attracted to you all right. I thought I made that clear last night, but since when do you use fuck twice in a sentence or fuck around with a guy like me?"

The words stung. "Stop calling me that." I punched him in the shoulder. It hurt my hand but not him.

"You're super sexy when you're mad, Princess." He laughed again.

I crossed my arms. He was pissing me off even more. "You think you know me, but you don't," I spat out loudly. "I grew up with four brothers, I can say fuck as much as I want." I moved a step closer and upped the volume. "And I can fuck anybody I want. Until a minute ago I wanted that to be you, but if you're going to be such an asshole—"

He closed the distance between us in an instant and pulled me into another one of his ferocious kisses.

His lips claimed mine, and his tongue and lips took control of the kiss, of my mind, and of me. A hand held my ass and pulled me into him, the other found my bra strap and had it unhooked with a single pinch of his fingers. "I dare you to show me," he said hoarsely into my ear, as he carried me into the bedroom.

I tried to squirm loose. "We haven't finished our talk." It was no use.

"Tomorrow," he said as he put me down and pushed me back onto the bed. His eyes said it all, the animal was loose again.

Tomorrow sounded good.

Nick

Her sassiness had made me hard again.

The minute she'd said she wanted to fuck me, my mind went blank. I couldn't resist her magnetic lips. The way she said it was more sensuously provocative than anything a girl had ever said to me. Talking went out the window. I kissed her, picked her up, and took her to bed. We could talk tomorrow. Talking was overrated, particularly with a hard-on that could drill granite.

She was even better than the night before. The tigress came out to play as she pulled at my clothes. Her hands and her lips were demanding as she kissed me with renewed abandon. She pounced on me and pulled at my pants as I wiggled out of my shirt. I'd gotten her topless quickly and those marvelous tits bounced for me as she struggled to undress me.

What a sight. I couldn't keep my hands from cupping them, supporting their weight, and teasing the hard raspberry nipples. The softness of the mounds of woman in my hands were such a contrast to the hardness of the tight little buds of the nipples that peaked at my slightest touch.

I was a tit man, alright, and hers were just right. Soft, supple, and large enough to fill my hand. Full enough to form enticing cleavage.

She unzipped her skirt and pulled it off. Sometime today she had put on the pink and black thong that I had slipped into her basket this morning. It was perfect on her, but it was going to be even better when it came off.

I flipped her over on her back, moving down between her legs, kissing her from the inside of the knee up to just before that pretty thong, before switching to the other leg.

She shivered lightly, and moaned softly, but she didn't try to push me away as she had last night.

I licked the length of her slit through the damp fabric of her thong as she stabbed her fingers into my hair and pulled me to her wetness.

I ran up and down the length, saturating the thin garment, circling her clit through the layer between us. I could only hold off tasting her for so long as anticipation destroyed me.

She pulled the thong aside, encouraging me to lick and suck her directly.

I did, only briefly, before pulling the thong down and off her legs. I wanted easy access to her delicious pussy. I dove in and teased her entrance with a finger.

Her taste drove me crazy as I licked and sucked on that responsive little clit. She was so sensitive there that I had her jerking and yelping her way closer to her climax. Her responses were perfection as she writhed her hips into me, and I teased the little pearl of her clit. "Fucking hell," she gasped as she panted faster with little whimpers.

I had to hurry. My cock was begging to have at her, to plunder the depths of her wetness. I kneaded a breast with one hand while I held her hips with the other and tongued lazy little circles around the swollen bud that was threatening to detonate her.

She opened her legs wider to me and pulled at my head aggressively, rocking her hips into me with each stroke of my tongue, each suck on her little bundle of nerves. Her sounds grew louder as I gave her a tongue-lashing.

Her moans grew, until she shuddered and clamped her legs on my head. She was a wild tornado when she came with an avalanche of tremors that I amplified with my thumb to her little pleasure button.

I got up and retrieved a condom from the drawer as she came back to earth. I was going to have to get another box soon.

She took the packet from me and started to roll it down my throbbing cock. Her hands on me were magic as she rolled the latex down, little by little, drawing it out on purpose, torturing me with the lightness of her touch, teasing my balls with each stroke.

She rolled over and got on her knees, her face down in the pillow, and that beautiful ass up.

I positioned myself behind her.

She put a hand between her legs to guide me in as my tip teased her pussy. She was slick and slippery, and oh so tight as I pushed in little by little. "I won't break," she said, grabbing my balls and pulling me forward.

I pushed in farther but not all the way, careful not to hurt her. Some women couldn't handle my length in this position.

"Is that all you got?" she taunted me.

I grasped her hips and rammed into her, fully to the root.

She cried out, but I had learned it was one of her screams of pleasure, my reward for pleasing her the way she did me.

I grabbed a fistful of her hair and snaked a hand around to fondle those great tits as I started to pump into her and she rocked back into me with equal fervor. The tension was building in me as her animal desire kept pace with mine.

She was so tight, and I couldn't last long with the way her walls constricted around me every time I pulled back. She didn't know it, but she had the perfect technique and her little yelps as I thrust into her were erotic music to my ears.

Her moans increased as she came again, convulsing around my cock, pulling me to my limit as the pressure built.

With one last push as deep as I could go, I tensed up and came with a shudder, breathless from the exertion.

I knelt back on the bed and pulled her back with me, sitting on my lap, with me still inside her. I wrapped my arm around her, held her breasts, and kissed her neck and ear, while I regained my breath.

After a few minutes I disposed of the condom. We settled into bed, with me wrapped around her, my cock up against her ass. One arm above her head, and the other wrapped around her, holding a boob.

The prim and proper girl hid a volcano of lust.

We still hadn't had the talk. That could wait until tomorrow. For tonight, she had said she wanted to fuck me, and that's what we were going to do, and not just once.

Tonight I was going to fuck the Covington Princess's brains out and her brothers could go fuck themselves if they didn't like it.

~

Katie

We'd had another three-peat last night. Sex in the evening, the middle of the night, and in the morning. My God, was he good. He was exactly what I needed. He made me feel alive, desired, and happier than I had been in what seemed like forever. For today, being with Nick erased the shit that was raining down on Katherine's life.

Katherine would've written down the pros and cons of sleeping with him in two columns on a piece of paper. Katherine would have decided against it. *Her loss.* Analysis over passion. Thinking rather than feeling. Planning rather than living.

Sure we didn't make any sense together, but we would not be together, we were just enjoying one another. Savoring one another was a better description.

At work Katherine dressed and acted to fit into the accounting world. She had to be better than the guys to be taken seriously. It was a man's club, and she had to conform and then outperform. It was a losing battle to try to change the expectations. The nail that stuck out always got hammered down. She had to be proper, professional, and boring.

It was Katie's turn to be irrational and do whatever the fuck she wanted to, merely because she fucking felt like it. Nick made me feel like it. Oh, did he.

Nick appreciated me as a woman, and I relished it. I could do without the bossiness, but mostly that had been him being deliciously protective. Protective I could deal with, it was even kind of hot.

This morning he'd cooked breakfast for me again. Imagine that, a guy who cooked breakfast. All my previous boyfriends, not that there were many, had all thought cooking anything more than toast was women's work. Joe had even put it in so many words.

Nick had mentioned last night that he wanted to talk, but we had put it off. He had jumped me last night as soon as I'd admitted how he turned me on.

I knew he would tell me that it had been fun, but I had overstayed my welcome. Too bad, I could do with more than two nights of his kind of therapy.

I steeled myself for the talk when I walked out to the kitchen in one of his T-shirts. I was braless and bottomless on purpose.

I jiggled my way over to him. His eyes never left my chest. I had guessed right; he was definitely a boob guy.

I made sure my breasts bounced as I strode up to him. It was empowering to be able to hold his attention so well.

He forced the predator in his eyes back under control as I reached him.

I rose up to kiss him briefly. "Good morning."

He put the spatula down and squeezed me tightly, pressing my chest to his. "Very good indeed, but it won't work." His smirk when he grabbed a handful of ass under the T-shirt showed he had figured out what I wasn't wearing.

He released me and I pulled the plates down from the cupboard. "What won't work?" I asked innocently as I sashayed my way over to the table.

"Trying to temp me like that. I know exactly what you're doing, you little tease."

I set the plates on the table. "Who, me?"

"Yeah, you."

"Is it working?" I asked as I ran my hands up the sides of the T-shirt to my chest and squeezed my breasts together.

His eyes bugged out, and he blinked a few times before turning back to the stove.

"Well?" I asked again.

"Yes, it's working so well I'm not going to be able to fit under the table." He laughed.

I came up behind him, reached around and stroked the bulge of his cock through his jeans.

He moaned his approval before he pushed my hand away. "Stop that or I'll have to punish you later."

I could come up with several ways I would like him to punish me right now with his tongue or the weapon behind the bulge. "What if I want it?"

"I won't let you come if you keep this up."

I stopped stroking him, went back to the table, and sat. "You're no fun." I'd had enough of that frustration with Joe, and I didn't need to travel that road again.

Nick had taught me what orgasms could be like with the right man, and I wanted more lessons. Before Nick, sex had ranged from okay to pretty good, but never great. It was like tasting strawberries or chocolate for the first time after years of eating nothing but oatmeal. I was sick of oatmeal, I wanted the real thing now.

He brought the omelets over to the table and served them onto our plates. "We need to talk," he said as he sat.

There it was. The end.

CHAPTER 8

Nick

SHE SUBTLY OFFERED ANOTHER ROUND THIS MORNING BEFORE breakfast, before the talk. Who was I to refuse the lady? My cock urged me to accept, but I hadn't gotten where I was in life by following my cock. It wouldn't be right to string her along, or safe for me.

This conversation couldn't be put off. I wasn't willing to make any commitments, ever. I needed to tell her that there was no way that this would go anywhere beyond what it was we had physically. Absolutely no way.

She was a Covington, and I was a felon. We were about as compatible as oil and water.

The conversation was a turnoff for women her age. They thought that the progression had to go from sex to a deeper relationship, and to love. That's why I sought out younger girls, ones who weren't at that point in their life yet, where they wanted a longer-term relationship. Girls out to have a fun time, and let the good times roll, until they didn't. Then we would both move on to the next non-permanent relationship.

Occasionally the girl thought I was kidding. When that happened it was a good idea to keep sharp objects out of reach, they could get insanely mad when the breakup came.

There weren't any nice ways to tell a girl that all I wanted was a temporary fuck buddy, but life was tough, it had to be done. It wasn't fair to her otherwise.

"Yeah, we should talk," Katie said.

"You know, the two of us are really from different worlds." I guessed she had no idea how different. Not many people knew my history since the last time we'd seen each other. I doubted she knew about my stint in prison.

She nodded. "Yeah, what else is new." She didn't make this easy, looking the way she did.

I was liable to talk myself into blue balls here, which was the last thing I wanted right now. She was the dessert I didn't want to pass up.

I wasn't sure how to word it with her. "I think…"

She stared down at the table. "So, when do you want me to leave?" She thought I was cutting it off. Dark disappointment showed in her eyes.

"No, that's not what I'm saying."

She crossed her arms under those marvelous tits and cocked her head. "What are we talking about, then?" The girl with the attitude was back. She was hard work, this one.

"Don't get your panties in a twist, Princess."

"You know perfectly well I'm not wearing any."

It seemed impossible but my cock got even harder. She was blowing my concentration.

Maybe this was her way of getting her brains fucked out before we talked. "We need to understand each other is all I'm saying. I don't want you having any expectations of me that I can't fulfill."

"What, like getting it up four times a night?"

"I'm not looking for a relationship is all."

She glared at me. "Well, neither am I."

I couldn't read if she was serious or not. "So we're cool?" This was too easy.

"Sure, just casual sex. Acquaintances with benefits. My life is so fucked up with the house and my job and everything." She smirked. "Just one condition."

There it was. The bargaining had begun. This was not good. It couldn't be that simple to get a girl like her to agree to casual sex so easily. Especially with a guy like me.

"I have one too," I told her.

She shrugged. "I get a ride on your Harley."

I laughed. "That can be arranged, but not until after."

"After what?"

I walked around to her side of the table, lifted her to her feet. I pulled the shirt over her head, releasing those tits that had been tormenting me all morning. "After this." I picked her up.

She bit my ear, not too hard, but hard enough. The tigress was back.

I carried her back into the bedroom and sat her on the edge of the bed.

She spread her legs, with an inferno in her eyes and a wicked smile on her face.

I loosened my belt and dropped my pants to match her nakedness. The breakfast menu had changed. Trying to explain my past could wait for a later time.

Katie

I WAS EXHAUSTED AND EXHILARATED. NICK MADE EVERY NEW

experience better than the last. He had made me come harder than even last night. I couldn't control my little yells of pleasure.

He followed me into rapture with a surge and a groan. "Oh, fuck, Katie, I can't take it, you feel so fucking good."

His compliment was exactly what I needed. I needed to give him back some of the pleasure that he heaped on me.

This was bliss. Our three-peat had turned into a four-peat and Nick wasn't throwing me to the curb. We had agreed, or rather both insisted, on acquaintances with benefits, just sex, no strings. Not that there was anything *"just",* about sex with Nick, it was on a dimension I hadn't contemplated before. Now that I had sampled it, I wanted more, definitely more.

Without the dating thing, I wouldn't have to be careful about what I said or did, worrying about hurting his feelings, or not acting the way a *girlfriend* should. I could be myself for a change. Thinking about it that way liberated me.

Katherine had lost out big time, and Katie was in charge. Katherine had denied herself for what? To end up with a charred hole in the ground where her house used to be, and a job working for the cruelest man on the planet, just so she could go on to another boring job where she had to go along to get ahead.

Katie was going to have some fun to balance out all the shit Katherine had put her through.

Later I would make a mental list of things I wanted to try with Nick, but right now he morphed in the bossy taskmaster again. We showered and now we had to get dressed and on the road in twenty minutes so we could be at the car dealers when they opened. It was no use arguing with his logic, no wasn't an option. Mr. Bossy was back.

He had a plan, and I had to stick to it. Yesterday had been clothes and a phone, and today was a car. After that he planned to check out the house on Myrtle Street. I needed a place to stay. Being casual sex partners or fuck buddies or whatever didn't mean moving in with him.

I turned off the hair dryer. "What was your condition?"

"What?"

"Your condition. You said you had a condition."

He pulled the razor up under his chin. "I don't share," he mumbled. "Ever."

So, he wanted monogamous casual sex.

It had never been any other way with me, the monogamous part, not the casual part. It hadn't occurred to me that for some people it might be different. "Me neither, or you might wake up short a few parts."

He laughed, but I was serious. I wasn't going to be the other woman. That was one thing that would not ever happen, not to me.

CHAPTER 9

NICK

SHE'D MODELED THREE DIFFERENT BRAS FOR ME THIS MORNING and asked me which one looked the sexiest.

I chose the red lacy push up one. It gave her tits the deepest, most enticing cleavage. She had sexy written all over her in those tight jeans as I followed her out, set the alarm code, and locked the front door. The jeans had rips in them. Why girls paid extra to get jeans with rips was beyond me but that was the trend. She had a rip just below the back pocket that made you wonder if she had any underwear on when her ass cheek showed. That was my kind of rip.

She turned around and put a hand to my chest. "Hey, baby, go get your motorcycle jacket. I need you in a leather jacket today." She'd never called me baby before.

That delicious smile of hers melted me, and I went back to get it.

She unfolded her laptop on her knees as I turned toward the

nearest dealer. It was a Ford store. I thought she could find something to suit her there.

"I want to go to the Chevrolet dealer down on Olympia," she said a few minutes later.

"The Ford dealer is closest. I'll take you there first and if you don't find what you want, there's a Chevy dealer right next door."

"I checked their inventories. The guy down South has a lot more on the lot, and I'll get a better deal down there because he needs to move them."

"You have more money than God so what's the difference?" I asked her.

She huffed. "Then let's go to the dealer you want to go to, and you buy me the car."

"Princess, I'll buy you a pizza, but a car is out of the question."

"So, you admit that what I spend on it matters. If it's your money it counts, if it's mine it doesn't. How's that make any sense? You think because rich people have money they can waste it. The only reason we have money, is we're careful about spending it. That way we keep it."

I turned the truck around and headed to the dealer she wanted.

She returned to tapping on her computer.

I stopped across the street from her dealer of choice.

She buttoned her shirt up all the way, hiding her nice cleavage. "Just play along. This is going to be fun. Now I'm ready," she told me as she stepped down from the truck. "Nicky, just be your normal ornery self, and disagree with whatever I say. Get it?"

"Got it."

"Good, and my name for today is Lily." She took my arm as we walked in, an unusual move for her. "Now let me pick the salesman," she said with a smile on her face and a bounce in her step.

I had never found dealing with car salesmen fun.

"Remember to disagree with everything I want, except if I want to leave."

"Sure thing, Princess."

She slapped my shoulder in her typical response to that name. It was the one thing that always got to her.

We wandered the outer rows of cars, peering in windows and perusing stickers. She shooed away the first two salesman who approached us, both middle-aged men. The third one to come up could have been fresh out of high school, barely old enough to shave. His name was Corey.

Katie introduced herself as *Lily Lust.*

I almost blew it by breaking up and laughing. Maybe this would be fun after all.

"Baby, I think I want a sports car. What do you think?"

"It's your money, darling," I responded.

She gave me a scowl when Corey turned his head the other way.

I'd screwed up. "But I think it's a bad idea, Lily," I said, correcting myself.

"But, baby, I wanna go fast. I think a Corvette would be nice. I might even let you drive it."

"Lily, it's so small."

"Maybe you're right, baby. How could I take all the girls to pole-dancing class?"

Young Corey's eyebrows shot up at that comment.

"I guess you're right. That is a problem." Katie wandered toward the showroom floor, with the young salesman in tow.

The little pervert was checking out the seductive rip in her jeans that showed a bit of her ass cheek with every step.

She stopped at the red Corvette inside the door. "I think this looks so cute. Do they make a four door model?"

Corey somehow managed to not roll his eyes. "No, it only comes with two doors."

"Too bad. It's really pretty." She traced her hand lazily along the hood on the way over to a pickup.

The guy tried to make small talk with her as she tried out the seats in the pickup.

"Oh, I do films," she answered to one of his questions. "Only part time now, but Nicky says he's going to get me some more parts real soon now, aren't you, baby?"

"Sure thing, darling, just around the corner," I answered, playing along with her bit of theater.

"Have I seen any of your films?" Corey asked.

"Well, you might have," Katie said giggling. "But they're not the kind that you find in theaters if you know what I mean." She winked at him.

He turned bright red. The little guy was way out of his league.

I took him aside to compound his embarrassment. "She has real talent," I whispered to him. "She can suck a golf ball through a garden hose. I shit you not."

The poor guy nearly died on the spot.

Katie moved to the sedans on the floor, checking out the small, compact one.

"I like this one, Nicky, it's cute, don't you think?" Katie asked.

That was my queue to steer her away from it. "No, love, you need something more substantial. That's like an eggshell on wheels. It's not safe."

Little Corey was eying Katie hungrily now and missed her question about the gas mileage completely.

She had to repeat it to get an answer out of him. "Hear that, Nicky, the mileage is better on this one."

"What does that matter when you're dead. I tell you, Lily, you need a bigger car."

She climbed out of the little compact and marched up to me. She crossed her arms and huffed. “You’re no fun to shop with. I’m done.” She marched toward the door.

“You need a bigger car,” I repeated.

“I’m leaving,” she said as she left the show room with the salesman trailing her, trying to talk her into staying.

I followed at a discreet distance, letting Corey try to reel her back in with no success.

He gave up at the sidewalk and she continued to my truck, waiting for me to open it.

We climbed in.

I closed the door after climbing in. “I agree that was fun, but we were supposed to be getting you a car.”

“But that was just Act One. Now we have them set up,” she said. “When you bring me back in, there isn’t anything he won't do to keep us from walking out again. He'll be falling all over himself to give me a deal.”

She had a real plan of attack for this.

“I dated a guy once in college, whose family had car dealerships. I know how they operate. They don't make much money selling the car on the front end. It's really the add-ons and the service that makes them all their profit.”

“What's the plan Lily?”

“I want the full-size sedan, but it needs to seem like I don't want it and you're forcing me. The sale price won't matter so much to them if they think they're going to make it back on financing and an extended warranty.”

“What's my part in this play?”

“He needs to think that you have the veto power over all this. But he needs to be negotiating with me instead of you. That puts him in an awkward position because I can always look to you to have you nix the deal. So we need to get him down at least 12 percent below sticker with him thinking that I’m going to finance the car and get an extended warranty.”

"But why do you want to finance it? You can afford this out of petty cash."

"I'll insist on no pre-pay penalty. In the end I write a check and they won't even know what hit them. Here's the plan: Every time I ask you if we can do it, you say it's not good enough until I say pretty please."

"I can handle that, Princess."

As if on cue, she hit me in the shoulder again.

Poking at her like that was fun.

Let Act Two begin.

~

Katie

Nick held the door for me as we reentered the showroom.

The underage salesman I had picked out earlier, Corey, hustled over to meet us.

I undid a button on my shirt.

Corey didn't miss it, his eyes were glued to my chest as he walked up.

"Corey, will you show Lily here the bigger sedan again?" Nick asked Corey.

Corey sensed this was going to be his last chance to get a sale with us. He took me over to the light blue sedan that had been the one I wanted to see all along.

I got in the driver's seat and checked out the interior, fiddling with the steering wheel and a few of the buttons. This was a newer model year of the car I'd lost in the fire, so I knew it pretty well. I asked a dozen useless questions about the car. We checked the back seat, the trunk, under the hood, everything I could think of.

"I told you this was the car for you," Nick said to me.

"But, Nicky, can I afford this?"

Nick checked the sticker and curled up his nose. "Maybe we have to get you a Ford."

Corey stepped up. "Before you do that let's see what kind of deal we can work for you."

Nick shrugged.

Corey pointed the way to one of the small sales cubicles on the side.

I undid another button on my shirt and started to fidget in my chair when we sat. "But, Nicky, I like it," I said.

"Let me work some numbers here for you, Lily," Corey said as he scribbled on his pad. After a moment, he came up with a number which was down a significant amount from the sticker, and showed it to us.

"Wow," I said. "Nicky, whatcha think? Can I swing that much?" I asked Nick.

"No way, Princess."

I glared at Nick. My character wasn't supposed to respond to the princess comment even though I wanted to punch him.

"How much better do you think we have to do, Nick?" Corey asked.

Nick shrugged. "I'm not the customer," he stated. "You need to be talking to Lily, here."

We went back and forth a few times, and I asked Corey what he recommended for financing.

I undid another button on my shirt.

Naturally he told me five years was the most popular, without mentioning that it also netted the dealership the most money, all while trying to hide his glances at my cleavage.

I had him add the extended warranty, another profit kicker for them. "Oh, Nicky, babe can you go get me a diet soda please?" I batted my eyes at Nick, and he grinned.

Cory shifted up in his chair, obviously eager to get Nick out of the room. "Machines are around the corner and down the hall," he said as Nick opened the door.

"I don't understand," Corey said. "Nick is?"

"Oh Nicky? He's my manager. And he's also my acting coach." I leaned forward giving Corey a good view down my shirt. "You know," I whispered to him leaning over. "Sounds are really important in my business. And I'm sort of a method actor, so I have to practice, if you know what I mean." I gave Cory an exaggerated wink before bouncing in my seat.

His eyes bugged out at what I was insinuating. He swallowed hard.

"He's a friend, so he gives me a discounted rate." I giggled.

"You pay him?" he asked incredulously.

"Sure. He's got a lot of experience in the business. But let's talk about the car before he gets back."

He nodded eagerly.

"Nick wouldn't want you to know this, but if we could take another five hundred off I know I can get him to agree."

Corey's face lit up like a Christmas tree. "Let me get my manager involved and get this deal done for you."

Corey stood and shoved his hands in his pockets to hide the bulge in his pants. He left the room as Nick came back with my Diet Coke.

Nick closed the door and sat down. "That little bugger has a boner for you," he said angrily.

"Yeah, that's the idea," I said, placing my hand on his arm. "Now we're ready for Act Three," I whispered to him. "He's going to send in his manager to close the deal. It always goes like this. If the sales guy has the ability to approve it, it's a lousy deal. They'll talk in the office for about five minutes or so to make us think that it's really hard for them to decide. When he comes back in, remember if I say pretty please then agree with me, but if I say please, please instead, then you're gonna take us out of here and out the door."

"Okay, Princess, you're in charge," he said, sitting back in his chair and opening his Dr. Pepper. "What did you say to the little guy to get him so excited, anyway?"

"I told him you gave me acting lessons to get the sounds right. He took the name Lily Lust and his imagination filled in the rest."

Nick grinned. "You little minx, you."

"A girl's gotta do what a girl's gotta do to get a good deal."

Several minutes later, Corey brought in his manager and introduced him as John Thomas.

John began by telling us how hard it was to meet my demands, and how the owner would kill him if he let the car go for what I wanted. "We could split the difference, though," he said. "How about two hundred less?" That wasn't even half way. He thought I couldn't have boobs and also do the math.

I turned to Nick. "Please, please, Nicky, can we get it?"

Nick stood. "I think we've had enough of this, Lily. Let's go." He yanked me up by the arm and pulled me to the door.

We only got five steps outside before Mr. Thomas came running after us. "Okay, we'll do the five hundred off," he called after us. "I'll figure out a way to explain it to the owner later."

Nick stopped us and turned. "Only if you throw in the floor mats and a car cover for free."

The manager hesitated, then agreed.

We were turned over to the credit manager to sign everything. I gave him my license to finalize the paperwork. "Lily is just my stage name," I explained. I also gave him the Myrtle Street address.

He appraised me oddly. "You're not by any chance related to William Covington?"

"I wish," I said loudly. "Then I'd be getting a Rolls now wouldn't I?"

That satisfied him and he gave me the paperwork ten minutes later.

"This isn't quite right," I told him. "I told that nice man Mr. Thomas I would think about the financing. I'm done thinking, and I think I'll just write a check."

He wasn't happy about it, but he was trapped now. We'd agreed on the price. He redid the paperwork without the financing and we signed it fifteen minutes later after a call to my bank. We heard the manager at the bank laugh at him over the phone for asking if a Covington had enough money in her account for the car.

I was driving away in a new Katherine appropriate car, very similar to the charred one sitting where my garage had been. It was appropriate for work, which I would have to get back to soon. Katie would have preferred a sports car, but Katherine won this round.

NICK HELPED ME LOAD MOST OF MY NEW CLOTHES IN THE BACK of the car. They wouldn't all fit, but I could make a second trip later.

I had one item on my list before I got to Myrtle Street. I parked at the electronics store, and quickly found a laptop identical to my work machine.

I didn't dare put my banking or other personal things like my email on the work computer. Also, our company had a policy against that and the IT department was pretty strict.

I pulled up to the Myrtle Street house. It was actually only a few blocks away from Nick's house on Maple. Easy walking distance for a visit.

There were two palm trees and a cedar in the front. The house wasn't much to look at, but Patrick had told me there was quite a large lot behind the house, and a pool as well.

I unlocked the door with the key he had left me. Somehow I wasn't surprised at what I found.

Patrick was a minimalist by nature, but this was extreme even for him. The walls were bare except for the occasional areas of spackle repair that hadn't been painted yet. A table with chairs, a couch, a chest of drawers, a coffee table, not even a television comprised the living room furniture.

I unboxed my new laptop, plugged it in, and let it start up. The contents of the drawers and the cabinets in the kitchen surprised me—a working set of kitchenware, silverware, plates, and miscellaneous foodstuffs. The fridge was mostly empty except for condiments, pickles and the like, and some ice cream still in the freezer.

The house was small but it would work for me for the time being. The mattress in the master bedroom turned out to be quite decent.

The backyard included a pool and some fruit trees. Patrick had told me there was a henhouse with laying chickens in the back. A neighborhood girl came by daily to feed the chickens and pick up any excess eggs that he hadn't already brought into the kitchen. He told me to try some; he bet I'd like the fresh eggs and not want to go back to store bought again.

It took me a dozen trips to cart all the clothes into the house. Back at the kitchen table, the laptop had finally come alive, and I went through the setup steps to get it launched.

I located the WiFi modem on the floor in the corner and got the login information so I could connect to the Internet. Naturally the computer wanted to do a few dozen Windows updates, but I postponed those until later.

My email was full of junk mail and I found a message that Uncle Garth had sent us all, giving us the details about Monica's arrest. I still couldn't believe that the evil bitch had torched my house. We had never even met.

There were two work emails regarding the LDSI audit that I was working on. I would have to do some more work on that in the next few days even though I was supposed to have the week off.

Then I found an email from Rosa, Mr. Downey's assistant, asking me to give her my new home address. The email had been sent on Friday. I'd been burned out of my house, and in one day they already wanted to know where my new home was. Rosa was okay, she merely had the misfortune to be assigned to work for Russ.

I responded to the email and gave her the Myrtle Street address, with a note that my cell phone number wasn't changing. I copied the email to the rest of our team, so they'd have it as well.

I finished unpacking my clothes, ripping the tags off things and putting them in piles on the bed to wash later. When it was done, I could be proud that I had accomplished several concrete things today. I had a car, clothes, a place to stay, and not least of all, a warm hard man, oh so hard, to hold me at night. I hadn't stopped to consider that he might not want me in his bed every night.

What was the appropriate etiquette for fuck buddies? Was it two nights a week? Five nights a week? It didn't make sense it would be every night—that got too close to relationship territory. I decided not to push it, I would take my cue from him. He had to have more experience with this than I did. Anybody had more experience than I did. No, not anybody, everybody.

I rechecked the refrigerator and the pantry. I needed a serious grocery trip to stock this place up. I locked up and drove my brand-new smelling car to the local supermarket.

A shopping cart full of grocery bags was the result of my trip down the aisles. Besides the everyday foods, I'd made sure to get a lot of apples, Pippins and Granny Smiths for the apple pies I planned to bake.

I usually made my own crusts, but tonight I wasn't sure I had time for that, so I had gotten several pre-made ones.

Back at the house, I turned the key in the lock. As I opened the front door I was greeted by a gust of wind from inside.

Then I saw it.

The back door was open.

The floor glittered with broken glass from the window pane.

CHAPTER 10

Nick

Shopping for cars had been a lot more fun than clothes shopping the day before. Katie had grown up to be quite a woman. Not that she had been an ugly duckling before, but the transformation to the elegant swan was complete. And she had the brains to go with the looks. The way she'd handled herself this morning had been eye-opening, and a hell of a lot of fun. She'd played those sales guys so well; they'd had no idea who they were dealing with.

I laughed out loud when I recalled her introducing herself as Lily Lust. What a name. That little pencil-dick of a sales guy couldn't take his eyes off her after that. Whatever minimal brain-power he had to begin with evaporated. I had to hand it to her; it was a great stunt, and not one I would have thought of.

She followed me back to my place in her new car where we loaded some of the clothes that she'd bought yesterday and I sent her off. She was going to move her stuff into the Myrtle Street house and check it out. It turned out to only be a few blocks away. A short jog.

I couldn't take every day off looking after her. I had work to do. After she was on her way, I disarmed the special cave alarm system, opened the solid steel door and locked myself inside.

The cave had started out as a standard bedroom, but was now a fortress with its own air conditioning and power supply. From the outside, the window appeared to just have a shade pulled down, but inside there was a solid wall this side of the shade. All the walls were clad in a copper mesh preventing any electronic signals from penetrating.

I had never let anyone more than peek inside. Nothing got in, and nothing got out. The room was as electronically impregnable as anything the government had.

It was a fitting workspace for the Network Knight.

I took my seat in front of the eight large monitors under the main gigantic screen and checked them one by one. So far my bots hadn't turned up what I was searching for. Each of them seemed to be running properly until I peered closer and noticed something odd about number three.

I switched over to that computer, took it up to full screen and scrolled back to see what it had found.

There it was. Ninety minutes ago it had found a trace of one of the transactions I was trying to follow. I copied the address and transaction details on the clipboard and dumped them into a new file in my Dropbox folder.

If this was what I thought it was, I had a good lead and this would turn into a quite profitable engagement.

An East Coast bank had been hacked and lost twenty-one million in a rogue Swift network transaction. It hadn't been publicized. It wasn't the kind of breach they wanted their share-holders to know about and I guessed they hadn't told the banking regulators yet either.

They gave me the particulars a little over a week ago and if I could track down the perpetrators before quarter end, I would net a nice sweet two-and-a-half percent reward.

I switched over to machine number nine. Lucky Number Nine, my most powerful machine running the sixty-two inch screen above all the others. I launched Badger, my custom drill down program on Lucky Number Nine. Given enough time Badger would find out where this trail led. True to its name, Badger would keep digging and wouldn't give up until it had cornered its prey.

Once I fed Badger the details I let it loose. The badger had the scent and would apply all the power of Lucky Number Nine to the task.

Leaving the cave I switched off the lights and locked the door behind me, resetting the alarm.

As soon as I was outside the room, my phone told me about the missed call and voicemail from Katie. The walls of the cave locked out everything electronic including cell phone signals, so the phone wouldn't work unless I attached it to the Wi-Fi inside. I hadn't done that.

My blood ran cold as I listened to first few words of Katie's voicemail. I ran for the door and jumped into the Tahoe.

The tires clawed for a grip on the asphalt as I punched the accelerator. Her place on Myrtle Street was less than a minute away if I ignored the stop signs.

KATIE

I DROPPED THE GROCERY BAGS I CARRIED AND RAN BACK TO MY car locking myself in. I was shaking. I dialed 9-1-1 while I backed out of the driveway. Screw the no talking on your cell phone while driving shit.

I told the lady who answered that somebody broke into my house, and no I didn't know if they were still inside.

She told me to stay on the line until the cops arrived.

I did.

They arrived quickly, flashing lights and all. The two cops went in guns drawn and came out a few minutes later with the good news. It was safe; the house was empty. They escorted me in.

The house was a mess. Every drawer had been opened and my new clothes flung onto the floor. They'd even ransacked the kitchen drawers, throwing all the utensils and such out. Lucky for me they left the cabinets with the plates and glasses alone.

From what I could tell, the only thing that was missing was my brand-new computer which had been on the table.

I called Nick, but didn't get an answer. I left a message about the break-in and asked him to come over. I was still shaking.

The police took a few minutes filling out a report, including the brand and serial number of my computer from the receipt I had. They told me they thought it was probably neighborhood kids, although it was pretty unusual in this neighborhood.

The thief had broken a window in the back to get in. The policeman mentioned that he didn't think my locks were very good quality either on his way out.

I was picking up in the kitchen when Nick came to a screeching halt out front.

He ran up to the locked front door and banged loudly.

I unlocked it for him and was happy to have him pull me into a tight hug.

"Precious, are you okay?"

I pressed my face into his solid chest, comforted by his hold on me. "Yeah, it's just not my day. Or week."

"You need to call the cops," he said.

"Already did. They've been here and gone. They wrote out a stupid report, now they're off to catch some real criminals."

He broke the hug and walked toward the back door and the broken glass on the floor. "What about fingerprints and stuff?"

"You've been watching way too much TV. They don't do fingerprints or anything like that for simple home burglaries anymore. Anyway, all they got was the computer I bought this morning. I didn't have a television or anything else they could pawn."

"They sure made a mess. Looks like they were looking for something."

"Maybe they expected me to have some hidden money or jewelry or something."

He examined the lock on the back door and came to the same conclusion the police had. "These locks suck. I can change them out for something better tomorrow. The doors are not too bad, though. As for the window I'll have to board that up tomorrow until we can get a glass guy to fix it."

I went back to picking up in the kitchen.

"It's not safe here. For tonight you're coming over to my place," he commanded.

"No." I stomped my foot, as if that would have some effect on him. "I'm not gonna let any juvenile delinquents run me out of my home."

"Why does everything with you have to be an argument?" He grabbed me by the shoulders with a fierceness in his eyes. He took a breath and loosened his grip. "It's not safe here tonight," he said slowly with a tone that still wouldn't allow any disagreement. "After I get your window boarded up and your locks fixed and some basic security in here, then you can stay the night if you want. But not tonight."

He was as bad as my brothers, what a Neanderthal, but I had to admit that he was probably right. "Only because you asked so nicely," I said sarcastically.

He stooped to pick up a whisk and a spatula. "Let me get this stuff for you." He put on the most disarming smile.

I couldn't be mad at him anymore, he was right. "Thanks, I'll work on the bedroom."

We cleaned up the mess in no time.

"Mexican or Pizza?" he asked.

"I don't really want to go out," I pleaded, crashing on the couch.

"Takeout then. The question still stands, Mexican or Pizza?"

"Mexican," I answered. It had been a while since I had eaten anything spicier than a Lean Cuisine for dinner. "But, I have to take a shower and go by the store and get another computer so I can get online again. I'll meet you over there."

He pulled me up off the couch. "Get started then, I'm not leaving until you do."

I didn't have the energy to argue; it wouldn't have done any good, anyway.

I set up the bathroom with the minimal toiletries I had collected at the mall. I wiped off my makeup. A quick rinse in the shower refreshed me. I brushed my teeth and brushed out my hair. I changed my mind and redid my mascara and only a touch of eye shadow and lip gloss. An evening with Nick was a minimal makeup event, but it didn't have to be no makeup. I chose a fresh tight, scoop-neck shirt to go with my Lily Lust bra.

The reaction I got from Nick when I emerged was wide-eyed with a shit-eating grin to go with it. It was exactly what I was after.

I glanced out the back window at the pool before I left. It looked inviting. I was going to have to get a bathing suit and some beach towels when I went out shopping again.

~

Nick

. . .

I HADN'T CALLED AHEAD, SO I HAD TO WAIT AWHILE AT THE restaurant. I rushed to get the food back to the house before Katie arrived. I hadn't given her a key, and I didn't want her to beat me back to the house and wait outside. I had never given a girl a key before, but I was considering it for Katie. I was planning on having her over more than just a night or two. She had changed into a real tease of an outfit. Just the thought of that made my cock come alive.

There was something about her that I couldn't put my finger on, perhaps it was her sassiness. Because of my size most people didn't have the guts to talk back to me.

When I opened the door, she took my breath away again. She teased me with lots of cleavage in that shirt with the plunging neckline and those tight skinny jeans. Her smile, the glint in her eye, and the bounce in her step indicated she knew exactly what she did to me, and enjoyed it. She carried in her new laptop in a box.

She grabbed the beer from the fridge while I opened up the styrofoam containers from Pedro's, the little Mexican hole-in-the-wall restaurant I liked.

"So, tell me what Katherine Covington has been doing all these years?" I scooped up salsa with a chip.

She took her seat opposite me and selected one of the beef tacos. "Well, after high school I went to USC."

"How did you choose that school? I thought you Covingtons went to UCLA."

"That's really the reason. I didn't want to go to a school where they had buildings named after my grandfather. And also I didn't want to be around my brothers anymore." She took a bite of her taco.

I finished chewing and raised my beer in salute. "I can drink to that."

She popped open her beer. "Anyway, I went to USC to get a business degree. At the time I felt like that would be the thing to do. I could be just as good as them in business if I applied myself."

"No doubt. But that's a pretty low hurdle to set for yourself. Your brothers are douchebags."

"They are not," she shot back loudly. "You just don't know them."

I was entitled to my opinion. They were douchebags, all of them. "Okay, no arguing about your brothers."

She eyed me warily. "I ended up with an accounting major in my business degree."

"How did you pick accounting? It seems pretty dry."

She took a sip of her beer. "I checked out marketing, but I just couldn't get into it. The idea of spending all day trying to figure out how to convince somebody to buy a new kind of soap they didn't actually need or want didn't appeal to me."

When she put it that way, it didn't appeal to me either. But then again a lot of people thought that sitting in front of a computer terminal for hours on end the way I did was boring too.

"And accounting is better?" I asked.

"Sure."

"I don't see it," I said. "Just doing numbers all day to figure out how much was spent on toilet paper or paper clips would drive me nuts."

"That's not the kind of accounting I do," she said between sips of beer. "I'm doing auditing, which is sort of like being in the police. We spend a lot of time checking things to make sure that nobody's cheating and everybody's obeying the rules, like a cop with a radar gun by the side of the road."

I finished off my burrito while listening to her. "Still, just checking a bunch of numbers is what it sounds like to me."

"The part I like is the detective work," she said with a smile. "When we are looking for how somebody might be cheating with the numbers. For instance, embezzlers are more common than you might guess. But none of them go around with badges that say embezzler on them."

I grabbed one of the tacos and started in on it while I waited for her to finish chewing.

"See, these guys have gotten pretty sophisticated, so it takes a lot of accounting detective work to figure out what's happening and to catch them, and to make it stick. That's the part of the job I find most interesting."

"That part sounds okay," I agreed. The cops and robbers aspect to her work sounded a lot like some of the things I did. "You like it, then?"

"In general yeah, but not so much right now. My boss has turned into a complete asshole for some reason."

I had heard the complaint often enough. "That happens. You can just quit you know." Being my own boss was the only way I operated.

"It's not that simple. I'm trying to get my CPA, and I've passed all the tests. The only thing I still need is for them to sign off on my experience hours. It's a racket they have going. The accounting firms are the only ones that can sign off, and I need two years or so. So while kids like me are trying to get signed off, they treat us like slave labor. If I quit I have to start all over at another place and it might be even worse." She finished off her taco and washed it down with a gulp of beer.

"How much longer do you have to go?" I asked.

"Just a few months. Then, as soon as I get signed off, I'm out of there. Right now my boss seems intent on getting me to quit before then. He's doing everything he can to drive me out of the company, but I won't let him. I put almost two years of my life into this and I'm not walking away empty-handed."

I admired her attitude. Katie was not one to be pushed around easily. "What's this guy's name, because I have some ways of making his life miserable if you want to get back at him." I had several ways I could screw with his electronic life.

"No thanks. It's just something I have to deal with."

I had expected somebody with her name and wealth to have folded with this kind adversity. The rich kids always seemed to leave when the game got too hard and they went off to do something else, or called daddy to fix it. They had the option of walking away from the obstacles that the rest of us had to face head on. Trust funds had a way of cushioning them from life's challenges.

Katie was working on her second taco when she put it down to go fetch another beer from the fridge. "You want another one?" She offered while she pulled a can out of the refrigerator.

"I'm good." I couldn't avoid watching the sway of her hips or the bounce of her tits as she walked back to the table. My cock thought she was seriously hot. "Then, why don't you just go to a different company to finish out your two years?"

Her face clouded with anger. "It's not that simple. A second year, Danielle, tried that last year. Not only did he refuse to give her a letter of recommendation, but after she moved to the other company, he sent a letter to her new boss saying her work had been completely unacceptable and he wouldn't count it as any hours toward the CPA requirement."

"Well, that sucks. If this guy is so terrible with everybody why don't your bosses fire him?"

"That's the problem. They don't see it because he doesn't treat anybody else like he's treating me. All the other first and second years seems to be getting along fine. So, if I complain about him, I become the problem. There's nothing I can do, but wait it out, I guess. This seems to be his game. Before she left, Danielle told me he did the same thing with a guy the year before. The guy couldn't take it so he gave up on his CPA and went into corporate accounting."

"Seems like a sick son of a bitch if you ask me."

"That's about the size of it. He just picked me as this year's target. Next year it'll be some other poor schmuck."

We finished off the rest of the tacos as she explained some of the torture her boss had put her through recently.

I decided sick bastard was too mild a description. I felt sorry for Katie. This was a perfect example of why I refused to work in a big company. Nobody was going to tell me what to do and give me shit about it. I was born to be a one man show, not a fucking cog in some giant machine.

Katie seemed like my type as well, but stubbornness wouldn't let her admit it. The cog was going to teach the machine a lesson if she got her way.

After cleaning off the table, Katie wanted to spend some time on her laptop doing work. It was just as well because I had to go spend time in the cave checking on my program's progress.

"I'll be in the cave. Knock on the door if you need me." I didn't like having her out of sight, but I had to tend to my work.

CHAPTER 11

Katie

"No problem, I have a lot of boring accounting shit to keep me busy," I told Nick. Even though my boss had told me I could take the week off, I knew deep down that if I came back without any progress on the LDSI audit, we would be in danger of missing our deadlines, and it would become my fault and possibly a reason to fire me. I would not give him that excuse.

I began reviewing the payables reconciliations. This had been where I had run into trouble at their site, and brought copies with me to the conference, expecting to work on them this weekend at least. I rolled my Susan B. Anthony dollar around in my hand.

Dad had given me the coin and told me that Susan B. Anthony's success with women's suffrage was the proof that there was nothing I couldn't accomplish with the proper application of effort and perseverance. I kept it with me always.

An hour later I had only made a small dent in the work when Nick came back out of his room.

He glanced at the still unopened computer box on the floor. "I thought you were going to get that set up tonight."

"That was the plan," I said. "But I still have a lot of work to go through here."

He pulled the box up onto the table. "Mind if I give you a hand?"

"Be my guest." I took another sip of my beer from dinner. There was still a quarter of a can left. Getting a buzz on while trying to do my work wasn't part of the plan.

Nick had the computer out and powering up in no time. He started the Windows installation process while I kept working through my reconciliations.

Having him this close was ruining my concentration. I found myself having to go backwards a step or two to recheck my work, but it would've been rude for me to ask him to go into the other room. It was his house, after all, and he was helping me.

He came over and stood behind my chair. His strong hands massaged my shoulders and neck.

I hadn't realized how tense I had gotten, hovering over the computer. His strong fingers elicited whimpers from me as he slowly worked the knots out of my muscles. "Keep that up and I won't get any work done at all."

"Sometimes work is overrated." He continued kneading my muscles, simultaneously draining the tension out of my body.

"You gotta stop that," I pleaded. "I really do have to make some progress on this."

He momentarily stopped the massage, but didn't pull his hands away. "Your boss gave you next week off."

"Yes and no. If I don't get this done by the end of the week and have it ready when I come back, the firm will miss the audit deadline. And I'll be blamed, assuming he doesn't just flat out fire me."

He pulled his hands away. "I still think you'd be better off if you just quit." He sat down and went back to setting up my new laptop.

Two hours later the payables reconciliations weren't going any better for me. I went back to last year's audit. It had been completed by DA and RD, Danielle and Russ Downey. I tried to follow the methodology that he had used, but I got stuck when it went to reconciling with overseas records.

I would need the offshore detail records to finish this. I had brought them home on a thumb drive last week before leaving for Vegas. I checked my laptop bag again without any luck. I thought I had put it in there to bring with me, but I must've left it at home where it now joined everything else I had owned in a giant ash heap.

"I could use a glass of wine," I told Nick in frustration.

"Wine is for sissies, Princess. One glass of scotch coming up."

I'd forgotten he didn't drink wine. Who doesn't have a single bottle of wine in the house?

He brought me over a tumbler half full.

I shut down my computer and took a mouthful. It burned going down, a lot stronger than what I was used to. My brothers all drank scotch, but Dad had always told me that *sophisticated* women didn't drink hard liquor straight. A Tom Collins was the strongest thing I had ever tried.

"Careful there, Precious, you're supposed to sip it not gulp it."

"Now you tell me." I took another large swallow. I was determined to finish this glass and call it a night. It took me several more attempts, but I finally reached the bottom of the glass. I got up, took Nick's hand, and led him toward the bedroom.

~

Nick

. . .

Katie was still asleep when I rolled out of bed Sunday morning.

I dressed quietly and left a note on the kitchen table telling her I was at her house getting the work done and she could join me later.

I rolled the Harley halfway down the street before starting it to avoid waking Katie. I brought the second helmet with me. She could have her ride this afternoon if all went smoothly.

Two big trucks with Hanson Security painted on them were waiting outside Katie's house when I rolled up at seven sharp.

I had done lots of contract work for Hanson security and Investigations in the past.

"Hey, Nick," Bob Hanson called out as he rounded the front of the nearest van trailed by Winston Evers. Though not as tall or strong as me or even Winston, Bob Hanson could take care of himself. I'd watched one of his self-defense classes that he gave some of his security guys. He knew more moves than I'd ever seen and I don't think he ever left the office without at least two weapons. The fact that Bob had come out himself to join Winston and the technicians was an indication that this was a top priority job.

When I had called Bob Hanson last night, his first reaction had been to tell me they didn't work on Sundays. His attitude about that changed as soon as I told him it was for Katherine Covington, Bill's little sister. They did a lot of work for the Covingtons, and mentioning her name got this moved right to the top of the list.

"Slumming I see, Hanson."

"Have to get out of the fucking office sometime," he responded. "I want to see for myself what the scope of the job is, in case I need to pull in more people. I know that computer weenies like you don't understand complicated shit like wires and cameras."

Winston, Hanson, and I all shook.

Winston was unusually quiet, probably in deference to his loudmouth boss.

I let them inside with the house key I had lifted from Katie's purse. It took us a little while, but we finally ended up agreeing on the list of items the guys would install. Bob didn't stick around, instead leaving Winston in charge after scoping out the project.

Winston sent one of the guys out to get better lock hardware for the doors and the windows.

We planned a complete installation with everything we could think of: motion sensors, cameras, and lights outside, sensors on all the doors and windows including the crawlspace, and the attic entrance. Sirens were to be located front, back, and two inside the house.

Most people didn't realize that a burglar alarm didn't keep the burglars out, it merely got rid of them with a lot of light and noise as soon as they broke in. Your average burglar was a coward, and not at all interested in drawing any attention to himself. They were like cockroaches—noise and a good dose of light always scared them off.

We decided on a couple of locations for panic buttons inside the house too. The cameras inside were a little trickier. I didn't want to pick exactly where they would be in the bedrooms without asking Katie.

All the cameras were going to be tied to the Internet with seven day storage.

I had a similar setup at my house with security cameras, except I had not included the master bedroom. That was because I knew how people like me could almost always find a way to get into the Internet feed.

Winston assured me he and his guys could get the entire job done today, which was a relief.

Bob had suggested a stronger door for the master bedroom with a deadbolt that could be set from inside as a semi-safe room. A determined attacker could still go around to the outside windows or spend time kicking his way through the wallboard, but at least it would buy some time in an emergency. That door was the only thing that we wouldn't get done today.

They started on the installation while I searched out glass contractors. It took a while, but I finally found a guy who would commit to doing it today. All it took was me telling him I would insist on paying cash and there was an extra hundred dollar tip in it for him if he got it done today.

~

Katie

The unmistakable noise of a Harley starting up and rumbling down the street woke me up. The bed next to me was empty.

Nick had said he needed to get an early start on work this morning. But when he'd mentioned it last night I hadn't paid attention to what the work was.

I checked the rest of the house and knocked on the metal door of the room he called the cave just to be sure. The door was locked.

He had gone.

I turned the shower up hot, rotating slowly under the spray. The big thing on my agenda for today was shopping for odds and ends for the house. I needed a few more things in the kitchen, some towels, lots of towels, because I needed some for the pool as well. I added a bathing suit to my mental list, and margarita makings. I could anticipate a nice afternoon lounging out by the pool soon, margarita in hand.

I pulled on a brand-new pair of jeans, triple checking that I had gotten all the tags off. I added a comfortable T-shirt and my new pair of Nike's from the mall. I didn't want to cook anything for breakfast, so I checked the cupboards for cereal. Naturally a guy like Nick only had Wheaties in his cupboard. I fixed myself a bowl.

That's when I noticed the note on the table. Nick had gone over to my house. Don't wear heels, it said.

He had left me a key to his house so I could lock up, at least that's what I assumed it was for. It was only my third morning here and already I rated a key to his house. The thought warmed me; I had never had a key to a guy's place before.

After a leisurely cup of coffee and my bowl of cereal, I pulled some money out of my wallet, stuffing a few twenties in my pocket. I left the oversized purse and laptop bag, put my shiny new laptop under my arm, locked the front door, and walked toward Myrtle Street. It was a pleasant sunny morning, and I wanted to walk instead of drive.

I already thought of Myrtle Street as my new home. I needed a place to call my own, and for the time being this was going to be it.

The neighborhood here was a quiet one with well-maintained cars in the driveways and neatly trimmed and watered lawns. This didn't appear to be the kind of neighborhood that had very much of a crime problem. It was a nice sunny slice of suburbia. Songbirds were chirping and singing in the trees. I passed two couples walking their dogs, and a pair of women jogging. Each of the groups greeted me with a warm "good morning" as we crossed paths. I could get to liking this area, a lot.

My previous neighborhood had been more upscale. Instead of walking they all got in their BMWs and drove off. Somehow the people here seemed more laid back and friendly, less hurried.

Rounding the corner on Myrtle Street, I saw the trucks in front of my house. Hanson security vans. Nick had mentioned he thought I needed a security system of some kind, but I had no idea this is what he meant. And worse than that, there was no way the Hanson people were going to keep this quiet. They'd blab it instantly to my brothers and my uncle Garth. I'd have to endure months of suggestions to move to some place safer, like their monster skyscraper.

This street had been fine when Patrick was living here because he was a guy. But I would be told it was too dangerous a neighborhood for a woman living alone.

Bullshit.

I walked up to find Winston on a ladder, mounting a surveillance camera on the porch.

"Good morning, Miss Katie," he called out as he saw me approach. I thought I had broken him of calling me Miss or ma'am, but apparently not completely.

"Winston, why do you have to keep doing that? If you call me Miss or ma'am one more time, I'm going to kick that ladder out from underneath you."

He chuckled. "Yes, boss."

I went inside. Three other Hanson employees in overalls were working, connecting up who knows what.

Nick was in the back talking with a guy who didn't have a Hanson uniform on, gesturing at the broken window. I put down my bag and went outside to join them.

Nick finished up with the guy a few seconds before taking me into a nice, tight hug. "Good morning, sleepyhead." He kissed the top of my head. "Jose here can have your window fixed this afternoon and Winston and the guys are going to have everything else done by the end of the day as well. What do you think about that?"

I stepped back. "I think you could've asked me before doing all this." I crossed my arms.

"You said you wanted to have your own place. I told you yesterday that you couldn't be here until it was safe. I thought I was doing you a favor by getting it ready today. Now, if you want, I'll tell Jose to come back next week and you can just live with a broken window for a week."

"You know that's not what I mean. It's just that you didn't ask me about any of the security stuff. And I didn't want to use Hanson."

"Why not? They're top-of-the-line."

I wasn't sure how to phrase it so I said it outright. "Because I didn't want this getting instantly broadcast to my brothers."

"If you think your brothers wouldn't find out about the burglary in the next day or two, you're nuts. Suck it up and deal with it. Tell them to fuck off and leave you alone."

He was right that they would find out about it soon enough anyway even if I used another company.

Nick ushered me inside. "Anyway, Katie, there is no way you are going to talk me out of installing the absolute best stuff. We do have one executive decision for you to make, but first, let me show you what we're doing. All new locking hardware for the windows and the doors. The system will monitor all the entry points and all the windows. There are motion sensors out front and in the back, and a full set of outdoor lights. We have cameras around the outside and also a few on the inside."

I stopped him right there. "I don't want cameras inside the house like I'm in some prison being watched twenty-four hours a day."

"Trust me, it's nothing like prison, and that's not how this system works, Precious. The cameras are on a feed and recorded for a week. Nobody's watching anything else unless the alarm gets triggered, or we have to go in and check out some suspicious activity in the last day or two. And that can't happen without your approval."

That sounded a lot better. "Nobody's watching?"

"The feeds don't go active at the monitoring station until the alarm goes off, that's the way it works. There's no peeping Toms watching you. But there is the one decision you need to make. Do you want to have a camera in the master bedroom or not?"

That took a nanosecond. "No way."

"I don't blame you. I feel the same way," Nick said as he led me out front. "See the cameras up here outside the door?"

I nodded.

"You'll be able to pull these up on your phone and see who's at the door before you answer it."

I liked the sound of that.

I was feeling a lot better about it as he explained the system.

Nick told me he had to go run an errand and rumbled off on his Harley.

I set up my computer out by the pool where it was a little quieter. It took me a while to get connected to my email again on this new machine.

In Las Vegas I'd emailed myself all the presentations from the conference so that I could review them when I got back. Now was as good a time as any to start that. The first one I went to work on was the second half of the presentation that I'd pulled myself out of when I'd received that terrible text about my house.

Since I hadn't heard the words that went along with the slides it took me a little while to understand the rest of the presentation. Following that, I went on to the session I'd missed entirely because I had left early.

It was a complicated one having to do with tax treatments of offshore entities and I would have to go through this more than once to be certain I understood it.

From out back I could hear Nick return. The sound of a Harley in the neighborhood was unmistakable.

He came out to where I was sitting, holding something behind his back. "Precious, close your eyes."

I did, and waited.

He handed me something heavy.

I opened my eyes. It was a leather jacket, shiny and black. "Does this mean what I think it does?"

"I hope it fits. Time for your first ride on the hawg, Precious."

I put on the jacket and zipped it up. It wasn't the same one he had given me on the ride back from Las Vegas. This was a brand-new women's jacket. It was form-fitting and snug. "You got this for me?"

"If you're gonna ride, you have to do it right," he said with a smile.

I followed him around front, giddy at the thought of my first ride on his Harley. Now I understood why he'd told me not to wear heels. I hadn't brought an elastic for my hair, so I did my best to tuck my hair into the back of the jacket and zip it up tight.

He patted the seat behind him, and I climbed on and took a good grip of him. With a full throated roar, he launched us down the street.

The ride was everything I had hoped it would be. The Harley was the complete opposite of the Honda. It was loud, making a statement everywhere it went. I could see people turn their heads as we approached, there was no ignoring a Harley roaring by.

And Nick was right; I was holding onto him with a hundred horsepower vibrator between my legs. Every girl needed to do this at least once.

Nick promised we could go on a longer ride another day, but today we had to get back to the house.

It was nearly lunchtime when we got back, and I offered to go out and get the guys something to eat. There was a Subway a few blocks away on the main drag, so I gathered up their sandwich orders. I would be hoofing it, so the Cokes and waters I had in the fridge would have to do them for drinks.

CHAPTER 12

Nick

I OFFERED TO GO WITH HER TO GET SANDWICHES, BUT SHE refused and I didn't push it.

The black town car pulled up out front. It had been quite a while, but I recognized him instantly when he climbed out of the backseat. He had filled out since I'd last seen him, and the clothes were clean business casual, instead of sloppy high school chic.

Katie's big brother Bill had come.

His driver got out, but stayed by the car. The arrogant son of a bitch had a chauffeur.

The scowl on Bill's face as he walked up made it obvious he recognized me, and he wasn't happy to see me here, or with Katie. But that was his fucking problem not mine.

I stood my ground. I was done being intimidated by this family. I would give him a nose to match his brother's if he was fool enough to take a swing at me. I smiled and waved to tick him off.

Winston was on the porch out front with me.

"What's going on here?" Bill asked, addressing his question to Winston.

Winston climbed down from the ladder he was on. "Putting in a security system for your sister, Bill. It'll be first-rate when we're done."

"I heard there was a break-in. Is that true?" Bill asked Winston, still refusing to address me directly.

"Yeah, that's what I heard. Nick here knows more about it than I do," Winston answered.

Bill Covington stared at me, expecting me to explain to his highness.

"Good to see you again, Bill," I said with a smile plastered on my face that was intended to bug him. He had probably heard from Patrick that I had brought Katie back from Las Vegas and he clearly wasn't any happier about it than his brother had been.

"Right," Bill said. "So, what happened?"

I let him stew for a few seconds before I answered. "She decided to move in yesterday. She brought over some things and left to go to the supermarket for food. While she was gone some punks broke a window in the back and ransacked the place. I called Hanson last night and asked him to get a crew over here to put in some security first thing today."

Bill pondered that for a second before the obvious question hit him. "I thought she came back to town on Thursday."

"We did," I said. I let the implication of what I said sink in.

His brow creased. He understood what I meant, and it bothered him even more than I had hoped. His little sister had shacked up with me for a few days and there was nothing he could do about it now. He marched inside.

Winston gave me a look, and we went back to working on the porch and door cameras without another word.

Fuck him.

~

KATIE

I ROUNDED THE CORNER ON MYRTLE STREET TOWARD MY HOUSE. Jason, my brother's driver, was leaning against the town car that he drove Bill around in.

What I didn't need right now was my big brother butting in. I quickened my pace back to the house, hoping to get there before the explosive mixture of Nick and my oldest brother turned my new home into another smoking hole in the ground.

Nick waved as he noticed me. He and Winston were working on the front porch. Bill was nowhere to be seen.

I waved Jason over and tried to convince him to come inside and join us for lunch.

He declined, saying his wife had made him lunch. It was so typically Jason.

I found Bill inside, asking the technicians detailed questions about what they were installing and how.

He always had to be in charge, as if Nick and Winston didn't understand well enough what they were doing.

Bill rushed over when he noticed me.

I emptied the bag of food onto the table. "Morning Bill, I didn't know you were coming over."

"Katie, why didn't you tell me what happened?"

"You were out of town, and Nick took care of me just *fine*."

Anger wrote itself across Bill's face. "He's not family," he said sternly.

"He may not be, but he was here, and you weren't," I shot back, not quite yelling.

The technicians were smart enough to stay away from this family argument.

The door opened and Nick and Winston sauntered in.

"Looks good, Katie," Nick said as he approached and put his arm around me.

Bill stiffened.

I turned and gave Nick a quick kiss. "Bill, want to stay and join us for lunch? I've got extra."

"No, thanks." He nodded his head toward the open bedroom door. "Katie we need to chat for a moment."

Nick let go of me. "I'll be right here, Precious," he whispered in my ear, low enough that Bill couldn't hear with the commotion the technicians were making choosing sandwiches.

Warily, I followed Bill into the room and he closed the door.

"I came here to bring you home," he told me flat out, as if it were a fact rather than a request.

"This is my home for the time being and I'm not going anywhere," I replied softly. I didn't want a yelling match that everybody in the other room would hear.

"Katie, you know this isn't a safe neighborhood."

Exactly what I had expected from him. "Not according to the police. This ZIP Code has a lower crime rate than the area around my old house."

"I can't let you stay here." There it was. His view that he could boss me around whenever he wanted.

"As the kids say, you're not the boss of me. I can do what I damn well please. You can see the Hanson guys are giving me a super system, and all the locks are being replaced too."

"You know hanging around Nick Knowlton is not a good idea."

I crossed my arms. "That's your real problem isn't it, Bill? You don't like Nick and you never have."

"Listen to me, Katie, you don't know him. He's a criminal, a felon who's been in prison and for good reason. He's not someone you want to hang out with."

An ex-con?

A momentary shiver ran through me. This was totally new. I

didn't really know Nick's history since high school, I hadn't asked him. Being an ex-con was not something I would've guessed, but I wasn't going to let my brother bully me into making a decision like this without talking with Nick.

"You're the one that doesn't know him," I told Bill. "He's a nice guy, and I'll pick my own friends thank you very much. We're done here, you can get in your fancy limo and leave us alone."

"Katherine you're making a mistake." He always used Katherine in big brother mode.

"I'm not twelve." He thought he could tell his little sister Katherine what to do. Katherine had always listened to him. Katherine had always obeyed. I was sick of being Katherine.

"It's my life and I get to make mistakes if I want to. Like I said, we're done here." I was in the other room before Bill could react.

He erased the disappointment that had shown on his face a few moments ago and waved to the gang as he headed out to his car.

"What did he want?" Nick whispered into my ear.

"Tell you later."

The guys finished off all the sandwiches they had ordered plus two of the extras I had gotten for them and went back to work.

I spent the early afternoon playing around with my new computer and checking several days' worth of email.

The later part of the afternoon, I went to the SEC Edgar website and re-read the last two years' 10K forms for LDSI, including the appendices. It was complicated and slow going. I hadn't brought my work computer over, and I hoped it would give me a clue as to what I was missing in my reconciliations. I wouldn't let this problem stump me and have Russ use it against me when I got back. I would solve this.

As my father'd taught me, *every accomplishment starts with the decision to try and only ends with perseverance.*

Winston and his people finished the system and got it hooked up to the Internet. They helped me load an application on my phone and Nick's that would interface with it. It was pretty cool, we could even pull up images from the video feeds.

Nick told me it was the same app he used on his phone to secure his house.

They assured me we were the only two who could see the video unless the alarm had been triggered, or I said okay to go search the history files for some reason.

The noise from testing the alarm sirens was so loud it hurt my ears. Any local punks who decided to break in were going to be surprised as hell and leave with a hearing impairment.

Before he left, Winston confided that the sign outside saying the house had an alarm was the most important part. He assured me that any crook with an IQ bigger than his shoe size would skip my house and find easier pickings without a security system.

I liked the sound of that.

I was sitting at the table still going through last year's 10K. It was just Nick and I.

Nick locked the door, came over behind me and started to give me another of those amazing shoulder and neck rubs.

"Keep that up, that's just what I need," I told him.

"What's the plan for tonight, Precious?" he whispered as he reached his hands lower and cupped my breasts. He was asking about tonight's sleeping arrangements, or at least the arrangements for tonight before we slept.

My missed shopping trips suddenly dawned on me. I hadn't gotten any sheets for the bed. "How about your place? I don't think I have any clean sheets here."

He was kissing and blowing in my ear and caressing my

breasts, keeping me from concentrating on the 10K in front of me.

I raised my hands up behind me. "How about if we christen this place tomorrow? I have to finish this report here." I grabbed his head and scratched his scalp. "If you pick up some dinner, I'll finish up here and then walk over to your place and meet you there."

He pulled his hands away from my chest, giving up for the time being on distracting me. "Chinese or Mexican again?"

I missed his touch already. "Chinese sounds great."

"Just don't be too long, you don't want it getting cold."

"Twenty minutes and I'll be outta here," I promised him.

He put a key down on the table in front of me. "This is your new key to the house." He locked the door behind him as he left.

After his massage I had to collect myself for a few moments before I finished this 10K. I told Siri to set a timer for twenty minutes so that I wouldn't be late.

An email showed up. It was from my brother Bill. The subject line was *Nick Knowlton's rap sheet*. My finger hovered over the key for a moment, unsure what to do. I deleted the email without opening it. I'd had enough of my brother's interference. He wasn't going to run my life.

I went back to studying the LDSI 10K report.

When the timer in my phone went off, I still hadn't gotten anything out of these that would tell me where my problem lay. But I refused to give up. I told Siri to set another timer for fifteen minutes, deciding to reread the last section.

The second timer went off as I finished. I would have to try again tomorrow.

Bill might have been right that Nick Knowlton was wrong for Katherine, but Nick was exactly what Katie needed: A high octane man, a mix of brains, brawn, and testosterone, extra heavy on the testosterone. He made me feel like a real woman, a complete woman.

I folded up my computer, put it under my arm, turned off the lights, set the alarm as Nick had shown me, and locked the door on my way out.

With the sun down, it was chillier than it had been on the walk over this morning.

Lights came on automatically out front as I moved away from the door, courtesy of the motion sensors. The lights did a pretty good job of illuminating the whole front yard all the way to the street. Cockroach repellent, Winston had called the lights.

I turned left at the sidewalk toward Nick's house.

The attack came from the bushes. He rushed out of the darkness and hit me solidly. My computer went clattering to the ground as I was thrown into the parked car at the curb. I hit my head hard on the car door window and fell to the ground.

A scream tore out of my lungs. My head hammered as I struggled to right myself.

I was instantly blinded by the bright light of a flashlight he shone in my eyes. Reflexively, I blinked and struggled to my feet.

He moved the light to search the ground by the car, and I took the chance to run toward the corner.

I couldn’t see a thing after being blinded by the bright light. I ran into the light pole near the corner, luckily only hitting it with my shoulder instead of straight on with my face. Regaining my balance, I ran as fast as I could. Luckily I had put Nikes on this morning, and I might not be able to fight, but running was something I was good at. I couldn't tell where the man behind me was when I turned the corner.

I ran straight into a wall.

CHAPTER 13

Nick

I CALLED THE ORDER INTO THE CHINESE RESTAURANT AS I WAS walking over. They had it ready right after I arrived.

I had noted the time when Katie said it was only going to be twenty minutes and I was going to hold her to it.

Thirty-five minutes later she still hadn't shown up, so I decided to walk back to her house and yank her away from her damned computer.

I turned the oven to one-seventy and put the food inside to stay warm.

When I neared Myrtle Street, I dialed her phone. It went to voicemail. I put the phone back in my pocket.

She came flying around the corner and ran straight into me in a high velocity version of how we had met a few days ago.

This time her momentum almost knocked me over.

I grabbed her and she started hitting me.

"Princess," I yelled as I struggled to hold her still. She was confused and panting. She blinked several times like she couldn't tell who I was.

The light of the street was dim, but I could see blood dripping down from her scalp. "Calm down, what happened, tell me what happened, what's wrong?"

She sobbed and clung to me. I hugged her and rocked her to soothe her. "Tell me what happened."

She shook terribly. Slowly she started to speak. "He hit me."

My heart raced as adrenaline filled my veins. "Who? Who hit you? Where?" I would kill the fucker.

She pointed behind her. "The house, near the house, he came out of nowhere." She was sobbing and shaking.

"Can you walk?"

She nodded. "Yeah."

I took her with me to the corner. I peered down the street but couldn't see anybody or anything. "Come with me. We're going back to my house. We need to get you cleaned up."

I held her tight as I walked her back in the direction of my house.

She was shaking and wobbly. "I don't understand," she mumbled.

Inside, I took her straight to the bathroom and pulled my first aid kit out from under the sink. I wet a wash cloth and handed it to her. She dabbed at her forehead and cheek.

The blood had dribbled down her face and gotten on her shirt as well. There had been a fair amount, and it hadn't stopped yet.

I soaked tissues in alcohol. "This is going to hurt." I dabbed at the cut with the alcohol.

She pulled back.

I cleaned it as best I could. It was long and deep and the bleeding hadn't stopped yet. The cut was just inside the hairline. "Precious, this is gonna need some stitches. I'm taking you to the emergency room." I tore open several bandage pads from my first-aid kit and put them on the wound. "Hold this," I told her. I located my roll of gauze and wrapped it around her head to help hold the bandage in place. She was going to arrive looking like one of those horror film characters.

She complained about going to the emergency room, but I insisted.

I grabbed more bandages for her to place on top of the ones that were held in place with the gauze, and loaded her in the car.

We walked into the emergency room at the nearby hospital a few minutes later.

With such an obvious bloody wound, they didn't make us wait. She got in to see a doctor right away.

They cut off my makeshift bandage and went about cleaning up her wound and controlling the bleeding.

My phone dinged with a text message. It was an automated text from Badger. The program had found something. I put the phone away and ignored the follow-up text. Badger would have to wait. Katie was my priority now.

The doctor concurred with me on the need for some stitches. He shot an accusatory glance in my direction. "How did this happen, young lady?" He probably thought this was some kind of domestic battery.

"I had just left my house when some guy rushed out of the bushes and hit me. I hit the parked car pretty hard right here." She pointed to her head and her shoulder.

"Do you know who attacked you?" the young doctor asked.

"No. It all happened so fast and it was dark. He got me with a flashlight in the eyes. I couldn't see anything. I just ran. Luckily I found Nick here."

The doctor seemed convinced that he wasn't gonna need to report me. That was the last kind of trouble I needed. "I'd suggest we call the police and you file a report if you're up to it," the doctor suggested.

Katie nodded.

"I'll have the nurse call them." He left and returned a few

minutes later. “I'm not bad at doing stitches, but we have a plastic surgeon available this time of night if you'd like him to do the stitches since it's near your hairline.”

It was thoughtful of him.

“Yes, please, that would be good,” Katie said.

“I'm also going to have to clip the hair away near the cut so we can put a bandage on,” he told her.

Katie wasn't at all happy about that.

It took us another hour to get out of there. The surgeon came by to do the stitching quite quickly, but we had to wait for the police to show up and Katie to give her statement.

There wasn't much for her to add beyond what she'd already said. She was pretty sure it was a man. She didn't see his face. He was bigger than her, and that was about all she could say. She mentioned that she was carrying her laptop at the time and she thought it skidded under the car.

We left there with the admonition that she should keep Neosporin on it as much as she could and the stitches should be looked at in a week to ten days.

Driving back, I went to Myrtle Street instead of straight to my house. I parked in front of Katie's and got the Maglite out of the door pocket. “How many houses down did you say?”

“Two or three.”

I went back that direction, searching the grass, the bushes, and under the cars. I didn't see her laptop anywhere. I located where it happened. It was pretty easy to figure out with the blood on the car door.

I went back to the car and gave her the bad news. “You’re now out a second laptop.” What I didn't say was the obvious implication of this attack.

The firebug lady was in jail, and Katie’d had her house broken into and been attacked twice now since then. This was not merely a case of bad luck. Somebody was after her.

As I turned the truck around heading to my little house, the choice became obvious. I could drive her to her brother's place and drop her off, where she would be safe with the Covingtons and the Hanson firm watching out for her, or I could take her back to my place. If I did that, I was taking responsibility for her safety, and not for only one night.

It was something I didn't do cavalierly. She would need a full-time bodyguard, nothing part-time about this.

She deserved the best, not some half-ass attempt.

I turned away from the big glass Covington tower. She was safer at my place.

I stopped at the gas station mini-mart. "Be right back."

I went inside and bought a bottle of champagne.

"What's that for?" she asked when I brought the bottle back to the truck.

"For when we catch this fucker," I told her.

That brought a grin to her face.

Once safely back at my place, she lay down on the couch to rest.

I turned off the oven and checked the food. I put the soup in the microwave to reheat.

She opened her eyes. She patted the edge of the couch next to her. "I could use a hug," she said softly.

I sat on the edge, kissed her lightly on the lips, and gave her the hug she asked for.

She sniffled and cried. "I was so scared."

"It'll be okay, Precious. I'll keep you safe." There was no way I was going to take her back to her brother's. She was mine to protect, and I wouldn't fail her. I would find this fucker and make him pay for what he'd put her through.

The microwave dinged.

Eventually her sniffling stopped. "I guess the food's ready."

I let her lie back down. "It can wait if you're not up to it."

She sat up. "No, let's eat."

The girl was a fighter.

~

Katie

I was famished, and the food smelled great. "What did you get us?"

"I hope you like Szechuan. We have hot and sour soup, Mongolian Beef, Kung Pao chicken, and Beef with Broccoli."

I pulled plates out of the cupboard and silverware from the drawer. "Sounds good to me."

He frowned. "Silverware is against the house rules. Chopsticks only for Chinese food."

Properly chastised, I put the silverware away except for spoons to serve the food from the containers. I wasn't very proficient with chopsticks, but I was game to learn.

We settled at the table and he spooned some out for each of us and poured the soup into two bowls.

The soup was spicy all right. We needed to talk, but I wasn't quite sure how to begin the conversation.

He understood. "I think we should talk about it."

He didn't need to explain what *it* was. "Yeah, I guess this means that the burglary might not have been random."

He slurped some of his soup down with a raised eyebrow. "Absolutely not random." He picked up a piece of Mongolian beef and started chewing, challenging me to continue.

"Yeah, I guess not." I picked up the Kung Pao chicken.

"This is serious."

He was right, of course, and I started to shiver lightly. It wasn't my imagination. Somebody was after me.

"Look, the firebug lady is in jail, and you get targeted twice in two days in this neighborhood. Somebody either wants to hurt you, or scare you, or you have something they want."

I was scared all right. A pit the size of a grapefruit formed in my stomach when he said they might want to hurt me. Today I'd gotten banged up, but it could have been much worse if the guy had been armed with a gun or a knife, or if he'd chased after me and Nick hadn't been there.

"You're not going to be safe until I figure out who this is and take care of him."

This side of Nick scared me. Perhaps I shouldn't have been so quick to delete Bill's rap sheet email.

"We have an advantage here because you just moved."

I finished chewing what I had in my mouth. "What advantage?" I had been listening to him but now he had lost me. "He knows who I am and I don't know who he is. How is that an advantage?"

"I was out front of the house a lot today. If somebody had been following you, I would've seen them. So it has to be somebody that knows you moved to that address."

What he said made sense.

"The obvious question is who knows? Who did you tell?"

"Well, you, and my brothers for one. Then there's the people at my work."

"Who exactly at work knows?"

"My boss and his secretary and everybody else on our team because I copied them on the email."

"How many people is that?"

I thought for a moment. "About ten, I guess."

"That's not too bad. Anybody else?"

"Well, there's the people at LDSI, I emailed and asked them to FedEx me some information."

"And how many people is that?"

"I don't know. I just emailed four people there, but they probably had to tell somebody else to actually ship it." I thought some more. I must be missing something or somebody. "There's the car dealer, and I told Bill's Secretary Judy, so some people at Covington could know."

"That's a bigger list than I thought, but at least it's a lot better than having to consider the whole LA phone book." He slurped more soup. "What's LDSI, anyway?"

"LDSI is Lindbergh Defense Strategies Inc.; that's the audit I'm working on now. I just don't see any of them wanting to hurt me."

"Somebody sure does, and we just have to figure out who it is. Did you piss anybody off at this fancy conference in Las Vegas?"

None of this made any sense. "Hell no."

He quickly told me what I could and couldn't do, to stay safe. It was as if he had been considering this for a while. He was in bossy mode again, but the throbbing of the cut on my head and my sore shoulder told me to not argue with him, at least not tonight.

I hadn't angered any of these people, at least that I knew of. The people at work were pretty much the same people I've been working with the last almost two years, and there were no obvious suspects there.

My hundred octane guy was in full protection mode right now and I had to admit he made me feel very special.

What had started out as a few days of hot sex, at least that's what I had expected, was going to turn into an extended time in the close presence of this man.

"You understand the rules?" he asked me.

"Yeah, I know, I don't go anywhere without you. That's the short version," I said, rolling my eyes.

"And?"

"And you monitor all my communications." I sneered. This part seemed a little over the top.

"It's the only way, Princess. Now give me your phone."

I was learning not to react when he called me that. It was his way of getting my attention or that he thought I was being snotty, which sometimes I was. I handed him the phone, and he took it down the hall into that locked room of his.

"When do I get a look inside?" I yelled down the hall after him.

He smiled as he unlocked the door. "When it's time."

While he was gone, I went through the list in my head again but didn't get anywhere. I had lived a pretty boring life recently, actually for quite a long time.

I cleaned up the dinner and plugged in my work laptop. I needed to get further on the LDSI reconciliations so I didn't get fired when I got back to work.

Nick came back out with my phone later. "You're all set to go."

"You're not listening in on me or anything are you?"

"No, of course not. But everything will be logged, we can get at it later if we need to."

The painkillers they'd given me at the hospital were wearing off. "I could use some Advil right about now."

Nick came back with the tablets and a full glass of scotch.

It didn't take me long to finish the glass and lose interest in my computer. I put it away, and we moved to the couch where he turned on the TV and scrolled through the movie listings.

He chose *Die Hard*, the original movie. "I like to watch this when I'm down. It reminds me that you can get out of even the worst jams if you just keep at it."

I got up and poured myself another glass of scotch and brought the bottle over because I wasn't done yet.

He was right about the movie, Bruce kept getting himself out of worse and worse situations as it went along, but then it was a movie and not real life. Nobody had burned his house down.

Nick's strong arm around my shoulders holding me into him, and the warmth of the scotch in my stomach, was precisely what I needed tonight. I emptied the rest of the glass and poured another.

CHAPTER 14

NICK

SHE HAD FALLEN ASLEEP DURING THE MOVIE AND SHE HAD BEEN pretty out of it when I'd finally gotten her into bed.

As the early morning light filtered in around the edges of the shades, I woke to find her sleeping peacefully behind me, her hair covering the gauze bandage on her scalp.

She was now my first. The first woman who had slept—and only slept—in my bed. My morning wood ached to rectify that situation.

Instead, I slipped out of bed, grabbed some clothes, and closed the door lightly behind me as I went about fixing breakfast. There would be plenty of time to sample her body later. Maybe on the kitchen counter after breakfast.

Katie was in worse trouble than she realized. These were no random events. The arson at her old house had been a thorough job, meant to obliterate the house and probably kill her if she'd been inside. The mere thought of that turned my stomach. The good news was that we had a limited set of suspects. Bad news was that we had no obvious motive, and without that we had nothing to go on.

She came out of the bedroom wearing one of my button up shirts, only a few buttons done. She was going to kill me if she walked around like that for long, with her cleavage on full display, and her bare hips.

"You like french toast?" I asked.

She came up from behind and wrapped her arms around me, pressing those warm, luscious breasts against me.

"You're in dangerous territory there, Precious. You want to get fucked before breakfast or after?"

"Cook's choice," she said, squeezing me tighter.

There was a knock at the door.

I went to check while Katie scooted toward the bedroom. Checking the peephole, I discovered Katie's older brother Bill at the door with Winston Evers in tow. "It's your douchebag brother," I said loud enough to be heard through the door by the dipshit in the suit.

She disappeared into the bedroom and closed the door.

I opened the front door and stood in the entrance. "What can I do for you two?"

"Can we come in, Nick?" Bill asked. He could stand outside all morning in his expensive suit for all I cared, but Katie wouldn't think that was cool.

I stood aside. "If your vaccinations are up-to-date."

Bill smiled at my joke, and the two followed me inside. "Where's Katie?" Bill asked in an accusatory tone, surveying the room.

"Oh, she's just getting dressed." I smiled. "She's a little tired this morning."

His smile gone, Bill gritted his teeth and took in a deep breath at the implication that I had been banging his sister all night long, which I hadn't, but I wasn't going to tell him that. He could stew and curse me under his breath.

Winston smirked in my direction, a gesture Bill didn't see. Winston understood that I was fucking with the boss man on purpose.

I went back to the stove and flipped the French toast. “So, like I said, what can I do for you this morning?”

Before Bill answered, Katie came out to join us, dressed this time. She had pulled the bandage off of her head and combed her hair over to hide the stitched up wound.

Bill rushed over to her and gave her a quick hug. “Are you okay?”

"Why wouldn't I be?” Katie asked innocently.

“Katherine you should know by now how connected Uncle Garth is in the police department. I've seen the report already this morning." Bill glanced in my direction. “Did *he* hurt you?” He clearly thought I was the one responsible for Katie's trip to the ER.

Winston was usually armed, and I wondered if Bill had brought him along as backup in case he wanted to try to teach me a lesson for fucking around with his little sister.

I balled my fists. I was pretty sure I could handle pretty boy Bill, but throwing Winston into the mix could certainly tilt the outcome in his favor.

Katie put her hands on her hips. “You should be ashamed of yourself. Nick is the one that saved me. You apologize to him right now.” The scowl Katie gave her brother could have killed a lesser man.

I looked away and turned down the burner under the french toast.

“I'm sorry,” Bill stammered. “The report wasn't very specific.” He straightened up. “Anyway, I'm here to take you home.” He tried to take Katie’s arm.

She backed away. It was obvious from Katie's expression that his approach wasn't going to get him very far. “I'm staying right here,” she said slowly as she walked in my direction. “I’m safe with Nick." She put her arm around my waist, sending her brother a clear fuck off message.

"Well, if you need to go out, Winston and the other Hanson folks are available and only a phone call away," Bill said, surprisingly giving up for the moment. He had come over here fully ready to take me on, but his sister was a force of nature that he wasn't prepared for.

"That's great, Bill," I said. "I'll call them if I need any help." Bill had directed his comment at Katie, but he needed to understand that I was the one in charge.

Bill's stare was icy. "You better keep her safe, Knowlton." His tone was as unfriendly as his gaze.

"Yes, sir, that's the plan," I replied cheerily.

"You guys want to stay for breakfast?" Katie asked them.

"Thanks, but no thanks," Bill replied. "I need to get into the office." Translation, he couldn't stand to be around me and was leaving as quickly as he could.

Douchebag.

I smiled at them as they left and was careful to give Katie a kiss as Bill glanced back in our direction.

I hugged my girl as the door closed.

"I'm sorry he was like that," Katie told me, burying her head in my chest. "He's just overprotective."

"I get it. He's a douchebag and he can't help himself." I let her go and walked back to the stove. I flipped over the french toast and found it had blackened during our discussion with her dipshit brother. I dumped the pieces in the trash and prepared some fresh ones.

After breakfast we agreed Katie would work on more of her accounting stuff so I could get back to work in the cave.

She had been bugging me about seeing what was in the room, so I gave her a quick peek before I settled in. I didn't take the time to try to explain what I did. That could wait.

The badger had found its prey and located the money last

night when it texted me. Unfortunately as I had suspected, I was now too late. The final hop late last night had taken the funds out of the system into Bitcoin and the money was now out of reach.

If I'd been here in the cave last night, I would've caught the bastard, but Katie took priority. I was at peace with that. I had promised to keep her safe, and that was job one. There were always fresh opportunities to make money, but there was only one Katie.

There was something special about this feisty vulnerable girl that I couldn't put my finger on. But she was mine to protect, no matter what. The strong took care of the weak, it was the way of the world.

I scrolled through the sequence of transfers that badger had uncovered. It looked eerily familiar. I kept a log of these on Lucky Number Nine.

I opened up the log and scrolled down. It took me a while to find them. I had found a similar sequence two other times I'd been asked to track down missing money. The similarities were plain as day, the last two hops were identical in each of the cases. Hong Kong to Singapore, and Singapore back to Macau, the same three banks used each time. With two incidents, it was luck, with three it was a pattern, not a coincidence.

Whoever had done this had gotten sloppy; they'd randomized all the early hops through the Caribbean, Europe, and Asia, but not the last two. Now I knew where to set up the roadblock if I got called in on another one of these. This was the signature of somebody who liked to repeat a working system, only changing up the victims and the timing.

With a little work I could set up to be ahead of him next time. My phone was on Wi-Fi this morning and the text came shortly before lunch.

BRANDI: Still on for 5 ??

I sent a quick reply.

ME: Yup

Katie made us soup for lunch and we both went back to our respective tasks for the afternoon.

By late afternoon, I had my trap set, and called the bank with the good news and the bad news.

They were completely focused on the bad news that this time the money had gotten away from them. They had hoped I would be able to recover it in time and they could sweep the whole incident under the rug. They weren't relishing reporting this to their regulators.

They perked up when they realized that if I caught the guy on his next attempt, they still might be able to tag him for this, and figure out how to get some or all of their money back. That was still an if, but it was better than nothing.

I added this trail to my log file. I checked my watch. The girls weren't due for another hour.

Katie

I APOLOGIZED PROFUSELY TO NICK FOR THE WAY BILL HAD acted this morning. My brother was only trying to do what he thought was the right thing. He didn't get that I was a grownup and he couldn't order me around.

After breakfast Nick wanted to work in the room he called the cave.

I had bugged him about it, so he let me peek inside. It looked like Mission Control in Houston, with huge monitors laid out in stacks around a central desk with another extra-large screen on the wall.

He told me it was a secure computing environment for him. One that couldn't be bugged, hacked, or monitored. I didn't understand what he was so paranoid about, but he wasn't eager to explain.

I hadn't received the extra copy of the overseas subsidiary files that the LDSI people had promised to send. The payables and receivables reconciliations would have to wait. I moved onto the capital equipment spreadsheets.

It was tedious work, but it had to be done carefully. I wasn't about to give Russ any more ammunition to harass me, or worse, terminate me.

Another two Advil with our soup at lunchtime to calm my throbbing head reminded me I was a prisoner of sorts in Nick's care until we figured out who the hell my attacker was. I asked Nick if he would take me out later for some more shopping. I had a list of things I still needed to get for the other house, my house. This called for a trip to Bed Bath & Beyond, and Nordstrom.

The LDSI capital equipment tests went slowly. There was only one of me.

It didn't help that I kept glancing down the hall, hoping Nick would emerge and want to do something to break the boredom. I recrossed my legs, knowing what I would suggest if he asked me.

Nick pretended to be the big bad biker dude, but he didn't fool me. I had gotten drunk last night after coming back from the hospital and he'd been the consummate gentleman. He was protective to a fault, but not the rough, hardass he tried to project. I decided he was like an M&M, a hard-shell on the outside and soft and sweet on the inside.

My musings were interrupted by a knock at Nick's front door.

They tried to barge right past me, but I blocked the way in. Twins from the look of them, pretty, but with too much makeup. They had huge boobs, as fake as their eyelashes, that were barely contained by their outfits. "Hi honey," the first one said.

"Yeah, we're, like, a little early," the second one added with a giggle.

"Can I help you?" I asked. Maybe their outfits worked, selling whatever they were peddling if the man of the house answered the door, but they turned me off.

"We're here for our date with Nick," they said almost in unison. "I'm Brandi," the first one said, "and I'm Candy," the second one added with another giggle. They looked barely out of high school.

"We're sisters," Brandi said.

Duh.

They were dressed in Halloween-like skimpy fake nurse outfits with white fishnet stockings. They looked like working girls.

"There must be some mistake," I said. Nick wouldn't call hookers over.

Candy's brows knitted with confusion. "No mistake. We have a date with Nick, Nick Knowlton."

"I don't think so," I insisted. Nick wouldn't be having girls over like this, we had agreed.

Brandi held up her phone. "We confirmed this morning."

I froze.

The text on her phone from Nick said just what she insisted. Nick had confirmed a date with these two bimbos. He had set a date with hookers. The asshole.

Nausea roiled my stomach.

Somebody had a nurse fetish. If that was what got Nick off, he was welcome to them, but this wasn't for me. I couldn't stay here if he was going to invite hookers over.

I let them in and quickly gathered up my things.

To think that I had thought Nick wanted to be monogamous acquaintances-with-benefits or whatever we were. How could I have been so dumb? Obviously no one woman could satisfy his appetite.

"He's all yours, girls. Knock on the metal door down the hall," I told them as I exited the house. I wiped the beginning of a tear from my eye and started the trek back to my house on Myrtle Street. I obviously didn't belong here.

I could kick myself. Bill had been right after all, Nick was completely wrong for me. I didn't understand who he was or what he was. A date with the two fake nurse bimbos, what the hell was that about?

It had only been five days, and already he was tired of me. Somehow I had been stupid enough to think whatever it was we had would last a lot longer than a week. I was a moron. I had convinced myself that putting me to bed in my drunken state last night without taking advantage of me had been a sweet thing.

A gentlemanly thing.

Now I understood: I'd failed my audition, and he was on to the next girl, in this case twins. Either that or he had a foursome in mind and that was not happening.

There was way too much I didn't know about Nick and right now I could kick myself for picturing him as an M&M, sweet in the center.

The screech of tires startled me.

My heart leapt to my throat.

The blaring horn went on for seconds.

I hurried to the other side of the street, and the pickup with the angry driver roared past.

I had been so lost in my pity party that I'd almost become roadkill.

Good going, Katie. Katherine never let a guy get to her like this.

What did a guy with one dick do with two girls, anyway? I only wondered for a moment before the visual sickened me.

Have to work. Work takes the mind off useless thoughts.

Katie had allowed her desires for a man to complicate her life.

Katherine knew enough to work hard and keep her life simple.

CHAPTER 15

Nick

I WAS GETTING READY TO BUTTON THINGS UP FOR THE NIGHT when a knock sounded on the cave door. I put Lucky Number Nine to sleep and pushed back my chair.

When I opened the door, it was Brandi and Candy. They were early. Way early.

Brandi was practically falling out of her outfit, or maybe it was Candy. I couldn't tell them apart. That was their allure. That, and their ample assets and willing desires. "The other girl left, so it's just the three of us, honey," she said, placing her hand on my chest.

"Oh, shit." I raced past them down the hallway to find Katie's laptop and her bag missing from the table and Katie nowhere to be found either.

The girls followed me. "We don't need her do we?"

I had no time for this right now. "Girls, we have to reschedule. I'll text you."

Candy, I think it was, pasted a pout on her face. She held out her hand.

I pulled out my wallet and handed her two Benjamin's. "There's more next time, Candy."

She quickly tucked the bills into her bra. "I'm Brandi," she corrected me.

"Fine. Now scoot, girls, I have to go."

The other one, Candy, held out her hand next.

This was getting more expensive by the moment. I pulled out some more bills and handed them to her.

"Just text us anytime honey," Candy said.

I shooed them out and locked up behind me. Both helmets were still strapped on my Harley in the driveway. I didn't bother with a helmet.

I cranked up and headed after Katie. She had to be going to her house, at least as a first step. Her car was there. I hoped she wasn't too far ahead of me.

I hadn't seen her yet on the sidewalk. I turned the corner onto Myrtle, and once again the sidewalk ahead of me was empty. I pulled up and parked in her driveway.

Her car was still here. The lights in the house were off. Either I was wrong about her choice of destination or she'd already made it inside and was hiding. Riding the Harley had the disadvantage that she could hear me coming from blocks away. I dismounted and pulled my phone out. I opened up the security app and scrolled through the incident log. The door been opened a few minutes ago, and the system disarmed and then rearmed.

At least I knew where she was.

I walked up to the door and knocked.

No response. She was playing possum.

"Princess, I know you're in there," I said loudly enough for her to hear me through the door. I knocked again.

Still no response. "We need to talk, Princess, you don't understand the situation."

I listened, but there was still no noise from inside.

She was probably calling her brother to rescue her. Wouldn't that be a bitch? I'd have to give him a bloody nose to match Liam's.

"I can stay out here all night if that's what it takes." That didn't get a response out of her either. "Are you scared to hear the truth?"

The faint sound of movement came from inside. A challenge like that was something she couldn't ignore, it was her weakness. "Go away."

At least now I had her talking. "Not a chance in hell, Precious. I told your brother I was going to keep you safe, and I keep my promises."

"Consider yourself released from that obligation," came the response from close behind the door.

"Like I said, not a chance in hell." I let that settle in. "I say you're scared to hear the truth."

"Are you going to lie to me now and tell me those girls weren't there to see you?"

"Are you too scared to come out from behind this door and hear the truth?"

"I don't hear you denying it."

Of course not. They had been there to see me, but, it wasn't the whole story. "You're just chicken to hear the truth. Because then you'd have to admit you were wrong. And a Covington can never admit she's wrong. She's too fucking perfect for that."

The door opened. Her eyes were red. "That's not true," she yelled at me. She slammed the door in my face.

"Then come with me and hear the whole story before you make up your mind." I let that sink in.

She didn't say anything back. The door didn't open, no response came.

I gave it my best shot. "You're just like your brother. You think people like me couldn't possibly have anything to say that's worth listening to. You're all so stuck up. You think you're better than the rest of us."

The door opened again. "How can you say that? You don't know anything about me." Fearful eyes peered out.

I stepped back to give her space. "I know you're scared to open up to me. You're scared to listen to me. You're scared to learn about me. You're scared to go on a date with me."

The fear in her eyes turned to anger. I might have gone too far in provoking her.

"Spend a day with me, Precious. It's a long story. I promise by the end of it you'll understand." I offered her my hand. "I'm going to camp out on your doorstep until you agree. If after a day you want me to leave, I will."

Hesitantly, she inched forward. The anger disappeared and confusion knitted her brow. "What about your hooker dates?"

"It's not what you think. Now get your shit, we're going on a little trip."

"Where to?"

"Why does everything with you have to be such a battle? Just get a change or two of clothes, put them in the backpack, and let's get going."

She returned a few minutes later with the backpack. We set the alarm and locked the house.

Katie

I SWUNG MY LEG OVER AND MOUNTED BEHIND HIM ON THE Harley.

"Hold on," were the only words he spoke as we took the short trip back to his house. Once there, he stuffed a few things in the backpack, I was carrying and we were off again, this time on the Honda.

"Long trip?" I asked.

"Long enough."

"Where are we going?" I asked.

He sped across the intersection and took the freeway on-ramp heading south. "On a date. Somewhere you will be happy."

He obviously wasn't in a talking mood yet. The traffic on the freeway was heavy and moving slowly. I grabbed him tight as he came very close to a yellow sports car on the left, riding down the lane markers between the lanes. "Is this even safe?"

"You're always safe with me, Princess," he said into my helmet.

I freed up one hand and punched him in the side for the comment.

"Good to see you're back to normal, Precious."

I hit him again, and he laughed.

"If it makes you feel better we'll go slower," he said as he pulled in behind a small Toyota and stayed in the lane instead of splitting the traffic the way he had been before.

"It makes me nervous."

"You don't trust me?"

"I don't know you."

"Fair enough."

We rode for about a mile or so without talking. It bugged me that he hadn't offered any explanation for the two bimbos yet. Not that they needed any explanation. He had needs, and it was obvious, two of them had to be better than one of me.

"I thought we were going to talk," I said.

The traffic slowed to a crawl, and a solid string of vehicles stretched ahead. I hadn't used the bathroom at his place and I was going to have to pee if we stayed here forever. "Okay, maybe now it's safe if you want to go between the cars."

He moved to the left and split the lanes of traffic. Thankfully he went slowly.

I was afraid one of these idiots in the cars we were passing might get mad enough to move over and squish us, but instead they generally gave us a little more room as we came up. Slowly I got more comfortable, and my bladder was happy that we were making better progress now.

Soon I saw flashing lights ahead, and it didn't take us long to get past the accident.

As the traffic sped up, he moved back into a lane. "Are you ready to listen now?" he asked.

"Okay what is it I don't know about the bimbo twins?" I finally asked.

"You mean Brandi and Candy?"

"They weren't nurses."

"Of course not. They're just friends of mine," he answered.

"I thought you said you weren't going to see anybody else." There, I had said it.

He laughed. "You're jealous."

"Am not," I lied.

"They were just coming by on business."

"Is that what they call it these days? They said it was a date," I said as sarcastically as I could manage.

"What did you think they came by for?"

"You know." Of course they'd been there to polish his pole.

"Maybe you should spell it out for me, Princess. You know I didn't go to college like you."

He thought I was stupid. "They looked like prostitutes."

"I told you we come from two different worlds. They're just doing what they can to survive. If a girl from Hollywood gets naked and pretends she likes it when some stranger licks her tits, you call her an actress because she went to college and is getting paid a million bucks. These girls just let a guy do more and get paid less for acting like they like it and you look down on them."

Nick changed lanes to pass an old Volkswagen bug.

"It's not the same," I said. I couldn't see having hookers as *friends*, and besides, they had said they had a date with Nick.

"Like I said, different worlds, Princess, those two didn't go to college like you, they never had the same opportunities as you had. They're doing what they can to survive. They're saving up to open a beauty parlor. They found something they're good at, and they're doing what they choose to do, nobody's making them. You invested in an accounting degree, and they put their money into silicone."

I had to admit it was a different way to view it. "And what exactly do you hire them for?"

"Certainly not what you are thinking," Nick said as he settled back into our previous lane.

I recalled the conversation quite well. "They said it was a date."

"In their line of work, a date is synonymous with a business meeting. And that's all it was. A business meeting. They're subcontractors. I hire them to distract people I need distracted."

I should have been relieved that he hadn't called them for their *services*. But it also made me uneasy, because it pointed out how little I knew about what he did for a living.

Different worlds for sure.

He moved over a lane and passed the little Fiat we had been following.

"When will you explain to me what it is you do?" I asked.

"You've never asked me before."

"I'm asking now."

"Over dinner."

We motored on down the 405 and turned north on I-5.

"If it's much farther, I'm going to need a pit stop," I informed him.

"Almost there, Precious."

CHAPTER 16

WE GOT OFF AT WEST KATELLA, AND A FEW MINUTES LATER HE turned in at the sign marked *Disneyland Hotel.*

"Welcome to the happiest place on earth," he said as he shut down the bike.

This was perfect. He couldn't have picked a better place to come. I hadn't been here since my dad had taken me when I was little, and I'd always wanted to come back. It had been only me and my dad. My brothers had been off on a Boy Scout camping trip.

It was the one time I recalled getting my father's full, undivided attention. Usually we made a point of doing things together as a family. I can still remember how giddy my father had been on the rides here. That weekend was my one real father daughter vacation. It was the way I would always remember him. Laughing, happy, and devoting his full attention to me. Two of the happiest days of my life.

"You can get off now, Princess," Nick said, waking me out of my joyful daydream.

I punched him in the side again for the Princess comment

and swung my leg over. My first few steps were a little wobbly once again.

It was a short walk from the motorcycle parking to the lobby. I let him go to the front desk while I searched out the restrooms.

Nick had gotten us a nice room upstairs facing the pools. We went back down the elevator in search of dinner after unloading our things.

Nick chose Steakhouse 55, which was fine by me, we were both a little old for *Goofy's Kitchen.*

I waited as Nick tried to get us a table and returned with the bad news that it was going to be a sixty to ninety minute wait. "Maybe I can help with that," I told him. I pulled out my black AMEX card and dialed the number on the back. I told the nice lady on the other end our predicament.

Five minutes later they called my name.

"I knew there was a reason I brought you along," Nick said kiddingly as they ushered us to our table.

"Friends in high places."

I ordered the filet mignon and Nick got the bone-in rib-eye.

Nick surprised the waiter by ordering Budweisers for both of us. He had this thing about wine, and I wasn't going to fight it tonight even if a nice Cabernet was calling out to me.

"Now I think it's time," I told him as I took a sip of my water.

"Time for?"

"You promised to tell me more about your past and what you do. Now it's time."

"It's a long story, you sure you have the patience?"

"Stop stalling."

The waiter brought us our beers.

Nick fingered his beer glass and fixed me with his gaze. "You look beautiful tonight."

The heat of a blush singed my cheeks. "You're stalling."

He nodded. "You know I went to prison right?"

I nodded again, waiting for him to elaborate.

"What nobody knows is why. On paper it was for dealing in stolen property. I spent two years in Folsom, the longest two years of my life." He took a sip of his beer.

I reached my hand across the table to touch his, to comfort him.

"But that's not the real story." He paused and twisted his beer glass around and around, trying to come up with the right words. "I took the rap for my little brother, Lester."

I had only known Lester briefly. He'd been kicked out of school even before Nick. Everybody knew he'd dealt drugs, and he wasn't particularly smart about it. It had probably only been a matter of time before he'd gotten caught.

"Because he'd been busted before, he would've gotten a pretty long sentence, so I volunteered to take the rap."

This was heartbreaking to listen to. Nick had been sent away for a crime he didn't commit to keep his little brother safe.

"Where is Lester now?"

Nick's eyes deadened as they drifted down to the table.

I dreaded the answer.

"Dead. The idiot tried to rip off a drug dealer and got himself shot. It happened while I was locked up. There was nothing I could do to save him."

I squeezed his hand. "You did all anyone could have done for him." He had done what he could to help his brother, and it had all been for naught.

My brother had been completely wrong about Nick. He was sure Nick was a bad guy, a criminal, and he had sacrificed himself to save his younger brother.

The waitstaff brought our meals, and we started in silence. There was nothing more to say about Lester and the predicament he had put Nick in.

I finished a forkful of my potatoes and I was still curious about what he was doing nowadays. "That's all in the past, so what is it you do now? You told me you were at the computer hacker conference, and you have a roomful of computers in your house."

"You're right it's in the past, or it should be. But that's not the way it works on my side of the street. I'm now an ex-con and I always will be. I go to apply for a job, there will be a line on the application asking about my criminal history. That will kill that job opportunity for me, and the next one, and the next one. To people like your brothers I'm just human trash."

"That's not true," I insisted.

"Bullshit. That's just the way it is, and I'm resigned to it. I did this to myself and there's no one else to blame."

In many ways he was right, but it didn't make me like it any better. People were always working on fixing discrimination based on ethnicity or gender, but never your criminal history. It was sad but true.

"I'm self-employed, which means nobody can refuse to hire me and nobody can fire me. That's my way around the problem. When your brothers got me kicked out of school, that nixed my scholarship, and took college out of the equation for me. I hung out with the computer geeks and taught myself everything I could about computers."

I put my cutlery down for a moment. I had known my family had been responsible for getting him kicked out of school after the fight with Liam. What I hadn't understood was what it had cost him. "I'm so sorry, Nick, I had no idea."

"It wasn't your fault, Katie, it was your fuckass brother Liam. He lied to the principal. Liam threw the first punch that day, but he lied about it, and based on my reputation nobody believed me."

All I'd known at the time was Liam had ended up with the broken nose and Nick had ended up out of school. It had seemed fair, but now I understood how unfair it had been. Liam had been the instigator. No one had asked me, and I hadn't thought to speak up, so it was partly my fault as well.

"Anyway, learning computers is the best thing that ever happened to me. I don't have to go into a stupid office to do my work, I don't have to put up with an asinine boss the way you do, and I make pretty good money."

"What do you do, then?"

"I'm one of the good guy hackers."

"Don't all you computer geeks have cool handles you call each other?"

He smiled and nodded.

"What's yours?"

"It's a secret."

"I'll just get Hank to tell me then," I said. "He's had a crush on me forever, he'll tell me."

"Okay, already." He leaned forward and whispered, "Network Knight."

"Get out. NK just like your initials."

He grinned.

"Tell me, what does a white hat do, anyway?" I asked.

"I find ways into systems that the bad guys haven't found yet and, at conferences like the one we just had, I tell the companies about the weak areas so they can fix them before the bad guys do much damage."

"That sounds pretty noble."

"Sort of. I don't tell the companies about these vulnerabilities they have in their systems right away. I use them for a while before I tell them. That lets me run my business."

"Your business?"

"I'm in the recovery business. When people lose money through various schemes, I'm the guy they come to, to help track down the money and the perpetrator. Can't always help them, but when I can I get a percentage as a reward. And sometimes the bad guys end up going to prison as well." Now he was smiling. This was something he was truly proud of, as well he should be.

I still didn't see how a couple of hookers could help him track down stolen money. "And how do the bimbo twins fit into this?"

"Please stop calling them that. They really are nice girls."

"Okay, Brandi and Candy."

"One of the prices of being an ex-con, is that I'm still on the radar of the cops. And not all of them are very ethical."

I leaned forward because he was talking softly now. "And?"

"There are two of them who have been on my case the last few years. A sergeant Delancey and his partner Stephanie. I have the technology to turn a guy's cell phone into an on demand bug. And every once in a while those two bozos need me to place one of these bugs on some guy they're chasing. The twins help me place the bugs. I pay well. They're smart, and they know how to distract the targets and get the job done quickly."

"Is that legal?"

"Of course not. These cops don't want to bother with a court order. I'm sure they use me because they couldn't get one if they tried."

"Why do you do it, then?"

"It's not like I have a choice."

"You always have a choice," I said.

"Maybe in your world, Princess, but not in mine. These guys threatened to send me back to prison if I don't cooperate. In my world you have to go along to get along."

"They can't just send you to prison because they want to."

"You are so sweet, Katie, but so naive. It's pretty simple. These are dirty cops, they don't play by the rules. Anytime they want to, they can plant stuff on me, and arrest me. End of story. With my record and their planted evidence I wouldn't stand a chance."

"But that's not fair," I complained.

"Haven't you heard a single thing I'd said? What's fair in your world doesn't apply to me. In your world cops are the solution, in my world cops are the problem."

It couldn't be as hopeless as he thought.

~

Nick

Telling Katie my past at dinner was the hardest thing I'd done in a long time. Admitting to her, and myself, what I had been and what I was had been a difficult thing to say out loud. It was one thing to know in my heart I wasn't a full citizen of the country—an ex-con never was. It was another thing to put it in so many words. It made it seem so much more final.

These last few days with Katie had been an elixir for my soul. I was starting to believe that there was hope that my life could change, that things could improve. Now, after seeing the horror in her eyes as I described my situation, that hope seemed to be slipping away.

After dinner we went for a drink at Trader Sam's Tiki Bar. She ordered a Mojito, and she dared me to order something other than my usual Bud.

I chose a drink called the Shrunken Zombie Head. It sounded cool, and it wasn't half bad. I ordered a second.

I needed the conversation to switch to something lighter than my history, so I had her fill me in on her time at college.

She entertained me with tales of parties at her sorority. She told me about one of the guys who'd insisted on coming to her beginning accounting class with a pillow to prop his head on as a way to antagonize the professor.

That sounded like a stunt I would've pulled. "Did that work for him?" I asked.

"He didn't come back for sophomore year."

Eventually curiosity got the best of her and she asked about my time in prison. Girls usually didn't do that, even the ones who liked to be bad. Even guys stay away from the subject—they couldn't relate unless they had been there.

"Folsom wasn't so bad, at least I didn't get sent to San Quentin where the real bad dudes are. It taught me two important lessons."

She waited for me to elaborate.

"First, never show weakness and never back down. The guys that did got pounded into the ground."

"Is that why you try so hard to project the tough guy image?"

I shrugged. "Always easier to avoid a fight than to finish one. If the other guy thinks I'll beat his brains in if he starts something, then it usually doesn't get that far."

She waited and when I didn't elaborate any further she asked, "and the second lesson?"

I smiled at her. "Don't ever bend over in the shower to pick up the soap."

She had probably heard that line before, but she laughed anyway. She didn't realize that it was only partly a joke.

CHAPTER 17

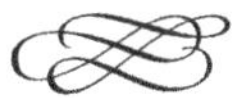

Katie

THE NEXT MORNING, WE RODE THE MONORAIL FROM THE HOTEL to the park.

We headed right from Main Street into Tomorrowland. Nick let me pick the first ride, and I chose the Star Wars Hyperspace Mountain ride. The line wasn't terribly long.

Nick had meant it when he'd said this would be a date. He held my hand as we moved through the line.

The warmth of his touch as he held my hand or placed it lightly on the small of my back while in the line had my head spinning. I'd been naked with him between the sheets, but somehow this light touch was different, more erotic in a way I couldn't explain. It held the promise of something unknown to come. I banished those thoughts as we boarded the ride.

Once on the ride, he put his strong arm possessively around me, pulling me close. It was going to be a very long day if we kept up this much bodily contact.

Exiting the ride, I glanced around but came up short finding some corner I could drag him to for the kiss he deserved. The kiss I was dying to lay on him.

He took my hand, and we strolled to the Matterhorn bobsleds. It had been one of my favorites when I was here with my dad, but it wasn't the same today. It was a single seat ride and I couldn't have Nick next to me. He was behind me yelling like a little kid as we went down the mountain. Still fun but not the same as having him next to me.

The lines were longer than I remembered and it was a good thing Nick had signed up for FASTPASS to reserve times for some rides so we didn't have to stand around as much.

Still, being in line wasn't half bad. It was a typically warm Southern California morning, bright sunshine and the gentlest of breezes. Nick kept his arm around me as we moved slowly forward, whispering in my ear. There was something strangely electric about his presence today.

I had asked him to try to explain more about what he did and how he tracked down the Internet thieves.

His work was very secretive, and his clients terribly paranoid about publicity. He whispered to me to keep the others nearby from hearing what he was explaining. The whole leaning over and whispering bit added a tingly sense of mystery to his explanations. His lips brushed ever so lightly against my hair and my ear as he explained, and each time he did I momentarily lost track of his words.

I had to admit that although I thought I understood a lot of accounting; I was woefully uninformed about the computer and Internet side of these financial transactions.

"You said you like the detective work part of what you do," Nick whispered.

I nodded.

"Well, it's much the same with what I do. There is no X marks the spot to tell me where the treasure is hidden. The bad guys don't telegraph who they are by wearing black hats. It's all a series of clues that have to be deduced from the raw data."

I nodded again.

"Like this last one I was working on, I recognized the last three hops of this most recent heist as a pattern I'd seen before. It turned out to be the same as two others I'd logged last month. Sort of like a signature. Now I know this particular guy or group of guys has done this at least three times and I've got a good chance of putting a road block in place on the next heist and capturing the money, and maybe them."

I stretched up to whisper a question to him. "Do you have to sit in front of computers all day to do this?"

"For a little while when I set it up." We moved forward another several paces. "In the final bit, the program trying to track this down sends me a text message when it finds something. That's when I have to get back to the computer." He had to stop his explanation as we reached the boarding station.

We logged a few more rides before lunch. Nick chose the Blue Bayou restaurant in New Orleans Square for our lunch stop. I hadn't had one before, so Nick ordered Monte Cristo sandwiches for both of us. They were delicious. Hybrids between a grilled ham and cheese and French toast.

I wanted to learn more about his work, but I could only ask generic questions out loud in the restaurant. "What is the going rate for your services on one of these?" I wasn't sure what the right term was for what he did. "Searches," I added.

Nick warmed me with a wide smile. "Would you believe two-and-a-half percent?"

I picked up my iced tea. "And what are the amounts you're tracking down?" I sipped from my glass.

He held up two fingers, followed by one, and whispered, "Million."

I spit up the tea I was drinking in surprise. Two-and-a-half percent of twenty-one was a half million dollars.

I had just made a complete fool of myself. "I'm sorry. You just surprised me." I tried to clean up the mess I had created with my napkin without looking even stupider. I looked around, lucky for me the place was loud and everybody else was engrossed in their own conversations.

"Half a million on one job?" I asked softly. "I am definitely in the wrong business."

He shook his head. "Would have. If I had caught them."

I finished dabbing my napkin at the table and tried for another sip of my iced tea. "But didn't you say you found the pattern?"

He held up a finger while he finished chewing. "Yeah, but that was too late. I was busy at the time."

"Too busy for five hundred K?" I asked quietly as I leaned forward.

He reached across to touch my hand. "I was at the hospital taking care of something more important."

His smile melted me. Then I realized what he was saying. He had been at the hospital with me, taking care of me. "Was that the text you got while we were in the ER?"

His gaze fell to his plate. "It doesn't matter."

"I want to know," I insisted.

He nodded. "Yeah, but it's not important."

"I was fine, you should have gone." Being with me had cost him a half million dollars and he wasn't upset about it.

Joe would have been livid. He would have dumped me out of the car and left me by the side of the road for that much money, or even a tenth of that.

How did I deserve such a man?

Steely eyes greeted me from across the table. "Your safety is my responsibility, Princess. Job one. That takes priority over everything else," he stated sternly. He tried to make it seem trivial by laughing. "Anyway, more opportunities come by all the time."

I was torn between being mad at him for doing something stupid, or being mad at him for calling me Princess, or being over the top happy I had a man like him watching out for me. I settled on happy.

He changed the subject by asking about my brother Patrick who'd recently left town.

I filled Nick in on what I knew while we finished lunch.

We had saved the water rides for the warmer afternoon. We hit Splash Mountain right after lunch, followed by the Jungle Cruise, and my favorite of the day, the Pirates of the Caribbean ride. Each of the rides evoked a child-like happiness from him. Laughter and full faced grins were my constant companion. Not to mention, a fair amount of tickling and hugging and playful kissing.

At the haunted mansion he took two quarters and put them through the coin press. It turned them into special elongated pressed silver Disneyland coins, with the Disneyland Haunted Mansion embossed on them. I'd seen penny presses before, but these did quarters.

He gave me one. "Now, don't lose this. Keep this with you so you remember today."

I put the coin in my pocket.

This truly was the happiest place on earth. A place where we could leave all of our cares behind and take these short rides that transported us to happier times. I was getting used to the warmth of his embrace and felt oddly naked if he left my side for a moment.

I was ready to go back to the hotel, but he insisted on one last attraction. The crowds were dying down somewhat, and he pulled me over in the direction of the paddlewheel boat.

We strolled aboard, and he took me up to the top level near the stern of the Mark Twain Riverboat. The steam puffed methodically out of the twin chimneys as the large paddlewheel churned and the boat started its journey around Tom Sawyer's island.

I leaned against the railing, snuggled up close to Nick's warmth and watched the trees and the people slowly go by. The magic of this place was how it transported you out of Los Angeles into another world. Logically I knew that there were millions of people in thousands of houses just outside the park boundaries, but you couldn't see any of that from here or hear it.

Nick corralled a passing couple and asked them to take a picture of us on his phone. When they were done, he kissed me on the top of my head, careful to avoid my sore stitched cut, and gave me a squeeze.

I squeezed his hand. "Thank you for bringing me. This has been a wonderful day."

He turned me to face him.

My breasts pressed up against his chest, I became lost in the depths of his eyes, and the fullness of his smile.

"I could tell you needed this. Ever since I brought you back, you've been working nonstop, even though your boss gave you the week off."

"I have to get this work done."

He stopped me with a finger to my lips. "What you need, Precious, is to slow down and enjoy your life. You know the saying about all work and no play right?"

I nodded silently. "But—"

"No buts," he said, stopping me. "You're a very special woman, Princess, even if you are a pain in the ass sometimes."

My instinct was to object, but I held it back. He was trying to be nice. Those were some of the nicest words anybody had said to me in a very long time.

"You deserve days like today. You'll see, when we get back, the world will still be there waiting for us. Anyway, that's half the reason."

I blinked back tears and pressed my face into his chest to

hide them. When I had them under control, I turned to look out at the water again.

"And the other half?" I asked without meeting his eyes.

"If you can't tell, then you're a lot stupider than I think you are."

I hoped I knew what his answer would be, but I had to hear it. "Oh, you know, I am sort of slow, so you're going to have to spell it out for me."

He put his elbows on the railing and leaned over. "I really wanted to have a day with you all to myself."

He had a knack for making me feel special. "The day's not over yet," I said without meeting his eyes.

"Or the night either," he added.

That was the part I anticipated. Each time I had tried to get a real kiss out of him today, all I'd gotten was little more than a peck, and an admonition to wait until tonight.

The anticipation was going to give me a stroke.

CHAPTER 18

NICK

SHE WAS NESTLED AGAINST ME AS WE WALKED OUT, HEATING UP my thoughts.

Katie wanted to go back to the room and get room service, but I vetoed that idea. I made her pick, and she chose Thai for dinner, so we found a small local hole-in-the-wall not far from the park.

It worked for me because I wanted something quick so I could get back to the room before long. I had plans for tonight and as they came to mind I kept having to adjust my pants.

All they had on the menu were Thai beers, so I ordered one while Katie stuck to water and tea.

One sip of the beer and I knew why you didn't find these in any respectable bar. I flagged down our waitress and asked for a Coke instead. Lesson learned.

"With all of your computer knowledge, have you ever thought about teaching?" she asked. That came out of nowhere.

"You have got to be kidding."

"No, seriously, you ought to think about it."

I ignored her. She had no idea what it was like to apply for a job with a record.

She broke apart her chopsticks. "I know I'm not missing any work today, but how can you afford to take the day off?"

I took a sip of my Coke. "I'm between jobs right now, so I'm not missing anything."

"Don't you have to be available for clients?"

"Yes and no. I'm my own boss so I get to set the rules. Rule number one is I work when I want to, and today I don't want to. My whole business is set up—that's not really right—my whole *life* is set up so that I can pick up and take off whenever I want to."

"I see," she said.

The soup arrived.

"After Folsom, freedom of movement is special to me. I can't be tied down. I have to be able to change my mind and go do something different tomorrow if I choose."

I slurped some soup with one of those crazy-big Chinese soup spoons.

Katie took a spoonful of hers. "Why did you do it?"

"Do what?"

"What you did for your brother."

"Lester may not have been the sharpest tool in the shed, but he was my brother. I had to protect him." I took another sip of my Coke. "Lester was not a strong kid. For him, prison would have been a death sentence. I did the only thing I could to save him."

"But two years in prison?"

"He needed my help, and I gave it to him. Shit, your fuckass brother Liam got his nose broken trying to protect you from me. It's what big brothers do."

She thought about that and nodded.

I wasn't certain she could ever truly understand a big brother's responsibilities.

As I asked her to tell me what she thought about today, her smile grew and the little girl displaced the in-control woman. This place had worked its magic on her and brought her to a happier place.

Suddenly her foot traced a path under the tablecloth up my leg as she smiled coyly. My girl was getting playful, and hopefully as horny as I was.

I took her hand across the table and traced figure eights on it with my thumb. "If we're done here, we could head back to the room."

She gave me a knowing smile and nodded. "Sounds perfect to me."

~

Katie

Nick had one hand around me and the other in his pocket trying to hide the bulge behind his zipper.

I loved that I could do that to him. It was unfair in a way. He had drenched my panties all day but nobody could tell, while his situation was hard to hide.

When nobody was watching, the thumb of his arm snaked around me would innocently stroke the underside of my breast as we walked.

I smiled up at him, catching the mischievous glimmer in his eye. "Careful there. We're in public," I mumbled softly.

He leaned my way. "You started it by playing footsies."

I had been yearning all day to get him some place private where I could kiss him senseless.

Once inside the doorway, he wrapped his strong arms around

me and held me from behind. He placed his chin on my head. "Tonight you do as I say, understood?"

I nodded as he pulled me firmly against the bulge of the monster cock lurking behind that zipper. I wiggled my ass against his arousal. In bed was the one place I didn't mind him telling me what to do.

He was the teacher, and I was the pupil. He had so much more experience than I did.

He picked up the phone and called down to room service. He ordered up the same drinks we'd had last night. A Mojito for me and a Shrunken Zombie Head for him.

I tried to pull myself up for the kiss I had anticipated all day, but instead he sent me down the hall with the ice bucket for ice cubes.

The drinks arrived quickly.

"Stand still," he told me as he slowly pulled my clothes off. I still couldn't get how he could unhook my bra with two fingers quicker than I could with two hands.

I stepped out of my pants and shucked my sneakers to the side. My anticipation for his touch grew by the second. I nodded to the window. "The curtains?"

"It's fine, if they know where to look, let them enjoy the show."

The danger of possibly being seen from the other tower made me instinctively cover myself.

"Walk to the window."

"What?"

He sipped his drink with the funny name. "You heard me. Face the window. Spread your legs and raise your arms," he said.

"No." I picked up the Mojito. "I need this first." I almost gave myself brain freeze sucking down half the drink in a few seconds.

"Now," he commanded as he pulled me to the window. "You promised to do as I asked."

I had promised, but this was humiliating. I relented and put my hands up against the window and spread my legs, completely vulnerable. I could see all the people down by the pools, and on the sidewalks. My heart clattered against my chest.

He came up behind me and wrapped his arms around me. "To grow, you have to be willing to step outside your comfort zone." He spun me around to face him and pulled me in for a kiss. He tasted of rum, sex, and power. He held me tightly, and the window and the people outside evaporated from my thoughts as our tongues stroked one another. I was in his arms and nothing else mattered.

I pulled at his hair and his neck to reach up to him. My breasts pillowed against his chest, my heart nearly beating out of my ribcage, as he finally gave me the kiss I had been waiting all day for. The kiss that claimed me as his woman. The kiss that drowned out all outside sounds. The kiss that told me I was the sole focus of his passion.

He carried me back to the bed and lay me down on it, and then handed me my drink to finish.

I watched as he disrobed, slowly and methodically, like a striptease but without the flourishes. The monster cock was finally loose and bobbed as he walked to the table to retrieve his drink.

He took a final sip of his cocktail and returned to sit next to me.

As he climbed on the bed I spread my legs, but he lay down by my side with his knees near my head and his head on my thigh. He put one arm under my leg and the other over my stomach. "You have the most beautiful pussy, Princess."

"I like your cock too." I grabbed the monster with both hands.

"The rules are you can only use your hands and the first one to make the other come wins." With a simple move the fingers of one hand parted my drenched pussy lips while the others finger delved into me.

Now I understood his position. I started to stroke and twist on his cock. I knew that the twisting motion really turned him on.

In mere seconds, he had started his finger magic on my clit, slowly circling with first one finger then the other, teasing me by coming close then backing away.

I tried to concentrate on stroking his cock, and ignoring what he was doing to me down there, but it was useless. With every circle and touch the clit whisperer was getting to me. I caught myself ready to lick him, but pulled back before I did.

He kept up the musical fingers routine on my sensitive nub and moved in for the kill, rubbing me slower, then faster, harder then softer. He kept playing me like an instrument.

I couldn't control the little moans that came with each stroke of his fingers. I lost the ability to concentrate on my task as I mindlessly pulled on his member. They called it jerking off, so I tried pulling harder with each stroke in hopes that I could still win the race, but what he was doing to me had my nerves tingling and my muscles tensing as he brought me closer to my undoing.

I redoubled my efforts on his cock, but it was no use; I could tell I was going to lose the race. I didn't have enough experience at a handjob to do it well, while he knew exactly how to manipulate my little love button. I was going to lose.

Two fingers entered me and stroked my G-spot as he continued on my swollen bud, sending me past my limit in no time.

My spasms came, and I was afraid I'd hurt his fingers I clenched down so hard. I screamed out loud enough to have the neighbors calling security, almost loud enough to break the glass.

I had lost the race, but I had won as well. Panting, I fell back flat as he released me.

He got up to take another sip of his drink. "I win."

"If this is losing, I'll take it any time," I retorted.

After a minute, he came back to the bed, but lay on the other side of me in the same position.

I was determined to learn how to win this game. I tried harder to give him the handjob of his life.

He was relentless in his attack on my little bundle of nerves.

In no time, probably because he already warmed me up to boiling and beyond, he had me nearing the edge.

I tried harder, but I couldn't concentrate as his fingers circled, darted, pinched, and stroked at my sensitive clit with abandon. The rushing of my blood was all I could hear. I was oblivious to the yelps and gasps I emitted as he took me even higher than before, seemingly lifting me off the bed.

As I came close, he backed off and renewed his attack, taking me to yet another plane.

There was no way I could win at this rate. I panted and shuddered under his touch.

Another coordinated attack on my G-spot and my swollen bud sent me into orbit again.

This time he pulled his fingers out as my contractions began, but he kept the pressure on my clit as I almost rolled up into a ball with my spasms.

It was no use, I couldn't match his finger mastery.

He got up again, and I figured out his trick.

I was getting him close, and he needed to get up and walk around to decompress.

"Come back here," I told him.

He ignored me and finished his drink. When he came back to bed, he straddled me and sat on my hips, reaching behind himself to stroke me.

I grabbed his joystick and started to pump him. Now I had a chance.

He could only use one hand and didn't have as good access as before.

I closed my legs.

He grimaced at my move. "That's not fair." He tweaked a nipple with his free hand.

"You chose the position," I reminded him. I pumped him faster. I spit into my hands to get some lubrication, and stroked again.

He went to work on me again, but I hoped he couldn't make me come as quickly without his G-spot trick, not that he needed it, but it had been his unfair advantage in making me come more quickly. His breathing became jerky as he tensed up.

I was getting close to breaking him, he couldn't hold out for ever, but neither could I.

He was doing my favorite circling motion on me as my nerves neared overload.

Then he went stiff, and with a groan and a shudder I won as a spurt landed on my chest, then a second, and a third.

He gasped and continued with his fingers, taking me around Jupiter a few seconds later with yells that I couldn't control.

I milked a few more drops of cum out of him before letting go.

He had marked me as his, and it made me proud that I could make him come undone this way.

The smile on my man's face said it all. We had both won, there were no losers in this bed.

He cleaned me up and lay down beside me.

I snuggled up against his heaving chest, warm and close.

CHAPTER 19

KATIE

AFTER DINNER HE HAD SATISFIED ME SO COMPLETELY AND ALL without using his marvelous monster cock.

We fixed that twice in the middle of the night. I insisted he do me doggy style, and then I rode him reverse cowgirl, so I could play with his balls.

This morning we were both exhausted, and we cuddled before breakfast.

Now, I had myself draped around Nick, feeling his steady breathing as we passed another truck on the freeway headed home. The morning overcast hadn't burned off yet, and it matched my mood. We were leaving Walt Disney's little oasis of happiness to head back to the dreariness of my fucked-up everyday life.

Nick had been right that I'd needed yesterday. My relaxation had been total and complete. It was now a reminder of what I had missed these last few years. My father had taught me the importance of setting a goal and working toward it each and every day. Nick had pointed out how I could still work toward my goals without allowing them to consume me.

I made myself a vow to not forget this, to schedule some decompression time, time to stop and smell the roses. Most importantly, time to enjoy those around me. Right now, that meant Nick.

The people I knew at work weren't bad people, but all we had in common was the work. Being with Nick for these days had shown me how much more there was to life. He poked at me when I was too serious and made me laugh. His situation with his brother and now the cops brought home to me how lucky I was to be born a Covington, something I had taken for granted.

He was right; we came from different worlds. Some of that was because I had made myself a world centered around my work goals and cut myself off from the real world.

As the miles rolled by and we came closer to our return to reality, I hugged him tighter. I didn't want to let go of him. He was now my indispensable anchor to the real world.

As we exited the freeway, he navigated back to his house, bypassing the turn to my place.

"I thought you were going to take me home."

"When it's safe."

I knocked my helmet against his. "I can't stay at your house forever," I complained.

"Like I said, when it's safe."

I appreciated the protection, but I wanted to be able to enjoy my new house, and not hang around his place forever. "How about we split our time between the two?"

He grunted his acceptance as we parked in front of his house and dismounted. "Let me get some work done today and we'll go over to yours tomorrow, how's that?"

I agreed that was a reasonable accommodation, so I got to work on my laptop as he headed into his cave.

A quick check of my email found dozens of useless things

and, surprisingly, no messages from work. The week off thing seemed to be working.

After lunch he took me over to Myrtle Street to retrieve some of my groceries and the package I'd been expecting from LDSI.

It had been two days, and I fumbled unsuccessfully with the alarm. Luckily, Nick helped me avoid the sirens.

A quick check of the mail box, the porch, and around the side of the house yielded no package. It should have been here by now.

"What's the problem, Precious, you lose something?"

"I was expecting a package with some data that I lost in the fire for this audit I'm doing."

"Give me a sec." Nick manipulated his phone for a minute. "According the security system nobody's been on your porch since we left, so no packages came."

I would have to call them and remind them again that I couldn't finish the audit without it. I gathered up the makings of a dinner and everything I would need for the apple pie baking session I'd planned for this afternoon. That had always been a calming activity for me.

We went back to Nick's house after locking up and he returned to the cave while I worked.

Before long I had finished the capital equipment section. I couldn't go any further without the overseas files LDSI had promised to send me.

It was time to bake a pie.

Apple was my favorite, although I dabbled in peach, cherry, and pumpkin. I'd gotten everything I needed at the supermarket before the attack. I located some pie tins. I didn't have a lot of time and decided I would use the pre-made crusts.

Naturally, Nick's kitchen didn't come equipped with an apple peeler. That little hand-cranked gadget saved an immense amount of time. Until I got one I was going to have to go the old-fashioned route and peel the apples by hand with a knife. I pulled out a big plastic bowl and started.

~

Nick

My phone rang. It was from DV. DV was the contact I had assigned to the burner phone the asshole Sgt. Delancey used to reach me. He had no idea the initials DV were short for Darth Vader, which was a bit of an insult to Vader.

Reluctantly, I answered the phone.

"*Hey, Nicky, I'm not getting any data yet from Jimmy's phone. What the fuck's the holdup?*" Delancey was being his normal charming self.

"It's taking a little while to get it set up." I didn't want to explain to them that I'd taken yesterday off to go down to Disneyland with my girl.

"*You had plenty of time. It should have been done by now,*" he yelled. He only seemed to have two volume settings and he liked to the use the higher one a lot.

"I'll get it done real soon. I was out of town last week. You got a choice. You want it done today or you want it done right?"

"*Don't fuck with me, convict, get it done.*" He hung up.

At least they didn't want to have a face-to-face meeting with me. That was always the worst. That was when the threats got more intense, and I was tempted to bash their skulls in and tell them to go fuck themselves. It was hard to keep my calm when I had to deal with these fuckers. One of these days I might lose my cool and end up headed back to Folsom, or worse.

This project of theirs hadn't been high up my priority list so I had delayed contacting Candy and Brandi again. Now I needed to get this done. I could delay those assholes for a little while but not forever. I texted Brandi.

ME: Can you come over for a few minutes?

The reply was close to instant.

BRANDI: 7 OK?

ME: Yup

Delancey and Stephanie wanted a special software bug installed on Jimmy Krasniki's phone, and Candy and Brandi were my only hope of getting it done.

Krasniki was Eastern European mafia, and I had no contacts with them and no interest in creating any. Jimmy wasn't his real name. They said he took that name because he got tired of guys mispronouncing his first name and having it sound like they said fuck you Krasniki.

Brandi and Candy were real pros. If anybody could get it done, the twins could. They looked like airheads but they were cunning as foxes.

I ventured out to the kitchen to visit with Katie and warn her they were coming over.

She beamed one of her magnificent smiles my way as I rounded the corner. "I hope you like apple pie."

"Sounds perfect to me. Need any help?" I came up behind her and wrapped my arms around her midsection as she was placing apple slices in the pie pan. "Can't you just pour them in?"

She rubbed her butt against me. "This is one of the secrets. You need to place the apple slices so there's almost no space between them. That way you get a firm piece that doesn't just fall apart and run all over the plate."

I tightened my grip on her and brought my arms up to caress her breasts, teasing her nipples through the fabric.

"You're making me lose my concentration," she complained.

I whispered into her ear, "That's sort of the idea." I pushed her forward against the counter and nibbled lightly at her ear.

She wiggled her ass against me again, daring me to take her. "Who called?"

"That's why I'm out here distracting you. Remember the two cops I told you about?"

She nodded. "Um hum."

"It was that asshole Delancey."

"I still think you shouldn't have to work with them." She was so naive.

"Not my choice, Precious. Anyway, I have to finish this job for them, and I need the twins' help. So I invited them to come over here tonight if it's okay with you?"

"Over here?"

Shit, I should have introduced the subject differently. "Yeah, but only if it's okay with you."

"Sure it's okay. You were right that I was wrong to judge them."

"They'll be here around seven." I kissed her and left her to finish her pie as I went back to the cave.

I didn't know if Krasniki used a Samsung or an Apple phone, so I made up transfer cords for both.

Each one looked innocently like a phone charger. A small wall plug box on one end and a phone jack on the other. One with the Samsung type plug and one with the Apple style.

They were my own secret design. If the girls plugged his phone into one of them, the malware would be downloaded to the phone in less than a second.

The malware would communicate with a special website that

Delancey and his asshole partner had access to. They could check it at their leisure and find out what Jimmy had been up to. All without a court order. Jimmy would never know why things weren't going his way anymore.

When I came back out Katie's pie was in the oven. It filled the house with a delicious aroma.

Katie fixed us a stir-fry for an early dinner.

When the pie came out, it looked as good as it smelled. It would've been a perfect candidate for one of those cooking magazines.

She shooed me away when I tried to get a forkful. "You have to wait."

"Wait for what?"

"You have guests coming over. It wouldn't be polite to eat it before they arrived." It struck me that she was referring to the twins as guests.

The knock on the door came promptly at seven. The twins were on time today.

Katie rushed to open the door for them and greeted them warmly by name. She even figured out which one was Candy and which one was Brandi. Something that usually stumped me.

~

Katie

AS ADVERTISED, THE KNOCK ON THE DOOR CAME AT SEVEN o'clock.

They had changed wigs, and they were redheads tonight. They wore matching slinky red dresses and tall bright red heels. Their lipstick matched their shoes. They waved, standing back from the door.

This was probably what they considered working attire, I thought before catching myself judging them.

They eyed me cautiously. "We're here to meet Nick, if that's okay?" Brandi said.

"Sure, come on in. He's expecting you." I beckoned them in.

"Hi, Candy, I'm Katie. We met the other day," I said offering my hand to the one I recognized as Candy.

Candy shook politely as the smile on her face turned warm and genuine. "I remember."

I also introduced myself to Brandi, reminding myself that these were just two young girls in a bad situation.

"Hi, girls," Nick said. "I'll get the equipment from the other room. Be just a minute."

I motioned to the table. "I hope you like apple pie. I baked a fresh one this afternoon, just for you girls." That wasn't exactly true, because I had started it before I knew they were coming over. But it wasn't untrue either. I always baked my pies for other people.

They giggled and perked up. "You didn't have to do that," Candy said.

"It's something I like to do. It keeps me busy and takes my mind off of things," I said.

"I do my nails when I need to keep myself busy," Brandi said giggling.

"Don't we all?" I responded. Quickly checking my nails, they definitely needed work. "I guess I know what I'll be doing tonight."

The girls both laughed.

"Please sit down," I said. I uncovered the pie and put it on the counter. I served up four healthy slices and brought them over.

I had to admit this is one of my better efforts, the pie looked great. And when it looked good, it never failed to taste good too.

"This looks better than our mama made," Candy said.

"Mama never really could cook," Brandi added with a laugh.

I went to the fridge. "What would you girls like to drink?"

"Water would be fine," Brandi replied.

I poured glasses of water for each of us, and opened a can of beer for Nick.

The three of us waited patiently for Nick to return.

Nick showed up from down the hall with some electronic gizmos in his hand and placed them on the table with a file folder as he sat down. "Girls, thanks for coming over."

They both nodded.

"Let me explain—"

I bumped his knee under the table and he glanced over at me. "Nick wouldn't it be more polite to let our guests eat first?"

"You're absolutely right, Princess," he replied trying to get a rise out of me.

I didn't go for it.

The two girls had surprising appetites.

"How long have you two been together?" Brandi asked.

Nick coughed.

I answered for him. "We're not together. We're just friends."

Neither of the girls seemed convinced, but they didn't ask any more embarrassing questions.

They finished their pieces in no time.

I could tell Nick was anxious to show them his electronics, and I was curious as well what they did for him.

Nick opened a folder and passed them over a picture.

I glanced at the picture they had in front of them.

"This is the mark," Nick said. "His name is Jimmy Krasniki."

"Krasniki, like what kind of name is that?" Candy asked.

"Albanian," Nick answered. "He hangs out in a bar at the corner of Pico and Saturn."

"What's the play?" Brandi asked. "Same as last time?"

Nick shook his head. "No, this is easier." He picked up the

electronics he'd put on the table. "Now, these look like two regular phone chargers. The white one is an Apple charger and the black one is for a Samsung. I don't know which phone he has. The job is to either plug his phone into one of them and bring the chargers back or, if you can't get that done, to leave the charger there so he'll use it sooner or later." Nick passed the chargers over in their direction.

The girls checked them over curiously.

"That's it?" Candy asked.

"That's it," Nick replied. "I handle the rest from here. "Jimmy here is a pretty nasty guy, so I don't want you girls hanging around him any longer than you need to."

The twins giggled. This was obviously not new news to them, and it shouldn't have been to me.

"I don't know how you want to get introduced, because I know it's not your usual territory."

"I think we can figure that out," Candy answered.

"Yeah, we got a lot of friends over there," Brandi added.

"Just don't let him figure out who you really are. This is not somebody you want to have come after you later."

That sounded ominous to me.

"What if we need to pay a third girl to get us introduced?" Candy asked.

Nick pulled out his wallet. He counted out twenty $100 bills and pushed the pile across the table. "You girls figure out how to divvy up the money."

I was impressed by how much they were getting paid for this. A thousand dollars apiece, and my accounting brain noted it was tax-free. It was more than I took home in a week.

Nick's phone and mine both buzzed at the same time. Mine was on the counter in the kitchen.

Nick jumped up as he read the screen. "Gotta go check your house, Katie. You stay here, don't you dare think of leaving."

A chill ran through me. This couldn't be happening again.

"Girls," Nick said addressing the twins. "Don't let her leave, and don't open the door for anybody but me," he said sternly.

They nodded.

He grabbed his jacket on the way to the door. "Tie her up if you have to," he added as he closed the door on his way out.

They laughed.

Nick's motorcycle roared off.

"Is there any more of that pie left?" Brandi asked. "It was delicious."

I brought the plate over and served us all some more.

"So, seriously," Brandi said. "How long have you two been together?"

The heat of a blush warmed my cheeks. "Like I said, not a couple."

"I see the way he looks at you," Candy said. "He's got it bad. You got him hooked."

What she said startled me. I had thought we were both being pretty levelheaded about keeping this at the acquaintances with benefits level. No entanglements, but really good benefits. Fantastic benefits.

"I can tell you're into him too," Brandi said. "Aren't you?"

"He's okay. He's been a good friend." I took another bite of my pie to keep from having to say anything more.

"That's okay, you don't have to say anything. We'll keep your secret safe. And I think Nick really is the nicest guy," Brandi told me.

Candy nodded. "Yeah, he puts on this whole tough guy act, but he's a giant softy inside."

Brandi checked her phone. "We have to get going soon. We've got an appointment."

I could guess what appointment meant. "You know you girls really don't have to do this." I hated that they had to resort to what they did for a living.

"Now, don't go giving us the speech. This is just what girls like us do," Brandi said matter-of-factly, reaching out to touch my arm.

"Nick said you're in accounting. That sounds hard," Candy said.

"Nick told you that?" I asked.

"Sure, Nick tells us everything. He's our best client."

I was too curious to let it lie. "You don't…?"

"Oh no, not Nick. He's not that kind of client. We're like family and everything," Brandi interjected.

"Nick, he hires us for odd jobs and stuff," Candy said.

"Like this Jimmy guy?"

"Yeah, like that, or keeping a guy occupied and away from his office for a while. Or watching a place for who's going in and out. Stuff like that," Candy replied. "We're sort of like invisible to people. They see us, but they don't, you know?"

Brandi's phone rang, and she answered it. "Uh-huh, is it important… Sure we can do that. Where do you keep the duct tape if we need it?" She ended the call and composed a text message. "Nick needs us to stay with Katie here till he gets back," she said to Candy.

"No. You girls can get going whenever you need to. I'm fine," I told them.

"Don't get any ideas," Brandi told me laughingly. "Nick says stay, we all stay. And, he said it's okay to use the duct tape on you if we have to."

Candy laughed.

They seemed serious enough that I discarded my thoughts of running for the door.

Candy gathered up the plates and took them to the sink. "Then we don't have to miss *The Bachelor* after all."

"What did Nick say?" I asked.

Brandi was still composing the text on her phone. "Just a sec, I need to call off our date." She turned to me after she sent the text. "Nick said he would be awhile and to keep you safe here." She pointed a finger at me with a smile. "You're grounded girl."

Candy finished at the sink and opened the coffee table drawer to retrieve the TV remote. She knew where Nick stashed things; they must have spent more time here than I would have guessed. She turned on *The Bachelor*. "It's a women tell all episode. I love those."

Brandi and I joined her on the couch.

I still wanted to hear what Nick was not telling me. Two more attempts at wringing information out of Brandi failed. I sat back, resigned to watch the stupid television show with them.

I had never watched the show, but I knew the premise. One guy dated more than a dozen girls who all pretended to love him. One by one they get eliminated until he gets down to two. In the end the guy picks his true love and they're supposed to go off and get married. Of course most of the time that didn't happen because the girls were only in it for publicity, anyway. The guys probably too, but having a dozen beautiful women fawning over you for a whole TV season was probably all it took to get thousands of guys to sign up.

Becca was up in the hot seat now next to the moderator. The other girls were tearing her to shreds and explaining why they didn't like her. It was pretty simple—she was even more devious than they were.

Then there was the girl who complained the other girls were monopolizing the bachelor's time. She didn't get it that that was the idea behind the show.

Brandi and Candy agreed with the comments of most of the girls. They had obviously watched the episodes and seen the behavior these girls were complaining about.

I never had the time. I was so focused on my career. Yesterday had been my first full day off without even thinking about accounting or my job responsibilities. It had been long overdue.

They seemed like such nice girls. I didn't understand it. "Why do you do it?" I blurted out before I realized how insulting the question sounded.

"Do what?" Brandi asked.

"You know," I said, afraid to be more specific.

Candy smiled at her sister. "You mean like why aren't we serving tacos for a living? We took a marketing course at the community college. It was really pretty interesting. They taught us that there's a couple ways to be successful."

Brandi continued, "You can either convince people that they need something you have, or provide something they really want. We figured out that we could provide something some men sure want."

"We provide a fantasy," Candy said. "That's all. For a little while the guy gets to pretend he's James fucking Bond or whatever and he's dating twins."

"Twins with big boobs," Brandi added.

Candy smiled. "Yeah, that too. A lot of men have had the dream, and for the right price we can make it come true for an evening."

"The course taught us," Brandi said. "Demand and supply. Scarcity leads to high prices, just like the professor said. Since our services are pretty unique, we get to be picky about who we date and still charge a lot. It's just an acting gig is all." That was the same way Nick had described it, although I couldn't agree.

"I'm really glad Nick made us take the course. He paid for it and everything," Candy said.

"Yeah, it was a turning point," Brandi added.

"Nick?" I asked. This was a whole new side to the tough biker; he made these two take a marketing course and paid for it.

Candy smiled at her sister. "We grew up on the same street as him and Lester. He was always sort of like the big brother we never had."

"Nick said you were saving up to start a business. That right?" I asked.

"Yeah, Nick makes us put money away every month in the bank, and we're over halfway there," Brandi replied.

"And our college fund," Candy added. "Nick made us set that up too, and it's almost full now."

"Nick made you?"

Candy laughed. "Of course. When Nick tells you to do something, it don't make a lot of sense to argue. But, you probably know that by now." It was certainly a lesson I was learning.

The girls had it nailed as far as marketing 101 went. It made sense that in their *business* a pair of attractive big-chested twins was a high-priced rarity. I still didn't approve of what they were doing, but at least they had a well-thought-out exit strategy. They were obviously smart enough they didn't have to be doing this if they didn't want to. And, personally, I couldn't imagine wanting to.

Tonight had certainly shed new light on Nick's character. He paid for their marketing course, made them save for their future, and encouraged them to work toward college. They were certainly lucky to have a friend like Nick.

CHAPTER 20

Nick

There were no lights on inside the house, no cars out front. I couldn't hear anybody or anything except the blare of the siren. I ran up to the window on the corner and peeked over the edge.

The window next to the front door was broken.

I went around to the front door. I tried the knob. Locked. I unlocked it and moved inside. After silencing the alarm I went through the house carefully, checking all the rooms and closets.

The house was empty. A rock with a paper tied around it lay in the middle of the floor. Broken glass littered the carpet near the window. Somebody had been intent on sending a message.

I went to the kitchen drawer and located a baggie. Careful not to touch the paper in case of fingerprints, I removed the rubber band holding it around the rock.

The message scrawled on the paper was simple.

Leave town or die bitch.

This had to be some kind of misdirection; it didn't make any sense. Katie had only spent a few days at this house and somebody wanted her to leave town? There was no sense in that.

A big black SUV came to a screeching halt out front.

Winston Evers exited the car and ran up to the house, his gun drawn. He came in through the open door and leveled his gun at me.

I didn't move a muscle. The last thing I needed was adrenaline forcing him to make a mistake. You don't surprise a man with a gun.

He lowered his Glock and holstered it. "Nick, I got the alarm and got here as soon as I could. What happened?"

"Neither of us were in the house and haven't been for days. When I got here, the siren was still going, but I didn't see anybody. I reset the system and cleared the house, nobody in sight. Whoever it was sent this nice little calling card through the window." I pointed out the rock and handed him the note in the baggie.

Winston scanned the note quickly. "Somebody sure isn't happy."

"Doesn't make any sense. She just moved in here, she hasn't had time to make enemies of the neighbors."

"You have any candidates?" he asked.

"A short list. Only a few people were aware she moved into this house. Some at her work, you guys at Hanson, of course."

He shook his head and gave me the evil eye for that comment.

"And some people at a company she's been auditing called LDSI. I'll send you the full list."

"I can tell you Bill's not gonna be happy about this."

"Yeah, so what else is new?"

"You know he's gonna want to take her back to the condo."

That's not happening.

"Over my dead body," I told him.

Winston chuckled. "Don't tempt him." Winston went to

check the other rooms. "Anything on the video," he called back to me.

"Haven't checked it yet, I was busy clearing the house."

His suggestion was a good one, so I pulled up the video feeds on my phone. My screen wasn't very big but at least I got a general idea if it held anything useful.

The front porch camera had an image of somebody in black with a mask over his face throwing something.

Then I got the surprise.

"Winston you need to see this."

He came back from checking the other rooms and watched as I replayed the feed. "A gun?" He surveyed the room.

"Looks like muzzle flashes to me."

Winston was checking the back wall up high. "Found one."

"I count three shots on the video," I told him.

It didn't take long, we located all three slugs inside the house. This definitely changed the complexion of the things. It had escalated from burglary, to a physical assault on Katie, and now gunfire. This was deadly serious.

"Where's she now?" Winston asked, turning to me.

"At my place."

"You might want to get back there in case this is a diversion. I'll pull these out of the wall and get them to our lab guys and see if they tell us anything."

"You have a key to lock up?"

He nodded. "Yup. Don't forget to send me that list."

I left him to finish up at the house and remounted my bike. I pulled on my helmet and zipped up my jacket. Foreboding filled me.

Something doesn't add up.

The lights had been off. Nobody had been in the house for days. Whoever this was had to have known that. He knew there was a security system with video. That's why he'd worn a mask and loose black clothing at night.

I started up the bike but sat there idling for a moment. This attack didn't make any sense. Making a lot of noise shooting at an empty house was stupid, it could only bring attention.

What if that's what he wanted?

I had an idea.

I lifted my visor and pulled out onto the road slowly. As I left, I carefully checked my mirrors.

There it was.

A car pulled away from the curb down the block, following me.

I turned left, and it followed.

That's why the guy had called attention to himself. He'd wanted us to rush to the house. He hadn't found where Katie was, and he needed me to lead him back to her.

No way.

I went at a reasonable enough speed that he could keep up without being obvious. I had a new destination in mind. Before long I turned into the circular driveway of the Covington's monster condo tower.

Getting off my bike I could see the tail had stopped down the street on Wilshire. I pulled off my helmet and was greeted by the same doorman who had been here last week.

"Oliver, I need you to do something for me," I told the old man.

"What can I do for you Mr. Knowlton." He remembered me from last week.

"I need you to call the police and get them to check on that black sedan down there that's been following me." I motioned in the general direction of where the car had stopped, trying not to be obvious about it.

Oliver picked up the phone at his station. "Yes, sir, right away."

I watched the car as discreetly as I could.

It left before the black and white arrived.

The cops were unusually deferential as they drove up and talked to Oliver and I. The Covingtons obviously had pull. The cops wouldn't have been nearly as nice if I had called for myself.

Ten minutes later I left and headed in the opposite direction of my house. This time fast, I ran two red lights, and doubled back on the freeway.

I only headed home when I was sure I wasn't being followed.

This person was crafty and dangerous. We needed to turn this around and become the hunters. Katie had to have a clue that would lead us to this asshole's identity. She just didn't realize what it was yet.

~

Katie

NICK CAME IN THE DOOR ABOUT THE TIME *THE BACHELOR* ENDED. He pulled some more hundred dollar bills out of his wallet and handed them to the twins on their way out. His wallet seemed to contain an endless supply of the bills. He hadn't used plastic once yet.

As soon as he locked the door, he came over and enfolded me in his arms. His hug was warm and comforting.

I pushed away to see his face. "You finally going to tell me what happened?"

He kissed my forehead. "Your admirer was by the house again. This time he threw a rock through your front window and then fired three shots into the house."

I froze. "Shots? You mean gunshots?"

"Yes. Winston joined me over there, and we found the slugs in the wall. His lab will go over them but I don't know if that will tell us anything."

"But why shoot at an empty house?"

"Very good question, Precious. He did it on purpose to lure us over there."

"You mean you think he wanted to attack you too?"

"No, nothing like that. He followed me after I left the house. He thought I'd lead him to you. But instead I went over to that stupid condo tower of your brothers'. Now he thinks you're hiding out there."

I shivered.

"Precious, this guy is getting more dangerous every day. You have something or you know something serious enough for this guy to want to get out a gun."

"But I don't have anything. Everything burned up in the fire."

"We have to turn this around on them," he said. "Like I said, maybe you know something that's dangerous to him and you just don't realize what it is. So tomorrow we have to re-examine everything you think you know or don't know. The job now is to find him before he finds you."

I still had no idea what it could be. "Okay. So we start from scratch."

"Tomorrow." He picked me up effortlessly. He bumped off the lights in the kitchen and carried me into the bedroom.

We would start tomorrow.

CHAPTER 21

Katie

Nick already had breakfast on the table when I got out of the shower. This morning it was sausage, eggs, and hash browns, with cantaloupe on the side. The man was surprisingly versatile in the kitchen.

"Why so much food?" I asked, giving him a quick hug before sitting down.

He poured grapefruit juice for both of us. "You need your energy for today. Today you're the hunter, remember that."

Him saying that gave me more confidence than I'd had yesterday. I took a bite of sausage.

"It has to be either work or this company LDSI."

Neither one made any sense to me. "I got nothing. I'm not a threat to anybody at work or LDSI."

"But you're doing an audit on LDSI right?"

I nodded with a mouthful of sausage.

"Have you found anything suspicious yet?" he asked.

I shook my head. "No, it's all pretty boring stuff and no discrepancies at all yet."

He cocked an eyebrow. "Yet?"

"Well, I'm not quite done, but it's not like I would, or could, tell if they were selling secrets to the Russians or anything."

"What do they do at LDSI?"

"Lindbergh Defense Strategies Incorporated, like it sounds they do defense work, mostly. They make some parts for airplanes and they do some consulting work for the Pentagon."

"That sounds more promising than your accounting buddies, so what does it take to finish up the audit and see if there is anything there?"

"Just the data I was expecting them to send me that didn't arrive in the mail yet."

We finished breakfast with Nick asking more questions about how auditing worked and what my job entailed. It didn't seem to lead to any obvious clues about who could be after me. Auditing was by nature boring, monotonous stuff.

When eight o'clock rolled around, I figured the LDSI people would be wandering into work. I emailed, asking for the tracking number on the package of the data they had sent me. It would let me figure out where it was in the FedEx system.

Two hours later a response arrived. It said they hadn't sent the data because my company said I'd been pulled off the account. Instead they'd sent it to my boss to forward to whomever he'd assigned as the new person on the account.

My temperature went up ten degrees. If I'd had something handy to throw I would have, instead I slammed my fist on the table.

What an asshole he was. That fucker Russ Downey he had given me the week off and taken the account away to give to somebody else. He was probably going to tell management that I couldn't handle it. That I wasn't good enough.

Nick came running in from the other room. "What happened? You okay?"

"No, I'm not okay," I yelled before I could control myself enough to realize that yelling at Nick wouldn't help anything. I took a deep breath. "I just got a call from LDSI."

"And?"

I tried to control my temper. "They were told I was taken off the account by my boss," I said as calmly as I could manage.

Nick came over behind me and started to rub my shoulders. "And what does that mean?"

"Besides that he's a fucking asshole?" I asked rhetorically. "What it smells like, is him taking the account away because I'm taking this week off, because some psycho lady torched my house. Then he's going to go tell management I couldn't handle the workload and it was a simple enough account. So, I'm incompetent as far as he's concerned, end of career, end of story." It sounded even worse when I said it out loud.

Nick rubbed my shoulders harder. "It sounds to me like you need to head this off at the pass before next week. You should go in this afternoon and have a sit down with this jerk and tell him how much you've already done and that you'll have it done by the end of the week like it should have been. And put it in writing too."

I liked Nick's suggestion. "Yeah, that sounds good. With him getting ready to fire me, how much worse could it get, anyway? I'll go right after lunch." I tried to calm down by controlling my breathing. It didn't work. I was jittery from the anger, but right now anger wouldn't do me any good. He was too far away to punch.

Russ usually left for lunch promptly at noon, and I didn't have a lot of time left to get my little memo ready for him. I liked Nick's idea of putting my side in writing.

I had only finished the second paragraph when my phone rang again.

It was Betty from HR at my company. "*Katherine, how are you feeling?*"

"Okay, considering."

"*Good to hear.*" She hesitated before going on. "*I'm calling to schedule your exit.*"

"What exit?"

"*Your exit interview. I thought you would be able to get through it. I know Mr. Downey can be hard to work with, so I understand why you quit.*"

I was so mad the pencil in my hand snapped. "I didn't quit," I said loudly.

"*He emailed last week to say you weren't sure you wanted to stay. And, he marked you as no-show no call Monday, Tuesday, and Wednesday. We terminated you yesterday afternoon.*"

I tried to take all this in. It was too much to process. "That's not what I said."

There was silence on the other end. *"I'm sorry, Katherine, that's what the record says. If you're not going to come in you're supposed to call us in HR and I don't have any record that you called.*"

"Of course not. My house burned down last week, and when I called to tell him about it, he told me take the week off so why would I call?"

"*Katherine, all I can tell you is what I have in front of me here. He wrote an email last Friday saying that you'd called, and you weren't sure you were coming back—*"

I interrupted her. "How can he do that? That wasn't the conversation."

"*Katherine, that's the email I have. Then Monday and Tuesday he told us that you were no call no show, and we didn't get any calls from you either. Yesterday when you didn't come in and you didn't call, he put in your termination paperwork. It's signed by Mr. Parker too.*"

Parker was Downey's boss. I'd never talked to him, and

almost never saw him. So, Russ had given him the same line of bull he was feeding HR. How was I supposed to fix that?

I refused to set a time for the exit interview with her and got off the call, still steaming mad. I turned to see Nick watching from the hallway.

He came my direction. "What now?"

"The asshole one upped himself. He told HR I wanted to quit and when I didn't come in the last three days, they terminated me." I sniffled and wiped the tear off my cheek.

Nick pulled me up out of the chair, and into an embrace.

He was warm and solid as ever. My rock, the one solid piece in my life that wasn't going to let me down. "But you didn't want that job, anyway."

"But not this way." He was right that I didn't want the job, but I intended to leave on my own terms and not Downey's. This was humiliating. I wiped another tear. I buried my head against Nick's chest and listened to his breathing.

Nick

SHE TOLD ME THE IMPORTANT THING TO HER WAS THAT SHE LEAVE on her own terms. It was something I could understand. She didn't want to be pushed around any more than I did, and it was also important to her to get this CPA certificate she'd been working on for so long.

"Then go and see your boss's boss," I told her.

She perked up at that. It wasn't something she had considered. She wiped her nose with her sleeve. "Yeah, I guess that's all that's left right now."

I left her to work on that while I went to make a call to

Winston. I wanted to be able to have a frank conversation with him out of Katie's earshot.

"*How's our girl?*" Winston asked.

"Not so good, but it has to do with her job, not the house." I didn't want to go into any more of it with him. "What do we have from your lab guys?"

"*Actually, more than I expected. We got nothing on the bullets, they're not in the system anywhere we can find. So, the gun's not going to help us except that the guy's no genius.*"

"How so?"

"*We got a fingerprint on the note. It's not much of one, just a partial. But the lab guys think it's enough for an ID if we find a candidate to match it to. What kind of idiot doesn't use gloves when he writes a threatening note?*"

"Well, that's good news," I said. "Is it anything we can use against the DMV database?"

"*No such luck," he said. "Looks like a partial left thumb print.*" The California DMV only took right thumbprints so that wouldn't help us. "*We didn't get a hit on AFIS either. So, the guy doesn't have a record, or maybe the print is less good for a match than my guys thought.*"

"Did you recover anything more off of the video?" I asked.

"*No, the guy's face is covered and there's not much light out by the street.*"

We hung up after agreeing to keep each other up-to-date.

I decided to attack the problem with the tools I had. Katie had given me names and phone numbers of her people at work that knew where she had moved. I started on the list.

Two hours later Katie came knocking on my door. "There are two beers with our names on them out in the kitchen if you want to join me."

I was up for that. I followed her out to the kitchen, and she handed me a can.

I took it and offered a toast. "To finding the son of a bitch."

That dragged a smile out of my girl. "Do you have any wizardry that can help with that?"

"I've got a start," I told her. "Using the cell phone numbers you gave me for the people at your work."

She nodded.

"I'm generating the call logs for them for the last month or so. It takes a little while the way I do it because I don't get to just ask the phone company to download it for me."

"How do you do that?"

"You don't want to know."

"You mean it's illegal?"

"Let's just say that I have ways to access information that other people can't necessarily get."

She nodded. She was smart enough not to ask any more questions about this and get in any trouble in the future.

"It'll take me a little longer, but I can also pull location data for most of these phones. That's what I'm hoping will be the motherlode. If we find one of these phones was near your house when you got attacked, we'll have him."

She took another swig of beer and fiddled with the can.

"And Winston has a partial print on the note that they threw through your window. That's also a good step forward."

Her phone rang. "Rosa, good to hear from you." Her lips quivered. "Why not?" she asked the person on the other end. Her eyes misted over. Whatever the conversation was, it wasn't going well for her. "I see. Thank you for trying, Rosa." They ended the call.

"And?" I asked.

The tears flowed. "Three weeks," she sniffled. "Mr. Palmer, my boss's boss won't see me until three weeks from now. He's out of town and after that he has a European trip for something."

I wiped a tear and pulled her up into a hug and rubbed her back. My girl didn't deserve this.

"You won't leave me, will you?"

"I'm always here for you, Precious." I meant it. The asshole tormenting her was going to pay for this. That was one thing I was certain of. Katie didn't deserve any of the shit happening to her.

~

Katie

NICK WAS HOLDING ME, CUDDLING ON THE COUCH AFTER TWO glasses of scotch.

I had never been a hard liquor drinker, but now it was the way to go. The scotch warmed me inside and snuggling with Nick kept me warm on the outside.

He was my rock. While everything else had gone wrong this last week, he was the one constant. He was a dominant, bossy, opinionated man, but he was one hundred percent behind me, and always there to put a positive spin on things and get me to focus on what I could do to improve things, rather than wallow in my own misery.

My life was in the shitter. My house and everything outside of one suitcase of now worthless work clothes had been burned by that maniac Monica Paisley. Two years of work for that asshole Russ Downey was down the tubes, I was no closer to getting my CPA, and some lunatic was after me.

The only good thing in my life was Nick.

My phone rang, and Nick picked it up off the coffee table.

"Miss Covington's line, may I help you?" he answered. "She's a little busy right now, why don't you tell me."

I sat up and grabbed for the phone, unsuccessfully.

Nick stood and kept it away from me.

"I understand, I'll let her know. Thanks for the heads up," he said before ending the call.

"My brother?" I asked. I wasn't getting calls from anyone else recently.

"Yeah, douchebag number one."

"He is not." I tried to punch his shoulder, but in my current state it had absolutely no effect on him. "Well, what did he say?"

"It's good news, and it's bad news. The bad news is that the Monica lady is out on bail again."

That wasn't bad news, it was terrible news. I grabbed the bottle and poured some more scotch into my glass.

"The good news is, he says they've got location data on her that proves she's not the one that took a match to your house."

That confused me. "How's that good news?"

"Instead of having to worry about two people trying to turn you into a crispy critter, it's only one. The Monica lady was never after you in the first place. It means the guy with the love note wrapped around the rock is probably the same guy that torched your house."

I tried to wrap my head around what Nick was saying, but it wasn't easy. "You think that's good?"

"Sure, it's always easier to defend against one person than two. It means when we find the one asshole you're safe."

I turned and leaned back against him. My protector had my back. Literally.

CHAPTER 22

(Three Weeks Later)

Katie

The envelope had arrived yesterday. It said that they weren't going to honor the insurance policy on my house. The fire department had ruled it arson, and a timer had been used. They didn't pay on arson unless a suspect had been caught. When I had called to complain, they had implied I had to prove I didn't burn my own house down. They thought because a timer had been used, I could have set it before I went out of town. I had cried for an hour.

Fucking insurance companies.

My luck had to change.

I was outside the restaurant downtown, waiting for Danielle Addison. I rolled Dad's coin over in my hand before returning it to my purse.

It had been three weeks since I'd been fired by the company.

I had my meeting scheduled with Mr. Palmer next Monday. My memo outlining why I thought I should get my job back and why I thought Russ Downey was incompetent had stretched now to ten pages.

I could tell Nick thought it was a waste of time. Nevertheless, he had been supportive. I couldn't let pessimism rule me.

My goal was to get a simple note from Danielle, saying that she agreed with what I had written. Two people telling Palmer the same thing would be more powerful than me alone.

I'd emailed her my memo last night. She'd agreed to read it and meet me for lunch.

Danielle walked up from the south with more spring in her step than I remembered and a smile on her face.

She greeted me warmly with a hug.

"Looks like life is agreeing with you, Danielle," I told her as we took our seats inside. Her face had lost the worried and worn appearance of last year.

"Absolutely. You have no idea how much nicer it is at Federated than working at Arthur and Company. Now I wish I'd been smart enough to move earlier."

That surprised me. "You don't regret having left when you were so close to finishing your hours?"

"Not anymore. At first I was mad, but now I realize it was my fault for not doing it sooner. I shouldn't have stayed and tried to deal with that dickhead Downey. He had given me the feeling for over a year that he had it in for me. If I'd paid attention to my gut, I would have left earlier. After what he put Paul through, the writing was on the wall. I was too slow catching on is all."

The waitress came by and took our lunch orders.

I craned my neck and spied Winston Evers having lunch along one wall and his partner from Hanson, Constance Collier, near the door. She had dropped me off out front and Winston had gone inside ahead of me. The Hanson people were thorough if nothing else in trying to keep me safe, but this was getting tiring.

"Everything okay, Katie?" Danielle asked.

"Sure. I thought I noticed somebody else I knew here."

I didn't want to broach the subject of my memo right away, so we spent lunch with her telling me all about Federated and her work there. It sounded like a dramatically nicer place to work than Arthur and Company.

I found myself wishing I had joined her a year ago, changing firms. I'd initially considered it, but decided it made more sense to stick it out in one place. Twenty-twenty hindsight wouldn't help me.

We were nearly finished and skinny Danielle seemed like a girl who didn't do desserts. "Danielle, I'd like your help."

"Sure." She leaned forward intently.

"I don't know if you heard, but Downey fired me a few weeks ago."

Danielle reached across the table to gently touch my hand with a kind look to match. "No, I didn't know. You always did such good work. Would you like a reference? Is that it?"

I shook my head and gathered up my courage. "No, that's not it. It wasn't fair at all. He told me take the week off, then he told HR that…" I wasn't sure exactly how to put this.

"He's such a bastard," she volunteered.

"Anyway he told them that I quit, but I didn't. So I made an appointment with Mr. Palmer."

Danielle cocked an eyebrow.

"I meet with him on Monday. I'm going to tell him how bad Mr. Downey is, and I was wondering if you'd give me a letter to take along about your experience with him last year."

Her brow furrowed. Not a good sign. She cast her eyes down at the table and shook her head. "I can't, Katherine, I'm sorry. It's not a good idea to burn any bridges. You should let it go and move on."

"I just know that if I'm not the only one complaining, Mr. Palmer will have to take me seriously."

Danielle exhaled a deep breath. "Katherine, don't be naive. That's not the way it works. If Palmer wanted to get rid of him, it would've happened a long time ago. If you go in there like that, it will be a suicide mission. It won't change anything. Assholes will be assholes, and nothing will change."

I slumped down in my seat. It was over. There was no way I was going to change Danielle's mind. If I wanted to fight this, I would be on my own.

And, she might be right. Nick agreed with Danielle, talking to Palmer would be a waste of time.

Maybe Dad had been wrong. Maybe there were things, certain things, that couldn't be fixed with an application of effort and persistence, no matter how hard I tried.

"Don't be down about it," Danielle said, sensing my despair. "A month or two from now at a different firm, life will be so much better. You'll wonder why you didn't get out of there earlier. I promise it'll be better."

I tried my best to digest her perspective. I wasn't used to giving up. Surrender had never been in my vocabulary.

I was suddenly alone. I needed Nick.

~

Nick

KATIE WAS IN ONE OF MY FAVORITE POSITIONS, AT LEAST IN public. She was wrapped snuggly around me on the back of my Harley as we motored north on the 405.

"Tell me again why we're doing this?" I asked her through the intercom.

"Because it's a family thing. We do it almost every month, and I don't want to miss it. Besides, you get a chance to meet my uncle Garth and lots of other nice people."

Meeting another Covington was not at the top of my list, but it was important to Katie, so I could suck it up and go along, even if her douche brother Bill was going to be there.

"And it's for a good cause. You should appreciate that."

"I do." They were doing something to help people who were on my end of the financial spectrum, the kind of people I'd grown up with. If it had been one of their fancy parties with other stupid rich people, I would've sent Winston to keep Katie safe.

But she was right, Habitat for Humanity was worthwhile enough to even put up with Bill fucking Covington for a day. It honestly surprised me when she first mentioned her family did this on a routine basis. I never would've guessed it.

I opened up the throttle to pass another Prius road boulder clogging up the freeway lanes. I slowed down alongside the driver of the hybrid tin can and stared at him.

The driver nearly shit in his pants and moved over a lane to get away from me. The self-righteous road toads were everywhere in LA, they thought they owned the fucking place.

"Hey, what is your problem," Katie said in my ears.

"What problem?"

"You've been in a bad mood since breakfast, and now you're terrorizing the other drivers. That's the third one you've done that to."

I hadn't been counting but there sure were a lot of them out here today. "Done what to?"

She punched me in the kidney, and not lightly. "You know damn well what you're doing." She gave me a squeeze. "I'll bet it's because you're scared."

"Nothing scares me, Princess."

"I'll bet you're scared to spend the day with Bill aren't you?"

"I couldn't give a shit about your douchebag brother."

"You know if you're scared, we can turn around and go back home."

I opened up the throttle and split the lanes between cars.

"Trying to scare me isn't going to work this time. Instead it proves I'm right."

I slowed down and took my place behind a pickup truck in the second to the left lane. "Okay, already. I don't want to be around your stupid brother. But that's not the same as scared. I'm just afraid I might have to break one of his arms if he says the wrong thing."

She hugged me tighter. "You'll do fine. He's really a nice guy, and if he starts to act up, let me punch him."

I laughed. "That'll be the day, Princess. If he starts anything I'll finish it. That's one thing you can count on."

"Just don't you start anything."

I wasn't planning on it, but I wasn't planning on taking any shit from her fucking brother either.

We rode along in silence until we reached the project.

The place was buzzing with activity. Katie introduced me to the amiable old man organizing today, his name was Lloyd Benson. The name sounded familiar but I couldn't place it.

He assigned us to a desk passing out helmets, gloves, and safety glasses to the arriving volunteers.

Captain douchebag was already there, and busy on the other side of the lot directing the unloading of a truckload of lumber. He was followed around by a beautiful blonde with a clipboard in hand who Katie informed me was Bill's wife Lauren. She was probably a saint if she could put up with that fucker every day.

After everybody had arrived, and we were done with our little pass-out chore, Benson assigned us to a group installing insulation in interior walls.

I had done a fair amount of construction work before and showed our little group of four how to place the cuts in the insulation so that it would fit neatly around the wires and piping in the walls when they encountered that. We finished all but one room before lunch.

Winston and Hank from Hanson Security were also there today, so at least I knew somebody besides Katie. Hank had mentioned once that he did this, but I hadn't paid any attention at the time.

When the lunch horn sounded, Katie had warned me we would be eating with her family group, including that fucker Bill.

We washed up by a faucet along the side yard and sat in camping chairs that Winston and Hank had brought along.

Her brother Bill eventually joined us along with another fellow he introduced as Phil Patterson.

I liked Phil as soon as we shook hands. He had the calluses and the worn leather tool belt of a man who did honest work with his hands for a living, my kind of guy, not a pencil-pusher like Bill.

"As the new guy you get first dibs," Bill said to me. He opened a big bag from Subway. He rummaged through the bag for a moment. "We've got turkey and cheese, roast beef, meatball, or Italian sub."

I chose the meatball sub. Katie went for turkey and cheese, and the two of us both grabbed barbecue from the pile of bags of potato chips.

Katie passed out paper plates and spooned out the potato salad she had made last night.

I was looking forward to the apple pie she'd also baked.

~

Katie

NICK HAD BEEN IN A ROTTEN MOOD EVER SINCE YESTERDAY when I'd informed him I was coming to today's Habitat for

Humanity project whether he came along or not. His foul mood had shown in his driving this morning as well.

He'd only calmed down when I accused him of being scared to be around Bill. Today was going to be a challenge.

Lloyd Benson assigned us to hang insulation and the morning went by uneventfully.

The beginning of lunch was a bit tense as Bill and Nick eyed each other warily like two lions sizing each other up before the brawl. Thankfully, neither man said anything to rile the other.

After all the sandwiches were consumed, I brought out my apple pie for today and dished it out to the hungry crowd. Nobody ever refused my apple pie.

"Hey, Winston," Bill said. "Are you going to make it to the scholarship fundraiser on Tuesday?"

I'd forgotten about that. We had the scholarship fundraiser for the local high school that we held every year at our country club coming up in two days and it had completely slipped my mind.

"Don't I make it every year?" Winston replied.

"How many pies you going to bring this year?" Bill asked me.

I fiddled with my potato salad for a moment. I'd brought my apple pies to the club for this fundraiser, each of the last five years. "I'm not sure I'm going," I said reluctantly.

Disappointment instantly clouded Bill's face. "Katie, you're on the social committee. How can you not go?"

I glanced at Nick. "Would you like to go with me?"

"Sure," he responded patting my leg. Something flashed through his eyes that I couldn't read.

Had he said he would go with me because I needed a bodyguard, or because he wanted to go with me? I couldn't tell.

My musings were interrupted by a visit from our project organizer Lloyd Benson. "Just the group I was looking for," he announced. "We're going to need a few strong backs after lunch. The roofing company couldn't spare a conveyor truck today, so we're going to have to get the shingles up onto the roof the old-fashioned way, with ladders."

"How many squares are we talking about?" Phil asked him. Phil had taught me that a square was a roofing term for a hundred square feet.

"Forty-six, son," Benson answered him. *Son* was what old man Benson called every man except his own son.

Phil thought for a moment. "You know that's about five fucking tons. That's gonna take a while."

Benson gave Phil an evil stare. He didn't like swearing on the job, and Phil had restrained himself up until now.

"I guess we better get a move on," Bill said, interrupting the silence. "Phil and Winston, how about you guys stack on the roof, while Nick and I get the bundles up to you?"

Phil nodded. Winston didn't say anything.

"That is, if you can handle it," Bill added with a smirk in Nick's direction.

"The only question is if you can keep up, pencil-pusher," Nick shot back.

It didn't take a genius to see my brother had challenged Nick to a race and there was no turning back now.

The men located two tall extension ladders while Hank backed the roofing truck up the driveway.

"Let me secure the ladders before you two amateur idiots hurt yourselves," Phil said as he climbed up the first ladder. He used clamps and nylon straps to fasten the ladders to the roof so they wouldn't move.

I wouldn't have thought of that.

Hank joined Winston and Phil on the roof as Bill and Nick grabbed their first packages of roofing shingles, and the race was on.

Each of the guys had to bring the packages to the rear of the truck before jumping down and grabbing them one at a time to take them up the ladder and hand off to the guys on the roof.

Lloyd Benson joined me, watching the two try to rush up the ladder and outdo each other. "They do know we have all afternoon, don't they?" he asked me.

"I don't think they're going to take all afternoon," Lauren told him. She had joined me to watch the guys compete even if they didn't want to call it that.

Nick wiped his brow with his sleeve. The sweat was soaking through his shirt, as was Bill's.

"I just hope they don't hurt themselves," I answered. "How much does each one of those weigh?" I asked Mr. Benson.

He leaned over and whispered to me. "Seventy-one pounds."

I shouldn't have been surprised that the old man knew the exact weight. He was a real stickler for details.

It'd been over a dozen trips up and down the ladder for each of them when Nick hefted two packages on his shoulder before starting up the ladder.

Winston had trouble handling the two stacks at once as Nick handed them over.

"Mr. Benson we're going to need some more help up here," Hank called down. The guys on the roof were not keeping up with Bill and Nick, even though there were three of them.

"Coming right up, son," Mr. Benson replied. He left to round up more strong backs to climb up on the roof.

Bill had noticed Nick had switched to carrying two packages each trip up the ladder and started doing the same.

They were over halfway done, which meant each of them had already carried three thousand pounds down off the truck and up the ladder.

Mr. Benson returned and asked Lauren to make a trip to Home Depot for some extra supplies.

She agreed reluctantly; she and I were both busy watching the duel. Both our men were getting noticeably slower at this point.

"Need a break, pencil pusher?" Nick asked Bill.

"Why? Getting tired?" Bill replied. He picked up three stacks of shingles on his next trip. Halfway up, he had trouble steadying himself on the ladder with that load. He leaned off to the side, trying to balance.

Nick dropped the shingles he was carrying with a thud and rushed over to the side of Bill's ladder.

I gasped.

Nick caught Bill just as the heavy load he was carrying sent him off balance and falling toward Nick.

Bill's hardhat went flying, and the packages of shingles broke open as they hit the ground.

Thankfully, Nick grabbed Bill on his way to the ground. The two men ended up in a heap on the ground.

They untangled themselves and Bill rose first, hopping on one leg.

"Thanks, Nick," Bill said dusting himself off. "Shall we call it a draw?" he asked panting. The knee of Bill's jeans were ripped and blood was dripping down. He had a limp.

"The way I count, I'm one ahead of you," Nick replied. "But that's close enough for me. Draw it is."

Bill offered Nick his hand, and the two men shook, followed by one of those bro-hugs where they slapped each other on the back.

Bill limped back to the truck and picked up a fresh package to take up the ladder.

Nick stopped him. "Bill, let me get the rest of them while you get that knee looked at."

Bill nodded and handed the shingles over to Nick.

The ice had been broken. The two lions had decided there wouldn't be a loser today.

Nick continued to take the packages of shingles up to the roof, now one at a time, while I retrieved the first-aid kit from Mr. Benson.

Bill sat down on one of the camping chairs, still breathing hard from the exertion of their race.

I took out the medical shears and cut open his pant leg from the ankle up.

"If you hadn't been such an idiot, this wouldn't have happened."

"We were only trying to get the job done by the end of the day."

I wet some gauze with the alcohol from the kit. "That's bull-shit and you know it. It would've been so much easier if you guys just pulled down your pants and put 'em on the table so we could measure."

Bill laughed.

The laughing stopped as soon as I poured alcohol on the wound. It probably stung like hell.

"Where would the fun be in that?" he asked.

"At least you wouldn't hurt yourself like an idiot. If you'd been up another rung or two on the ladder this could have been a lot worse."

He didn't argue it.

I cleaned the wound, added the antibiotic ointment and wrapped it tightly. "You're on injured reserve for the rest of the afternoon," I told him. I liked giving my brother orders for once, instead of the other way around.

"Oh my God, what happened? Are you all right, honey?" Lauren exclaimed, rushing up.

Bill put his best smile on and lied to her. "It's just a scratch, SP." SP was a nickname Bill had called her ever since they had met.

When I had asked him, Bill had told me SP meant sugar plum. But the way Lauren smirked when he said that told me it was really something else that he didn't want to say in public.

Lauren turned to me. "What really happened?"

Bill gave me the evil eye, his order to shut up.

"As usual, he was being an idiot. He tried to carry three packages of the shingles at once up the ladder."

Lauren shook her head.

"Nick caught me or it would've been worse," Bill admitted.

"Then you should thank him, and stop acting like he has the plague or something," Lauren lectured her husband.

"Already did. We're best buds now."

Lauren turned to me for confirmation.

I nodded. "It's about time they both stopped being idiots." I took a sip of my Coke.

"What did you want to talk about?" Lauren asked me after Bill left.

CHAPTER 23

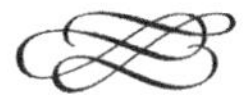

Nick

Katie's pencil-pushing brother Bill, had turned out to be an okay guy. None of the rich kid college boy weenies I had known before would've kept up with me schlepping those god-awful shingles up to the roof. Every one of them would've complained about it and given up earlier, passing the work off to somebody else, somebody lower down the food chain, somebody like me.

I regretted my pushing him so hard had gotten him injured, but it wasn't that bad. At the end of the day when the girls were off talking together about whatever girls talk about, he and I were sharing a beer and bitching about the Lakers.

If anybody had told me yesterday that Bill fucking Covington would be out here helping at a Habitat for Humanity project on a Sunday instead of on the golf course punishing little white balls I would've laughed. But he'd been here all day working hard like a regular guy. All the college weenies would have just written a check and deducted it on their taxes. He had real character.

On the Harley heading home, Katie gave me a squeeze. "A penny for your thoughts, big guy," came through the intercom.

"I'm thinking I'm gonna need one hell of a back rub tonight."

She giggled. "That can be arranged." She paused. "I want to thank you for catching Bill when he fell. It could have been pretty bad."

"I just didn't want to have to listen to his bitching all afternoon. He probably would have cried like a baby."

Katie did her typical thing when she didn't like what I said. She punched me in the side. Not hard enough to hurt, but hard enough to make her opinion clear. "I saw you two at the end of the day. Lauren and I could tell you like him."

"Like is a pretty strong word. But he's an okay guy in my book, unlike your fucking stepbrother Liam."

She didn't respond to my bringing up Liam's name.

"What were you and Lauren gossiping about over there on the side?"

It took her a while to respond. "She agrees with you, that I should drop the idea of meeting with Palmer tomorrow."

It hurt her to say that. She was the stubbornest woman I had ever met when she got an idea into her head. I had spent the last three weeks trying to explain to her how it was a lost cause and a waste of her time.

"And are you?" I asked.

"No, that would be giving up."

She had this thing about giving up. She thought it showed weakness, and that was against her religion.

~

Katie

. . .

DISMOUNTING FROM THE BIKE, NICK CLAIMED FIRST DIBS ON THE shower, and I knew he'd be in there for a while.

I decided to get my things in order for my Palmer meeting tomorrow. I also needed to return my notebooks, and the company laptop.

I emptied the contents of the laptop bag onto the table. There was no sense turning it in with my eyeliner pencils and mascara in the pockets.

That's when it fell out.

The bright blue thumb drive.

The one with the LDSI foreign data on it. The one I thought had burned up in the fire. It'd been hidden in the pocket of my laptop bag all along.

I powered up the computer and inserted the drive. The data was all there. I transferred it to the hard drive and opened up my audit files. Now I had a chance to convince Mr. Palmer to take me back. If I finished the LDSI audit tonight, I could make it clear to him how Mr. Downey had lied about it.

I began inserting the foreign data into my sheets and going through the calculations.

"Shower's all yours, Precious," Nick called out.

I ignored him. I pulled Dad's coin out and put it on the table next to my laptop.

Hard work and perseverance.

Nick made us chili, hot and spicy. He pulled out a beer for me, but I chose water instead. I needed a clear head to get this done quickly.

By ten o'clock I had a clue, but I didn't say anything to Nick because I wasn't sure, and I didn't want to get my hopes up. By eleven I was sure.

This was the smoking gun, it was so damned obvious. Somebody was embezzling from LDSI. I'd gone through about three quarters of the transactions and the amount was already over seven hundred thousand dollars. There was a good chance that the total could reach a million.

"Nick, you need to see this."

Nick slowly picked himself up off the couch, moving with obvious discomfort. "I'm still gonna need that back rub," he said as he came over and stood behind me. "Tell me. What am I looking at?"

I pointed to my $700,000 number on the screen. "He stole more than that from the company."

Nick whistled. "Who is he?"

"I don't know, but I know it went to these two accounts here." I pointed to the bank accounts I'd determined the money went to. "They're both accounts in the Cayman Islands. Most of it went into that top one."

Nick sat down. "Now this makes sense. One of those fuckers at the company didn't want you to find this out. So first he burns down your old house, then he rifles through the new house, and grabs your laptop from you out on the street. It all makes sense. He needed to make sure you didn't have the data."

I'd only gotten this copy of the data because I'd asked one of the junior accountants who didn't know any better.

Now I really had something to tell Mr. Palmer.

"I've got to finish this tonight so I have it ready for tomorrow."

Nick was dialing his phone. "Hey, Winston. We don't have a name yet, but we've narrowed it down." He gave him the particulars we had.

I CHECKED MY BAG ONE LAST TIME BEFORE OPENING THE DOOR to the Arthur and Company building. I had the company laptop with me, a printout of my findings on the LDSI audit, and my memo to Mr. Palmer. My heart stopped for a moment when I thought I had lost the thumb drive of LDSI data, but it had merely been hidden beneath the computer.

I told the receptionist I was here to meet with Mr. Palmer.

She asked me to have a seat while somebody came down to get me.

"Nervous?" Nick asked, rubbing my back lightly.

"A little." That was a lie. I was more nervous than I'd been in a long time. Today the building didn't seem like my work anymore. I felt like an interloper here. This was my last chance to get my career back on track.

Nick picked up one of the magazines while we waited in the lobby.

I froze.

Russ Downey, of all people, walked in from the street. Anger clouded his face as he noticed me sitting with Nick in the lobby. He looked away quickly and hurried off to the elevator.

At least I didn't have to meet with Jerkus Maximus today. I almost threw up when I realized that if I got my wish and was reinstated by Palmer, I very well could end up back working for Downey this afternoon. That was an outcome I hadn't fully considered.

At least Nick was here with me, the one solid thing in my life these days.

A few minutes later, the stainless doors of the left-hand elevator parted. Rosa, Mr. Downey's assistant came over. She escorted me to the elevator and upstairs with her standard cheery good morning.

The secret to maintaining that attitude while working for Mr. Downey was something I would have to ask her about later.

The elevator doors parted on the fourth floor, and Rosa stepped out, urging me to follow her.

This wasn't the right floor. Palmer was on sixteen.

Betty from HR appeared from around the corner. "Good morning, Katherine, so good to finally meet you." We had actually met once when I'd joined almost two years ago, but obviously she had forgotten that. "Right this way."

I followed her into a small conference room.

My hand started to shake.

They were obviously taking this seriously if HR was going to be in the meeting with Mr. Palmer and me.

Rosa left, and Betty closed the door. She opened a folder and read from a piece of paper. "I see you brought your company computer."

Pulled the laptop out of the bag and slid it across the table to her. "Yes, and the audit results are on there."

She took a moment and flipped the computer over, checking the serial number against her piece of paper. Smiling as she checked it off. "And your work papers?"

I slid over my notebooks, and the hard copy of my LDSI audit results.

"Is this all?"

"Anything else that I had in hard copy burned up with my house."

The comment about my house burning down didn't faze her one bit. She checked off another box on her paper. "And those papers?" she asked, pointing to my memo for Palmer.

I guess they were company papers as well. "Yeah, this is for Mr. Palmer when he gets here." I slid the papers across to her.

"I'll give these to him." She checked her paper again. "Any customer confidential data?" she asked.

I retrieved the thumb drive from the bottom of my bag and placed it on the table. "This is the foreign data from LDSI that corroborates the audit results."

"Very good," she said. "And LDSI is?"

"Lindbergh Defense Strategies Inc. The audit engagement those other papers relate to."

She seemed unimpressed, but she was in HR, anyway. Understanding what we did wasn't in her job description. She pulled out several more papers stapled together and handed them across to me.

It was a set of questions about how happy I had been working at Arthur and Company, what I thought of the hiring process, what I thought of the review process, what I thought of my supervisor, and on and on.

"All these are answered in that memo there," I told her. I didn't want to go through it a second time.

She seemed happy with the answer and took her papers back. "Your badge was deactivated three weeks ago, I'll need that as well."

I took the lanyard off and handed it and my badge to her.

She closed her little file with a smile, placed it on the laptop and pick the bundle up. "Well, I think we're done here," she announced. "Now if you'll come with me," she said, leading the way.

I followed her out of the conference room back to the elevator. Finally we were going to see Palmer.

She dialed a number on her phone as we walked. "On the way now," she said before hanging up.

As the elevator doors closed, she pushed the lobby button.

I blinked hard and checked again. The lobby button was lit, not the sixteenth floor. "Shouldn't we be going up to see Mr. Palmer now?"

The friendliness disappeared from her face.

The doors opened to the lobby. Security was waiting there.

I couldn't believe what was happening. "I have an appointment with Mr. Palmer."

"No," Betty said sternly. "I have my instructions."

When a security guard grabbed for me, I wrenched my elbow away from him but followed him toward the front door.

"Done already?" Nick asked as he strode in our direction.

The tears rolled down my cheeks, luckily Nick didn't see them until we were outside.

"What happened, Precious?" he asked, pulling me into him.

I hugged him as strongly as I could. It had all gone wrong, and I needed him, the one thing I could hold onto that was real. "I didn't get to see him," I sobbed. My world was falling apart.

He could have reminded me that he'd told me this was a waste of time, but he didn't. He held me. "It'll be okay," were his only words as he led me back to the car.

It didn't feel okay. It was over. I had lost my house, my job, and my career. I had tried my hardest but it wasn't good enough. I wasn't good enough.

I had applied as much effort and persistence as I could, and it hadn't been enough.

CHAPTER 24

Nick

I tried to console her, but she didn't want to talk about it. It was actually for the best. She wasn't meant to work for that company, no matter how hard she tried. They didn't deserve her.

When we got home, she went straight to bed to take a nap.

I called Winston to find out what progress he'd made, which amounted to zip. The kind of standard methods available to him weren't going to work in the Cayman Islands.

I locked myself in the cave to finish tracking down this LDSI asshole who was at the root of all her problems. Well, nearly all. This was my area of expertise. I had the accounts she'd located, and it was up to me to track the money and find the owners.

I had started last night, but some of my methods needed to be used during business hours to avoid detection.

I was surprised by the results an hour later. This guy was an idiot, he hadn't taken any of the standard precautions to avoid having the money tracked.

By dinner time, I'd located the owner of the larger of the two accounts, Frank Sabbatini. He wasn't on Katie's list of LDSI people who knew where she lived, but a quick deep dive of his local bank account showed him getting direct deposits from LDSI, so he did work there.

The smaller account at the second bank I hadn't traced back to Sabbatini yet for sure. He hadn't made any recent outgoing transactions, which made the task harder.

Katie was still in the bedroom, but she would be getting hungry soon. She hadn't eaten since breakfast.

I pulled a pizza out of the freezer. I added extra sauce, pepperoni, mushrooms, and cheese. Thick and gooey the way she liked it. I popped it in the oven and grabbed a beer.

She had been through one hell of a day. Her accounting job at Arthur and Company that had meant so much to her was officially done. On the upside, she had located the information that would allow us to put this fucker Sabbatini behind bars. She wouldn't have the job she wanted, but at least she'd be safe.

Getting up off the couch to pull the pizza from the oven reminded me how sore I still was from yesterday. That had been one shitload of shingles Bill and I schlepped off of the truck and up to the roof.

Katie appeared at the bedroom doorway, rubbing her eyes.

"Sleep okay?" I asked.

"No. I just couldn't."

She wandered over, wrapping her arms around me from behind as I cut the pizza into slices. "How did I ever deserve somebody like you? My own personal pizza chef," she murmured.

I was the lucky one, with the press of those soft breasts up against my back. My cock swelled with the anticipation of how their softness would fill my hands later tonight.

"Only the best for my girl, Precious," I told her as I finished the final cut. "Now get the plates."

"I'm not done hugging you yet," she said squeezing me

tighter.

"If you keep this up we won't get a chance to eat, or drink your champagne."

"Champagne? You figured out who it is?" she asked excitedly.

"That's what we were saving the champagne for, right?"

"Who was it… is it?" she asked as she raced to the fridge and pulled out the champagne bottle.

I carried the pizza over the table. "Ever hear of a guy named Frank Sabbatini?"

~

Katie

Frank Sabbatini, that little weasel. "Sure, he's the payables manager at LDSI. Are you sure it's him?"

Nick took the champagne bottle from me. "No doubt about it. I linked him positively to the account. And, he's been sending the money back here to himself like an idiot." He popped the champagne cork and brought the bottle over to the table along with two glasses.

I served us both a slice of the pizza. "I never did deal with him very much, but the people in his department didn't care for him. That much I could tell, but nobody likes payables managers." They all called him Frankie, which sounded a bit like a mobster to me, and he reeked of garlic the few times I had talked to him.

He poured the champagne and raised his glass to me. "To the end of your troubles. You're safe now, Katie."

We clinked glasses, and I downed mine and asked for more. I deserved it.

After dinner, we went to the store for supplies. We had

agreed to go to the country club fundraiser tomorrow night, and everybody expected me to bring my apple pies.

Nick became chief apple peeler for the evening. Instead of baking, what I wanted to do was peel his clothes off, but these pies needed to be done first.

I behaved myself, with only a few sexual innuendos, and occasionally rubbing up against him. I liked how every *accidental* brush of my breast against his arm got a reaction.

The peeling and slicing had taken the most time. After that, the rest was sort of a production line. The club was getting store bought crusts, but they would have to deal with it. I didn't have the time to refrigerate and roll out the crusts for this many pies tonight. I brushed the tops with an egg wash and added a strip of foil around the edges to finish them off.

We ended up with extra filling, which I used to make about two dozen small apple tarts. We baked those first. Nick added a rack to the oven to fit all six pies at once, and we were off and cooking.

An hour later the finished pies were a perfect light brown, and the apple fragrance filled the house.

Even though he was probably in more need of one than me, Nick had insisted he give me a nice long back rub.

"What if I want a front rub instead?" I had asked as he'd peeled my clothes off.

"In due time, Precious."

I gave up and lay face down on the bed.

As he got undressed I grinned. My earlier flirting had gotten the desired result. My man was ready for action, his erection hard and vertical.

They told you it was really hard to find a good man, but they didn't tell you how good it was to find a really hard man.

He straddled my thighs and started to knead my lower back.

I groaned as the intense pressure of his fingers released my pent up tension.

"This too hard for you?" he asked.

"Hard is good," I responded, with more than one meaning.

He worked his way up my spine to my shoulders, kneading the stiffness away. As he worked my shoulders, he leaned forward and teased me with the brush of his cock on my back.

Twice I tried to reach back and grab him.

He swatted my hand away both times.

I couldn't reach the good stuff. "You're no fun," I complained.

"You want to have fun?"

I nodded. "Um hmm."

"You know you need to let go."

"Let go of what?" I asked.

"The idea that your job defines who you are."

"I know it doesn't."

He punished me lightly for lying with extra hard pressure of my lower back. "Liar."

I winced. "Okay, already. I admit that maybe I've been a little obsessed with getting my CPA this year."

He went back to his normal obscenely hard pressure on my tight muscles. "Maybe? You know, Princess, the first step to recovery is admitting you have a problem."

"I don't have a problem, except maybe you."

He pushed harder again, an unsubtle indication of what he thought of my response. "I'm cutting you off. You're going cold turkey."

"And what is that supposed to mean?"

He leaned forward to rub my shoulders, this time with only moderate pressure.

"That feels good," I mumbled as I relaxed into the bed.

The tip of his cock teased my back once more, getting me even wetter. He had his hands all over me, but I was unable to reciprocate.

"I'm telling you, you're going to stop working for a while.

You need to relax a little and learn how to take a little bit of time for yourself," he said.

"Am I?" He was alternating between getting me excited and getting me angry. "You're not my boss." I tried to push up to roll over, but it was no use, he held me down.

"Get used to it, Princess." He spanked me.

"Stop calling me that!"

"Suck it up. You're going to pay attention and do what you're told. Because it's obvious you don't know what's good for you."

He was back to telling me what to do and trying to run my life. I'd had way too much of that. Between him and my brothers, everybody was always trying to run my life.

He stopped the massage for a moment. "I seem to be the only one around here that cares enough about you to be honest with you and tell you when you're fucking up. And girl, you're fucking yourself up."

I stayed quiet. Tears pricked my eyes. With my head in the pillow I couldn't see his eyes, but I was sure if I did, they would see straight through me. I couldn't hold the tears back.

He moved to massage my neck.

I nodded. It was the only response I could manage. I had thought he was being mean. He wasn't. He was doing the one thing I had hoped he would do for weeks now. He was telling me he cared. It was the one thing I wanted most today. The one thing I needed.

"Are we clear?" he asked.

I nodded again and kept my face in the pillow to hide my tears.

"And are you going to do what I tell you?"

I managed a giggle. "Do I have a choice?"

"Of course not," he said, giving me another light spank.

He couldn't see me smile.

Only one thing mattered tonight.

I am his and he cares.

~

Nick

I WOKE UP WITH HER HOLDING MY MORNING WOOD. IT WAS THE perfect way to start the day.

We'd taken our time pleasing each other this morning. She'd been so warm and soft in my hands, so tight and wet on my cock, perfection in every way.

Her moans and yelps had made perfect music. Her movements in sync with mine.

The face she'd made when she came, her O-face, was something I could never get tired of. It was the picture of her I carried around in my head all day.

We had all day to prepare for her country club shindig this evening, so we were lounging in bed when my phone rang.

It was Winston with news. Sabbatini had skipped town and left the country yesterday. Winston said he was certain that based on the information we'd given him, the feds would have a warrant out for him within the week.

Then he told me the even better news. I put it on speaker so Katie could hear.

"Winston you're on speaker now with Katie. Why don't you say that again?"

"*Morning, Miss Covington,*" Winston started. "*I got fingerprints off of some of his work papers yesterday, and we have a positive match. It's his print on the love note that was attached to the rock that went through your window.*"

"And?" Katie asked.

"*The LAPD conducted a search of his house and found a gun matching the caliber of the bullets that ended up in your wall. An arrest warrant has been issued for him, and I'm betting ballistics will show that his gun was the one that shot up your house. That should be enough to put him away.*"

"So it's over?" Katie asked.

"*Looks that way. At least as soon as we get our hands on him. As I told Nick, the bugger left the country yesterday,*" Winston responded.

Relief washed over Katie's face. "But he could come back, right?" Katie asked with a note of concern.

"*They put a flag on his passport too,*" Winston continued. "*He'll be nabbed as soon as he comes back into the country.*"

"How'd you manage that?" I asked.

"*Let's just say Katie's uncle Garth has a lot of pull with the cops. There's not much the old man can't get done.*"

After the call, we reluctantly left the bed to take a shower.

The combination of the hot water, soap, and her hands on me was heavenly.

She didn't want to turn into a prune though, so she left me to go make breakfast.

I had told her she was going to stop working for a while.

She took it better than I'd expected. Perhaps deep down she realized how destructive it had been for her to let that job destroy her.

She needed more days like our day at Disneyland. She needed to slow down and allow herself to take her work seriously without obsessing over it. She promised she would do what I told her, and I intended to hold her to it.

She was curious about how I had found Sabbatini and linked him to the missing money she had highlighted.

So, I did something I had never done before. I invited her into the cave and had her bring an extra chair. I proudly showed her what some of my programs could do.

She didn't understand any of the programming, but she was smart, and she quickly understood most of my tracking methodologies.

I had never let anybody join me in the cave, not even Hank. I had jealously guarded this information and the scope of my work from everyone.

I took her out for a ride on the Harley. Sunshine, the wind in your face, and the noise of the bike was always a good antidote to what ails you.

I parked at Venice Beach. We walked down the beach-front sidewalk until we found a nice little place to eat. We shared tacos and a nacho plate while watching the tourists and the surf.

The sunshine and fresh air had always lightened my mood, and it was working with her.

After lunch I turned north, and we cruised the Pacific Coast Highway up past Malibu and back. Nothing but sunshine and the salty ocean breeze. We returned home in the early afternoon, having accomplished absolutely nothing.

"I have a task for you," I told her when we got inside.

"Yes, Sir, Mr. Boss, Sir," she said sarcastically. This was on the mild end of the talk-back spectrum for her.

"Your job this afternoon is to sit down and watch television. You can pick between *The Bachelor*, *Survivor*, and *Judge Judy*."

"What if I want to watch something else?"

"Then you ask nicely," I told her.

It appeared she was about to say something back, but she kept it to herself. She walked over, turned on the television and grabbed the clicker. She scrolled down until she found *The Bachelor*.

She lifted her computer off the coffee table and opened it up.

I snatched it away from her, earning me the evil-eye but she held her tongue.

I joined her on the couch for her relaxation lesson.

She snuggled close and kissed my ear. "Thank you for caring," she whispered.

I didn't say anything, I merely pulled her closer.

She deserves it.

CHAPTER 25

NICK

NATURALLY THERE WAS A GUARD SHACK AND A GATE AT THE entrance. They couldn't let just anybody get into this exclusive acreage. The unwashed masses might trample the neatly trimmed shrubbery or steal a golf ball.

The guard recognized Katie, raised the gate, and waved us through.

The clubhouse was situated at the top of the hill. I stopped in the circular drive by the entrance while Katie fetched some help.

She returned with one of the waitstaff and a cart to carry her desserts inside.

I found a parking space at the end of the large parking lot filled with a shiny clean cars. Naturally, my Tahoe was the only American steel here. I spotted a lone Cadillac among the sea of imported luxury cars.

Some snob had even brought his Lamborghini. A lot of good a two-hundred-mile-an-hour car did him in LA traffic.

Katie had forgotten her tarts in the back seat. I carried the cardboard box of apple tarts to the clubhouse. Past the massive doors, the entrance hallway was lined with trophy cases, filled with silver cups and the like. They sure liked to congratulate themselves on hitting the little white ball around.

A few men were conversing a few yards past the trophy cases as I scanned the area for Katie with no success. "Deliveries are around the side," the closest one said, sneering at me and pointing back toward the door I had come in.

He could stuff it for all I cared. I ignored him and continued inside, looking for Katie.

The group mumbled among themselves, like the pussies they were.

Bite me.

Katie came rushing around the corner. "Oh, I forgot those," Katie said with a warm smile to match the spring in her step.

The sight of her made me forget the group of jerks I had just encountered.

She raised up on her toes and gave me a kiss. "Just bring them over here." She led me around the corner into the kitchen where we deposited the tarts. We moved out to the dining room. "You can just mingle out here for a moment. I need to go check on the silent auction setup."

One whole wall of the dining room was windows that overlooked the entire LA basin. Yesterday's wind had blown the smog out, making for quite a breathtaking view. This was a nice place for LA's movers and shakers to observe the rest of us.

An older gent walked up and offered his hand. "Garth Durham. You must be Nicolas Knowlton."

I shook with him. "Mr. Durham."

"Please call me Uncle Garth, the whole family does."

"Young man. I wanted to thank you personally, for all the help you have given Katherine. The entire family appreciates it more than you will ever know."

"I didn't do much," I told him.

“A fair bit more than that, if my sources are correct,” he said leaning closer. “Locating that Sabbatini fellow was quite good work.” He had the thinning hair of an old grandfather type, but his sharp gray eyes indicated a man who hadn’t slowed one bit.

We looked out the window for a moment.

“A very nice view is it not?” he asked.

“Sure is.”

“My sources in law enforcement tell me it was also very impressive the way you intercepted that money from Southeast Federal before it made its way to North Korea last year.”

This was a problem. “I'm not sure I know what you mean.” He knew way more than he should have. I thought only four people in the world knew about that.

“No need for modesty, Nicholas. I understand your work is quite brilliant.”

I didn't respond.

“Be that as it may.” He pulled out a business card and handed it to me. “The family is in your debt. Should I ever be able to be of assistance, do not hesitate to call.”

I took his card and pocketed it, with a smile. If Winston thought this guy had impressive contacts, then a favor from him could come in handy some day.

We shook again, and he excused himself with another thank you.

I turned back to the window, contemplating how he could have found out about Southeast Federal.

The view from here still reminded me of the zookeepers watching over the animals.

The rest of us down on the valley floor had a view that ended at our backyard fence or the neighbor’s house.

I tensed as I noticed another older man approach. The crease of the geezer’s brow didn't bode well for pleasant conversation. “Young man, young man, I'm afraid you're going to have to come back when you locate the appropriate attire.”

"What the hell's the right attire?" I demanded, in no mood to be told what to do by this bozo.

Bill Covington appeared out of nowhere. "Afternoon, Bob, what's the problem?"

"I was just asking this gentleman to comply with our dress code," Bob explained.

"It'll be okay for today, don't you think?" Bill asked, calmly placing a hand on the old man's shoulder. "Nick here is on Katherine's protection detail and a close personal friend. I can vouch for him."

Last week he'd wanted to punch my lights out, and today I was his close personal friend. Go figure.

"Yes, sir, Mr. Covington, but just this one time," Bob said as he shot me another disapproving glance before he turned on his heels and walked away.

"What's that all about?" I asked Bill. "Those turkeys over there are wearing shorts," I said, motioning to a pair of middle-aged men who had walked in the side door, wearing shorts and short-sleeve shirts.

Bill grinned. "That's golf attire, which is allowed. Bob's a stickler for the rules here. Men have to wear collared shirts, and denim is not allowed. Bob's the manager here, worked for us an awfully long time. We only removed the dinner-time tie requirement a few years ago, and he has a hard time letting go of the old ways."

"Count me out." I was wearing jeans today, same as any other day. Who needs a dress code, anyway? Half of Hollywood considered jeans with rips in them to be the height of fashion.

"You get used to it," he offered. "Enough of that. I really wanted to thank you, Nick, for all you've done for Katie. I understand from the Hanson folks that you ID'd the guy."

"Katie's really the one that did all the work. She figured out embezzling was going on at that company she was auditing. I just got the name to go with the bank account."

Bill grinned. “You're being too modest. But I want to thank you anyway,” he said, his hand on my shoulder.

“I promised I'd keep her safe,” I told him. That was certainly true, but was only part of it. It had started out as a commitment, but had become more than that, much more.

Katie appeared and snuggled against my side, wrapping her arm tightly around me. “I hope you're being nice to him,” Katie said to her brother. Her warmth up against my side reminded me why I was here.

“Absolutely. Now if you'll excuse me,” he said, “I have to mingle.”

“Was he? Was he behaving himself?” Katie asked.

“I guess, for a Covington.”

She hip-bumped me.

“At least he got that geezer over there to lay off,” I told her, pointing out Bob. “Even though I'm wearing jeans.”

“Yeah, he can be a grouch. I completely forgot about that, it's been a while since I've been up here.”

“Tell me again what the party is all about.”

“This is an annual fundraiser that the club holds, to raise money for a scholarship fund.”

“How much are we supposed to fork over?” I asked her, pulling my wallet out of my pocket.

“Put that away, she admonished me. “It doesn't work like that. Fifty dollars a plate goes to the fund, plus whatever we raise from the silent auction in the other room.”

“Should we go bid on something?”

Katie smiled. “That would be nice.”

The adjoining room contained several long tables with items and clipboards for the bidding.

The three creeps from the entrance hallway followed us, eyeing Katie.

“Who are those three bozos that just walked in after us?” I whispered to Katie.

She glanced back. "Joe, Vince, and Peter. They think of themselves as the Three Musketeers, but they're more like the Three Stooges."

We approached the first table. "And why are they staring at us?"

She leaned in. "Because they're losers. And because I used to date Joe in college."

"I knew there was a reason I didn't like them."

I'd never been to a silent auction, but I'd heard how they worked.

As we went down the tables, I didn't see anything particularly appealing. Who needs a spa day, or a wine and cheese basket, anyway? Eventually, we reached an item which was a one week getaway in Hawaii for two. It was something I could get behind.

There were already four bids on the clipboard. I added my name and doubled the last bid. I was going to get this for Katie.

Katie glanced at the bid I'd put down and elbowed me. "You must really want that."

"Part of your therapy. One week alone with me, sand, sunshine, and surf. And, plenty of beer, can't forget the beer."

"Can I bring my computer?" She knew the answer to that one.

"Books, you can bring books, bikinis, and sunscreen. Nothing else."

She reached up to kiss me, nothing too obvious in this setting, but enough for me to see Stooge number one over in the corner get ticked off. "Thank you for caring," she whispered. "I promise to be good."

I moved my hand from her waist down to her ass and gave her a squeeze. "Only during the daylight hours, I hope."

"Katherine, how have you been?" Stooge number one said, as the group walked up.

"Great, just great, Joe," she responded curtly.

So, now I knew that stooge number one, the guy that had told me to take my delivery around the side was her ex, dipshit Joe.

"Katherine, aren't you going to introduce us to your date?"

"Nick Knowlton," I offered.

I smiled and gave the weenie a vise-grip of a hand shake.

He winced, but didn't cry.

A shame. I should have tried harder.

Then the inevitable happened. "Knowlton? I seem to remember a Knowlton that we went to school with. Did you ever go to Brentmoor?" stooge number two asked.

"Sure did, Vince, for a while that is. Then he moved on," Katie answered for me.

Vince seemed puzzled "And where'd you go after Brent-moor?" he asked.

"SHK," I told him.

"SHK? I'm not sure I've heard of that. Where is it located?"

"Of course you guys wouldn't have heard of it," I answered. "It takes a special invitation to get in."

These bozos weren't smart enough to understand that SHK stood for the School of Hard Knocks. The Three Stooges were completely puzzled, but seemed afraid to admit that there was something they didn't know.

Total dipshits.

"You thinking about joining the club?" Joe asked.

"I hadn't thought about it. How does that work?" I asked, pulling Katie closer.

"Pretty simple, really. First, you need a referral from a current member," stooge number three, Peter, told me.

"I think he's got that handled," Katie said looking up at me before giving them her warmest smile.

"Then there's the net worth check. They don't let slackers in," Vince added.

More snobbery.

"Then the interview with the membership committee," Joe added.

I didn't bother to respond.

"And of course the background check," Joe said.

My jaw clenched.

Asswipe.

Joe's smirk indicated he might know about my problem with a background check, but I couldn't be sure.

"And it helps if you went to USC like we all did. They're kind of partial to USC grads," Peter added.

"You mean the University of Spoiled Children?" I shot back.

I thought it was funny, but only Katie laughed. The Three Stooges didn't appreciate the dig.

Hank, who had gone to UCLA, had taught me the moniker they used referring to rival USC people.

"You must have gone to UCLA then," Joe said.

I shook my head. "No."

"Where'd you go to school?" Vince asked.

I hesitated. "Folsom."

"Is that a state school, or what?" Vince asked.

"It's a state institution all right," Joe told him, giving him an elbow to the ribs.

Katie pulled me away. "We should check the other room."

"I don't care for your friends much," I told her softly as we passed into the main dining room with the view.

By the window we ran into two more of Katie's friends who she introduced as Marlene and Jessica.

A waiter meandered by with wine glasses on a tray. "Cabernet or Chablis," he offered.

"What vintage?" Marlene asked.

"The Cabernet is a Beringer 2012, and the Chablis is the house white," the waiter told them.

They each took a glass of the red.

Jessica complained that she would have preferred the 2011 vintage.

The poor waiter merely shrugged.

Katie picked a glass of the white.

"You don't want any wine?" Marlene asked.

"I'll wait for the beer," I said.

The two snobby ladies thought that was funny.

"Angelo, could you fetch a Budweiser for Mr. Knowlton," Katie requested of the waiter. "Please."

He nodded and left.

"They don't serve beer in the dining room," Marlene snickered.

"They do now," Katie responded.

I took a deep breath to calm myself.

The two snobs excused themselves.

"They aren't all like that," Katie whispered to me after they had left.

I hoped she was right.

Angelo returned with a can of Bud and a glass.

I grabbed the can, left the glass, and thanked him.

I pulled her into my side and took in the view.

Katie and I stayed by the window for the longest time. You could see the hills of Palos Verdes. The houses of several million people were in sight from this vantage point.

Katie put her empty glass down. "I'm going to go check on the kitchen for a moment. Don't get into any trouble."

I scanned the crowd for a few minutes before deciding on a bathroom break.

Even the restroom in this place was beyond upscale. Marble for the floors and mahogany for the walls. The gold faucets in the sinks might have been real gold. The urinals were occupied by two older gentlemen, so I took a stall. Moments later the familiar voices of the Three Stooges told me they had entered the room.

"You're kidding right?" the voice that belonging to Vince asked.

"You're such a dunce Vince," Joe said back. "Folsom isn't a state school you idiot. It's a prison, up near Sacramento. Sometimes I don't know how they let you graduate."

"He's an ex-con?" Vince asked.

I clenched my fists.

"Well, he wasn't a fucking guard," Peter said, piling on poor Vince.

"You know, you should tell your dad. Inviting an ex-con here might be just the thing he could use to get those stupid Covingtons off the board, and make a slot for you," Vince suggested.

I stayed quiet, waiting for them to leave, biding my time, lest they lock me up for murdering one of these motherfuckers.

"That's a good idea, I'll talk to Dad on the way home," Joe said.

"I can't believe Katherine's standards have fallen so low," Peter added.

It took all of my will power to keep from opening the stall door and flattening the three creeps.

"Yeah, Joe, you were engaged to her once, I bet you could probably get her back easy now," Vince said.

"That's a good idea too," Joe said as I heard them finally leave.

Over my dead body.

I waited a minute before leaving. I returned to my spot by the window. Admiring the city was more appealing than striking up a conversation with anyone in this crowd.

From the other side of the ficus tree I heard the distinctive nasal twang of Katie's snobby friend Marlene.

"I thought Katherine Covington had more class than that," Marlene said.

"Poor girl. She was fired from Arthur and Company and now she's involved with a man like him," her friend Jessica said.

"I'll bet he has tattoos," a third voice added.

"Who did he murder?" a fourth voice asked.

"No, it was drugs. I'll bet he spiked her apple pie," voice number three said.

"I'm certainly not touching it," Marlene said.

"Me either," Jessica added.

It was too much for me, so I left for the far end of the room.

CHAPTER 26

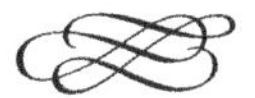

Katie

Bob, the club manager, called the guests in to sit down to dinner. We were seated at a family table with Bill, Lauren, Uncle Garth, his wife, Bob Hanson, Nick, and I.

The dinner was quite pleasant, with Bill behaving himself, and Lauren taking a particular interest in talking to Nick.

Uncle Garth made an interesting comment about Nick's abilities that I didn't understand, but Nick's knowing glance indicated he did.

Because we had such a large crowd and a limited kitchen, the entrees were either chicken or fish.

I had chosen chicken for both of us.

The desserts were potluck serve yourself from a long table. I had brought my pies as I always did, and there were Mrs. Huddleston's cherry cobbler, the chocolate mousse cake Mrs. Barry always brought, and a new addition—strawberry shortcake.

Surprisingly, at the end of the dinner, very little of my pies had been eaten. It appeared the women in particular were avoiding my pie this year.

I must've done something wrong with it because it had always been gobbled up before.

When Bob started announcing the results of the silent auction, I waited anxiously to hear Nick's name called when they got to the week in Hawaii.

Nick scowled when Joseph E. Hunsinger the third come over the speakers as the winner.

Joe had probably done it on purpose to spite us, the weasel.

"It'll be cheaper for us to buy it ourselves anyway," I whispered to Nick to console him.

It didn't seem to help, as his eyes shot daggers in Joe's direction.

At the end of the presentations we said our goodbyes to my family.

"I liked your pie," Nick said as we walked past the dessert table.

"I guess this is the year for cherry cobbler," I said, snaking my arm around him. "Usually I beat Mrs. Huddleston by a mile."

Nick stiffened, pulled me close and kissed the top of my head. "They don't know what they missed."

"And remember to call me if you need anything," Uncle Garth mentioned to Nick as we reached the door.

"Sure thing," Nick said as he shook Uncle Garth's hand.

"I think he likes you," I said as the door closed behind us.

"I guess that makes one of them."

Nick was quiet as we drove back to his place. We crossed the freeway before he opened his mouth. "Is it usually like that?"

"Like what?" I wasn't sure what he meant. The dinner had been pretty much the way those things normally went. Not the part about Joe being rude and trying to upstage him by grabbing the Hawaii vacation, but everything else.

"Pretty normal," I told him.

"That's what I was afraid of," Nick said, implying more than he was saying.

"What do you mean?"

Nick sighed, shook his head, and drove on.

I didn't bring it up again, the scowl on his face said it all. He had not enjoyed the evening.

He opened the door and ushered me inside.

He silently walked to the cabinet and retrieved his scotch and a glass. "You want one?"

"Sure. Are we going to talk?"

"About what?"

"About what your problem is."

He poured himself a glass and took out one for me. "I don't have a problem. I'm not so sure I like your friends very much."

"Yeah, Joe has always been a dick, not that I'd ever call him my friend."

Nick poured a smaller one for me and handed it over. "Is that why you got engaged to him?"

That was certainly not something I was expecting. We'd been engaged for all of about two weeks before I called it off. Hardly anybody knew about it at the time. "I'm sorry, I didn't say anything about it because I didn't think it was important. He's still a dick."

Nick emptied his glass. "I agree."

I took a sip of the scotch as I watched him walk into the bedroom. Where did this leave us now? We hadn't discussed it.

Nick had promised to keep me safe, and he had. I'd been protected, knowing as long as I was in danger he would keep his commitment, as he kept all his commitments, and be by my side. Now the danger was over, and I was afraid he wasn't bound to me anymore.

Acquaintances with benefits I had said, and I had meant it. This had certainly morphed into friends with benefits, and more. Nick had grown on me in a way I certainly hadn't expected.

Katie had gone home with him, in an impulsive anti-Katherine moment, but it was no longer impulsive attraction. No longer just hormones, or pheromones, or lust. I had fallen for him. Hard.

I did my best to banish the thoughts from my consciousness as I finished the glass and followed him into the bedroom.

He was standing there, silently waiting for me in the partial darkness.

"Nick," I said as I reached him. Words failed me.

His finger to my lips commanded silence.

Silently, and slowly, he unbuttoned my blouse.

"Nick," I whispered as it slid to the floor.

A finger pointed at me reminded me of his previous command. He didn't want me to talk. This wasn't a time for words, it was a time for touching, a time for hands and lips and tongues.

I worked at the buttons of his shirt as his fingers traced the outline of my bra and teased the sensitive skin up to my collar-bone out to my shoulders and back to my neck.

He traced my cleavage and slipped his fingers inside my bra, coming teasingly close but not touching the hardened little peaks of my nipples.

When I finished the last of his shirt buttons and slid the fabric off his shoulders, he slipped a hand behind me and with a quick pinch of practiced fingers undid the hooks.

I unzipped my skirt and slid it past my hips, kicking it aside as it pooled at my feet. I stood in front of him naked, save for a thong and my heels.

"My God, you're so fucking beautiful," he said in a voice raspy and coated in lust.

I couldn't control the blush rising from my chest to my cheeks. He'd said it before, but tonight the conviction in his voice conveyed more than the words ever had. The passion in his eyes sent heated liquid to melt my thong.

I didn't have the words for him, and he had commanded my

silence. All I could do was show him. I circled a hand behind the nape of his neck and speared his hair with the other, pulling myself up to him, my mouth to his. I kissed him like I had never kissed a man before.

I covered his mouth, my tongue demanded entrance and began the dance with his. I tasted the whiskey on him as we exchanged breath, hunger for each other, and lust. I tried to give back to him as good as he gave me. It seemed I never could.

His hands found my back and my ass, pulling me into him, against him hard. I could barely breathe. I didn't care.

I broke the kiss and pushed away enough to reach his belt. I fumbled as I tried to undo the thing. Finally it loosened, and I was able to pull the zipper down. I wasted no time hooking my fingers into his underwear and pulling them and his pants down to his ankles, freeing his cock.

He shucked his shoes and stepped out of his pants. He grabbed the sides of my thong and with a forceful yank snapped the garment free.

We fell back onto the bed, me on top of him, heels and all. My legs straddled his as I rubbed my soaked slit the length of his cock. I leaned over, my breasts scraping against his chest, my eyes conveying my wordless wishes to him.

He kneaded my breasts as I sat up and he tweaked my nipples, sending shocks through me.

I moved down and took him in my mouth for a moment to finish the act that I had never fully performed for a man. I could do it tonight, I could swallow it. I wanted to, for him.

"Not tonight, Princess," he said as he pulled me up to him and rolled us over.

Pinned below him, I clawed at his back to pull him closer. I was his to take, to have as he wished. I wanted him inside me. But he stayed there pushed up on arms extended at my sides, his eyes devouring me.

"You are so fucking beautiful," he repeated, with hunger in his eyes.

A tear came to my eyes. The truth of his emotions shone in his eyes.

I worked my hands over his torso, his arms, his neck, feeling the bunched muscles as his eyes continued to dance over me.

He leaned and reached for the nightstand to get a condom.

I pulled his arm back. "Not tonight. Please. I'm on the pill and I'm clean."

He lowered his head to mine and kissed my nose. "Me too," he whispered.

I spread my legs to welcome him.

Slowly he positioned himself at my entrance and pushed in.

He laughed as I pulled my knees up and grabbed my ankles. "Brought your shoes to bed. I like it."

The sensation as he entered me was pure bliss. We fit so perfectly and he filled me so fully it was as if his cock was made for me and me for him.

He completed me when he was inside me, gliding in and out, thrusting in and out, pounding in and out, it didn't matter. The way he made me feel was nothing I had ever expected to find.

With every thrust I clenched tighter around him. He was bringing me closer and closer to the cliff, building pressure within me I couldn't withstand as the sensations crashed through me. The tension built. I didn't want to come, I didn't want it to be over.

I held off my orgasm as long as I could. All I wanted was to stay like this, joined with Nick. I wrapped my heels behind him and pulled him in.

I rocked into him. I gave him all I had, all I could. I was his, completely. I needed to be his, to stay his.

With several more powerful thrusts, Nick reached the end of his rope and exploded inside me. He pushed harder and deeper pounding into me, pushing me over the cliff into my soul-blistering orgasm, as we screamed out each other's names.

I untangled my legs, and he collapsed on top of me, panting, sweating, spent.

All I could hear was my pulse banging in my ears. The pounding of our hearts beating together against each other's chests filled my thoughts.

I had given him all I had, for him to take. My body and my heart.

He had taken the first, but I feared he didn't want the second. I needed more time to show him, to convince him, to win him.

As our jagged breathing slowed and the pulsating of his cock inside me dissipated he rolled off me to the side.

I nestled up against him, my arm over his chest, my head on his shoulder, sensing the beat of his heart. The heart I wanted so much to win.

I shed my heels and spooned with my man before sleep won out. One of his legs over one of mine, his arm around me cupping my breast, a tear in my eye, and a longing in my heart.

He owned my heart. I longed for his.

ONLY A HINT OF MORNING LIGHT SNUCK BY THE EDGES OF THE shades.

I woke to find Nick out of bed and getting dressed. I rubbed the sleep out of my eyes, trying to understand the scene in front of me.

He was packing clothes in his backpack. He was leaving.

I had lost. He was leaving and I couldn't help the apprehension. He wasn't coming back, at least not for me.

We had said this would be casual, with no attachments, no commitments, nothing to regret. I only had myself to blame for my feelings. I had told myself I could handle it. I had been wrong. This I couldn't handle.

I couldn't hold him. I couldn't demand he stay. I wouldn't beg him to stay. I longed for him and needed him to feel the same way.

I'd sensed a change after the country club party last night. I had lost him, but I'd really never had him, had I?

Last night he'd made love to me. Real love, not just sex, not just fucking our brains out. Not last night. He had given me all he had, and I had returned all I had from the bottom of my heart. My broken heart.

But now he was leaving.

If I thought crying could keep him, I would've bawled all morning. If I thought arguing would've kept him, I would've yelled.

My uncle Garth once told me "*The heart wants what the heart wants. You can't fool it and you can't convince it to change.*" The problem was, mine wanted Nick's, but his didn't want mine.

"You're awake," he said.

I commanded my eyes to stay dry. I wouldn't be the weeping woman today.

"You leaving?" I asked, knowing the answer before he said anything.

"I've got a job I've been putting off for a while,"

He zipped up the backpack. "You're safe now with Sabbatini out of the country and a flag on his passport. I have to do this job and get back to work."

I hoped I might be wrong. That it might be only a temporary absence, to return to me.

"How long will you be gone?"

"I don't know."

"Any guess?" I should have held my tongue. I sounded like the clingy woman. Even I didn't like how I sounded.

"As long as it takes."

"Will you call?" Another thing I regretted saying as soon as the words escaped my lips.

"Not sure I can. I'll see you around when I get back."

There it was. *Not sure he could call* meant clear as day he didn't want to call. He didn't say he would see me as soon as he got back. He said he would see me around. It was as noncommittal as it could get. He didn't want the clingy woman. He wanted me to disappear.

I'd pushed too hard. I'd lost him.

I had asked for a commitment he couldn't make. I hadn't given him the space he needed.

I closed my eyes and put my head in the pillow. I heard him walk out, and when I looked up again, the room was as empty as my heart.

I heard the door close.

It was over.

Slowly I got up and willed my legs to take me to the shower.

Once under the hot water I couldn't control my tears anymore. The wall was the only thing keeping me upright as it all came out. I grabbed the soap and told myself I was a survivor. At least I hadn't left tear stains on his pillow.

I finally emerged from the shower, dried off, and pulled on clean clothes.

An hour later I'd packed all the things I had brought over to Nick's into my car and drove the few blocks back to Myrtle Street. The place I belonged. At his house I was merely a temporary guest.

Once inside I busied myself unpacking my clothes and putting things away. As I placed my toothbrush and deodorant back in the bathroom, I realized how final this move was.

Being at Nick's house had only been a temporary arrangement anyway, a safe haven away from the maniac Sabbatini. It had never really been meant to be permanent, even semi-permanent. It was so Nick could take care of me exactly as he had promised.

He'd promised to get me safely back from Las Vegas and he had.

He'd promised to keep me safe from my attacker, and he had.

He'd promised to fuck my brains out without any strings, and he had.

I was the one who hadn't kept the promise I'd made to him and myself. The promise to keep it casual. It had become so much harder than I realized.

The sex had been great, better than great, fantastic, but that wasn't it. Falling for Nick had been so natural, so inevitable, so right for me. He was the right man for me, the complement to Katherine's obsessive nature, the antidote to Katherine's risk-aversion, the patch to everything missing in Katherine's life.

But he didn't want me.

I climbed back into bed and the tears started all over again.

After lunch I finally got up and dressed for a walk. I needed some activity to take my mind off of my situation.

CHAPTER 27

Nick

I COULDN'T BEAR TO MEET HER EYES AS I LEFT. I SO WANTED FOR her to have everything she deserved, and she deserved better than me, much better than me.

I drove my truck south. I needed to put miles between me and her, before I changed my mind and made a mistake I would regret, she would regret.

I'd promised to protect her, and I'd failed. I'd kept her safe from Sabbatini, that part was true. But I hadn't kept her safe from me. That's where I'd failed. I hadn't realized the danger to her.

Katherine Covington and I were from different worlds. I had told her as much when we'd started whatever it was we had become to one another. Fuck buddies, transitioning to friends and lovers. And yes, I loved her.

How far apart our worlds were, though, had actually escaped me until last night at her country club, among her friends.

I was the fish out of water. As far as they were concerned I was the fish to be stuffed, mounted on the wall, laughed at and ridiculed. I had the smell of loser, the smell of ex-con, the smell of high school dropout on me. Staying around Katie risked having it rub off on her and corrupt her in her own world.

I hadn't realized how closed-minded the people in her circle were. It shouldn't have been a surprise. Those who had it all often looked down upon those who didn't. Theirs was a closed society. Entrance was controlled by birthright. Even to those born into it, the wrong actions could get you ridiculed and banished.

I couldn't doom her to a life of ridicule from her peers. I couldn't make hers a lifetime of explaining me, of justifying me, of protecting me from them. I wouldn't be the cause of her destruction, I couldn't.

Two days ago I'd told her I was the only one who cared enough about her to tell her when she was fucking up. Today I had to be the one who cared enough about her to leave her in order to save her. Save her from me.

It was clear she wanted me to stay, but it was only because she didn't understand what was good for her. The same way she didn't understand her own destructive tendency to obsess about her work.

I had to be man enough to do the right thing for her and leave before it was too late. It was the hardest thing I'd ever done, even harder than going to prison to save my brother, but no less right.

I was doing the only thing I could to protect her. The right thing, the honorable thing.

The thought made me laugh out loud. The last thing those Three Stooges last night would've suspected me of was doing the honorable thing. They wouldn't understand an honorable motivation if it bit them in the ass.

Cocksuckers.

I was well on my way to San Diego when seven-thirty rolled around. I grabbed my phone and dialed my contact, Gavin Krause, at Bensonhurst Aerospace. They'd been after me for two months to come in and do a security sweep and locate the intruder and the hole in their systems. I need to be on-site to do it right, which was where I was heading now.

I reminded him what my obscenely high hourly rate was. It didn't bother him one bit. I demanded a bonus if I managed a quick resolution of their problem.

He put me on hold, and three minutes later agreed to my demands. They needed me, badly.

He gave me the address of a Denny's in San Diego to meet him and set up my undercover ID at Bensonhurst.

I need work to take my mind off of Katie.

Katie

I WALKED SEEMINGLY FOREVER. I STOPPED AT A SMALL restaurant for a very late lunch. I hadn't eaten anything all day, but all I ordered was a small BLT.

With the distance I had come it would be near dark by the time I retraced my steps. The house on Myrtle Street wasn't really my home, but it was the closest thing I had to one.

I came close to crying again at the thought. I had lost everything: my house, my job, my career, and now my boyfriend. I been reticent to apply the label to Nick, but it was the label that stuck. He had been that much and more. Definitely more, much more than an acquaintance with benefits, as we had started out.

He certainly wasn't an acquaintance anymore, he had become a good friend, no, a dear friend, but better than *a friend*. My only best friend.

The one man I had felt truly close to, truly at ease with, the one I could trust implicitly.

He had always said our worlds were different, but when I

was with him, they overlapped. He could get me to laugh and see things I hadn't seen before. He both took care of me and cared about how I took care of myself.

I realized now how endearing his bossiness was. In his way he was showing me how much he cared. If I hadn't been important in his view of things, he wouldn't have tried to tell me what to do. Instead he probably would've ignored me.

What he had done was the opposite of ignore me. From the first day, when he'd changed his schedule to give me a ride back to LA, he had put his entire life on hold for me. He had put his work on hold and passed up untold commissions or fees, or whatever he called them.

Outwardly I had complained to him when he'd tried to make me take time off of my work, to relax and do simple things. Inwardly I cherished his concern for my well-being.

He had become the ultimate cure to what afflicted me.

A drug to my system is what he had become. I needed to be around him. I needed to make love to him to show him how much I cared. I needed him to boss me around to show me in his own way how much he cared.

But now I was in withdrawal, and it sucked. My heart ached from his absence. With every motorcycle I heard, I turned, hoping to see Nick riding toward me. Every man in a leather jacket walking past reminded me of him. Couples holding hands reminded me of what I had lost.

I followed the endless sidewalk back to Myrtle Street, one foot in front of the other, dreading the emptiness awaiting me there. It was nearly dark by the time I dragged myself up to the front door.

Opening the door, the chirping of the alarm panel sounded. Even it reminded me of Nick, and the day he had spent overseeing the installation, all to keep me safe.

After a microwave dinner, I didn't have the energy to watch television. I finished my beer and realized how he had changed me. Before Nick, I had only drunk wine it seemed. Except for the night at the club, I hadn't had wine in a month.

I had hoped all the walking would exhaust me to the point where I could get some sleep. It didn't work.

Every time I turned over in bed I reached out my arm, hoping to find his warmth next to me. Hoping for the opportunity to cuddle again. Hoping for the opportunity to wrap my legs around him again and join our two bodies as one. Hoping he was here.

NICK HAD LEFT THREE DAYS AGO. THREE HORRIBLE EMPTY DAYS, and three sleepless nights.

Each day I had walked farther along the boulevard. Each day I had hoped it would exhaust me enough to force sleep when I lay down at night.

It hadn't worked.

I'd asked if he would call. I heard his words from that morning in my head. He wasn't sure he would be able to.

I had hoped, however, that being apart would make him miss me so much he might actually want to call. Take the time to call. Care enough to call.

Each day I had been disappointed.

I composed myself before I pressed the doorbell.

Bill opened the door. He peered down the hallway.

He expected to see Nick behind me. I lunged forward and hugged my oldest brother.

He pulled me inside and closed the door. "Katie, where's Nick?"

I didn't answer I only hugged him harder.

"What's wrong?" He rubbed his hand over my back.

I needed to toughen up. I released him and walked inside.

"Katie," he called after me.

"You got anything here a girl could have for breakfast?" I

asked as cheerily as I could manage without turning back to face Bill.

Lauren came out of the other room with a questioning look. "Katie. You're here early." She gave me a quick embrace.

"I could use something to eat." It was no joke, I was trembling, and I needed something in my stomach to calm me.

"Sure," Lauren said, as she pulled orange juice out of the fridge. "Would you like to start with OJ?"

"Sounds great," I responded.

I barely had the glass in my hand before my bullheaded brother yanked me over to the couch. "What did he do?" He tensed up. "So help me if he hurt—"

"No, it's not that," I said cutting him off. "Nick would never hurt me."

Lauren left for the other room as Bill sat me down.

"Tell me then," he said in the tone he used when he was trying to stand in for Dad.

I shook my head. How could I admit to my brother how I'd agreed to a friends-with-benefits arrangement with a guy? A guy he'd never approved of in the first place.

Bill sat next to me and pulled me into his side.

I could barely breathe. I was so ashamed.

"Katie. You need to talk to me. Did you two break up?"

I nodded, trying in vain to hold back the tears flowing down my cheeks. I threw my arms around him and sobbed into his chest. My oldest brother was the one who had always been there for me.

I'd lost my house, my job, and now my man, even though he was never really my man. I wanted to have my stupid job back even if it was the job from hell with the devil himself as my boss. I wanted to have the house I'd spent so long decorating back.

I wanted it all back the way it was, but it was a wish no one could grant, not even Bill.

My brother held me in his arms without saying a thing. He gave me the silence I needed right now, instead of the lecture he normally would have given me. My tears soaked his shirt.

I sat up and sniffled. "Nick's gone." Saying it out loud made it seem even more final. I'd come here to talk, but I'd suddenly lost the courage. "I was so stupid, silly when you think about it."

Bill gently brushed the hair away from my face, silently urging me to go on.

"We said it was…" I didn't know how to explain casual fuck buddies to my brother. Acquaintances-with-benefits didn't sound right. "We said we were gonna keep it casual. No strings, no attachments, just two friends."

My brother's eyes were filled with knowing kindness. "Do you love him?"

I sniffled again and nodded.

"We can't choose who we love," he said, "Or who we don't. Our hearts choose for us. It can't work any other way."

"I ended up thinking we could be more than…" I couldn't say out loud how I expected the sex to progress to love.

"You don't need to tell me any more."

I managed a weak giggle. "I wasn't going to."

"I had Uncle Garth and the Hanson firm look into him," he told me. "He's really not the guy I thought he was."

"He's a good man. He's had it rougher than you'll ever know, and he's had to make sacrifices. Bigger sacrifices than you can imagine."

"You mean his brother?" Bill asked.

It startled me. "You know about that?"

"Uncle Garth found out a few days ago."

I picked up the glass and took another sip of orange juice.

"What happened between you two?" Bill asked softly.

"I don't know," I said peering into my orange juice. "At the club Tuesday night Joe and those stupid friends of his were mean to him."

"Joe Hunsinger? That little prick?"

I nodded.

"The little shit," Bill spat.

"Nick was sort of sullen on the way home, and in the morning… The next morning he said he had to leave to do some work."

I took another sip of orange juice to give myself time to think. I couldn't explain this to myself, much less my brother. I wiped my nose on my sleeve. "He said he would see me around."

I put the juice down and hugged my brother again burying my face into him. "I asked if he'd call," I sobbed. "He said he didn't think so."

My brother held me tight and kissed the top of my head. "Then he's not as bright as I thought he was. Or he's just a pussy if he couldn't take a little shit from the likes of Hunsinger."

I stayed in my brother's arms until my tear ducts dried out from overuse. I sat up and brushed my hair back. "What about the breakfast you promised?"

After breakfast Bill said he needed to go to work.

Lauren told him she would follow along later, obviously wanting to keep me company for at least a while.

I appreciated the gesture. I needed to talk to another woman.

After Bill left, Lauren pulled white wine out of the fridge and poured us both glasses.

"Isn't it a little early to be drinking?" I asked.

"I think you need it," she said. "Or at least you deserve it."

I nodded. I downed the glass quickly, needing something to dull the pain.

She poured me another, and we took a seat on the couch.

"It all seemed to be going so well," I told her.

"What happened?"

I took a cleansing breath and tried to compose my thoughts. I hoped to get through this without more tears.

"I think the visit to the club the other night scared him," I said.

She put down her glass. "He didn't seem to be having a terribly good time, but the club can be a bit much."

I took another sip of my wine. "I think it was Joe Hunsinger."

"Who's he?" she asked. I hadn't ever told Lauren about Joe. He'd been a distant memory by the time she married Bill.

Trying to make this glass last longer than the first I twisted it in my hand. "Ex-boyfriend from college, ex-fiancé actually, but only for two weeks."

She waited for me to continue.

"He and his stupid buddies were mean to Nick. They insinuated he couldn't get into the club, he couldn't qualify."

"Maybe it's not important to him," Lauren offered.

I hadn't considered that. "And I guess some of my friends also weren't very nice when Nick wanted to get a beer instead of wine."

Lauren laughed.

I needed more laughter. Laughter was good for me now.

"Over a beer?" Lauren asked.

"Seems so stupid doesn't it?"

Lauren reached over to touch my arm. A simple gesture but quite comforting. "You want to know what I think?"

I nodded.

"Something upset him that night at the club. I don't know what it is, but what you told me doesn't sound right."

"But I don't remember anything else happening," I replied.

"I can tell you what I saw on Sunday at the Habitat project was a man head over heels in love with you."

Her words shocked me. I knew Nick cared, he had said as much. But caring was not the same as love. I was sure the morning after the club, when he'd rejected me, that he didn't want my love, that he couldn't return my love.

"You really think so?" I asked hopefully.

"You'd have to be blind, or a fool to have missed it."

I had missed it so I guess I was blind and a fool. None of this made sense.

"But he left. When I asked if he would even call, he said no." I was losing the battle to keep my tears at bay. "All he would commit to was he would see me around maybe." He hadn't actually said *maybe* but it was my interpretation.

"Look," she said slowly. "I can't tell you about that. But I've seen you two together a few times, and on Sunday the man was one hundred percent in love with you, girl."

I drank some more wine. "But what do I do now?"

"Figure out what you did to spook him maybe, or sit and wait a little while. Men can be pretty stupid creatures sometimes. They're physically strong and they can be courageous, slay dragons and more, but emotions scare them. They have the emotional intelligence of lizards."

I giggled.

"The feelings in his eyes when he looked at you are the kind that don't disappear overnight," she added.

I tried to absorb what she was saying and hope.

"Give it some time. I doubt you're the only one hurting right now. I have no idea what it is, but he may have something he has to sort out."

CHAPTER 28

Katie

It was early Monday morning, and I hadn't gotten a call or a text. Nothing.

Nick didn't care about me. He'd been honest about that part from the beginning. We were supposed to keep it casual, no emotional entanglements. He'd kept his promise.

He didn't care the way I did. It was obvious now. Not only had he left, but he hadn't called or sent so much as a text message saying good morning, or a message saying he'd be back next week, or next month.

My father had taught me long ago to work with the way things were rather than wishing they were different.

Nick didn't care. I had to face my reality. Wishing for it to change wouldn't do any good.

After a quick breakfast, I picked up my Susan B. Anthony dollar and rubbed it between my fingers. I had never needed a man before, my work or my school goal had always kept me occupied. Compared to today those had been happier times. I was writing off Nick Knowlton as a failed experiment. I needed a goal now, something to do to keep me busy, to focus me, to heal me.

I picked up my phone and dialed.

He'd be up at this time of day because he worked in construction.

"*Katie, what are you doing calling me this time of the morning?*" Phil asked when he answered his phone. Phil Patterson was one of my brother Patrick's best friends from high school.

"I want to buy the house on Myrtle Street, I'm going to enlarge it," I told him matter-of-factly.

"*You fucking nuts?*"

I rubbed my coin between my fingers again. "One hundred percent serious." I was standing in the house right now and I knew what my goal was going to be, at least for the short term.

There was silence on the other end.

"Well?" I asked.

"*You have no fucking idea what you're getting into. The place is a dump. You can't just add on to it. It needs to be completely redone. All these idiots on TV make it look like it's a piece a cake. But it fucking isn't. It's hard work=*"

I cut him off. "And you think I can't do hard work? Is that it?"

"*No, that's not it at all. Patrick will fuckin' kill me when he finds out I let you get in over your head,*" he yelled.

I wasn't going to be deterred by any asshole yelling at me through the phone. "How much do you want for it? I'll make it worth your while."

"*I was going to split the lot. I can't just sell it to you.*"

"Philip Patterson, if you don't agree to sell it to me right now I'll make sure Patrick kills you, and then breaks you in two, and then kills each half again."

He finally believed I was serious, and two minutes later we agreed on a price.

Now I had a project to keep me busy, to keep my mind off of Nick. A project to keep me sane.

I know what I'm going to do.

~

Nick

It'd been a week. I had tried everything: long runs, hot showers, extra glasses of scotch before bed, nothing worked. Sleep continued to elude me. Every time I closed my eyes a vision of Katie painted itself on my eyelids; I smelled Katie; I felt Katie.

After a fitful hour or so of sleep I would awaken, and stretch my arm out, only to find empty sheets alongside me, before trying to fall asleep again. She wasn't anywhere here except in my mind, and it was killing me.

Women had always been so easy. What was the saying? *Find 'em, fuck 'em, and forget 'em.* It'd always worked for me. The variety had always been entertaining, and once onto the next I'd never considered going back.

Not until now. Katie had a hold on me I couldn't deny. The distance should've provided relief, but it didn't.

A dozen times I'd picked up my phone and considered calling her. Each time it was a harder decision than the last to put the phone down.

Unable to get back to sleep again, I powered up the little coffee machine in my hotel room.

After a quick shower I grabbed the coffee and opened my laptop.

I was awfully close to identifying the culprits at Bensonhurst. The key to finding the pattern had been to recognize how only half of the company data came from the obvious suspect.

When I reformulated the problem to search for the communication path to two suspects instead of one, I'd found the similarities.

After a few hours of work I had the answer.

It was six in the morning, but I suspected Gavin wouldn't mind a call this early, given the news I had.

It took a few rings to get through, and his answer was even groggier than I'd expected.

"Better get your checkbook ready, Gavin, I think I got the evidence for you."

That woke him up. "No shit? Who is it?"

I hadn't mentioned to him yet, my conclusion: He actually had two moles in his company.

"I caught not one fish, but two," I told him.

"Are you sure?"

"Pretty sure. No, make that absolutely sure. I know they're responsible for the breach, but I don't have the goods on them yet if you want to charge them criminally. For that I'm gonna have to go back to my home base and pull the matching financial data. I think it should sew it up for you."

"Who is it? Who are they?"

"I'll let you know the names as soon as I have the financial tie-ins. Shouldn't be more than a day or so."

"I need them now. We can't risk any more disclosures."

"It won't be a problem," I told him. "The communications have been running on two week cycles like clockwork. They're not due again for another ten days. I need to be absolutely sure and have everything tied up for you with a nice red bow on top. I have this thing about accusing somebody of a crime without perfect evidence."

"So, tomorrow maybe?"

"Get your checkbook ready. I'll give you one name and the second and all the evidence as soon as I get the wire transfer."

"Not very trusting are you?"

"No, and I don't take Visa or MasterCard either."

He laughed, and we agreed to be in touch later.

I skipped a shower and headed down to the breakfast buffet. A little food, a full tank of gas, and I was out of this godforsaken town.

Maybe I'd be able to get to sleep if I was in my own bed. I could always hope.

~

Katie

I HAD MOVED INTO PATRICK'S CONDO. IT MADE MORE SENSE TO be up here next to Bill and Lauren for meals with a kitchen and a bedroom, instead of living in the middle of a remodel.

I had met with three architects and gone over a half-dozen different plans. When I introduced myself as William Covington's sister and told them I had a rush project, they couldn't wait to meet me and tap into a Covington bank account. I'd also made sure to tell them that there were bonuses involved for early completion.

Each had asked about the budget and telling them there wasn't one had gotten their attention.

It'd been tiring, but it's what I'd wanted. Something to occupy my time and my mind.

I was back at Myrtle Street with the latest set of plans laid out on the table. I checked the plans again and every time I did, I saw Nick's face.

He still prevented me from sleeping.

I laughed at the thought. Nick had always kept me from sleeping very well; we kept waking up and getting busy. Those nights had been the best of my life even if I hadn't always gotten as much sleep as I'd wanted. I'd never felt cheated in the morning, instead I'd always felt cherished.

I had no idea if it was the right word; I had no idea about a lot of things anymore.

Life had been so simple as Katherine. Katherine would get up and put on her nice, sensible clothes. She would put on her nice, sensible makeup and go to her sensible job—even if it wasn't nice.

Katherine had had a routine, and she'd stuck to it. It had kept her busy, kept her occupied. There wasn't a minute of the day that hadn't gone by where she wasn't working toward her goal.

Now what did I have?

I had a small old house with a nice pool and a large lot. I could turn it into a nice large house with a nice pool on a large lot.

But the house still had an emptiness about it.

Katherine had been used to living alone, she always had. She'd never even moved in with Joe, or he with her.

Katie, though, had spent several weeks moved in with Nick, unable to live here because of the threat from Sabbatini. It had been nice, better than nice, it'd been homey, and comforting. It had felt right.

After waking up next to Nick day after day, an empty bed all to myself didn't seem right. It was lacking, and what it lacked went by the name of Nick Knowlton.

Nick Knowlton, former high school bad boy and breaker of my stepbrother's nose. Nick, the ex-con who'd gone to prison to save his brother. Nick, the ex-con who couldn't get out from underneath the blackmail of two dirty cops. Nick, who didn't fit in at the club. Nick, who'd stolen my heart.

He was the Nick I wanted and couldn't have.

I leaned over the plans again. The front room and the front wall stayed where they were, along with the master and its outside wall.

The architects had told me that in order to get this through the city as a remodel, we needed to keep the front wall. Seemed pretty silly to me, but those were the rules.

As long as I kept the floor to the front room, the front door, and the front wall, I could tear everything else out and replace it. I was only doing a remodel. If we moved the bulldozer over a couple of feet and took out the front wall as well, then it became a new house, and all the rules changed.

I was going to take the second bedroom next to the master and use it to expand the master suite, the bath, and turn part of it into a walk-in closet.

I used my ruler on the plans to see how long it would make the master bedroom. I paced it off from the outside wall through the hallway.

I decide I needed to have them move the wall over another two feet and extend the back of the house the same amount.

Without a doubt they'd tell me how it would cost extra, but what was the fun of being a Covington if I couldn't ignore costs and have what I wanted?

I went to pull my Susan B. Anthony dollar out of my purse and found the pressed quarter from Disneyland Nick had gotten me. I held the coin in my fingers and remembered back to that day.

It had been a perfect day, surely the best day I had had since Dad died, and quite a while before as well. I longed to be back there with Nick. I knew now I should have done it differently. There had to have been a way I could have kept him.

A knock came at the back door.

It was the little girl from next door Patrick had hired to take care of the chickens and the excess eggs.

I opened the door.

"Would you like any today?" she asked.

"Two would be fine," I told her.

She handed me two of the still-warm eggs from her basket.

Then she dragged her dog along and left with a spring in her step. There went a happy child.

I put the eggs in the fridge. I wished to be as happy and carefree as she was.

Maybe that's what I needed. Maybe I needed a dog.

CHAPTER 29

Nick

THE DRIVE HOME HAD BEEN A LONG ONE. LIKE AN IDIOT, I WAS making it during rush hour.

I opened the door, and the alarm started beeping.

"Good job, Katie," I said to the empty room as I entered the disarm code.

She'd set the alarm like I'd taught her. I hoped she was still doing it at her house to stay safe.

I'd been in such a hurry when I left I hadn't brought enough clothes, only what would fit in the backpack, so what I was wearing was getting a little ripe. I emptied the contents of my backpack into the washer and stripped.

I went to grab my laundry basket and make it a full load when I noticed them.

In the corner behind my laundry basket were those stupid tiger striped yoga pants, the ones my Katie had worn on the trip back from Vegas.

Seeing them brought back memories of her wrapped tightly

around me for the long trip. The way her hair looked when she'd let it loose at the stop in the middle of the desert. The sorrow in her eyes as she'd told me about losing her house. The way she'd turned an instant beet red the moment I complimented her, and the happiness I had found when she'd come running down from her brother's condo and told me she wanted to go to my place.

It had been a truly wonderful day, the first of many.

I threw the yoga pants into the basket and added them to the washer along with the rest of my clothes. Maybe this would give me a reason to see Katie. I could stop by to drop them off. Or, if I didn't have the courage to face her, I could leave them on her doorstep. Either way, it was a decision for tomorrow.

After a long hot shower and a microwave meal from the freezer I was ready to get back to work.

This Bensonhurst problem was easier than most. After a few short hours in the cave I had concrete proof the two dirtbags I had identified were the true culprits. The money trail was incontestable and clear as day.

They hadn't been at all creative in trying to hide their tracks. They were so convinced nobody would guess their identities that they didn't think they had to cover up the money trail.

Idiots.

I emailed Gavin the name of the little fish and told him I had a bigger one that would surprise him when he learned the name.

As expected, the company was foaming at the mouth to get this closed out. He even offered to have cash hand-delivered to me.

I assured him I wasn't dumb enough to want to carry that much cash around. I would wait for the wire transfer tomorrow.

I pulled out the scotch and poured myself a short one. With time on my hands, and nothing to lose, I decided to call Bob Hanson. Maybe his firm had some quick job I could do for them. Right now I wanted something to keep me busy and keep my mind off of Katie.

"*Did you finally decide to crawl out from under that rock you've been hiding under?*" Hanson asked.

I'd been expecting a slightly more cordial greeting. "What do you mean?"

"*Bill Covington tells me you're a fucking pussy. You've been hanging out with his sister and then you go and disappear as soon as things get rough.*"

"That's not it at all," I complained.

"*Yeah? Some country club asshole calls you a name, and you curl up and run away. I call it being a fucking pussy.*"

I couldn't explain to him what had really happened.

"*Winston told me you were a hard ass, and Hank swears you're fucking brilliant. But from where I stand you're a stupid lightweight if you can't handle a little prick like Hunsinger. If the little fucker got anywhere near my girl, he'd be six feet under.*"

"Look, I didn't call you to get fucking yelled at. You got any work for me or not?"

"*Not until you grow a set, you fucking computer weenie! And stay away from Bill Covington. He's likely to shoot you on sight.*" He hung up.

The call hadn't gone as planned. Something was fucked up big-time, and it was me.

I was a fucking idiot, and maybe Hanson was right, maybe I was a pussy. I had gotten scared and walked away from the only good thing to ever happen to me.

A big fucking idiot.

I GOT UP EARLY THE NEXT MORNING FOR A RUN.

I had told Gavin yesterday I would give the name of the big fish as soon as he wired my fee.

I kept checking my account, and at ten-thirty the money arrived. Eighty-five thousand including the bonus for finishing in less than ten days. Not a bad sum for a week's work; it would keep me in Bud and motorcycle parts for quite a while.

I transferred it into my brokerage account with the press of a few buttons and dialed up my friend Gavin.

"I was about to call you, Nick," Gavin said as he answered the phone. "It should be there any minute."

"I got it, it arrived safe and sound," I told him.

"I'm waiting."

"Dirtbag number two is none other than your new products manager Darren."

"Are you sure?" The astonishment in his voice was clear.

"I told you it would surprise you."

"Why would he do that?" he asked.

Gavin could ask the stupidest questions sometimes. "Money, of course," I told him. "If you want me to psychoanalyze them, it'll cost extra."

"But you're sure about this, right?"

"Give me a second to send you the data." I quickly composed an email to him with the evidence files I had compiled yesterday, and copied their CFO.

"It's on the way now. Should be everything you need. It includes a full tracking of all the money straight to these two guys. The way I understand the laws, you should be able to get the FBI to nail them for ten to thirty years each. And it doesn't count, whatever tax evasion charges the feds may cook up."

Gavin cleared his throat. "Nick, would you be interested in coming on board full-time, or even part-time? Our guys worked on this for a year and you finished it in a week."

"No, thanks, the corporate life is not for me. And don't be too hard on your guys. They were pretty close, but they made a mistake. They had assumed there was only one leaker and didn't consider a second. That was the brilliance of the plan. On every event one guy or the other arranged to have a perfect alibi."

"Let me know if you ever change your mind," Gavin said.

"Don't hold your breath," I told him.

"The email just arrived. You mind walking me through it?"

I spent the next twenty minutes going through the evidence I'd collected, to make sure he understood it completely.

We hung up, and in spite of my outrageous fee they were more than pleased. And, two more dirtbags were about to get what they deserved.

I needed some sunshine and fresh air. I decided on a walk down to my local Mexican restaurant, Pedro's, for lunch. A nice big burrito or two and a beer lay in my future, not to mention the chips, lots of chips.

Leaving the house, I noticed my little bloody clothes pirate flag was getting a little tired. At some point I would have to redo it.

The day was another perfect southern California day. The fronds of the tall palm trees swayed in the light breeze, and the sunshine on my face was welcome after a week indoors staring at a computer screen. A perfect day to take the Harley out for a spin. Maybe a nice ride up the PCH this afternoon.

I hadn't gotten much exercise, so I changed my destination from the closer Pedro's to a restaurant further down the main drag. It would add about twenty minutes each direction to my walk.

When I got there, I checked out the menu and recalled why I preferred Pedro's. This place had smaller everything. Smaller tacos, smaller burritos, smaller beers. Who served beer in little eight ounce paper cups, anyway?

I took a table and told the nice waitress I wanted two burritos and two beers and please keep the basket of chips topped up.

She brought me two baskets of chips instead, with a smile, and two salsas: one red and one green. The nice thing about Mexican restaurants around here was that you got to start eating the chips as soon as you sat down.

My meal arrived after I'd consumed about half a basket of

chips. I admired the symmetry of it. Two little burritos on the plate, two little beers past the plate, and two bowls of salsa next to two baskets of chips.

I stared at the meal for a whole minute. Something bugged me.

Then it hit me.

My gut tightened with the realization.

The LDSI embezzlement had involved two bank accounts in the Caymans, and the bank accounts behaved differently. I had assumed they both belonged to Sabbatini. What if there were two people in on the embezzlement?

It would explain two bank accounts behaving differently. I'd fallen into the same trap of intellectual laziness I'd accused the Bensonhurst guys of.

I called over the waitress and asked her to box the meal up for me; I was going to take it to go. I needed to get back to the cave and continue the LDSI investigation where I'd left off. It was possible I hadn't finished it.

I jogged back home carrying my lunch in a bag, trying to keep it from getting shaken into a mush as it swung back and forth.

I grabbed utensils, a Coke from the fridge, and some extra napkins before I opened up the cave.

I put the LDSI account information I had from before up on the big screen in between forkfuls of mashed up burrito.

I double checked for new information, but there wasn't any on the second account. So, I changed tack and went back further in time to the opening of the account.

Two hours later I found a clue. A phone number on a reference to one of the transactions.

I was able to find phone history between that phone number and the main number at LDSI. The critical discovery was the location data for the phone. It was a burner with no registration data and had rarely been turned on. Some of the locations were on random freeways around town, a good way to hide your actual location.

But four times it'd been turned on for a few minutes each time in downtown Los Angeles. Plugging the location into my maps only narrowed it to within a block, but resulted in a disturbing find. It was the same block as Katie's old work address. The place I had taken her for the meeting with Palmer that turned out to be her exit interview.

There was a second culprit and he or she had worked for Katie's company.

I grabbed the yoga pants out of the dryer and stuffed them in my back pocket. I wasn't prepared for this, but I had to talk to Katie today. Only she knew enough about the people at Arthur to narrow down the search. Walking made the most sense; I needed the time to figure out what I would say when she opened the door.

~

Katie

I WAS BACK AT MY HOUSE ON MYRTLE STREET. THE TITLE company had called this morning to say my purchase from Phil had been filed with the county this morning, the house was now officially mine. Having the flexibility to pay cash had made the transaction go quickly.

Today I was meeting with contractors. The plans hadn't been completely settled yet, but I had chosen my architect. And, I had a preliminary set I was using to discuss scheduling with these men.

I'd interviewed three this morning, and so far I liked Roy Thompson the best. He had had an easygoing way about him, and he was already working on a house a few blocks away that I had driven by. They seemed to be making good progress, and best of all, the construction site looked tidy to my inexperienced eye.

My little next door chicken watcher had come by the back door while Roy was here, and I had given Roy some eggs to take home.

He'd said his wife would be tickled to get them. Roy's easy-going nature was easy to like, and he could start as soon as I had the demo permit in hand.

I had one more fellow coming by this afternoon; if I didn't like him better than Roy, I'd have an easy choice to make.

I pulled another Coke out of the fridge and went out the front door to check the mail. Nothing there, same as yesterday, not even any junk mail yet.

A breeze in my face greeted me when I reopened the door. The back door was ajar; I must not have closed it when the young egg girl had stopped by.

I closed and locked the front door behind me, went to the back, and pushed it closed. I headed back to the kitchen.

I passed the hallway to the bedrooms.

He grabbed me, then I heard the click.

The sound I'd heard a hundred times on TV or at the movies.

My heart stopped. I turned to see my worst nightmare.

Russ Downey held a gun he had just cocked aimed at my face. "You stupid fucking bitch," he spat.

I froze.

He shoved me back.

My foot caught on the edge of the coffee table. I couldn't catch myself and I landed on my ass and one hand hard enough to loosen my fillings. My wrist twisted and hurt like the devil. My tailbone was probably broken.

I couldn't breathe. My pulse hammered in my ears. There wasn't anything to hide behind, there wasn't any place to run. I wasn't close enough to try to grab the gun and wrestle with him.

Slowly I was able to pull in a breath and then a second.

"You couldn't just fucking quit like you were supposed to," he said, waving the gun at me.

I struggled up slowly. At least he wasn't here to shoot me dead in cold blood and take off. He could have done it ten seconds ago. One wrist was toast, and my ass hurt like hell, but at least my legs were good enough to make a run for it if I got the chance.

His hand trembled violently, but not half as bad as my knees were shaking.

I tried to control my breathing. Slow deep breaths. I had to calm myself.

I needed him to be calm too, or at least calmer. I'd seen plenty of TV where they emphasized negotiating with the gunman and getting them to calm down first. "How did you get in?" I asked, regretting my tone as soon as I said it.

"You left the back door unlocked, bitch. I came in when you went out front. Now it's you and me in here. Locked up nice and tight. Nice and cozy. Our own little party."

"What are you doing here?" It was a stupid question but was the only one I could come up with for the moment. Of course he was here to shoot me or abduct me or something.

He didn't answer the question. "All you had to do was quit, and everything would've been fine," he said, raising his voice, still waving the gun around.

"I don't understand." I needed to keep him talking to get him to realize that murder was not a step he wanted to take.

"You had to go and finish the fucking LDSI audit. You were supposed to quit and let me finish it. Instead you have to go and ruin my fucking life, bitch."

Now I understood the pattern. Every year he'd apply pressure to the person he'd assigned to the LDSI audit.

"You had to go and write a fucking memo to Palmer. Why

couldn't you leave well enough alone?" he yelled, waving the gun in the air.

Now it made sense. Each year he'd get the person assigned to LDSI to quit so he could finish the audit and sign it off as clean, probably for a portion of the money.

"I should kill you," he said coldly, pacing back and forth.

"No, that's not a good idea," I said quickly.

"Why? You going to offer to blow me or something?"

The thought was sickening. If it came to that I was going to bite it off, and maybe he'd bleed to death.

"No. But a murder charge is a whole other thing. A lot worse than a simple white collar crime."

His brow creased and his face became even redder. "You and your fucking memo to Palmer. You think LDSI was the only one? Palmer fired me, and then they did an audit of my work and now the fucking FBI is on my case. They're threatening eighty years. You think I'm going to last eighty years?"

He couldn't seriously want me to answer.

"What the fuck's the difference if its eighty years or eighty years plus twenty-five to life."

This was definitely getting worse. He was talking himself into killing me. "Tell me how you did it." I asked as calmly as I could.

"You think by getting me to talk to you it's gonna save you?" He walked around me in a circle, poking me in the back with the gun.

A drop of sweat fell into my eye. I didn't dare move to wipe it away. Any sudden move could be the one that pushed him over the edge, but I couldn't still my legs. My willpower was no match for the fear and the adrenaline coursing through my veins.

Before I could answer there was a knock at the front door.

Downey put a finger to his lips, ordering me not to make a sound. "Who the fuck is that?" he whispered.

"I'm expecting a contractor," I said softly, still frozen in place.

"Don't answer it."

I considered screaming instead, but didn't. It would have forced his hand, or gotten the contractor shot. At least Russ worried about getting caught, which is why he wanted me to be quiet. That was good. I might be able to convince him he couldn't kill me and get away with it. At least I had a possible way out.

The knocking stopped and whoever it was trundled down the steps.

I had to keep him talking. It was my only chance.

CHAPTER 30

Nick

On the walk over I failed to cobble together a coherent first sentence for when she opened the door.

Hi, Katie, I brought these over.

Hi, Katie, I was in the neighborhood and wanted to stop by.

Hi, Katie, I want to ask you about your ex-coworkers.

Hi, Katie, I have some information you might be interested in.

Like a pussy I slowed down. I still didn't have a good first line yet.

Hi, Katie, I saw your light on.

Hi, Katie, I saw two burritos on my plate and I had an idea.

They were getting worse. Every one I ran through in my head ended up with a door slammed in my face, or worse.

She had to hate me by now. She had asked if I could call her, and like a cold bastard I had said I wouldn't have the time.

Who doesn't have the time to call the one girl he loves? Who? *Nobody with a heart, that's who, you dumb shit.*

I am so fucked.

At the time I had thought I needed to make a clean break with her, like how ripping a bandage off quickly was better than doing it slowly.

I had been wrong, and Bob Hanson had been right. I was a pussy. I had owed it to her to explain myself. She was a smart girl, she would have understood I was right, and it was the best thing for both of us if I stayed away from her. It would have been difficult, but it would have been right. It is what a gentleman would have done.

Talking to her was what I should have done last week, and what I needed to do now. Right after I told her what I had found.

If she would listen to me.

As I neared the house, a man came down from the porch of her house. He was older, balding, and overweight.

I might not be country club material, but I was a damned sight better than him. Katie's standards had slipped.

I sped up and yelled to him. He ignored me and drove off as I reached the house.

The side gate was open.

"Precious, you have to learn to close this," I said to myself as I went to shut it.

I observed Katie through the window, talking.

I went through the gate where I could see through the window; she was talking to another old schmuck.

He waved his hand in the air.

He had a gun.

My pulse raced.

I ducked down, moving closer to the house. I quietly called 9-1-1 and gave them the address while I worked my way around back. I hung up the call.

Katie was in danger. I had no idea who this asshole was, but we were about to meet in a most unpleasant way for him. I snuck around to the window by the back door and peeked in.

I could only see the two of them.

He was yelling at her, "bitch" was the only word I made out clearly. His back was to me. He waved the gun up in the air and back down again. He paced back and forth nervously. The dude was agitated as hell. Agitated and armed was a very bad mixture.

I slowly tried the back door handle. It was unlocked. I eased the door open, hoping it wouldn't squeak.

Katie noticed me and immediately yelled at the guy, "You have to tell me how you did it."

Good girl. She was trying to distract him.

"What the fuck for?" He yelled back, swinging the gun wildly.

"It was brilliant…" she said loudly.

That was my queue.

As soon as the guy raised the gun over his head again, I charged.

I grabbed the gun arm with both hands as I launched myself and body slammed him.

The gun went off.

Katie jumped back.

I landed on top of the bastard, knocking the wind out of him with a loud grunt.

The gun skittered across the floor.

He tried to crawl toward it, but I grabbed his collar and yanked him back.

I punched him in the side, which resulted in another grunt. I grabbed a wrist and yanked it behind his back and up to his shoulder blades.

He screamed.

Katie backed farther away.

I brought my elbow down on top of his head and smashed it to the floor.

With a knee on his lower back, and his arm wrenched up behind him. I had him under control. "You okay?"

She had her face in her hands. She didn't speak.

"Talk to me."

"Yeah, I guess," she said shakily, wrapping her arms around herself.

"Bitch," came from the guy underneath me. The guy definitely needed to use more deodorant.

"Did he hurt you?" I asked.

Katie shook her head. "I just didn't know…" Her voice trailed off.

"Trust me, it'll be okay. Can you get the gun?" I nodded in the direction the gun had slid.

Stinky squirmed but wasn't getting away from me. No fucking way. I punched him in the side of the head, twice.

Katie nodded then stumbled to where the gun had landed. She slowly brought the gun to me.

I took it with my free hand and stuck it in my waistband behind my back, in case.

The jerk continued to grunt and struggle. He tried to hit me with his free hand.

I yanked his arm up behind him harder. "You do that one more time and I'll tell her to get me a knife so I can cut your balls off," I hissed at him.

He settled down.

I could hear the sirens in the distance now.

"Who is this joker?" I asked Katie.

She didn't speak. She had her arms wrapped around herself, twisting one direction and the other. She was crashing. The girl was in shock.

"Who is this?" I repeated.

"Russ, Russ," she mumbled.

"Your asshole boss?"

She nodded after a second.

Her boss had been the other one involved in the embezzling.

He was probably covering it up and getting paid handsomely to do so.

"Now I can see why you didn't like him," I said, fishing for a laugh or at least a giggle.

I didn't get either of the hoped for responses.

Her ex-boss tried to get loose once again, but a quick bang of his head on the floor again stopped it. Stinky kept hissing and mumbling. *Bitch* was the only intelligible word.

Katie was losing it. She stared off into space.

I needed her to pull herself together before the cops arrived.

I grabbed the yoga pants I had partly stuffed in my back pocket.

I laughed. "I came over to bring these back to you," I told her as I quickly tied Stinky's hands together behind him with the yoga pants.

I hoped to help her mood with the humor. It didn't work, she stared at me blankly.

The LAPD announced themselves and banged on the door.

"We're getting the door," I yelled to them. "Precious, you have to open the door, can you do that?"

She didn't respond.

"Get the door, Precious."

She went to the door slowly as if in a trance.

The cops rushed in, guns drawn, as soon as she unlocked the door.

I stayed seated on the jerk and put my hands up. I knew the drill. "There's a gun in my waistband behind me," I told them.

They secured the gun, shoved me to the floor, and kept their weapons trained on all of us. They forced Katie up against the wall.

All three of us ended up getting cuffed. They weren't taking any chances while they sorted it out.

Katie was so scared she had trouble speaking to explain the

situation. The cops had run my license right away and with my record and the gun in my belt, they had already pegged me as the bad guy here. Downey complained he was the one being assaulted.

Soon after, both her uncle Garth and her brother Bill arrived.

Katie's uncle Garth showed the cops some cards from his wallet and had a quick conference with them.

The officers removed Katie's cuffs and apologized profusely. They said something about getting her statement tomorrow. Being rich, she got better treatment from these officers than I ever had.

Her brother whisked her away instantly.

Her uncle Garth eventually convinced them to uncuff me.

Uncle Garth gave me a pat on the back on his way out. "Don't forget to call me."

The cops kept asking me the same questions over and over.

It took a long time for my adrenaline jitters to dissipate.

I pointed out the video cameras and told them if they checked with the Hanson firm, they could get the video of the whole thing to answer all their questions.

They said they would get to the video in due time and kept on questioning me. As an ex-con I wasn't allowed to have a gun, and they were focused on that. It didn't seem to matter to them I said I had taken it away from Downey. They had been deferential to Katie's uncle, but he was gone now, and I got the standard ex-con treatment.

I spent two hours with them, giving my statement to two different officers and a detective. Because of my record they still didn't trust me; it was the story of my life. It didn't seem to matter that I was the one who had made the 9-1-1 call.

~

Katie

When I had caught sight of Nick slowly opening the back door, I couldn't believe my eyes. I knew I had to do something to distract Russ.

If he'd heard Nick come in, we both would've ended up dead.

So I had raised my voice to cover the sound of Nick coming in.

It had given Nick the time he needed.

I didn't remember much about the whole ordeal anymore. I wanted to forget it.

Bill seemed to arrive almost instantly, followed by my uncle Garth.

It was Uncle Garth who had convinced the cops to let me go home with Bill.

I was numb as Bill drove me home in his car and took me upstairs to Pat's condo.

Bill held me in his arms seemingly forever; all I did was shake. I had thought I might die. I almost had died.

Eventually, I made it into the shower. I scrubbed forever, getting all traces of Russ Downey off me.

When I came out, Lauren had food ready for me, and best of all a large glass of wine.

I winced as I sat. My butt was bruised, not broken. I'd heard that if you broke your tailbone you couldn't sit for a week. I finished the wine before I took a single forkful of the food.

Lauren understood and filled the glass again. "Bill told me what happened. You want to talk about it?"

I shook my head. The last thing I wanted to do was revisit anything having to do with Russ Downey.

I took another forkful of spaghetti. "This is good," I told her.

"Bill said Nick came back."

I nodded and took another forkful of spaghetti. I didn't want to talk about it.

She stared at me, daring me to explain.

"He needed to return some pants of mine," I told her.

Her face said it all. She wasn't impressed.

Neither was I. I had to face the fact Nick didn't love me, and I couldn't rekindle hope that I had been wrong about it. I needed to stay strong. My future was one I would have to write by myself, without Nick in the story.

I'd seen this movie play out before with my college roommate Susanna.

Susanna had had an on and off again boyfriend Jason. Jason had been around for a while, then he wasn't. He'd come back again, claiming to love her. The cycle repeated, and each time Susanna thought he was back for good.

Each time he would stay for a while, before leaving and breaking her heart again. Senior year, I don't know if it was the third or the fourth of these on again off again episodes with Jason, but she finally had been through enough. She didn't take him back; she had learned his actions meant more than his words. Six months later she was head over heels in love with another guy. The last time I saw her, they had two children, and she was immensely happy.

Nick had shown me how he felt, and I needed to accept it.

I couldn't repeat Susanna's mistake. I couldn't go through what she had. I didn't have the strength for it. I needed to be strong and learn from her lesson.

Lauren and I ate in silence.

Suddenly I heard a commotion in the hallway. It sounded like Bill arguing with Nick.

Nick

. . .

"I WON'T LET YOU SEE HER," BILL COVINGTON SAID, BLOCKING my path to Patrick's condo unit. The same one I had brought Katie to the night we'd returned from Las Vegas. Bill's jaw tightened, and he braced himself for my attack.

He was right to get prepared because I was going to wipe the floor with him if he didn't get out of the way.

"I'm going to see her. And frankly I don't give a fuck what you think," I said loudly. I clenched my fists.

"Over my dead body," he shot back, bending his knees and lowering his center of gravity. Somebody had taught him well.

"If that's the way you want it," I spat.

He might have been taught well, but I had the experience of street fighting, where there were no fucking rules, except win at any cost, and I had never lost, not outside of prison nor inside.

As I prepared to make my move, the door behind him opened.

His wife Lauren emerged. "Hi, Nick, why don't you come in," she said nicely.

Bill let out a breath and relaxed. He gave in to his wife's suggestion to let me pass, and moved aside.

I patted him on the shoulder on the way in.

Lauren gave me a quick hug at the door, and closed it, with her and Bill in the hallway.

Katie sat at the table, it was only me and her now.

Lauren and Bill had a muffled conversation I didn't pay attention to. I was focused on my woman.

As I approached her, she came to me, planting her face in my shoulder, crying.

"I was so scared," she said.

I rubbed her back and stroked her hair. "You're safe now. I told you I'd keep you safe."

"I just needed to say how grateful I am that you took care of him."

"No problem, Precious, it's what I do, remember."

She hugged me tight for a moment, then let me go. "You need to go now. I'll see you around." She backed away.

"I fucked up," I blurted out. There it was. "I'm sorry," I added.

She didn't move. Her face was blank, more suspicious than anything. She didn't utter a word as if I were a stranger. "You need to go," she repeated.

I had expected something more; I didn't know what.

I moved toward her. "I didn't want to hurt you."

She stepped back again. "What," she practically yelled. She raised her arms and yelled at me. "What the hell?"

"I couldn't stand to hurt you, but I realize now I fucked up."

She was hysterical. "What the hell are you talking about?"

I took in a breath and tried not to match her volume level. "I'm sorry. I didn't want you to regret being with me."

"Since when does that make any sense? You left. You told me you couldn't even be bothered to call me. You made it pretty fucking obvious how you felt. Do you have any idea how that made *me* feel."

I could only imagine how badly I had hurt her, and it killed me.

"I was wrong, I shouldn't have left." As soon as I said it, I knew I had screwed up the words.

"That's the stupidest thing anybody has ever said. If you cared at all, you would have stayed and talked to me. You left because you didn't want to be with me because you didn't want to talk to me."

"I know. I was wrong."

"You have no idea… Wrong isn't anywhere near… You are beyond stupid."

"You're right of course. I'll say what I came to say and leave."

"I don't want to hear it. Nothing you say can change anything, anyway. You didn't even call."

I had fucked up big time.

I turned and walked to the door.

How do I fuck everything up?

CHAPTER 31

Katie

He latched the deadbolt on the door, locking Bill and Lauren out, and returned.

"Come here and sit down," he said.

"What?"

He pulled two chairs out from the table facing each other. "Sit down with me," he repeated sternly

I straightened my shoulders. I folded my arms. I was sick of being told what to do. I stood where I was.

"Now," he added sternly with the tone he used when he wouldn't allow any negotiation.

"No," I shot back.

"Should I have let Mr. Stinky shoot you?" I liked his name for Russ Downey; I should have thought of it.

I didn't see any way to avoid it, so I took a chair and sat.

He settled into the chair facing me. His eyes shifted from firm and demanding to soft and caring. He took my hand in his.

I should have pulled it away, but the warmth of his touch

welded my hand to his. I was powerless to pull it away. His magnetism still had a hold on me I couldn't overcome.

"Katherine," he said. The word surprised me. He never used my name. It was always Precious or that obnoxious Princess nickname.

"Hear me out," he continued.

"Why? I know what you're going to say."

"Princess, you suck big time at listening," he said.

"But—"

He silenced me with a quick finger to my lips. "Listen," was all he said. All the men in my life were always bossing me around.

I lowered my eyes and waited.

"Katie," he used my name again. "I shouldn't have left you," he said slowly.

What the fuck?

That much was obvious. "Then why did you?"

He took a breath. "I told you several times, our two worlds are very different."

"But I told you it didn't matter to me." And, it hadn't, I had been more at ease with him than any man before. Certainly more than my ex, Joe.

He placed his other hand over mine. "Katie, I love you, and I couldn't bear the thought of you coming to regret being with me."

I rolled my eyes and pulled my hand back. "That is the stupidest thing you've said yet."

Now he was making no sense at all. "What the fuck do you mean, anyway? Why would I regret being with you?"

"Maybe not today, but after what happened to you at the club."

"What do you mean what happened to me? If you can't take a little ribbing from the likes of Joe and the two stooges, then you seriously need to toughen up."

"I can take a hundred Joes and wipe the floor with them. He's a fucking rodent."

"Then why did you let him get to you like that?"

"He didn't. I left because of the way he and those women treated you. I didn't want to put you through that anymore."

"They didn't do anything to me. And if you don't have enough respect for me to let me make up my own mind, then you should leave right now," I said, pointing to the door.

"I'm staying. That's the realization I came to. I can only give you everything I have to offer and let you decide if it's enough."

It was the first rational thing he had said. But what would happen when he decided to leave again?

"Nick, I can't… I can't go through this again. You need your freedom, and I need my sanity. You told me once how you built your life around being able to pick up and leave on a moment's notice. I can't live like that." Tears pricked my eyes.

I hadn't wanted him to leave and now that he was back, I was the one telling him to leave. It didn't make any sense. But I couldn't go through what had happened to Susanna.

He fished something out of his pocket and held it in his closed fist. "I was going to give you this at the club, but after… Anyway, I want you to have this."

He opened his hand. It contained a small velvet pouch. He extracted a ring from it. "I'm never leaving you alone again."

My heart thundered against my rib cage. Oh my God, I couldn't believe this was happening. Tears pricked my eyes.

He held out the ring. A ring with a diamond on it. "Katherine Mary Covington, I want you to take this ring, and my name. Will you marry me?"

My tears came in earnest. Tears of joy this time. I nodded and reached out and offered my left hand to him.

"Is that a yes?" he asked.

"No." I sniffled. "It's a hell yes."

He slipped the ring on my finger. It was a perfect fit. He

pulled me up out of the chair and kissed me in the same possessive way he had our first night. The same way I wanted him to every time we were together. Our tongues played hide and seek as I grabbed his hair and clawed at his back.

He lifted me up, and I wrapped my legs around him.

I'd gone without him for a week, an entire week. It seemed forty days too long.

He broke the kiss long enough to ask, “When's Patrick coming back?”

“I'm not sure he is coming back.”

“Then he won't mind,” Nick said, starting to pull the clothes off of me.

I reciprocated. Yanking his shirt and his belt. We clawed at each other's clothes and he had me naked in no time.

Nick picked me up, and I wrapped my legs around him grasping his neck.

“He won't mind if we use his window.” Nick backed me up against the window and pinned me there. He lifted me up and slid me slowly down on his waiting cock.

He thrust into me and pushed me against the window. The lights were still on, but I didn't care. We were twenty-two floors up and I didn't care if anybody was watching from outside.

All that mattered was my Neanderthal man was back. He was mine, all mine, and I was his.

WE WERE EATING BREAKFAST AT PATRICK'S CONDO. NICK HAD cooked me waffles. I still couldn't believe I’d found a man who made breakfast for me.

After he proposed, we had made love against the window, in bed, and in the shower this morning.

Nick had wanted to send Patrick a text with a selfie of us in his bed, to piss him off.

I had successfully vetoed the idea.

Until now, the time hadn't seemed right to ask Nick why he had really left.

"Last night," I began. "You said you didn't like what they were doing to me at the club. I don't understand what you meant, exactly." Exactly wasn't the right word. I had no idea what he was saying. But after his proposal it hadn't mattered.

He reached forward and tenderly tucked a tendril of hair behind my ear. "They were talking behind your back, criticizing you, looking down on you, because you were with me."

It was a curve ball. I had missed it completely; I had thought he was feeling bad about how they'd treated him, not me. Nobody had said a thing to me all night.

"You know why they weren't eating your pies?" he asked.

I shook my head.

"Those lady friends of yours were telling everyone that I had probably spiked them with drugs."

I gasped. "That's ridiculous."

"They did that to you because of me. And your ex, Joe, was going to get his father to force Bill off the board at the club for the same reason."

I laughed.

Nick didn't understand the humor in what he had said.

"Joe's father tried it the day before yesterday," I told him. "He got laughed out of the room. My grandfather founded the club, and Joe's father is an even bigger jerk than Joe is. Nobody can stand either of them. Trust me, Bill can handle himself."

Nick's thought process hadn't been at all what I had expected. I had thought he hadn't cared enough, or maybe he couldn't give up his freedom. Instead, he had once again been trying to protect me in his own Neanderthal way.

"Nick, you don't understand. I don't care what those people think, not one bit. They're not my friends."

"Good, because the next time I meet that little Joe prick he's going to need emergency dental work."

I laughed. "That's not the right way to get to him. If you really want to piss him off, break a couple of his golf clubs."

The doorbell sounded.

Nick opened it and Lauren entered.

"Good morning, Nick," Lauren said with a wink in my direction Nick couldn't see.

I smiled back, and when she got close enough, I showed her my ring.

"Oh my God, Katie, it's gorgeous."

"Nick, you sly fox you," she said to him. "Tell me, did he get on a knee?" she asked me.

I laughed. "My man doesn't kneel for anybody, even me."

Nick grinned as I'd known he would.

"Well? How did he do it?"

"He said he was stupid," I told her. "And I agreed with him. That was about it." I wasn't about to tell her any more.

Nick grimaced, but he deserved it after what he had put me through in the last week.

Lauren called Bill to give him the good news.

He'd already gone to work, and he congratulated me over the phone. I could tell from his tone he absolutely meant it. "*Welcome Nick to the family for me,*" he told me before we got off.

It wasn't five minutes before Uncle Garth called to congratulate us. Afterwards he wanted to have a word with Nick.

A smile grew on Nick's face, and he nodded as the conversation went on. "Sounds like a good plan to me," was all I heard him say.

Lauren was already busy on her phone, passing the news on to Patrick.

CHAPTER 32

(One Week Later)

Nick

I could hear Katie busy in the kitchen when my phone rang. It was from DV. Delancey again. I was not relishing this call.

"*Nicky, oh Nicky, do we have a problem,*" Delancey said as soon as I got on the phone.

"My only problem is you," I told him.

"*Careful there, convict. That kind of attitude could get you in serious trouble.*"

I didn't respond. I had poked the bear maybe a bit too hard.

"*Ya see, a little birdie told me that you've been holding out on us.*"

I closed the door to the bedroom so Katie wouldn't overhear this conversation.

"Is that so? You know birds don't know shit."

"*It seems you haven't been paying all your taxes, Nicky.*" He didn't mean the IRS either. Their demand had been that I pay them twenty percent of everything I made if I expected to stay out of prison.

"*It seems you have an account at First Federal. And Steph's source at the bank says you have seven figures there.*"

They had found my account, all right. I had four million plus a little at the bank. I had paid them a little, but nowhere near the twenty percent they wanted. Until now, they'd had no idea how much I really had or made in my work.

"*What you gotta say about that?*" Delancey asked.

There wasn't any good response. I hadn't paid *his* taxes on the money.

"*Here's what were gonna do, Nicky. You're gonna come meet us down on the corner by the smoke shop on Pico. You bring your checkbook with you. Maybe then we can settle this amicably. If you know what I mean.*" What he meant was pretty obvious. Write them a big check or he and his partner would bring the hammer down on me.

A knot formed in my stomach. "I'm busy."

"*Be there one hour from now, or so help me, I'll have you back in the system before nightfall,*" he snarled.

"Okay. One hour," I said before hanging up. I couldn't stand to talk to this fucker any longer.

There were several ways this meeting could turn out badly for me. I grabbed my checkbook and my coat on the way to the door. "I need to go out for a while," I told Katie.

She blew me a kiss. "This'll keep me busy for another two hours," she said. She was busy baking two more apple pies, one for us, and one for Bill and Lauren.

I blew her a kiss in return before I closed the door.

I started the truck and hoped I didn't have to bring her back bad news.

THE LAPD WERE MORONS WHEN IT CAME TO UNMARKED CARS. Instead of buying random used cars, the budget weenies made them buy fleet vehicles, and never imported. It was so easy to pick out the Ford or Chevy sedans they used.

I'd gotten here early and parked about a block away, surveying the scene.

Today Delancey and his partner were in a light blue Ford sedan. They might as well have had Los Angeles Police Department stenciled on the trunk. They parked right before the intersection on Pico, exactly where they had said they would be.

I checked my pockets carefully. I had what I needed and opened the door of my truck. I had met with them before, but it had never been a pleasant chat. The closer I approached, the more nervous I got. I crossed my fingers, hoping I would at least get out of the car alive. With these bozos there was always a risk.

I walked past their car to the intersection and doubled back toward them. I had walked up from behind, and it was never a good idea to surprise a man with a gun. This way they saw me before I rapped on the passenger side window.

Delancey was driving and Stephanic was in the passenger seat. Neither man's face bore a welcoming expression. Stephanic motioned for me to get in the back.

I opened the door and slid across to the center of the back seat.

Stephanic checked his watch. "Two minutes to spare, convict. We were about to leave and swear out your arrest warrant."

"Bring your checkbook, convict?" Delancey asked.

"Yes, sir," I said. Starting off confrontational with these two was *not* a good plan. "But I think you guys have bad information."

"Really?" Stephanic asked. "We think our information is pretty fucking good."

He pulled a piece of paper out of his pocket and unfolded it. "This says you owe us four hundred and three thousand dollars, dirtbag."

"Your math is wrong," I told him.

Stephanic waved the paper. "It says here you deposited two million and fifteen thousand into your account at Federal in the last twelve months. You want to look at it, convict? So, by our calculations," Stephanic chuckled, "Twenty percent is four oh three, but since we're such reasonable guys, we will let you off for four hundred grand even. Or else…"

This was getting dangerous. "Or else what, you write me up for fucking jaywalking?" I was treading very close to the edge here. There was a point beyond which I couldn't push these two assholes.

Delancey turned around with a murderous scowl on his face. "Very funny, convict. Steph give me the gun," he said to his partner.

Stephanic pulled out a Glock wrapped in a plastic bag and handed it to Delancey. "This is how it's going to go. You write us the check in thirty seconds or else we cuff you and take you downtown with this gun that we found on you."

"It's not my gun, you guys brought it."

Delancey continued. "You know that, and I know that, but the fucking DA doesn't know that. And when Steph and I swear we found it on you, that's the way it's going to be."

This was going from bad to worse.

"It worked when we planted the stolen shit at your house the first time you got sent up. It'll be even easier this time."

I stopped breathing. I had thought Lester actually did steal the junk. They were telling me the thing had been a setup from the beginning. It didn't make any sense, but I couldn't allow myself to go down that road. First, I had to get out of this car alive.

"The bad news for you, convict, is that this gun was used to kill a cop. In this state, that means special circumstances. You might even get the needle."

It was time to capitulate. I waved my hands. "Okay. Okay already. I got it." I pulled the checkbook out of my pocket along with a pen.

Delancey smirked. "Now you're being sensible."

I wrote out the check for four hundred thousand and signed it. I left the payee blank the way we had always done before. I tore the check out of the book and handed it over.

"So now you got the money and we're square right?"

"Until next month, convict," Delancey said.

Stephanie laughed. "Yeah, next month."

They were both still laughing when I climbed out of the car and closed the door.

Assholes.

I walked back toward my car, still jittery from the adrenaline. "They're all yours," I said out loud.

Four LAPD cars converged from different directions, lights flashing, but no sirens.

The officers jumped out of their cars and trained their guns on the unmarked blue sedan with Delancey and Stephanie inside.

I stopped on the sidewalk twenty yards back to watch as the two detectives were pulled out of the car, patted down, and cuffed.

Their protests and swearing had no effect.

A firm slap on the back, and I turned to find Katie's uncle Garth.

"Very good job, Nicholas," he said.

He was joined by Lieutenant Mitchell of Internal Affairs whom I had only met yesterday.

"Did you get enough?" I asked Mitchell.

"More than enough. You know, you ran a real risk by making them spell out the arithmetic. All we needed was for them to make a demand and you to hand over the money," Mitchell said.

"Only trying to do a good job," I told him. "And I can't thank you guys enough."

Mitchell shook my hand. "I've been after these guys for a year, but until you came forward, I had nothing. It now sounds like I might have them on murder, and of a cop no less. But we'll see about that later."

"Hey, make sure you guys don't cash the check," I told him.

Mitchell laughed. "No guarantees." He walked off to join the party, and no doubt to tell Delancey and Stephanic what kind of deep shit they were in.

Stephanic turned my way, and I waved to him.

Bite me.

He spat in my direction and yelled. "Better watch your back, dirtbag."

I ignored the threat. He was going to have a lot more than me to worry about. A cop on the inside would be in a constant battle for survival.

"It must feel good to be out from underneath them," Uncle Garth said.

"You have no idea." There was no way an outsider could possibly understand what I had been through with those two.

"What can I ever do to repay you, Mr. Durham?" I asked.

"Uncle Garth, please, and no need to thank me. You are family now, or at least you will be soon, and family always comes first." He patted me on the back. "Just make Katherine happy is all I ask."

That was an easy one. "She's my number one priority."

"I have no doubt," he replied.

I took a deep breath. "It took longer than I thought for them to call me."

"It took time for them to understand the clues we left leading to your bank account. Not the sharpest knives in the drawer, those two."

He excused himself and wandered off to join the gaggle of police.

Somehow the policemen accepted him as if he were one of their own.

I took another deep breath. My first real breaths of fresh air as a truly free man. I hadn't realized until today they had set up my brother and me for the conviction that had changed my life. It was infuriating to think about how unjust it was, but getting mad now wouldn't help anyone, and I had gotten even in the best way possible. I still had most of my life ahead of me, and all I could do was make the best of it from here on out.

I had known from the day I went in, I shouldn't have been there, but it had been my choice to protect my brother. If I had known it was a setup, it wouldn't have changed anything. They had been experts at planting the evidence, and the conviction had been assured, the only question I'd faced was me or my brother. I had made the sacrifice willingly and would have made the same choice even with what I knew today.

Getting mad about it would only eat away at my soul.

I turned and walked back to my truck with a renewed vigor. Now this was over, and I could go back and talk to Katie about it.

Now we could get on with the rest of our lives.

EPILOGUE

"THE SOUND OF A KISS IS NOT SO LOUD AS THAT OF A CANNON, BUT ITS ECHO LASTS A GREAT DEAL LONGER." -OLIVER WENDELL HOLMES, SR.

KATIE

NICK HAD LEFT THE WINDOW CRACKED OPEN LAST NIGHT. THE muffled sounds of Mr. Busy's crowing slipped into the room as the faint light of the coming sunrise filtered around the edges of the shades.

Mr. Busy was the name Patrick had given the rooster in the backyard. Mr. Busy because he was always busy chasing the hens of his harem. The no-crow collar around his neck didn't completely silence him, but it kept his noise down below nuisance level.

I rolled over to face Nick.

He was still asleep. He could sleep through most anything, it seemed. As I watched my husband, his chest rose and fell rhythmically.

With the heavy comforter over him I couldn't tell yet what I would find when I reached down to grab him, warm and soft or hard and ready.

I was getting wet thinking about it and planning my attack.

Cosmo said a man's testosterone levels were highest in the morning. Based on my man's average morning hardness I would say they were right.

I waited and lay watching him sleep peacefully, wondering how I had been so lucky to find such a perfect husband. I'd had no idea how my life would change the day I'd accepted his offer of a ride back from Las Vegas.

When I'd seen him come out of the elevator in Las Vegas with those two motorcycle helmets, I'd almost refused. It was hard now to contemplate how much different my life would be if I hadn't taken the ride with him.

I chose the slow attack. I slipped my hand over his abdomen and slowly made my way down south.

"Morning, Mrs. Knowlton," he said groggily as he opened his eyes.

I loved it when he called me that. Covington had been a fine name, but the day he'd asked me to share his, he'd made me the happiest woman on the planet.

I moved closer and brushed my lips against his. "Good morning, Network Knight."

My hand found him, and I knew the answer even before I asked. "Are you ready?"

"Always ready for you, Princess."

I'd forced myself to stop objecting to the Princess nickname. He meant it in a loving way.

I stroked his hard length with a light grip, and moved down to cup his balls.

He reciprocated by pulling me closer for a kiss as our tongues tangled and we exchanged breath with one another. He tried to roll toward me, but I let go of his balls and pushed his hip down firmly. This morning was my turn to be in charge.

Releasing him from the kiss, I moved down to bite his nipple lightly.

He tensed as I did.

I blew on the tender flesh and moved farther down. I gave his cock a long slow lick from root to tip before taking him in my mouth. A few quick strokes and he was well lubricated with my saliva. It was sexy the way his cock would jerk slightly as I blew cold air on the wet underside.

I climbed up over him and positioned myself over his super-hard cock.

He kneaded my breasts and thumbed my nipples with the circular motion that always sent tingles through me.

I held his cock and lowered myself slowly, a bit down and then back up, and a little more down, pulling my juices out and lubricating his length all the while teasing him with my slow approach.

His gentle moans as I lowered myself, and his gasps as I pulled up, were my guide. I slowly took more of him with each stroke until I reached his root. I rocked into him and he guided me up and down with his hands on my hips.

He moved to thumb my clit, but I pulled his hand away, not once, but twice he tried.

"No," I said. "My rules today. You first," I told him as I shoved down fully and his steely cock stretched me fully.

He was always making me come, and often twice before he did, but not this morning—it was my turn to set the rules. He relented and went back to guiding my hips with his hands and thrusting up into me as he pulled me down onto him, each thrust seemingly deeper and more filling than the last.

I neared my climax as every cell of my body tensed with the thrusts of him into my core, and all my nerve endings tingled with every lift off of him, but I held off. I had to. I had to make him come first today.

His breathing became shallower as he tensed up, nearing his limit.

I rocked down hard on him with one hand reached behind me

to grab his balls, and used the other to pinch his nipple as he came, gushing into me with a loud groan and a final deep push.

His legs shook and his cock continued to throb inside me as I ground down on him. He moved his thumb to my clit. His circling pressure on my sensitive nub quickly took me over the top in a shudder as he pulled me forward to kiss and nibble at my nipples. He truly was the clit whisperer.

I couldn't catch my breath as the spasms shook me and my body dissolved in my climax.

He pulled me down farther to hug me tightly. "You can wake me up like this any morning you want, Precious," he groaned into my ear.

The smile on his face in the dim morning light had been all the reward I needed.

I relaxed down on his chest as the pulses of his cock inside me slowly diminished. This was always the best part, the ultimate closeness between husband and wife. The perfect beginning to a new day in our life together.

Nick had saved me. Not only from Sabbatini and Downey, but also from myself. Each day he was teaching me how to live more fully in the moment.

I rolled off of him and headed to the shower. I had a conference call with a new client this morning at seven, and I wanted to be prepared.

We had started a business together, the two of us with our combined talents had a knack for unraveling financial fraud.

Nick wanted to name the business Network Knight Consulting, but after our first three potential clients laughed and then hung up the phone, we decided to change it.

His next suggestion had been Knowlton Financial Consulting, but sharing the KFC acronym with a fast food restaurant wasn't going to work either. We settled on KFA Knowlton Forensic Accounting.

Nick came up behind me and rubbed my shoulders. It was one of his most endearing habits. And one I got the routine benefit of, now that we worked together.

I leaned back in my chair. “Keep it up. It feels great.”

“I can think of something else that feels even better,” he whispered into my ear as his hands roamed down past my shoulders to caress my breasts.

As much as I wanted to, now was not the time. I reached up behind me to pull his head down so I could nibble on his ear. “You don't have time before class, Mr. Knowlton.”

“You can be such a killjoy sometimes,” he growled.

I giggled as he tickled me. “Cut it out. I refuse to be the reason you’re late.”

He released me and gave up for the moment. This would only make him hornier when he returned, and I could look forward to a satisfying afternoon.

Bill had talked to the Dean of the engineering school at UCLA and convinced him it would be a good idea to let Nick teach a programming course at the school. It didn't hurt that three of the buildings on campus were named after our grandfather, and Covington Industries’ history of substantial yearly contributions to the school didn’t hurt.

The department head had originally been opposed because Nick didn't have a degree. His objections evaporated though when Nick walked them through a half dozen papers he had written for the Black Hat Conference. They also balked at Nick's suggested title for the course, Elementary Hacking Techniques, he’d wanted to call it. They settled on Unconventional Programming, which somehow sounded more legitimate but didn't change the content of the course.

So now my high school dropout husband was teaching the college kids how the real world worked and loving every minute of it. It seemed to be what he was meant to do, even if he was the only Harley riding member of the department.

Nick pulled on his motorcycle jacket and packed up his backpack. Every time he rode up in those jeans and jacket it reminded me of the afternoon I had literally bumped into him in Las Vegas and he'd changed my life forever. He was one walking hunk of sex appeal and he was all mine.

I only had to put up with his insistence on moving his brand of pirate flag over to this house. He had been right though, it kept the front lawn clean of dog poop.

Riding the Harley to school meant he could park closer to his building, to say nothing of how much easier it was to navigate the Westwood traffic on two wheels instead of four. He could have ridden the Honda, but preferred the outlaw image of the Harley.

I finished up my spreadsheet, saved the file, and pushed back from my desk. All they had provided us with at Arthur and Company had been laptops. The huge monitor Nick had gotten me made this work so much easier than working hunched over a laptop.

I glanced at the two frames on the wall above my monitor. They represented my past and my future.

The elegant frame on the wall was seventeen inches high and twenty-one inches wide with a shiny mahogany border, but what it framed was much bigger than a small piece of paper.

Above the gold seal it said the California Board of Accountancy granted Katherine M. Covington the right to practice as a Certified Public Accountant. It represented my work future and also six hard years of Katherine's past.

The other held a blowup of the picture of our day at Disneyland. It was Nick and I on a sunny afternoon against the railing of the riverboat with trees in the background. It reminded me of the day Nick had taken the time to teach me how to relax and enjoy doing nothing at all. It'd been my first real day off in six years, nothing but sunshine, laughter, and the man of my dreams.

It signified Katie's future—one free of self-imposed pressures—one shared with the baddest boy in high school who had grown up to be the best man in town.

My haunted house pressed coin sat on my desk next to my keyboard where a simple touch of the coin could bring back memories of Nick holding me on the rides that day. He had brought me to the sunny side of reality, relaxed and contented.

"See you when I get back, and say hi to the twins for me," Nick called back from the door.

"Don't scare the kids too much," I warned him.

"No promises." It meant he would be moderately nice to them, but probably still call them all weenies. He thought the college kids he was teaching were mostly pampered brats. Nevertheless, he had invited the class over for a barbecue this weekend. Quite a nice touch, I thought.

I blew him a kiss before he closed the door behind him.

I had an appointment at *The Twin Belles* beauty spa for a mani pedi and highlights.

I had put money up for Brandi and Candy's business and was now a one third owner. The ownership didn't matter to me, it was the opportunity to help those two girls leave *the life* earlier and achieve their dream that I wanted to participate in. They deserved it.

I stood up to stretch, and spent a moment contemplating the framed certificate on my wall. I had come so far from the day I'd walked out of the Arthur and Company building with my plans of becoming a CPA shattered.

It turned out Russ Downey had seen me in the lobby as he'd walked in and sabotaged my plans to talk to Mr. Palmer. He'd told Palmer's assistant I wished to cancel the meeting, and convinced Betty in HR to expedite my exit interview.

What Russ hadn't counted on, though, was me having a

memo ready, and Betty unwittingly forwarding it to Palmer. The memo had started the inquiry that was Downey's undoing.

The turnaround day for me had been when my uncle Garth walked in with me to Palmer's office on the top floor of the Arthur building.

My uncle had always seemed like a kindly old man to me. That afternoon I got to see the other side of him. Uncle Garth had contacts throughout the state, and beyond. I'd been told there was little he couldn't accomplish with a phone call or meeting, but I hadn't witnessed it until then.

He'd walked us into Palmer's office with no notes, but confronted the man by rattling off no fewer than seven itemized ethics and accounting standards Arthur and Company was guilty of violating. He had memorized the code numbers and the text of each item. He proceeded to pull the business cards of five separate members of the State Board of Accountancy out of his pocket and placed them on Palmer's desk.

The poor man's face had drained of all blood as my uncle had accused him of running a criminal enterprise, no less.

We walked out of the office with an agreement that my experience hours would be signed off by the end of the day, and poor Danielle's as well. As compensation for the injustice of having had to work for Russ Downey, we were both also receiving an additional twelve months of pay.

It'd been a lesson in the real power of knowledge and connections.

My uncle was a good man to have at your back.

Russ Downey finally was getting what he deserved. He and Sabbatini were sitting in jail awaiting trial. The DA had asked for and gotten a substantial bail set for both of them, based on all the video evidence of his attack on me at the house.

Neither had been able to make bail since the FBI had frozen their assets while they lodged money laundering and additional federal fraud charges against them. The men wouldn't be getting out anytime soon.

Nick had helped by providing the FBI with the account numbers for all of their offshore accounts as well.

Once Sabbatini had been charged with the arson of my old house, the stupid insurance company finally decided to honor their policy and pay me for the loss. I'd had the lot cleared and decided to sell it as raw land.

Nick and I were now living in the remodeled Myrtle Street house. Nick had sold his old house to Phil, who had wanted to have a property to rehabilitate in the area, so now he didn't hate me for making him sell me his property.

My phone dinged. It was a reminder to pick up the food for tonight.

Bill had started inviting Nick to the weekly poker games at the club. Nick had been reticent at first, given his previous treatment at the club. Bringing home eight hundred dollars the first night, changed his mind. According to Nick the club guys were lightweight suckers.

When the boys were playing, Lauren and the twins came over for girl time at my place. Tonight we had a *Bachelor* marathon planned.

After lunch I was surprised to find Uncle Garth at the door. I hadn't seen him since the last Habitat weekend. Nick had been modifying his travel schedule to make sure we could both attend the projects regularly.

"Good afternoon, Katherine," my kindly uncle said as he gave me a quick hug and a kiss on the cheek. "Is Nicholas around?"

"He should be back from class any time now." I invited him in and served him coffee while we waited for Nick to arrive.

It didn't take long for the distinctive sound of his Harley to announce Nick's arrival out front.

I opened the door for him. "Uncle Garth is here to see you," I told Nick as he entered.

The two men greeted each other warmly and took seats across the coffee table.

"Nicholas, as you may know, I have certain contacts, friends, in legal circles."

Nick nodded as I took a seat next to him.

Nick's expression indicated he didn't have any clearer idea than I did what Uncle Garth was leading up to.

My uncle inched forward. "I am afraid you will not get to testify at the trial of those two police officers, Delancey and Stephanic, after all."

Nick's face fell.

"They have pleaded guilty, so it will not be necessary," Uncle Garth continued. "A stipulation of the plea deal is that all monies they extorted from you over the years will be returned."

"Well, I guess that's it then. Thank you," Nick said. His smile had returned.

"I didn't think you would mind," my uncle said. "I took it upon myself to encourage certain authorities to re-examine your case in light of recent developments." Uncle Garth opened the envelope he was carrying and placed the piece of paper on the table facing us.

It was from the Superior Court of California.

"Nicholas, your original conviction has been vacated, and your record expunged."

Nick's jaw dropped, he rushed around to embrace my surprised uncle. Over the backslapping Nick said, "Uncle Garth, I don't know how to thank you."

I couldn't believe my ears. Nick was getting his life back. He couldn't get the years back, but he was no longer an ex-convict.

The men separated and Uncle Garth encouraged Nick to take a seat again. "As I told you before, the only repayment I require is for you to keep this young lady happy."

"My top priority each and every day," Nick replied. Hearing my husband say those words brought tears to my eyes because I knew he truly meant them.

~

IF YOU ENJOYED THIS BOOK, PLEASE LEAVE A REVIEW.

THE FOLLOWING PAGES CONTAIN SNEAK PEEKS OF BOOKS 5, 6 and 7 of the series: **Picked by the Billionaire**, **Saved by the Billionaire**, and **Caught by the Billionaire**

SNEAK PEEK: PICKED BY THE BILLIONAIRE

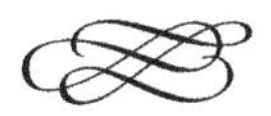

CHAPTER 1

LIAM

I PANTED RAGGEDLY AS I SLID OFF MELINDA AND ROLLED ONTO my back, the final aftershocks of pleasure fading slowly away.

She playfully nibbled my ear before laying her head on my shoulder.

I returned the favor by pinching her nipple.

She made her delightful little purring noise as I pulled her into my side and she slid a leg over mine.

It was comfortable here, almost too comfortable. She was warm and soft against me as I stroked her long blonde hair. She deserved some cuddle time while I caught my breath and let my cock deflate enough to be able to dress. The time would be shorter than she liked but it couldn't be helped.

This evening Melinda Nixon and I had entertained Jeremy Sanders and his wife at the Boston Opera. It had been tolerable, as such things went. Thankfully tonight's performance of *Aladdin* had been in English.

The only distraction had been the reappearance of my shadow during the intermission. The petite redhead had tried to look inconspicuous while taking pictures of me with her phone. With hair like hers, she didn't exactly blend in to the scenery. This had been the third time I'd noticed her following me around, but accosting her with Jeremy Sanders in the vicinity had been out of the question.

Next time, you little redheaded minx. Next time.

I wanted to add an outdoor footwear line to the company, and hoped to persuade the Sanders family to divest theirs. Since coming to Boston, I had learned evenings like this were a necessary part of the company courtship dance prior to making a formal offer.

A year ago I had thought it was just a matter of spreadsheets and check writing to acquire a business. Three consecutive failures had taught me how wrong-headed I had been.

My sister-in-law Lauren deserved the credit for teaching me how to conduct this corporate foreplay. She could schmooze with the best of them, and she would have been proud of our efforts this evening. Mrs. Sanders in particular had been quite taken by Melinda's knowledge of Arabian mythology.

I checked the clock, the dim red numerals displayed one-twelve in the morning. An energetic session before the opera and now another after had thoroughly relaxed me. It was time to go home.

Josh and I had a squash court reserved at the club a little over five hours from now. I discarded the condom and pulled on my clothes, not bothering with the cummerbund or my cufflinks.

Melinda didn't ask me to stay; she understood. The rule was simple: I didn't spend the night. Not ever.

I pulled the velvet *Cartier* pouch from my pocket and left it on the front table for her; earrings with black pearls on white gold hoops. Flicking off her hall light, I closed the door behind me, and latched the deadbolt.

Once inside my car, I punched start and the V-12 roared to life.

Eat your heart out, Daniel Craig, you get to drive an Aston Martin in the movie. I drive one every day.

Melinda served as intelligent and stunningly attractive eye candy when I needed a date for an event like tonight. In return, I accompanied her to a social event of her choosing every few months. She had looks, class, and also wicked smarts.

We fit well together. We weren't exclusive or attached. I fucked other women when I found an appropriate target, and I didn't care if Melinda did the same. She understood our arrangement: no commitments, no entanglements, no expectations, and no relationship.

I had dared to love once, and lost. I intended to never repeat the experience. Not ever.

The scar weighed on me every day.

~

AMY

I HUNG UP MY JACKET BEFORE CLOSING THE DOOR TO MY OFFICE. I needed quiet time to finish the presentation for Friday's funding meeting.

The purple and orange FedEx envelope dominated my desktop.

It was from the devil himself. I had tried once telling my assistant to stop signing for these, but it had only worked for a week. He'd arranged a process server to wait outside my office and added the fee to my bill.

My hand trembled as I ripped open the package and the envelope slid out. The envelope inside was an innocuous white. The return address was the problem. Forrester, Forrester &

Jenkins Attorneys at Law: my ex-husband's choice of divorce lawyers.

Maximilian Forrester was the face of the firm. He appeared on late night commercials on every local television station. I doubted there was anybody in Boston who hadn't heard of Max Forrester, the divorce lawyer who specialized in handling the man's side of the case.

Translation: when you were done fucking your wife, and you really wanted to fuck her over in the divorce, Max was your guy. The man had no moral compass and knew no limits. Calling him a human shark was an insult to sharks. I'd shaken hands with the man once, and it took two applications of my hand sanitizer to remove the slime. Just the man's name was enough to make me want to retch.

I dreaded what the letter inside would say. An envelope like this never brought good news.

Samantha Tiffany knocked on my door once as she invited herself in the way she always did. She reached my desk in three paces.

"Friday's investment meeting just got moved to tomorrow afternoon at two. I hope that's not a problem," she announced.

"Sure, not a problem." It would mean less time to prepare, but handling meetings like this was my job.

Samantha and I had started Tiffany's Fine Chocolates together three years ago. Her name was on the packages, but we were equal co-founders. Amy's didn't sound as sophisticated as Tiffany's, and T&A Chocolates didn't make the cut either.

Our specialty was organic, preservative-free, GMO-free, kosher, confections for those who cared to spend a little more for the very best. She was a wizard in the kitchen we called our lab and had concocted kick-ass chocolates with her bakery background. Samantha was the product wiz while I handled the marketing and finance sides of the business.

Samantha noticed the envelope. "What's in it? Do I need to go get my earplugs?"

The last time I had gotten one of these fucking envelopes I had screamed bloody murder. It had scared the receptionist Lucy so badly she'd almost called 9-1-1.

I plopped my ass down in my seat. "Don't know, and right now I don't care."

"Maybe Matt remarried, and you don't owe spousal support anymore."

"That's about as likely as me winning the Mega Millions drawing." An actuary would tell me it was even less likely than the lottery.

Matt Hudson, my worthless ex-husband, knew a good deal when he saw it, and was too mean to let me off the hook so easily. He would milk this for as long as he could. Hard work and Matt were not well acquainted with one another.

If Matt had filed for divorce in Massachusetts, my alimony payments would have ended. But no such luck; Forrester filed in Rhode Island and convinced the judge to extend the payments for another four years while Matt supposedly went to school.

I had taken a marketing job at a tech company after graduating from Brown. We'd been married a month later, and rented a place in Lynn, but he kept his studio apartment in Providence for his weekend job. Somehow he never found a full-time job that suited him, and he hadn't worked a day since our divorce, from what I could tell.

I didn't have the emotional strength to deal with the bad news inside the envelope right now. I slid it into my purse for later. Preferably when there was nothing breakable within reach.

"If you want to leave early and get shit-faced, I'm up for it," Samantha offered. With all the work we had piled up, she had to be seriously worried about my sanity to suggest leaving early.

I shook my head. "Thanks, Sam, but no. I need to work on this presentation."

The evil-Sam grin overtook her face, which always meant something totally off-the-wall was coming. "We can make a little voodoo doll and stick pins in him." She giggled. The doll didn't sound as good as going out with her to get drunk.

When I didn't go for her suggestion, she retreated to the door. "I'll leave you to it, then." She stopped before shutting the door. "You know, if you want to get back at him, Gary down in shipping has some pretty inventive ways."

The suggestion tempted me to laugh, but I didn't want to encourage her. "I don't even want to know how you know that."

Samantha closed the door on her way out.

Knowing Gary, I imagined he might have perfected the exploding package of dog-shit prank I had seen on the Internet.

The funding meeting tomorrow afternoon was important, too important to jeopardize by taking time away from today to feel sorry for myself.

My phone vibrated with the arrival of a text message.

VIV: See you 2nite

It had slipped my mind; I had agreed to meet my sister Vivienne for drinks. She was my rock even if she was off-the-wall crazy half the time. I had canceled on her last week and didn't dare cancel again.

ME: Might be late

VIV: Then drink fast to catch up

I opened my PowerPoint presentation.

~

Vivienne had gotten us a table with a good view of the place, as was her specialty. Deer hunters had blinds for hunting their prey. Vivienne selected tables the same way.

A glass of yellow mush sat in front of my seat. "I got you a Margarita to start." She was trying to break me of my habit of always ordering an appletini.

I pasted on a smile and took the seat across from her. "Thanks." I sipped the concoction slowly. These tended to give me a brain freeze if I wasn't careful.

"Okay, what's wrong?" she asked. "You've got that look again."

No matter how cheery I tried to be, Vivienne could always tell when I was hiding bad news. I pulled the letter out and placed it on the table.

Her face dropped, and she huffed. "What does the fucker want this time?"

I slumped in my seat. "Another hundred a month. This never ends. It's just not fair. And he's…"

Vivienne cocked an eyebrow. "He's what? Are you still trolling his Facebook?"

I stared down at my drink and took another long sip to avoid answering the question.

"Who is it now?" she asked.

I sipped more of my yellow mush.

"Never mind." She pulled out her phone. "I'll check myself." She fiddled with her phone for a few seconds. "Not MaryJo Mulvaney?"

I nodded. I had been checking Matt's Facebook using Samantha's phone so he wouldn't know it was me.

"This is great," Vivienne said with a laugh. "That slut's got, like, every STD known to man, and probably a few they haven't named yet."

I laughed. MaryJo never had been very picky. "You think?"

"It's what Linda at the hospital told me. Serves him right. He'll be on antibiotics for a year trying to get rid of the warts on his dick."

I laughed. Vivienne could always come up with a way to cheer me up.

She pointed her finger at me. "You really need to get over this loser."

She was right, but it was difficult after devoting years of my life to trying to make it work.

Vivienne lifted her drink to me. "Like Oprah says, don't get mad, get even."

"She wouldn't say that," I objected.

"Who cares? It's still a good rule. You need to get yourself laid tonight and put him behind you."

"Shh, not so loud." Luckily the bar was loud enough nobody had heard my crazy sister.

"How did the date with Jester go? Is he worth banging?" She always harangued me about my dating, or often the lack of dating, since my divorce from Matt.

I shook my head. "It's Jasper, and no he was a waste of a dinner," I told her.

"Not that I'm counting or anything, but you're now oh for fourteen. You seriously need to up your game." Of course she was counting, and if I had told her about Todd or Jerry last month, she would have known I was officially zero for sixteen since trying to dip my toe back in the dating pond.

"You can't have your vibrator be the only thing getting you off. Tell me I missed one and you've had one good fuck since your divorce."

I glanced down into my Margarita with embarrassment.

"Look, your vagina is like an ear piercing, if you don't put something in it every once in a while it might just close up on you."

She was just teasing me, but I felt ashamed because she was

right, my vibrator and my fingers had been my only release since Matt. I hadn't taken that big leap in the dating scene and gotten hot and naked with a guy yet.

The guys I had dated were not all bad, but I couldn't make myself take the final leap. Some, like Jasper, were complete losers, but with the others, as soon as the question became his place or my place I broke it off and powered up my computer to select another name from the list.

I hadn't been this prudish in college. But now none of them seemed special enough to sleep with. "It's tough, I'm just not ready," I told her, stirring my drink with the straw.

"Stop making excuses. Stop thinking and start acting," she said. "It's just like riding a bicycle. Once you've done it you don't forget. Just two people exercising together. You don't even have to do much of the work."

"But I haven't found the right guy yet."

"You're not marrying the guy for Christ's sake, any guy with more than a three-inch penis should be good enough to get it done. You need to pop that post-divorce cherry of yours, and move past Matt."

My rational brain agreed with Vivienne—sex shouldn't be such a big deal. I had been active enough in college, and it had worked out. Logically I agreed with her, but emotionally I was terrified.

"We agreed you would get past this. Get over the hurdle with one guy, and the rest will be easy. Have a one-night stand. I know it's not your thing, but it's the easiest way to get over this phobia of yours and rejoin the human race. Trust me, everybody else is doing it, and not just once a month either."

I stirred my drink again, contemplating her words. It seemed a big step to sleep with somebody other than Matt and accept I had screwed up that phase of my life; accept it was over. It made the mistake more real. I didn't want to make the same blunder again and become a pro at failed relationships.

"I guess," I said.

"He doesn't even need to speak English. Once his head is between your legs, it won't matter."

I clamped my thighs together at the visual.

"With your looks and that rockin' bod you could land any one of the guys in this place tonight and get it done."

"You think so?" I didn't believe it for a moment. I wasn't homely, but I never put myself high up on the sexpot scale.

"Sure, if they've got red blood cells in their veins, they'll definitely go for you. Just let him do what comes naturally to a man. It's easy, and if you're too nervous about the whole thing, just do the starfish."

"Starfish?" I asked. Viv was always teaching me things I hadn't heard before. She was my younger sister, but in middle school she'd had to explain what Mickie meant the first time he said he wanted me to *blow him.* He had laughed when I'd puckered up my lips and made like his face was a birthday candle. I'd been too ashamed to talk to Mickie again all year.

"Starfish. Just lay on your back, go spread eagle, and let him do all the work. It's better if you participate, but it'll get the job done. He gets his rocks off and you get past this hang-up."

I took another sip of my now-thawed drink.

"Amy, I'm not going to stop bugging you about this. You have to get on with your life. I know you don't want to become a nun, so stop acting like one. So what if your marriage failed? A lot do. You don't have to be mental about it. You know Matt's banging every chick in Brockton he can get his hands on. Look forward instead of back."

Vivienne had warned me about Matt before I dated him, but had been polite enough to not remind me more than once after the divorce.

"But I'm not ready for that kind of relationship yet," I told her.

"That's the most fucked up thing you've said all night. We're talking sex, fucking, boinking, not marriage. You don't have to be in a relationship with a guy to have sex with him. This is the twenty-first fucking century. Just have a random hookup, a good time with a stranger. You'll never see the guy again. You can let yourself go."

I shook my head and played with my glass.

"Didn't you ever have a one-night stand in college?"

"No," I admitted. I had let guys get to second base on the first date, but never anything further. I had always been more prudish than my hall-mates in the dorm.

"Then you start tonight. Think of it as the first night of the rest of your life. No backing out."

"I don't know how," I said. Pick up a guy? I had never picked up a guy. They always made the first move, I had no clue what to do.

Vivienne grinned and took two swallows of her Moscow mule. "Good girl. The first step in recovery is admitting you have a problem."

"So what do I do? If, on the off chance I want to take your advice tonight?"

Her grin increased to a full-on megawatt smile. "Pick a guy, preferably one who's alone, and looks like he showers on a regular basis." She scanned the room.

I waited for her advice on picking out an example. She was the expert at this.

Vivienne tipped her head toward the bar. "Dark hair, navy suit, looks like he showers regularly."

The man she pointed out was alone at the bar and had been there ever since I'd arrived. He was nursing a drink and pondering the state of the world in the bottom of his glass.

"He's hot," Vivienne said. "But I can't tell if he's wearing a ring from here."

A quick chill ran through me. I hadn't considered that some

men here might be married. I would not be a home-wrecker. "What if he just took it off to come in here?"

"Don't get all paranoid, sis. This time of year you'll see a tan line on his finger if he took it off. What I was going to say is, you can check for a ring first."

"Or if he had one on recently."

"Sure, that too. If it looks okay, then pick him up."

That was all the instruction she was offering? *Pick him up*? If he was a pencil or a stapler, I could pick him up, but I was clueless on how to pick up a guy in a bar or anywhere. "But—"

"No buts, just go up and meet the guy."

"How?"

"Find a reason to get close to him, maybe look sideways at him, catch his eye. Talk to him."

"And just ask if he wants to fuck?"

"Of course not. Undo another button on your top."

I undid a button as she suggested.

"That's not enough; you need another one."

"But I don't ever—"

"Trust me, sis. Another button. This is advertising, you understand advertising, right?"

I undid another, and now you could see my cleavage and my bra.

"That's nice," my sister said. "Black lace, they go for black, or red, that gets 'em too."

I might be a prude, but I liked nice lingerie.

"Now go do it." Her eyes bored into me. My sister would not let me back down from this tonight. "Remember you're doing this to get back at Matt for those damn alimony payments."

Her statement riled me enough to do anything. Matt had said I wasn't talented enough to land the marketing job at the tech startup, and he had scoffed at my and Samantha's idea of starting our confectionery company. I had been successful at both those things and could learn to do this too.

I got up, straightened my skirt, picked up my glass, and started for the bar. It felt uncomfortable to have so much cleavage showing, but that's what my margarita was for. I sucked down the last of my liquid courage.

I can do this.

CHAPTER 2

Natalie

In line at the coffee shop, no one recognized me. No one gave me dirty looks or spit on me.

Finally a moment of anonymity, a moment of peace.

The clientele at this Peet's was more businessmen and fewer neurotic housewives than the one I'd been frequenting near home. The fireman at the counter was rattling off order after order at the poor barista.

"But Lucy, I don't know if I have time for that… But I can't… Okay, you win." The whiny male voice came from behind me.

I glanced back at the lengthening line, held up by the guy ordering for a dozen. Mr. Whiny on the phone to Lucy was the short, bald guy directly behind me.

The broad-shouldered man ahead of me moved up to the counter after Mr. Infinite-list finished reading his written orders. Ninety-seven dollars and change was a lot of coffee.

I closed my eyes and listened to Broad Shoulders order. I

couldn't see his face, but the deep, seductive voice with a hint of gravel predicted a chiseled jawline and stubble——a high-octane man, a real man, unlike the whiny wimp jabbering on his cell phone behind me.

The sound of Broad Shoulders' voice had me visualizing a deep, dark chocolate pudding——something I could lick all day long.

He ordered a medium caffè mocha, my drink of choice as well.

"Ryan," he said when the barista asked his name.

Ryan, a very lick-worthy name.

I gulped, realizing how inappropriate my daydreams had become just four months after my divorce. I knew it was four months because the final decree had arrived yesterday. I was finally free of Damien Winterbourne.

When I opened my eyes, Broad Shoulders had paid and moved aside, making room for me to order. I'd been right about him being a high-octane man. He had the deep blue eyes, the chiseled jawline——everything except the stubble, but that could be cured quickly. Tall and imposing, he tugged at his collar, apparently ill at ease in his expensive suit and tie.

"Miss?" the barista said, pulling me back to reality.

I advanced to the counter. "I'll have the same."

She rang me up and smiled. "And your name, miss?"

I slid my AmEx card into the reader. "Natalie."

The card machine beeped twice, and the little screen read *declined.*

The barista shot me a questioning glance. "Try it again. Sometimes it acts up."

I removed the card and shoved it back in.

The reader complained loudly again.

"Perhaps another card?" the girl behind the counter offered with a sigh.

I located my Visa card and tried that with the same embarrassing result. The line behind me was restless, and the muttering increased. Nothing nice, no doubt.

"Get a clue, lady," was the only thing I could pick out of the mumbling.

This is not my day.

I cringed as I pulled back the second card. "Something must be wrong. I'll have to call and get this straightened out."

I left the counter, looking down at the floor to avoid the stares, and scurried to the corner of the store. I dialed the number on the back of my Visa. When the annoying mechanical voice asked for it, I keyed in my card number. Instead of giving me my balance information, I was told to wait for the next available agent. I settled into a seat while the telephone hold music played.

"Caffè mocha, right?" That same one-hundred-octane male voice said.

I looked up to see Mr. Broad Shoulders, Ryan, holding two cups with an iPad tucked under one arm.

He held one out for me. The sight of this man froze me in place, now that I got a good look at the features and size of him. His deep blue eyes captured me and wouldn't let me go.

"Here, take it; I can't drink two." The voice was even deeper and more chocolaty than at the counter.

"You shouldn't have," I offered feebly, reaching for my purse to pay him back.

His brow knit, and he thrust the cup forward. "Here, I can't miss my quota."

I accepted the cup. "Quota?"

His smile returned. "When I was ten, I promised my mother to do at least one good deed a week."

My grin nearly broke my face. "Really?" A man who kept a promise to his mother couldn't be all bad. Or it was the most off-the-wall pickup line I'd ever heard.

He turned and walked toward the door.

Not a pick-up line, evidently.

"Thank you," I called after him, watching his tight ass like a pervert. Hell, it had been a long time, after all. I deserved to watch if I wanted.

My phone buzzed with an incoming text. I moved the phone from my ear and checked the screen.

BROSNAHAND: Call me - we need to talk

Another chat with Brosnahand, my ex-husband's lawyer, was not going to rise to the top of my list today, and probably not even tomorrow. Whatever information he had to pass on was unlikely to brighten my outlook. Even after agreeing to the divorce, Damien still wanted to talk to me. The feeling wasn't mutual.

Becoming Damien Winterbourne's wife had been the worst mistake of my life. He'd fooled me, along with all the people that now regretted ever having done business with him. To every one of my previous so-called friends, sharing his last name meant sharing his guilt. The Winterbourne name was now radioactive in Boston, at least until the memories faded. As soon as I sold the house, I'd get as far away from here as I could, as fast as I could.

Damien was cooling his heels in jail, awaiting trial——a good place for him to be. The judge had been perceptive enough to see him as a flight risk.

I ended the call with the credit card company. Waiting on terminal hold would be more comfortable at home. I hadn't remembered to charge my phone last night, and the notice on the screen told me I had less than twenty percent battery left. I ignored the warning. The phone went back in my purse.

I collected my free mocha, my purse, and added a packet of sweetener to my cup before heading out. Coffee wasn't the purpose of my trip to this part of town. Cartier Jewelers next door was about to open.

Turning right out of Peet's, the sight stopped me in my tracks. I stifled a laugh.

With his coffee in one hand and his iPad in the other, Ryan was trying to use his chin to scroll the text on the tablet as he read a page and chin-scrolled farther down to read some more.

I ventured closer, stretching my smirk to a smile. "Thank you for the coffee, Ryan."

He glanced momentarily in my direction. "You already said that." He went back to his reading.

Somebody has a stick up his ass today.

Thankfully I didn't mouth the words.

"You're welcome, Natalie," he added after another chin-scroll.

He'd noticed my name, a point in his favor.

I found myself glancing at his profile in the morning sun as I waited. His face was one a Roman sculptor would have chosen, I decided.

After a few minutes of silence between us, Jonas Gisler, the store manager, came to unlock the door.

As I entered behind Ryan, the time on the wall clock read ten exactly. Gisler was Swiss and proudly precise, I'd learned earlier.

Ryan went directly to the ruby counter.

I waited.

"Mrs. Winterbourne, what may I help you with today?" Gisler said with his Teutonic smile.

Surprise overcame Ryan's face. "I was here first," he announced loudly.

Gisler was unmoved as he continued to watch me for a response to his question. My status as a repeat customer seemed to trump Ryan's position in line.

I pointed toward Ryan. "It's Spencer now, Mr. Gisler, and he's right. He was first."

Gisler's smile broke down to a mild grin. "As you wish." He moved to the ruby counter. "What may I help with today, sir?"

Ryan pointed through the glass. "I'd like to see that one, please."

I shuffled closer, pretending to scan the cases for a purchase.

Gisler pulled out a ruby necklace with a huge heart-shaped stone, set in a circle of diamonds, and laid it on a velvet mat.

Ryan looked at it, perplexed. "No, that won't do." He didn't bother to check the price tag as any normal person would. "Let's see the next one over."

Gisler complied, bringing up another gorgeous necklace.

Ryan shook his head.

"Perhaps if you were to tell me your parameters, I might recommend a few pieces," Gisler offered.

Ryan ignored him and pointed to another necklace and then two more. None of them pleased him.

Gisler sighed. "Perhaps a feminine perspective might help? Mrs. Spencer here has exquisite taste."

I blushed at the compliment.

"Sure," Ryan said, casting a glance my way.

I moved next to him, but avoided eye contact, lest I freeze up. "I'll try, and it's Miss."

"I don't have a lot of time," he said. "I'm due in court soon." His body heat became perceptible as he shifted closer.

"A lawyer, huh?"

He tugged at his collar. "No," he said curtly, my hint to shut up.

That explained why he seemed uncomfortable in his expensive suit. A lawyer also would have used a page of words instead of one.

A quick peek at the tags on the necklaces he had chosen first showed prices from forty to seventy thousand. This was one lucky woman.

"Special occasion?" I asked.

"Her birthday," he replied, choosing more than a single-word answer this time.

"Mr. Gisler, those three in the back, please." I pointed out three more modest stones than he had originally chosen, a little less ostentatious, more ruby and less diamond surround.

I'd checked his left hand earlier, no wedding ring, which most likely meant special girlfriend gift. If he went too big now, he'd have a hard time topping it with the engagement ring.

"Those are too small," he said quickly.

"She must be very special. Wife? Girlfriend?"

He shook his head. "Sister."

"Right," I said, letting too much disbelief color my voice.

He turned toward me. "Yes, sister." Annoyance tinged his tone.

"Then we want to avoid these heart-shaped stones." I pointed out the first set he'd selected. "Mr. Gisler, the third from the end please."

The jeweler pulled out a beautiful cushion-cut solitaire ruby on a white gold chain. It was way too large for any normal person to give his sister, but the smile on Ryan's face said we'd found the one.

The price tag was face down, and he didn't bother to turn it over. Instead, he handed his AmEx card to Gisler. "I'd like it gift wrapped and overnighted to this address," he said, pulling a piece of paper from his wallet.

"I can take care of that for you, sir." Gisler took the card and the paper to his register.

I moved back to a more respectful distance. "What'd you do wrong?" I asked.

He cocked his head. "Pardon?"

"That's an awfully expensive birthday gift." I couldn't believe he didn't see how absurd it was.

His eyes flicked downward. "I forgot her birthday last year."

Even if I'd forgotten my sister's birthday, she'd be getting something like a scarf.

"And you think she's expecting something like this?"

The man would rate as totally clueless if he agreed with my question.

"I think she'll complain like crazy, actually, but that's just tough. She'll have to take it."

He didn't seem to understand the difference between expecting something this extravagant, and accepting such a beautiful gift.

If I opened something like this on my birthday, you wouldn't be able to pry it away from me with dynamite.

Gisler returned with the credit card and charge slip.

I couldn't resist peeking. Fifty-eight thousand dollars. If I had a brother, I would want one like Ryan, although right now my hormones were casting him for a different role than brother—way different.

He replaced the card in his wallet. "You can get it there tomorrow?"

Gisler stiffened as if that were an insult. "You can rely on me, sir."

I shocked myself by reaching over to touch Ryan briefly on the arm.

He didn't recoil. Instead, a warm smile tugged at his lips.

"Ryan," I said. "You know, flowers and a phone call go a long way as well."

He nodded. "Appreciate the advice, Miss Spencer."

"Natalie," I corrected him.

He checked his watch and collected his receipt. "Thank you again for the help." He reached the door in a few quick strides. "Natalie," he added before the door closed behind him.

Gisler huffed loudly. "Now, Miss Spencer, how may I help you?"

I opened my purse and pulled out the red velvet pouch. "I'd

like to get these cleaned, if I could." I handed him the pouch. "And the post on one of them needs some looking after."

He gently opened it and slid out the earrings, my pride and joy. "My, they are even more lovely every time I see them."

"Thank you." They were the best pair of diamond earrings I would ever own, eight total carats of beautiful brilliance.

He held them up for a closer inspection. "Yes, I see. I can have these ready for you after lunch, if that's acceptable."

I nodded. "Perfect. I'll be by around one." That would give me time to pick up Murphy and also get to the gym before returning. I'd been told some cats liked car rides. Murphy was not among them, as the long scratch on my arm proved.

Once I'd gotten him to the groomer's this morning, his mood had changed, as it always did. He loved the attention. Now I just needed a Star Trek transporter to get him there without having to load him into the car.

I bid Mr. Gisler goodbye and sucked down half my mocha on the way back to the car.

As I started the engine, the radio came alive with Frank Sinatra singing "That's Life." His tune could be my theme song, a reminder to never give up.

First, there had been Damien's arrest, followed by the ridicule and shame, and then the divorce. Now I finally had my name back. Once I sold the house and left this city, I could reclaim my future, in a place where the Winterbourne stigma wouldn't follow me. Natalie Winterbourne's life was over, but Natalie Spencer's was ahead of me. I could feel it.

Like a sign of things to come, the road bent left, and the sun beat in through the windshield, lifting my spirits. I turned the music up high.

The drive home went quickly in light mid-day traffic, with fewer crazies than normal on the road.

I turned the corner onto my street, and there they were: two police cars and three black SUVs in front of my house.

I pulled up to the garage and climbed out of the car with my battle-face on. I'd had enough of these searches already. They'd been here only last week, for Christ's sake.

This one was different. Some of the windbreakers had US MARSHAL in bold yellow lettering on the back, in addition to the usual FBI jerks.

A uniformed cop held up his hand as I reached the walk. "Hold it, ma'am. You can't go in."

I started past him. "The hell I can't. This is my house." In the past, the only way to deal with these assholes had been at high volume.

He grabbed my arm. "Agent White," he called.

I wrested my arm loose, but stopped where I was. The last thing I needed was some stupid cop tasering me in the back, on my own property.

One of the agents from last week trotted over. He flipped open his badge momentarily, as they all did. They could be dime-store replicas for all the time they *didn't* give you to inspect them.

"Special Agent White," he announced like it should mean something to me. "Mrs. Winterbourne, I'll need your car keys."

This had happened each time. They wanted to search the car as well as the house.

The key fob was still in my hand. I hadn't stashed it in my purse yet. I handed it over with a huff. "It's Spencer now, and how long is this going to take? I have to go pick up my cat."

He pocketed the key. "Mrs. Winterbourne," he said, intentionally trying to piss me off for sure. "This house and automobile, and all the contents, are being seized as products of a criminal enterprise."

"That can't be right," I complained.

"For any questions about this forfeiture, you may contact the United States Attorney." He offered me a business card.

I couldn't be hearing this right.

He forced the card at me again.

I took it. *Kirk Willey, Assistant United States Attorney*, it read.

The agent pointed toward the street. “You need to step off the property now, Mrs. Winterbourne.”

With my legs shaking, and my breakfast threatening to come up, tears clouded my eyes. “But this is my house.”

“Not any longer,” Agent White said coldly. He moved his hand to the butt of his gun.

CHAPTER 3

Vincent

The man in the suit had followed me all the way here from work this evening. It was the third time I'd noticed him in the last two weeks.

I stepped inside Holmby's Grill and peeked out the tinted window after the door closed. After a few seconds of not seeing the suited man, I found my way to my usual table in the corner. I mentally kicked myself for not getting a picture of him for our security team to check out.

Less than a minute later, *she* walked up on her tall black heels with the self assurance of the runway model she had once been. Her tits jiggled under the loose fabric of her low cut dress ——a dress that flaunted her ample cleavage and threatened to open just a bit too far, but unfortunately never quite did.

Half the men in the restaurant stared as she greeted me with a warm hug. No doubt they wished they were me. And rightly so. Staci Baxter and I would be getting hot and heavy between the sheets before the night was out. She had a body to die for, and knew how to work it. A night with Staci never disappointed.

"Vince," she purred as I pulled out her chair.

She liked to tease me by going braless in low-cut dresses, and it was working tonight. A quick peek down her dress before I rounded the table to my seat jolted my cock.

Staci had no doubt gotten a million teenage boys off via her body-paint pictures in the *Sports Illustrated* swimsuit issue. Since retiring from modeling, she had devoted all her time to her new clothing line.

Her jaw showed an uncommon tenseness this evening.

"You okay? I asked.

She glanced down. "I'm little nervous is all. I could use some wine."

I waved our waiter over. "That I can help with."

He arrived quickly.

"A bottle of Opus One Proprietary Red, please," I told him.

She managed a pasted-on smile after he left and sipped her water——a definite off night for her.

I asked about her sister, and that seemed to calm her while our waiter sought out the wine.

When he returned I approved the bottle, and she guzzled down most of a glass.

She fiddled with her silverware. "I'm not sure I'm ready."

"Don't worry, tomorrow's meeting with the bank will go just fine with the presentation you've got."

"Vince, you've been such a help. I just don't know if it's good enough." Her nervousness was understandable; asking for a half-million dollar bank loan would make anybody stressed.

"You've got this."

Our waiter returned, and I ordered the gorgonzola truffle-crusted New York strip steak, and Staci chose the lamb chops.

"Do you want to go over it one last time?" I asked.

She smiled. "Please." She pulled the presentation folder from her oversized purse.

She placed it on the table and began the spiel I'd worked out with her. "Gentlemen..." she started out.

The food arrived just as she finished the presentation.

I topped off our wine glasses and raised mine to her. "Sounded damned good to me. You don't have anything to worry about."

The blush that rose in her cleavage was enticing.

I cut my first piece of steak. "Now, tell me more about how your little sister is getting on in New York."

She perked up and started with how hard it had been for her sister to find a place to live in the city.

An hour later, we had finished dinner and decided against dessert.

We had long since left the topic of her presentation tomorrow, but the undercurrent of nervousness in her demeanor hadn't dissipated.

"Staci, do you want to talk about what's really bothering you?"

She hesitated before retrieving her purse. After a moment of rummaging, she pulled out a piece of folded paper and extended it across the table with a shaky hand.

I opened it.

Stay away from Vincent Benson unless you want to become collateral damage, the note read.

My stomach turned over.

"What is going on, Vince?"

The meaning was clear enough. Someone was messing with me and using her to do it.

"It's probably nothing... I can arrange some security for you, though."

"I live on the safest street in town. The chief of police lives next door. It looks like you should be the one watching out."

I took a picture of the note before grasping it with my napkin and folding it up. "Mind if I take this?"

She nodded.

There was probably nothing worthwhile on it, but I folded it inside the napkin and stuffed it in my pocket nonetheless.

I turned the conversation back to her clothing business while I mulled over who would be messing with me. No faces came to mind.

Sensing our meal had come to a close, I offered, "I've got a really nice bottle of port upstairs."

She wiped her lips with her napkin, but her eyes telegraphed the answer before the words arrived. "Not tonight, Vince. I've been stressing over this presentation all day, and I'm bushed. How 'bout a rain check?"

It wasn't the first time she'd begged off from our after-dinner gymnastics, but it *was* unusual. This was a standing date we had pretty much every Monday night.

No strings attached, just a good time. Neither of us did commitments, so neither of us expected anything more than companionship and physical pleasure. "Casual intimacy with friendship on the side," she had once called it. She seemed to be the only woman in town who didn't want or expect anything more from me——except Barb, of course.

My situation with Barbara was more commercial in nature. Gifts changed hands, but never cash. She was attractive arm candy when I needed it and an enthusiastic bed partner when I wanted some variety, but the side of friendship I had with Staci wasn't the same with Barb.

"I'll call you," Staci said when we made it to the door.

It wasn't a call I expected soon.

I opened the door for her and waited while she hailed a cab. I checked up and down the street for the suited man. All clear, for now.

After she entered the cab, I checked again in the direction of my condo on Tremont Street. Its safety was not far away.

Before starting out, I rubbed the ring I always wore.

Ashley

"I'm going to beat you out for that LA promotion," my opponent, Elizabeth Parsons, said as she stepped sideways on the mat, looking for an opening to attack me.

I slid to my left and dodged her first attempt. "Try all you want, Liz. But a brunette like you will stand out like a sore thumb in the sea of blondes in California."

She lunged at me again.

We tumbled to the ground, and she initially had the upper hand, but I had the leverage and weight advantage and pinned her fifteen seconds later.

She patted out.

"That makes three," I said.

"Best of seven?" she asked.

As the only women in the office, we usually sparred against each other——and Liz hated losing.

I checked the wall clock in the gym. "Out of time today."

We had gone through Quantico together. At the Academy and every day since, she had made up for her lack of stature with competitiveness and pure determination. She was shorter than me, and more buxom, which meant men often underestimated her. More than one bad guy had taken her for a pushover and ended up with a cracked skull thanks to her baton skills.

We grabbed our towels and headed to the showers. There wasn't a lot of time before our eight o'clock bullpen meeting.

~

FORTY MINUTES LATER, FBI BOSTON FIELD OFFICE SPECIAL Agent in Charge Randy White looked up when we entered the bullpen precisely on time. He checked his watch. "You're late."

Liz started to complain. "But——"

"New rule: no less than three minutes early, understood?"

Anybody else would have accepted our arrival or told us five minutes early. Only SAC White would come up with something asinine like three minutes. He invented another stupid rule every few weeks——something my partner, John McNally, called Caesar moments.

"Yes, sir," Liz and I said in unison.

From across the room, John rolled his eyes just enough for me to see.

White had been promoted six months ago to the SAC position. Before that he'd been one of us in the bullpen, and only a little difficult to get along with. Now he was the boss, and beyond difficult. *Randy* was no longer allowed, either. *Sir* had replaced it. The running joke was that the new budget would have to have a remodeling line item for changing out the doors to ones his ego could fit through.

The special agents had started betting on how long this phase would last. My bet had been six months——that's how long it took SAC Sinella, the previous occupant of that office, to settle down. Sinella's transfer to Nashville had triggered White's promotion to Asshole Behind the Glass.

Liz and I both had to kiss up to him because he would ultimately recommend one of us for the Los Angeles opening.

White motioned for Liz to join him in his office. "Parsons, new assignment."

She followed him and closed the door.

"What the fuck's with this stupid three-minute rule?" I asked John.

He shrugged. "He told us just before you two got here." He shook his head. "I'm changing my bet to nine months. The guy should be over his stupid Caesar routine by now, but he's definitely not."

"I'll call the agency," Liz said as she left White's office a few minutes later. "Sweet undercover assignment," she mumbled as she passed by my desk, trying to get a rise out of me.

The men in the office seemed oblivious, but it was clear to me: White had gotten balls deep into Liz during that ski weekend in New Hampshire last year.

She'd denied it when I confronted her about it, but the shift in her had been easy enough to see. Back when we were all in the bullpen together, she would walk in front of his desk on her way to the coffee room, and although he tried to hide it, his eyes would follow her.

And now, it seemed White had given her the plum assignment.

I wasn't in a mood to make a scene. My last undercover had netted me a month in a cockroach- and bedbug-infested cover apartment that still gave me the shivers when I thought about it. When your cover persona was down and out, the bureau went out of its way to make the entire experience realistic, and the latest budget cut had us going even further down-market in arranging cover locations.

The Bureau didn't reward people who rocked the boat.

Liz opened the folder on her desk. "Jacinda? Do I look like a Jacinda to you?" she mumbled rhetorically. She shook her head and kept reading.

I didn't answer. She didn't expect one.

CHAPTER 4

Vincent

The next morning started with fireworks.

This one had a temper. “Fired? You can’t fire me. I quit,” she yelled.

The stapler she threw missed me and hit the wall with a bang. Security grabbed her arms and escorted her out.

It took Wes Parker, my number two, all of a minute to end up in my office and close the door. “What the hell did you do this time?”

“Nothing,” I insisted.

Nothing more than I ever did. I insisted on accuracy with my PA, and that didn’t suit Marcy what’s-her-name very well.

He plopped down in the red chair he always chose. “At this rate, in a year there won’t be anybody left in Boston willing to apply.”

“Fuck you.”

“What’s got you in such a piss-poor mood this morning?”

I pulled up the picture of the note Staci had received and

handed my phone to Wes. "Staci found that on her car yesterday."

He scanned it. "Somebody's messing with you."

"No shit, Sherlock. Now you tell me who."

He handed the phone back. "Fuck anybody's wife lately?"

"Fuck no, and you know that."

I had played the field, but married women were never my style. And after Marilyn last year went full-house psycho on me when I wouldn't call her back, I'd ended up limiting myself to Barbara and Staci: the only two that were certified commitment-phobes, safe dates without emotional expectations, merely material ones.

As long as they were supplied with expensive dinners, shopping trips, and the occasional extravagant gift, those ladies were happy and supplied me with enjoyable interludes in the bedroom. The gifts were most often jewelry, but never, never would they expect a ring.

My mission here in Boston was simple and clear: grow the Eastern division of Covington both in size and profitability to a point my father couldn't ignore.

He hadn't wanted to give me control of Benson Corp. back home in California. He said I wasn't seasoned enough, or experienced enough, and I intended to show him he was wrong, completely wrong.

"Just checking," Wes responded. "You ought to give it to security."

"Already did."

"At least you have the advantage now."

"How so?"

"They've given up the element of surprise. You know somebody's coming at you."

Wes left after badgering me for a few more minutes about who I might have pissed off recently.

I called down to Judith in HR.

She was expecting my call. "I'll have another candidate here tomorrow morning, Mr. Benson."

"Not soon enough. After lunch," I said.

"Yes, sir" came the immediate response.

I glanced at the picture of the note another time. The question remained: who was coming after me and why?

The why could only be answered by knowing the who.

I returned to my spreadsheet on the Semaphore acquisition. Getting our hands on them would be my crowning achievement so far, and it was looking good.

An hour later, the numbers were all swimming on the screen in front of me. I needed a break to clear my head.

Once on the treadmill downstairs, the hum of the machine and the pounding of my feet relaxed me. Exercise always cleared the slate mentally and allowed me to return to a problem with renewed focus.

AFTER LUNCH, A KNOCK CAME AT MY OFFICE DOOR.

I checked my watch: half-past one. "Yes?"

Judith from HR popped in. "I've got your new PA outside, if you're ready to meet her."

I closed the spreadsheet and rose.

The girl walked in with plenty of hip swivel and offered a firm handshake. Tall red heels, a short blue skirt, and an only partially buttoned pink top were meant to distract——and had the desired effect.

She extended her resume. "Jacinda Wilder."

Judith excused herself.

I accepted the resume and caught myself drawn to the well of her cleavage as she sat——definitely deep enough to get lost in. I glanced down at the resume and asked her about her experience.

She had an impressive list of prior jobs, but none had lasted very long.

"The nature of temporary work," she explained. "I often get called to fill in for maternity leaves or unexpected vacancies."

The way she smirked when she said *unexpected vacancies* made me guess she was the revenge the boss brought in when his wife decided the old assistant had been too good looking.

"This position can be quite demanding," I told her.

She smiled. "I'm available any time of the day or night, as much time as you need, and whatever services you need."

I wasn't interested, but her implication was naughty.

I liked this girl. Her answers were all couched cautiously, not divulging very much information——exactly the kind of discretion we needed here.

Ashley

Liz was back early after her first day undercover, and not looking happy from where I could see her through the glass of the boss's office.

I couldn't make out what was being said, but White was gesticulating in a menacing manner.

He opened the door. "Newton, get in here."

I hustled over.

"You fucked up," White said, pointing at Liz. "Getting blown after less than a day? What were you thinking, Parsons?"

Liz wisely didn't answer.

"This is way too important a case for you to screw it up."

"It's not screwed, not yet," Liz argued. "They threw me out, but we can still get Ashley in, and I don't think they made me, actually."

"What do you call getting caught in the subject's office on the first day, and getting walked out?"

"I got them thinking I worked freelance for a tabloid. The guy is a gossip magnet. They'll think I was looking for dirt to publish, not connect me to here. That tabloid identity just has to be fully backstopped, and they'll stop looking. We're not blown yet."

Liz had thought ahead, if she had that already worked out. It sounded plausible enough to me.

White scratched his chin. "Tabloid could work. Get Randy to help you backstop that front."

"In the meantime," Liz continued, "we send Ashley in right away. They have no way to connect the two of us."

White closed his eyes momentarily. "Newton, you're up then." His eyes bored into mine. "And you better do a better job of this than Parsons here."

"Yes, sir," I answered.

Nothing else would have been acceptable.

Still newly promoted, White's reputation would suffer for a long time if he messed up a big case. Translation: I was cannon fodder, and if anything went wrong, it was my fault. I'd fall on the boss's sword for him, or suffer the consequences.

"Newton, a word," he said, indicating it was time for Liz to leave, which she did without argument.

The door closed.

I took a seat.

"Parsons has better evals than you," he said.

I schooled my face to not show the anger I felt. As far as our evaluations under Sinella went, I knew the statement to be a lie. Liz and I had shared once, and our evals were identical. It could only mean that Liz's evals had been helped by her hide-the-salami sessions with our new boss, and that wasn't fair. I wasn't traveling that road.

"This is DOJ's top priority, so I really want to get this guy," he said. "If you close this case quickly and solidly, I'll make sure you beat out Parsons for the LA slot."

"Thank you, sir" was all I said. I had no doubt he could swing it whichever way he wanted it to go.

My new boss was a much bigger pig than I had thought possible yesterday, but I could only deal with the situation presented to me. The only option for escape was to nail this assignment and get the hell out of Dodge.

He tapped the closed folder in front of him. "DOJ has information that this guy is running drugs through his import business. Oxy and fentanyl mostly. The objective here is to cut off the head of the snake, not just the low-level minions. We want the top guy. Wiretap warrants have been turned down, so you're going undercover inside this guy's business so we can nail him."

"In what capacity?"

White opened the folder on his desk. "His secretary."

I nodded. This certainly beat out my last assignment, an executive assistant wouldn't be getting the crap cover motel I'd gotten last time.

"This won't be an easy undercover," he added. "Since Parsons isn't the first one he's fired this month, you have to figure out how to last longer than she did."

"Not a problem, sir."

"Good. I'm counting on you." He handed the folder across the desk.

"Our contact in the personnel agency is listed on the first page, and she'll be expecting your call. Develop a cover and use John for whatever backup you need."

"Is that all, sir?"

He went back to his screen and flicked his hand toward the door, shooing me away as if I were a fly on the desk.

After I closed the door behind me, I gritted my teeth and realized the faint odor in his office wasn't the new carpet. It was the stench of the swine inhabiting it.

Catching the local DOJ's top target was a career-making assignment. Back at my desk, I opened the file. The problem was on the second page: the name of our target.

Turning this down wasn't an option. Randy Turnbull had refused an assignment White gave him last month and was now in the Alaska field office chasing caribou rustlers or something.

Vincent Benson had taken me to our high school prom, and I had just been assigned to nail his hide to the wall.

I am so fucked.

Made in the USA
Las Vegas, NV
13 October 2024